MARY'S NECK

BOOKS BY
BOOTH TARKINGTON

MARY'S NECK

By BOOTH TARKINGTON

FRONTISPIECE BY
WALLACE MORGAN

MCMXXXII

DOUBLEDAY, DORAN
and Company, Inc.
Garden City,
N. Y.

PRINTED AT THE *Country Life Press*, GARDEN CITY, N. Y., U. S. A.

TO SUSANAH

MARY'S NECK

IN EXPLANATION

THE middle-aged stranger whom I met by chance upon
the lower rocks at Mary's Neck, that salt-washed prom-
ontory of the New England coast, was at first taciturn
but became voluble when a little conversation developed
the fact that we were both from the Midland country.
We were indulging in the unexciting pastime of fishing
for rock-cod, and the reason for his taciturnity, he explained, was that he had mistaken me for a native of
Mary's Neck; and, when I informed him that nothing was
more unlikely than that a native would be fishing for
rock-cod, he expressed astonishment that I, a fellow-
Midlander, should seem to know anything about what a
native would or would not do.

It was certainly a relief, he said, to meet a fellow-
being from the Middle West—from "back home" was
the way he put it—and I was the first person he could
really talk to that he had encountered since his recent
arrival at Mary's Neck. He had been through a great
deal in that short time, he told me, and he shook his head
ruefully; then, with the confidential trustfulness that one
Midlander on foreign soil nearly always reposes in another, he began straightway to tell me all about his
troubles. We ceased to annoy the rock-cod with murder,
sat upon a ledge over the salty sea-weed that heaved and

fell with the Atlantic surge, and I listened while he spoke fully of what lay disturbingly upon his mind.

A man's vocabulary reveals him, and from the first I was interested not only in what this exile said but in how he said it. His manner of speech was characteristic, I thought, of what we sometimes call the "average well-to-do American" of these times; thus, just as one guesses the engine by its sound, so I caught at the creature through words seldom divested of a half-concealed plaintive humor and now and then unintentionally eloquent, and found him genuine. The sun was overhead when he began by informing me that his name was Masscy and he came from Logansville, Illinois; but the broken shadows were stretching eastward across the rocks and the light was rosy before his narrative concluded.

Not long after this, we chanced to meet again, in the same manner, and, abandoning our humble pastime, again he talked and again I listened. I have noticed that many of the northern New England people fortify themselves within their reticence, and even in time of distress seem to feel that an open mouth is a breach through which the foe may leap; but when we Midlanders are in difficulties we always need to tell somebody about them. Mr. Massey's troubles were more like perplexities, those that bemuse the foreigner treading a strange soil and hearing unfamiliar tongues, though sometimes his bewilderments were the deepest indeed, when concerned with his own family. Moreover, as this family of his consisted of a wife and two daughters, he seemed to feel that he would not invariably be understood if he talked freely at home; it was necessary to him to open his heart to a fellow-man.

For the greater part of the year my own habitation is at Cobble Reef, several miles distant from the much more populous, lively and affluent resort at Mary's Neck. After our second meeting, Mr. Massey drove over to Cobble Reef to see me and express himself in a long talk on my modest but breezy verandah; he came again and formed the habit of coming when he had something on his mind. Once, when he telephoned plaintively that he had twisted his ankle, I went to Mary's Neck, and, without much inquiry, found his cottage, for it was the largest on the crest of the coastal rocks and of itself rather conspicuous evidence of Mr. Massey's worldly prosperity. He was in a long wicker chair upon his verandah; he welcomed me heartily but expressed regret that his wife and daughters were absent, and then, frowning thoughtfully, added that perhaps it was just as well for us to have the place to ourselves. In fact, I had at no time the pleasure of meeting the Massey ladies, though a moment after I had left him, that day, I saw a shiny big limousine turn into his driveway and caught a glimpse of three charming faces and some pretty clothes.

I had a better view of one of the daughters late in the season on a day when he came to see me. The manner of his arrival was pleasant; he descended from a fine, fawn-colored runabout driven by a dark-eyed pretty girl of twenty, who seemed to take it as entirely a matter of course that three young men of similar age should have squeezed themselves into the rumble-seat. All three scrambled to take the place at her side vacated by Mr. Massey; muscular force was involved, and she used some of this, herself, to settle the contest. When two had been established beside her and the other forced to retire to the rumble, she leaned back, patted the defeated one upon a towsled head, then called to Mr. Massey that she would return for him later, and, settling herself to the controls of her lively machine, whizzed away down the white road that crosses the salt marshes and leads to Mary's Neck.

From his chair on my verandah, Mr. Massey a little anxiously observed the speed of her departure, but sighed resignedly. "That one was Clarissa," he said. "Pretty much any time you'd happen to see her it would be about the same way—dashing off for somewhere else with three or four of 'em hanging on as well as they can. As a matter of fact, it seems to Mrs. Massey and me that about all we're getting this end of our summer at Mary's Neck is just glimpses of both our daughters. Enid's eighteen and more serious than Clarissa; but they're both in and out all the time—mostly out."

He sighed again and went on to speak of intimate family matters. Indeed, I suppose that seldom has a man spoken with a more copious freedom to another man not a relative or of old acquaintance. There were times when he related the details of episodes mortifying to himself —told me of things he had thought and done that were of a kind not unknown in other people's experiences but that most of us feel it is more becoming not to impart. Gradually he formed in my mind a fairly clear impression of contrast or even conflict—something like a semi-historical picture of a Midland family a little convulsed by being out of its native environs; and, since there appears to be something of possible value, or even entertainment, in such a picture, I have here transcribed what presented it to me. The effect seems to be the homely narrative of a Logansville family's accommodating itself to a New England summer; but there may be something more generally applicable, here and there beneath the surface of Mr. Massey's talk, or, as I should say, his many talks. In recording them it has seemed only fair to him to preserve them in his own congenial Midland manner and to let him speak for himself.

B. T.

CHAPTER I

You see the Masseys have always had a great name for being home-bodies. Maybe it's been a mistake, I don't know; but anyway for three generations—ever since pioneer days—we've stuck pretty close around Logansville and done mighty little travelling. For my own part, Logansville's always been good enough for me and I never did see much use in getting very far away from home. Not that I couldn't afford it, because I've done as well in business as any man could ask—my father owned the gas-plant and I've still got it, and I'm president of the Logansville Light and Power Company besides—but two or three trips a year to Chicago on business and to other large cities, maybe, to look over Plants like ours, have usually been enough to satisfy me in the way of gadding about, so to speak. Of course I don't mean that my family and I practically haven't ever been out of Logansville. Both the girls went East to school, and they and Mrs. Massey have been to New York pretty often— I've had to go there myself sometimes—and they've been to Atlantic City and Florida. One or two summers we've spent a month or so at a hotel up on Lake Michigan; but it's a fact I never did see the ocean until we came here to Mary's Neck this summer, and to tell the truth

5

I didn't have any particular anxiety to see it. Mrs. Massey and Enid and Clarissa had just about all they could do, I expect, to persuade me that my duty required me to come and look at it.

They'd read about this place in a newspaper article by a summer correspondent, a lady-writer that was pretty enthusiastic about the quaint old Down East fishing village, full of quaint old interesting characters and quaint old interesting furniture and fashionable summer people and storm-bound rocks and sun-washed beaches and all this and that; and so last winter nothing would do but Mrs. Massey should write to a real-estate agent in Boston and rent a cottage here for the summer. That article hit her and the girls right between the eyes; they'd read books about just such places, and they'd already pestered me into remodelling our old house to make it Colonial or something—all out of place in Logansville, I told 'em, but they had their way, and they got their way about landing the family here in Mary's Neck for this summer, too.

They were so excited and so anxious to see the quaint old Down East characters and buy some of the quaint old furniture that they couldn't even wait for warm weather and hustled me up here with 'em right in April —yes, sir, outside of a taxicab ride in the rain across some of Boston, my first experience of old New England was spang in the middle of a snowstorm. "Stern and rockbound coast", I should say so! Mrs. Massey and the girls stood out on the front piazza, shivering and taking on about what a grand view it was, while I took the keys the Boston agent had given us and opened the front door and went inside to see what chance there was to get warm. There didn't seem to be much hope. The fireplaces were all empty, so I went out to the kitchen, and, happening to think, I turned a faucet of the sink and nothing came out. Then I opened the kitchen door and there was a man in rubber boots and these yellow slickers they call oilskins sitting on the back steps.

"Howdy do," I said. "I expect you're probably Zebias Flick, the man Mr. Avery in Boston told us was the caretaker here and would have everything nice and ready for us."

He didn't move, or even turn his head; he just sat there on the steps with his back toward me.

"Here!" I said. "Aren't you this Zebias Flick?"

Well, it didn't seem to register with him; he didn't pay any attention at all; he didn't budge—just sat there like a stone man, and I couldn't see even his profile because his head was all covered with one of these sou'wester hats that had snow on it. Mrs. Massey and the girls had been delighted in Boston when Mr. Avery told us the caretaker's name was Zebias Flick; they said it was "too perfect", that name! But as I stood there in the doorway looking at him, it began to come over me that if this was Zebias I wasn't taking a great liking to him at first sight.

"Listen!" I said. "Are you snowbound or are you Zebias Flick?"

At that, he stretched out one of his legs, then he stretched out the other one, then he put 'em both under him again and hoisted himself up. He didn't turn all the way toward me, just part way; but I could see that he had a weazened sort of face with kind of a scattered mustache, and his mouth was moving around underneath it because he was chewing a splinter. But he didn't say anything; he just gave sort of a cough. That is, it was more like a muffled bark—as if he was afraid if he let himself out in a good hearty cough he might commit himself to something.

"Well, that's a comfort," I told him. "Anyhow you can cough a little! Listen, are you Zebias Flick?"

"Well—" he said, "yes." He took his time to say it, too, and the way he said it struck me as if what he really wanted to say, and would have said if he hadn't got caught in a jam, was, "Yes and no."

So then I asked him why in the name of conscience there wasn't any heat in the house, and he loosened up enough to answer that there might be some wood in the cellar.

"The water isn't turned on, either," I told him, and I asked him if the current was on for the lights and the electric range in the kitchen.

"Dun't know as 'tis," he said.

"Well, how do we get our water and light?"

This question seemed to strike him as one that opened up a field of thought entirely new to him, and I had to repeat it twice. Then he came back at me with the snappy suggestion: "Telephone mebbe."

"All right, where's the telephone?"

"Dun't know as it's been connected."

"Listen!" I said. "Mr. Avery told me you were supposed to be the caretaker here, and the people that rent this cottage are more or less expected to employ you during the summer as kind of a hired man. Do you think if I made a settlement with you right now at a reasonable figure you could take up your duties and get some fires going in the house and the water connected and the lights on and kind of brighten things up generally? What about it?"

"Well," he said, and he turned more away from me, "I dun't know as I cal'lated on being around here this season. Had a mind to lobster some down Kitter's Cove way."

"Listen!" I said. "How much do you want?"

"Well—" he said, and he stopped chewing his splinter for so long that the end of it that stuck out beyond his mustache got snow on it.

I began making offers to him, raising them pretty fast because I'd only brought a light overcoat and I was pretty shivery. Finally, when I thought I'd gone about as far over the limit for a hired man as even an Eastern summer resort could expect, he began chewing his splinter again, at least enough to wobble the snow off of it; and pretty soon after that he seemed to make up his mind to come into the house and start in to be fairly busy, so I concluded that the terms were satisfactory. Then, the next day, the cook and a couple of housemaids Mrs. Massey had hired in Boston came up, and, feeling that we were beginning to get settled a little, I went out to take a look around and see where I was going to find somebody to talk to.

Of course Mrs. Massey and Clarissa and Enid are just as pleasant a family as a body could wish for; but they incline a good deal to topics that don't appeal to me so terribly and that pretty often are 'way out of a practical man's field of thought, and over my head, maybe. And besides that, a man always has a kind of powerful need to talk to other men quite a little, instead of just to women, no matter how nice those women are. Out our way in the Middle West everybody knows how easily talking goes on between man and man, so to speak; nobody's ever afraid to talk to anybody else, and of course in Logansville everybody knows everybody else and there's quite a power of talking goes on all the time. Well, I always supposed it was just the same all over the country, and that a man could hardly go anywhere where it wouldn't be the easiest thing in the world to start up a conversation—but when I thought that I'd never been to Mary's Neck in New England.

I went into the grocery store in the village and bought some supplies right liberally. There were several men in there; one or two, I could tell from their clothes, were fishermen, and they kind of seemed to smell like it, and two or three were in overalls. "Well, gentlemen," I said, "I hope we'll have some better weather before long." I said this because that's always a good way to start a conversation, and besides, I'd already heard some of the inhabitants of Mary's Neck calling out things about the weather to one another as they passed on the road. The very day we arrived I heard one of the villagers shout across the street to another in the midst of the snow-storm, "Snowin'!" and the other called back, "Yes, 'tis!" So I thought this might be an agreeable way to begin. But nobody paid any attention; nobody even looked at me, and I felt a little embarrassed.

"Well, most likely," I said, trying to make myself feel more comfortable, "I guess most likely it's liable to clear up pretty soon."

They just stood there, mostly with their hands in their pockets, and looked out toward the village street; so I waited to see if they weren't going to have a little politeness, maybe. After a while, one of 'em began to move his lower jaw, which I've learned since is a sort of preliminary sign a citizen of these parts makes to indicate that if you stand around and wait long enough he's liable to say something. When this one got the motion worked up to where he was ready, he spoke to a fisherman standing near him. "Cap'," he said, "you hear about old man Lingle's mistake?"

"No," the one he called "Cap'" told him. "Ain't."

"No?" the first one said. "Ole man Lingle was settin'

front his prop'ty at Pebble Cove when a little vessell come
round the Point. She sprung a plank and went right down
to the bottom with a young man aboard of her. He was
makin' a mite of a fuss; but he scarcely left a ripple, and
it turned out to be old Mrs. Cadwalader's son that keeps
the fish store over t' the Cove. After the funeral she
come around, and it seemed like she wanted to take old
man Lingle to task. 'Mr. Lingle,' she says, 'why didn't
you rescue my son? There you stood right on the shore
with your dory as handy as need be and my son hollering
for help only a mite of a distance away in the water. Why
didn't you git in that dory and go out and haul him
aboard?' Ole man Lingle seemed to feel bad about it.
'Why, Mrs. Cadwalader,' he says, 'I wouldn't 'a' had
such a thing happen for the world! If I'd 'a' dreamed it
was your son you know me better than to think I'd ever
stood there jest lookin' on like. Mrs. Cadwalader,' he
says, 'you'll have to excuse me; I thought it was one o'
them summer people.'"

Then, when he finished, nobody said anything and they
all stood just the way they were before, without any
expressions on their faces, staring out through the front
windows of the store as if they didn't have anything
except that to do for the next day or so. It struck me
as kind of chilling, so to speak, and I gave up trying to
be sociable with that lot; but I didn't do much better with
any of the other inhabitants I ran across, though I made
quite a number of attempts to strike up pleasant relations
with them if such there were.

There was only one person showed any willingness to
be friendly; but it didn't turn out very well. He was an
elderly-looking man with a right nice likeable kind of
face, and he was sawing wood just outside of a big barn
that stands close to an old stone fence on the back road;

I was walking by there and I stopped and sat down on the fence and watched him for a while. By-and-by he quit sawing and wiped his forehead, and I spoke to him.

"Pretty good exercise, sawing wood," I said; and he put his hand behind his ear and came up close to me.

"Wha'd you say? I'm hard o' hearin'."

So I got up and leaned close to his ear and said it again, louder, and he astonished me because he broke into a right amiable smile, the first thing of that kind I'd seen since I came to Mary's Neck. Well, sir, it warmed me all up, and I thought to myself that here at last I'd found one fellow-being, as it were, that I could come and talk to, and I was lonesome enough to take the trouble of trying to make him hear me. He said he'd always enjoyed sawing wood; and we began to have a real nice conversation until I happened to ask him whether he was a Democrat or a Republican. He didn't seem to understand me at first, so I shouted the question louder in his ear, and then, all at once, he reached out and grabbed my hat off my head and went into the barn with it. He stayed in there a minute; then he came out and walked up to the stone fence where I was and put my hat on my head again. He didn't say anything while he was doing all this and it seemed so peculiar that I felt kind of embarrassed and didn't say anything, either. Then he went over to his bucksaw and picked up a stick of wood and threw it at me. I dodged it; but he threw another one and was reaching down to get more, so I left.

On the way home I got to wondering why he'd taken my hat into the barn, so I took it off and looked at it. It was a new grey soft hat with a black band around it, and he had written DAMU on the front of the band in chalk. It struck me as a singular word; but I thought I saw what he meant, and when I got back to the cottage

I told Zebias Flick about this old man and where he lived and what he'd done to my hat, and I asked Zebias if he knew him. It was warmer, and Zebias had found a blade of grass that he had in his mouth; afterwhile it began to move up and down where it came out between some of his mustache, and finally he said:

"Might be I might; might be I mightn't."

"Well, who is he?"

"I couldn't say," he told me. "I couldn't say even if I was a mind to."

"Look here," I said, "that old man isn't right in his head. I might have known that, myself, at the start, from the willingness he showed to talk to me; but naturally a person that begins to throw cordwood at you just because you ask him whether he's a Republican or a Democrat—well, in a place as small as this, of course everybody would certainly know who he is. Do you mean to tell me you've never even heard of him?"

"I couldn't state," Zebias said. "I dun't take no interest in politics."

That's all I could get out of him. But our cook, a woman named Joanna Gillwife, was originally from somewhere Down East, herself, and had made some acquaintances in the village, and the next evening she came into the living-room and told Mrs. Massey and me all about that old man. Of course, as anybody knew, he wasn't right in his head; but he was strong and handy and perfectly gentle—except to strangers—so his family had always kept him in Mary's Neck instead of sending him away, and he was Zebias Flick's own cousin.

So that's the way it was, you see. I was kind of thrown back completely, as it were, on the society of Mrs. Massey and the girls.

CHAPTER II

WELL, of course they'd found out by this time that we'd come to Mary's Neck pretty early in the season—a good deal before the season was due to get ready to commence, in fact. "It isn't like Atlantic City," Mrs. Massey said, "or those other places where people go practically at any time. Joanna Gillwife has cooked several summers for families in other places along the shore and she tells me none of the cottagers to speak of will be here before June and most of 'em won't be along until a couple of months from now, and the hotels won't open till then, either. I thought Mr. Avery did seem rather surprised about our wanting to come in April and I s'pose we really were rushing things a little."

But of course Clarissa and Enid both said they'd known all about that. Anybody that knew anything understood that the season at places like Mary's Neck didn't begin until along in June, at least, they said, and they told me the kind of people that had cottages at Mary's Neck were probably mostly resting themselves at home in the eastern cities for a while after being in Florida and other southern resorts for some of the winter. The fact that they wouldn't be here for quite a while yet was a great advantage for us, Enid and Clarissa said, because when the season opened everything would be in such a sociable rush they wouldn't have time for anything, and now, the way things were, we'd have a long, peaceable period to get acquainted with the neighborhood in and find the quaint old characters and do some antiquing. What if we did have a few snowstorms, they asked, and they said they wished they had even more time before the pow-wowing and ruckus of the sociable season opened.

Enid is the artistic one, and for the last year or so she's had artistic theories I don't understand at all, and she gets sensitive about 'em, too; but she claims she isn't bigoted against the old in art because she's just as much interested in antiques as her mother and sister are. Sometimes she gets me nervous about both art and antiques; she has a way of looking as if she knew secrets about both that I couldn't ever hope to learn, and now and then if I ask questions in such matters she has a cold, hurt look that's right upsetting for a parent to endure. Clarissa and Mrs. Massey, too, can do a little in that line when it comes to antiques, and, during those first days of ours at Mary's Neck, the three of them were pretty often frosty with me, besides being expensive. They weren't having the same kind of oppressive time I was, not a bit of it. They were just revelling, as they said, in the delicious old quaintness of Mary's Neck and everything else up and down that strip of coast. They had magazines and read books about all such matters—getting themselves posted up on whatever was old enough to be worth anything—and already they'd gone fairly wild antiquing, as they called it. Our car and the chauffeur had got here from Logansville, and they went out antiquing all over Mary's Neck and up and down the coast and through the country and to inland towns as much as sixty or seventy miles away, almost every day; and what they brought home with 'em—my soul!

Of course, they'd had the fever a good while back before we ever thought of coming to Mary's Neck, and they'd bought a few terrible-looking things on their trips away from Logansville; but I hadn't got myself accustomed to the idea at all. The way I was brought up, my father and mother, like everybody else in our part of the country, always used to feel a little set up and superior whenever we could afford to buy something new. The principal idea people had about the pleasure of being well off was getting rid of old things and buying new ones; and that's always seemed to me the natural way of human nature, because it's the way of progress. Even the ancient orientals must have had that idea or else why was everybody so anxious to trade old lamps for new in the Arabian Nights story of Aladdin? I can't seem to keep myself from feeling that there's something upside-down about all this antiquing; but Enid and Clarissa and their mother fairly hoot at me when I air such notions, and they tell me I'm a barbarian and then start in to try and educate me some more. It's pretty uphill work for them, I guess.

They came home late one afternoon when we'd been here about ten days, and the car was so full that about all you could see of the three of them was their heads sticking out above the packages; and when the chauffeur and I had helped to carry all that truck into the house I couldn't make myself heard, there was so much going on in the way of exclamations. Enid and Clarissa just danced around the dining-room table where they had their plunder laid out, and kept shouting: "Look at this! Look at that!" till I was pretty nearly dazed.

"We're going to re-furnish this whole cottage with

antiques," they told me. "Just look at the treasures we've found!"

Well, I looked at them; and all I saw seemed to me to be the worst kind of second-hand truck I'd ever laid my eyes on. A good deal of it was pewter, and if there's anything on earth I despise——we used to be ashamed to have any of it in the house when I was a boy——it's pewter! Then there was a good deal of that cheap old kind of glass we used to use in Logansville before we could afford cut-glass; there were rusty iron candle-sticks with snuffers; there were some ratty old stable-lanterns, and heaven knows what all! The worst thing in the lot, I thought——even worse than a glass hen sitting on glass eggs in a glass basket——was a great big china dog. He was lying down on kind of an oval plate, and too sizable for a mantelpiece ornament——he was kind of spanielish; but you couldn't tell what kind of a dog he was, unless being a china dog made him some kind of a dog. He had four awful-looking yellowish spots on him; but for the rest of him he was glistening bald all over, and the expression on what was intended to be his face honestly made me sort of sick. As a matter of fact, this dog was one of those things you don't want to look at but you can't help doing it. I'd look at him a while; then I'd walk away and try to forget about him; then I'd have to come back to see if he really did look as horrible as I thought he did, and then I'd just stand staring at him and swallowing.

"Isn't he wonderful?" Enid asked me.

I said he was. "You haven't got it in mind to take him back to Logansville, have you?" I asked her.

At that, all three of 'em went for me. This dog, it seemed, was the finest thing they'd found in all their ransackings of the country around Mary's Neck; it was old Chippingale ware or old Cheswood or something——

I never could get the antiquing lingo straight. Anyhow, it was a great find and they'd got it at a tremendous bargain; but that seemed to be true of everything they bought. They were always talking of the "finds" they made; and they seemed to consider themselves pretty remarkable discoverers. It didn't matter if something they bought was sitting right out in the show-window of an antique store, they always said they "found" it, and pretty often they were sure the antique dealer hadn't understood the value of the things they bought, or maybe had got confused and put the wrong price-mark on something that was worth at least three times what they'd paid for it.

What they "found" was mostly the kind of extinct ornamental efforts I've just been talking about, though they'd also brought home a few old chairs with rush-seats, a couple of farmerish-looking tables and a ghastly sort of thing with mushmelon sized knobs on it that Clarissa told me was a "beautiful old Colonial wig-stand", and I hate to think what she paid for it—she could have bought a gas-driven lawn-mower with the same money. What they wanted most, of course, was furniture; but Mrs. Massey said that "really good things" and "fine, rare old pieces" in that line were scarce; the antique stores seemed to have been pretty well combed over for Colonial furniture.

"What I wish," she told me, "is that I knew some way to get inside of a few of these delicious old houses in this neighborhood. There's where the best old pieces are —if there were any way in the world to get at them! Some of these families have been living in the same house for generations, and the place is just full of the most wonderful old concealed treasures. The girls and I have done everything we could to get a look at them; we've used every bit of tact we possess; but these people up here in New England are so queer! We haven't got inside a single old house."

"No," I said, "I should think maybe you mightn't have. That seems fairly plausible to me."

"But we're going to keep on trying," Clarissa put in. "It makes my mouth water to think what must be inside some of these houses, and we're not going to rest until we see for ourselves. We'll make it before long; you just wait!"

But they had to go on waiting quite a little while longer; then one day they didn't get home till so late that dinner had been ready half an hour before they drove up and came bouncing out of the car. They were just wild, though they hadn't bought anything and didn't have any packages with 'em at all. They'd got into one of the delicious old houses at last, and the three of 'em tried to tell me all about it at the same time, and they were so excited it took me quite a while to make out what had happened. We were half through dinner before I could get the girls to let their mother have the floor to herself and tell me.

"There was never anything so absolutely perfect in the world!" she said. "I never dreamed they would let us in, and at first they weren't going to; but Enid looked so pretty and so pleading the dear old man simply couldn't resist her!"

"What dear old man?" I asked. "What dear old man?"

"The old man at this wonderful old house," she told me. "He's simply the sweetest old thing I ever——"

"And don't forget his darling old wife," Clarissa broke in. "They were simply the dearest, quaintest, sweetest old couple in the world! The most perfect old New England characters!"

"Absolutely!" Enid had to have her say. "You could see right away they were absolutely characters. They were the most perfectly quaint——"

"Yes," Mrs. Massey said, "they certainly were! And even after they let us into the front parlor, and we saw how wonderful it was, I was just sure they weren't going to consent to our seeing the rest of the house. I think if Clarissa hadn't developed such a crush on the old lady they never would have done it. You never saw such a place in your life—absolutely a treasure house!"

"Why, it's absolutely a museum!" Enid told me. "There's hardly a thing in it that isn't a museum piece, father. And all that priceless, wonderful stuff has been there for generations and generations in the old couple's family! That's the most wonderful thing about it all— they haven't the remotest idea of what it's worth themselves; so that if we ever get around the dear old things enough to persuade them to sell us such treasures, why, the bargains we could make would just take your breath!"

"Didn't you offer to buy anything?" I asked her.

"Offer to buy their family heirlooms? No, we certainly didn't! We knew too much for that; they'd have been insulted. That isn't the way to handle these people; you'd never get anywhere if you spoke of buying anything the very first day you got into the house. You have to lead up to it gradually; but after you once get them into the mood to sell——"

"Yes," Clarissa said, "that's when you begin to get the bargains. Why, Moses Brazinga told me, himself, about a woman that picked up a Hayes-and-Wheeler butterdish for two dollars at a farmhouse, and he offered her a hundred and twenty-five dollars for it and could have sold it to a New York collector for three hundred;

but she knew what she'd got, and she wouldn't sell it. She was from Chicago, he told me."

Maybe "Hayes-and-Wheeler butterdish" wasn't what Clarissa said, exactly—I never can get the straight of these things—but it was something like that, and Moses Brazinga is an antiquity dealer Mrs. Massey and the girls were always talking about. He has an antiquity store over at Lodgeport, a town about twenty miles from Mary's Neck, and they'd bought some coal-oil lamps from him only the day before. (I thought these lamps would look out of place in the house of the president of the Logansville Light and Power Company; but the girls said that didn't matter.) Anyhow, after Clarissa had told about the Hayes-and-Wheeler butterdish and Moses Brazinga and the Chicago lady, Mrs. Massey said that was just nothing to what happened to a picture collector she'd been reading about. He'd found some old paintings stored in a wood-shed up in the White Mountains and bought them for eight dollars and a half, and they turned out to be worth over seventy-five thousand. So then Enid broke out and told about things like that she'd heard of, and they all three began talking at once about old pieces of glass and iron and pewter and rags or rugs or something that people had "found" or "picked up", and that turned out to be worth enough to buy a first class automobile. And they said it was going to be just this way about the delicious old house they'd been in that day and were raving over.

"Well, but look here!" I said. "Hold on a minute! I thought you were telling me what a sweet old couple they are that live in this house you're talking so much about. If their furniture and bric-à-bric and all this and that are worth such a lot of money and they don't know it, you ought to tell 'em, oughtn't you? You wouldn't want to persuade them to sell you something for four dollars that's worth four hundred?"

I didn't get very far with that. They all three began to educate me again in the methods proper to antiquing; and then Enid got the floor to herself.

"You see, father," she told me, "these things that old couple own are only worth a certain amount to *them,* and that's what we'd pay them; so they'd get the full value as far as they, themselves, are concerned. If they sold to a dealer, they'd hardly get anything at all and probably be terribly cheated. Besides, you see, we don't propose to sell what we buy; we just want the things to keep, for our own pleasure in their beauty. We wouldn't dream of selling them to make *money!*"

"I see," I told her. "I'm glad you wouldn't expect to. I won't worry about it any more."

Well, they talked about that old house and the things in it and the quaint old couple off and on till bed-time; they talked almost as much about the old couple as they did about the coming sociable season that'd begin when the cottagers got here. This was such a regular subject with them that by now the cottagers were usually referred to just as "they". Probably more than a dozen times a day I'd hear Mrs. Massey and Clarissa and Enid saying something about what we ought to do "before they come" or "after they get here", and once I even overheard a whisper when the three of 'em were in the next room—I couldn't tell which of 'em said it: "Joanna Gillwife says nobody is practically anybody unless they own their own cottage; we ought to get him to buy this place before they come."

That was kind of a disturbing whisper to me, and the evening I'm speaking of I preferred hearing them talk about the old couple. As a matter of fact, they got me

kind of stirred up and curious to see these two old characters and where they lived, though of course I knew I
wouldn't understand a thing about their rare old house
and furniture, even if I went there. The girls and their
mother held off the next day and didn't go near the place
—they said it would be better policy—but they did go
the afternoon after that and a couple of times more,
and then they told me they thought the old couple were
kind of coming round to the point where they'd be willing to sell a few things maybe. Mrs. Massey had almost
come out in the open and talked price with them, so she
was beginning to feel right encouraged.

"Why don't you come with us to-morrow?" she asked
me. "It would help you to learn what beautiful fine old
things really are if you'd see them in their natural surroundings in that exquisite old house."

I said no, at first, though the truth is I had kind of
a hankering to go, and pretty soon I let them persuade
me. They told me to be careful not to talk much, and I
think they were a little nervous about my possibly saying
something that might offend the quaint old couple; but
the next afternoon we drove out there—it wasn't far
beyond the village—and stopped the car outside the white
picket gate at the end of a brick walk that led up to the
house. It was a nice-looking, white-painted farmhouse
with green shutters; but it was so old-fashioned and
plain that for my part I never would have made any great
fuss over it. The old couple were sitting on a wooden
bench out in the front yard, and when I got a good look
at them I thought probably that if I hadn't been told so
much about how perfect they were I wouldn't have made
any particular fuss over them, either.

Their name was Cheever, Mrs. Massey said when she
introduced me, and they were so much alike you could

almost have taken him out of his own rusty black clothes and put him into hers without seeing much difference. They had grey hair and weazened faces and silver spectacles, and they didn't look like people that ever gushed much. I guess maybe they were a right nice likeable old couple, if they wanted to be; but they hardly said a thing when Mrs. Massey and the girls began making a to-do over them. Most of the time when they were paid a compliment they'd just put a hand behind their ear and say, "Hey?" and then, if the compliment was repeated loud enough to hear, they'd scratch somewhere.

At least that's the way they impressed me; but I was glad I'd come, because I'd never seen anything like them before.

CHAPTER III

AFTER I'd stood around looking on a while, the old man seemed to notice me; then he took a big brass key out of his pocket and opened up the front door with it—it seems they're great people around here to keep everything locked up, even when they're right on the premises.

The girls followed him and the old lady into the front parlor; but Mrs. Massey gave me a pinch on the arm and kept me in the little front hall.

"Just look at that!" she whispered. "Just *look* at that staircase!"

Well, I looked at it, and it was certainly as mean a little staircase as I ever saw in my life. It came almost right down to the front door, and it was steep and narrow and twisted enough for a monkey, and had a miserable old strip of faded carpet running up it.

"Yes," I said. "Terrible." Because of course I thought that was why she wanted me to look at it.

"It's gorgeous!" she told me. "Look at the spiral of that mahogany rail! Maybe they'd sell that darling old stair-carpet with it."

I looked at her. "With it?" I asked her. "You mean you want to buy their staircase? Buy their staircase?"

"We'll have to talk to 'em about that," she whispered. "Look at that low boy!"

"Where?" I said, because I wanted to see one. I'd been hearing a lot of talk about low boys and high boys, and of course I understood by this time that some sort of furniture was implied. "Where's any low boy?"

She pointed to an ornery little table with some drawers underneath the top of it. "It's got cubbyhole legs and duck feet," she said. Anyhow she said something like that; I'm pretty sure it was duck feet. "Now come in and see the high boy," she said.

So we went into the parlor and I looked at the high boy but didn't think much of it. Then old Mr. and Mrs. Cheever took us all over the house. To me, the whole place seemed to be just a plain farmhouse full of kind of homely old-fashioned things with nothing in it I'd ever care to buy or feel I had to see around me; but I never heard anything like the way Mrs. Massey and the girls carried on together in whispers. Every minute or so one of 'em would come and grab me by the arm and whisper to me, too, sort of fiercely, "Carved knees!" they'd say, or "Will you *look* at those snake feet!" or something like that. Most of the time I was walking with old Cheever; but he never said a word except when we got to the kitchen where there was a flint-lock musket hanging over the miserable old fireplace among a lot of out-of-date cooking utensils, and I asked him how old it was.

"Seventeen-thirty-six, B. C.," he said, and I never heard a hoarser voice. "Either Seventeen-thirty-six, B. C. or Seventeen-thirty-seven, B. C."

"B. C.?" I asked him. "B. C.?"

"No," he said, "A. D." That's everything he said all the time we were in there, so I could see that Mrs.

Massey and the girls were right about his being a pretty quaint old New England character.

In one corner of the kitchen there was a contraption that Enid went just crazy over. It didn't amount to anything. I could have made one like it, myself, out of old pine boards if I'd wanted to, which I certainly didn't; but she dragged me over to it and made me look at some figures that had been scratched near the base of it with a nail or something.

"Look at that!" she whispered. "Seventeen-fifty-nine! A pine corner-cupboard dated Seventeen-fifty-nine with a scallop-shell impediment and chock full of absolutely priceless pewter. I'll simply die if they refuse to sell it!"

"What were you thinking of offering 'em for it?" I asked her.

"I don't know," she whispered to me. "It's worth hundreds and hundreds of dollars without the pewter, and I've simply got to have that pewter, too. Mother and Clarissa and I have made up our minds that we simply cannot live unless we get this corner-cupboard with the pewter, and the high boy and the low boy, and the three four-poster beds and that wonderful duck-foot dining-room table, and the Chippingale chair and the harp-backed chair and the set of blue china and the old silver tea-set and ladle and the staircase and——"

"Hold on," I said, and I wiped my forehead. "What on earth do you think you're doing? These old Cheevers intend to go on living here, don't they? How on earth could you expect 'em to do it with the staircase ripped out—and all these other——"

"Never mind," she told me. "They're used to living in the simplest way. Come on." So we went back to the parlor where the others already were, and Mrs. Massey was talking to the old couple about the high boy.

"Of course I know it's a delicate matter," she said, "to press you to name a price for a thing that's associated in your minds with former members of your family. But of course, since you feel you *could* bring yourselves to part with it——" She was being so polite about it that she just stopped there and waited for them to speak; but she had to wait so long that finally it got embarrassing. "Well," she said, "if you could just bring yourselves to name a price——" And she laughed a little, as if she were apologizing.

I saw that Mrs. Cheever was going to say something because her under jaw was beginning to move a little; so afterwhile, when she got herself ready like that, she said, "It's got clor and boiled feet."

It seemed to me that Mrs. Massey was surprised that the old lady knew so much about her high boy's feet. "Oh—has it?" she said. "I'd hardly noticed that." But here, it struck me, that she was trying to be diplomatic, because she went on, "Of course it's nice; but so far as rarity is concerned it isn't very——"

"It's got clor and boiled feet," the old lady broke in, "and it's got the original brasses and cubbyhole legs and a broken impediment."

It seemed to me from the way she said this that she was fixing to drive quite a bargain; but Enid began talking to me in a low voice—we were standing over by the doorway—and she told me the old lady didn't know anything at all about the high boy. "Those points are just some she picked up from hearing us talk about it," Enid said. "We ought to've been more cautious, I guess; we made altogether too much fuss over the high boy the first time we came. I think mother ought to've begun with the chandelier."

"My goodness!" I said. "You don't expect to buy the

chandelier right out of these people's ceiling, do you?" It surprised me, too, that anybody'd want a chandelier like that; it was a little old glass one with candles.

"Sh!" Enid told me. "It's waterproof; but they don't know it." Then she stepped forward and kind of took charge, as it were. "We might as well begin by telling Mr. and Mrs. Cheever exactly what we're interested in, I think. Now, in this room, there's the high boy and the chandelier and the two samplers and the wing chair——"

"And the secretary," Clarissa put in. "Don't forget the secretary and the andirons and the——"

"Wait a minute," I said; because I thought we'd be there a pretty long time if things weren't put on a more businesslike basis, so to speak. "Why don't one of you just sit down here and write out a list of all the things you want in the whole house, in case Mr. and Mrs. Cheever are willing to sell 'em to you; then they could take your list and look it over and write down whatever price they decide on opposite the articles. Wouldn't that be the best way to get somewhere?"

Mr. and Mrs. Cheever didn't say anything; but my family fell in with the plan, and Clarissa sat down at the secretary and wrote out the list, with her mother and Enid bending over her and putting in whatever she happened to forget. When they had it finished, I looked at it, and it made me feel pretty embarrassed—though of course I realized the old couple could buy new household goods to begin their life over again with.

I handed the list to Mrs. Cheever. "Here," I said, and I could feel myself getting red, I felt so apologetic. "You and your husband just write down the prices you think would be right. Of course I don't know how much you'll feel willing to part with——"

"That seckatary's got the original brasses on it, too," she said.

"Has it?" I asked her. "Well, if you and Mr. Cheever will just sit down here and work through the list, my family and I will step out in the yard and wait while you two do the figuring."

So that's what we did. Mrs. Massey and the girls and I went outdoors, and I never did see three women in a greater state of unsuppressed excitement. Enid and Clarissa were so exhilarated they just grabbed each other and began to dance on the brick walk; but Mrs. Massey stopped them for fear the old couple would look out of the window and see them. Then Clarissa got to standing in a kind of trance, staring at the front door and I noticed her and went up to her. "What's the matter?" I asked her.

"I wish we'd put that in," she said, in a dreamy sort of way.

"Put what in?"

"The front door."

I just walked away from her. I strolled around the house and noticed a shed in the back yard, and went in. There were quite a number of wonderful old things in there—mostly broken, though—and with its face against the wall there was one fine old piece that I turned over and looked at; but when I went back to the front yard I didn't say anything about it. The quaint old couple had just come out of the house, and Mrs. Massey and both girls couldn't restrain themselves—they made a dash for that list and fairly snatched it out of Mrs. Cheever's hand. Then they put their three heads together over it, and ten feet away I could hear 'em breathing.

Mr. Cheever was carrying a red-painted cylinder with a bottom to it and a rope handle. "Here," he said to me.

"This is an ancient Revolutionary fire-bucket. I cal'late to make it a present to ye in case ye buy the hull list."

Well, of course that would have made anybody understand there was something wrong, and the way my family were standing as they looked over the list seemed to have quite a little significance, too. None of them moved a muscle. They just stood and stared; but I could hear them breathing louder. So I went over to them and took the paper out of Mrs. Massey's hand, and she didn't resist any or hardly move her fingers as it slid out of them. Just one glance showed me that the Cheevers were certainly willing to sell because they had written a price after every article on the list, and then they had added the whole thing up and set down the total at the bottom.

I didn't bother much with the individual items, though, as my eye ran down the paper, I noticed that they had marked the high boy eighteen-hundred and fifty-two dollars, and the waterproof chandelier twelve-hundred and sixty-nine dollars. The staircase was cheaper; they only wanted eleven hundred for that, and ninety-one dollars for the old strip of carpet on it. The total at the bottom of the second page interested me a good deal; it was eleven-thousand, eight-hundred and twenty-two dollars and sixty-five cents.

"Yes," I said to Clarissa, "you could get the front door put in, I expect. I don't believe they'd make any particular fuss about selling it."

Well, we didn't get the present of that Revolutionary red fire-bucket; the two New England characters were carrying it back into the house with 'em as we drove away, and Mrs. Massey and the girls were pretty quiet. They seemed kind of staggered, so I didn't mention right then what I'd seen in the shed behind the house. I didn't want to make my family feel any blanker until they'd got used to the shock they'd had. I just said, "I expect you used the right word about Mr. and Mrs. Cheever—I mean about their being a dear old couple."

Probably I shouldn't have gone even that far; I might have been wiser if I hadn't said it, because the three of them stiffened up a little but didn't look at me, and right away I could see they regarded me as occupying the position of an enemy, you might put it. When members of our opposite sex have been too confident about something and are feeling let-down about it, there's hardly ever anything at all a man ought to take a chance of saying to them. I saw it was a mistake, so I kept quiet until we got home; then I took Mrs. Massey aside and asked her how many people she thought knew about her wanting to get inside one of those wonderful old houses in the neighborhood.

"Why, nobody," she said in a cold way, staring at me. "We don't know anybody."

"Did this Moses Brazinga at Lodgeport tell you about the Cheever place?"

"Certainly not! We never talked to him about anything except what he had to sell right there in his shop."

"Well, who did tell you about it?"

"I think it may have been Zebias Flick," she said.

I went out in the kitchen where Zebias was sitting, talking to Joanna Gillwife. He had his woolen-stockinged feet in the oven of the electric stove; but mainly on account of habit, I expect, because the current was off.

"Listen!" I said to him. "Joanna here tells me that pretty nearly everybody in Mary's Neck is kin to everybody else, especially yourself. Have you got some cousins named Cheever?"

"Cheever?" he said; then he ruminated a while and

took a pin out of his mouth and looked at it. "Cheever,"
he said to himself in a low voice, appearing to be puzzled.

"Yes, Cheever!" I said. "Cheever!"

"Well," he asked me slowly, "where'bouts do they
live? Do you mean the Philo Cheevers or the Cheevers
at Sloan's Point or the Cheevers around Nist Hill or
some o' the other Cheevers? I have hear," he went on,
"I have hear they was Cheevers 'way further on Down
East. Mebbe it was them you had a mind to 'quire 'bout;
but ef you was to 'peal to me I never see any of them
Cheevers and I dun't know as I'd want to. They might
be kin to me, and they mightn't. I couldn't give you no
inf'mation 'bout them Cheevers 'tall."

"I don't want any," I told him. "I just want to know
if you've got any relatives named Cheever anywhere."

"Cheever," he said, and he put his pin back in his
mouth. "Cheever." Then he took it out again and seemed
to brighten up a little. "I can tell you where you can git
some inf'mation 'bout the Cheevers. That's from ole Miss
Caroline Willingsworth; she lives back in the country
quite a ways but it'd pay you to go up there ef you got a
mind to hear 'bout the Cheevers. She's got family albums
and old dockments and——" Then he stopped himself
with the air of a man who remembers something important, made a regretful sound with his tongue, and let
his feet slide down from the oven to the floor. "No, I
guess she ain't, though. She passed away, come to think
of it, some little time ago, and I don't know as anybody'd
be able to tell you what become of all her albums and
dockments. They must be scattered far and wide, by this
time, because she didn't have anybody to leave 'em to, and
mebbe the neighbors got 'em, or then mebbe they didn't. I
wasn't there so I couldn't tell you. Mebbe they had an
auction——"

"Listen!" I said, and I guess I was getting kind of mad. "Listen! I simply asked you——"

But just then he put his pin back in his mouth again and began to roll it around with a sort of faraway expression on his face. I looked at him, and I knew it wasn't any use in the world.

CHAPTER IV

At the dinner-table, that evening, I didn't get a chance to make any mistake about being still in disfavor on account of my unwise remark about the Cheevers being a "dear" old couple, and I knew by experience I was going to be held in that state until the family got over their disappointment. Likely enough it's the same way with other families: I expect they split up temporarily pretty often, with one sex on one side and the other on the other, and it's my personal belief that up to this present date, A. D., my own sex never won—not when the complete results were examined. One of the things that makes me doubt my sex's intelligence in such matters is that the same experience over and over doesn't teach us how to save ourselves from being pushed into the opposition, as it were. We make some little careless remark on the wrong subject, or at a poor time to say anything, and right away the ladies establish us as hostile. When we see 'em doing this we ought to have sense enough to withdraw from their sight, or anyhow to become as unnoticeable as possible; but our natural impulses nearly always make us do otherwise.

We get ruffled inside, and, what's most damaging to us, we never remember that when the ladies put us in conflict with them, they regard us as their enemies on all subjects, not just the one that started the trouble. A man may think he's winning an argument with his daughter about socialism and right in the middle of it find he's trying to defend himself to her for something inexcusable he said to his aunt when he was fourteen years old and got his bad conduct into the family records. The truth is we don't know how to look out for ourselves at all, and that's something I made the big mistake of forgetting, the evening after we'd been to the Cheevers'. Like a fool, I congratulated myself upon having something up my sleeve that would put the family in their place whenever I chose to bring it out, and I thought that just about the right time for this was after we'd left the table and got settled in the living-room for the evening.

Mrs. Massey was sewing by the fireplace, and Enid and Clarissa were teaching each other to play backgammon from a set of rules, because they said backgammon was "coming in" and they ought to familiarize themselves with it. "We've simply got to be good players," Clarissa said, "before they get here."

"We certainly must," Enid told her. "It's a good thing we came when we did and are getting so well established in certain ways before they come."

I was sitting by a lamp over on the other side of the room, reading some reports from the Logansville gas plant; but I noticed what they said and thought I'd begin and lead up to the little triumph for myself I contemplated having. " 'Before they come'," I said, and chuckled to show I was good-naturedly making a little fun of the girls. " 'Before they come! Before they get here'! They, they, they! Seems to me we're hearing quite a good deal lately about 'they'. 'Before they come'!"

Both girls stopped playing backgammon right away,

and Mrs. Massey let her work sink down in her lap and
turned and looked at me. "Yes?" Enid said, not addressing me as if I were her father, "Before they come.
What is your objection?"

"Why, none," I said. "Why should there be? I only
meant——"

"Yes?" Clarissa cut in, speaking even less as if I were
any relation to her than Enid did. "What, please, did
you mean?"

"Why, nothing," I told her, and I knew I was getting
sort of red. So I decided to show them right there the
full extent of the mistake they'd made about the
Cheevers. "I just thought Enid was right about getting
so well established 'before they come'. I suppose she
means getting acquainted around the neighborhood, for
instance, the way we did to-day with the dear old
couple."

Enid and Clarissa looked away from me and at each
other, both pretty stony. "He will have his joke," Enid
said. "Usually the same one."

"Yes," Clarissa told her. "Over and over."

I laughed again, to show them I was still entirely good-
natured, though I could hear, myself, that the sound I
made wasn't just right for the purpose. "Did any of
you notice anything," I asked them, "over that front
door Clarissa wanted to buy? I expect you didn't; but I
did. There was an oblong space up there on the wall
where the paint was of a little different color from the
rest. Did any of you notice it and think what it might
signify?"

"No," Mrs. Massey said, in a rebuffing way, and then
spoke gently. "Go on with your game, children."

"Well, I did," I said. "I noticed that oblong space,
and, being just a man with an ordinary sort of mind, I

thought it had to mean something. So I browsed around till I found what must have been in that space until lately. It was out in their wood-shed, facing the wall; but I turned it over and looked at it. It was a signboard, and I got to wondering if maybe somebody hadn't heard how much you all wanted to see the inside of one of these quaint old houses. It struck me that something or other must have had something to do with their taking this signboard down, because it had 'Brazinga and Cheever, Antiques' painted on it."

Then I laughed again, because now I felt this news would put them in their place, so to speak. I thought I'd come out of the little contest pretty well, and that in their hearts they'd understand it was really a good thing for the head of the family, so to speak, to be their superior in practical matters. Of course what I'd told them must have been quite a blow; but they didn't show it. They didn't say anything; their expressions just got more reserved, and then Mrs. Massey began to sew again and the girls went on with their game. I thought it better to pick up my reading again, and so I did, now and then making a sound like chuckling to get myself back to normal with.

Pretty soon Clarissa said something to Enid, in a way that showed she was making an objection to me. No man alive could put that into it; but Clarissa did and plenty of women can. All she said was, "Stuffy, this room, isn't it?"

"Dreadful!" Enid told her. "It's because it's too small for the size of the house. That's the only objection I'd have to our owning the place. Still, if we bought it, we could tear out that wall and build the room out to any dimensions we wanted it."

"Certainly we could," Clarissa said. "The property

runs out over two hundred feet on this side. If we hired a contractor that knows his business he could get it done before they come."

It was just the way I'm describing;—without saying a word more than this, they made it appear to be my fault that the living-room was stuffy and too small for the size of the house they'd persuaded me to rent for them. As a matter of fact, the living-room wasn't stuffy at all—but there was more in what they were doing than just putting me back in my place, a great deal more! And I went right on from one mistake to another. "Here!" I said. "If you two expect to be helpmeets for a couple of poor fellows some day, you ought to learn to be more practical. A living-room built two hundred feet out into a yard might lack some in coziness, I expect; but in the first place you can't tear walls out of a rented house because the owner——"

But Enid got up and stood looking at me with her eyes so wide open they scared me. "Did you hear me say 'If we bought it'? Did you hear me say 'If we owned it'?"

"Well, Enid, I——"

"No!" she said. "I don't think I'd try to explain if I were you. When a father's so anxious to be critical of his daughter that he utterly disregards the truth and deliberately misquotes her, I think it's about time——"

But she didn't go any further with it; she put her hand over her mouth in a tragic kind of way, as if her duty made her do it to keep her from stating more and worse facts about me, and then she gave a gasp and hurried out of the room. Clarissa swallowed so that I could hear it, and went right out, too, and for a minute Mrs. Massey seemed as if she intended to do the same, but decided to sit looking at me, instead.

"Why, good heavens!" I told her. "Aren't they old enough yet to see when I'm only in fun?"

"Don't you think," she asked me;—"don't you think it seemed a little uncalled-for?"

"I should say I do think so! They hadn't any business in the world to take what I——"

"No," she said, "I meant you. I meant your critical attitude toward them. I think you could be more tactful, especially at a time like this when you must see how nervous they are about the impression we'll make on the other summer people when they come. If you weren't a man you'd see they're getting more anxious about that every day and how much they worry about what'll be our position here. Joanna Gillwife says in a place like this everything depends on how a new family starts out, and as a mother I'd naturally like to see my daughters have every possible advantage we could afford to give them. Joanna says that families who already know other families here can rent cottages and be just as much sought after as if they owned them; but for a new family, in particular, renting certainly doesn't make the very best impression. The girls can't help feeling what we're depriving them of. They've been very sweet—they've hardly even spoken of it and have been careful not so much as to hint at it to you, for fear of upsetting you; but of course they know that it's a handicap, and I do think, when they're so self-sacrificingly considerate of you, that for you to criticize them and attack them——"

"Look here!" I said, and I put down the gas works' report, "What on earth are you talking about? I didn't——"

But she stopped me. "Didn't Enid really prove that you'd deliberately misquoted her?"

"But only in fun. I——"

"No," Mrs. Massey said. "Not entirely, I'm afraid.
Not under the circumstances. If we *had* given them
all the advantages we can afford, when they're so nervous,
and if we *did* own the house, and *then* you talked like
that, they might have thought you were only joking;
but, knowing that we don't own it, they can hardly be
expected to think——"

"Look here!" I said, "You don't mean to tell me that
their feelings wouldn't have been hurt by what I said if
we'd happened to own this house? What dif——"

She shook her head, looking sad. "Of course it
would make the greatest difference. We've all fallen in
love with the place, especially if we did enlarge this room
a little, and, as Clarissa said, that could be done very
easily before they come. I wrote Mr. Avery and he said
the owner's lost practically everything and is so anxious
for ready money he'd just give the place away for a
song. Mr. Avery said the deed could be ready in a couple
of days, and the price—simply ridiculous for what the
place is worth——"

"My soul!" I said. "You don't mean to sit there and
tell me you propose——"

"Simply as an investment it'd be worth twice what we'd
give for it," she told me. "Mr. Avery said he'd send up
a contractor about the living-room from Boston, himself,
and a decorator, too, for that matter. Mr. Avery said
he'd take charge of the whole transaction and put it
right through, though of course I've been merely considering it with him and haven't told him anything
definite yet. The thing that made what you did to the
girls this evening so painfully tactless was that being a
man you didn't see how disappointed they are over not
getting those antiques this afternoon. They'd really set
their hearts on them—and yet, after all, I think it's a

good thing we didn't get them because it saves all that money in case we do buy the house. I don't mean we ought to think of it for my own sake, of course, though I don't deny I'd like to begin a garden here. I suppose Zebias Flick wouldn't do for that, and we'd have to hire another——"

"Listen!" I said, and I was putting myself more and more at a disadvantage because I was getting flustered. It made me dizzy. Here, right when I thought I was trying to explain how I hadn't meant to hurt the girls' feelings, I found I was arguing against buying the property, something I had never dreamed of doing. Somehow she'd made it seem as if Clarissa and Enid had a right to be hurt with practically anything I said, so long as we didn't own the cottage, and that I owed it to them to buy it to make up for what I'd done, and also that I was depriving them of their rightful advantages by merely paying rent. "Listen!" I told her. "I'm a business man. Suppose we bought this place and then decided we didn't want to come back next year and——"

"We could rent it. Easily! Mr. Avery says——"

"I don't like him," I told her. "I don't know anything about him except he's an agent. I don't want to hear any more about him, either. I won't do it!"

She gathered up her work and stood up, dignified. "Oh, if you're beginning to take that tone!"

"Why, dammit," I said, *"I* want to give my daughters all the advantages they can have; but when it comes to buying a house simply because this Joanna Gillwife told 'em——"

"Please lower your voice," Mrs. Massey said, and she went to the door. "If you're going to swear and quote the servants at me, I think perhaps I'd better leave you to yourself."

"Listen!" I said, just about bawling at her. "If you think I'm going to be forced into buying——"

"That will do," she told me. "We'll never speak of it again."

So she went out, too.

CHAPTER V

I DON'T like to go into the details of the next few days.
I'll only state roughly that I had to be the one that
insisted on buying the house, and that by the end of a
week we owned it and carpenters were tearing up the
living-room before extending it thirty-five feet out into
the yard. The family were letting me get this done and
looking at me now and then as if I were still a good deal
of a trial to them; but sometimes they'd forget and break
out with expressions denoting excitement and pleasure,
then perhaps notice that I was around and restrain themselves suddenly. Mrs. Massey naturally got back on a
customary footing with me sooner than our daughters
did; she said as long as the carpenters were here anyway they might as well enlarge the butler's-pantry and
put up a new lattice around the laundry yard, and do a
few other little things, though of course, as she'd told me,
her principal interest in owning the place was the garden
she could have. There are a couple of acres of ground
behind the cottage; she'd dreamed all her life of having a
New England garden, she said, and now she was going to
do it. I told her to go ahead, thinking it would look well
in me to give her this permission because she was already
going ahead anyhow without asking for it.

I anticipated she might have a little trouble finding a gardener. I've mentioned how this Zebias Flick kind of came with the cottage when we rented it; our owning it didn't seem to make any difference with him, and he appeared to have established his own line of duties. He kept the grass cut and weeds out of the gravelled walk and driveway—to some extent—and was supposed to look after the ashes and do a little window washing and so forth. I was pretty sure Zebias wouldn't care to add gardening to the other duties he performed, not at any price; but Mrs. Massey said it wouldn't do any harm to ask him. So she did. He just ate a couple of spears of grass and said he'd been thinking of laying off work entirely for the summer in order to rest himself. Even after two or three weeks of acquaintanceship, Zebias didn't talk much—at least not with any person his mind connected with summer—and the other original inhabitants of Mary's Neck were the same. Eternal vigilance still seemed to be their watchword, especially whenever I made any sickly effort to get chatty with them, and when I did find the one exception, it first startled me and then turned out to be a disappointment.

This exception was the gardener Zebias found for Mrs. Massey. She didn't know where to look for one, herself, so after quite a little pressure on her part Zebias said he wasn't sure that he didn't know somebody who'd be willing to give the position a try, if he was a mind to, and the next morning the person he'd induced to consent to make the trial began work in the back yard under Mrs. Massey's direction.

She'd already had about half an acre ploughed up and fertilized by a farmer Zebias had hired for her, and also she had on hand two or three truck-loads of young plants from greenhouses over at Lodgeport, besides a gallon or so of seeds from mail-order houses. You see, she was going at the thing in earnest, and from where I was sitting by an open window in my own room upstairs, trying to read—because the carpenters were tearing out partitions pretty noisily below—I could hear how brisk and interested her voice was sounding down there in the yard. I could hear another voice, too, a high-pitched one that struck me as about the nasalest and twangiest I'd ever heard in my life, and it seemed to be going on most of the time and usually in a surprised kind of a way.

"Hee-uh?" it would say, and I'd already heard that expression often enough in these parts to know it's meant for the word "here". "Hee-uh? You mean you want them little bushes lugged right hee-uh? Well, if 'twas me I wouldn't do it," I could hear this funny, twangy voice saying. "Hee-uh? You want them seeds stuck in hee-uh? Well, if they was mine I wouldn't do it. What I'd do with this gaddin if 'twas mine, I'd plant me 'bout eight nice, good rows o' potatoes and the rest I'd put into nice, good tunnips and cabbages, somethin' you'd git pleasure out of later on. Course though it's yours and you know what you want. 'Tain't my respons'bil'ty, so I'll take and do what you say. If you tell me to I'll do it; but if 'twas me I wouldn't. You mean you want 'em hee-uh?"

I could hear Mrs. Massey telling him yes she did, and sometimes she seemed to be calling the new gardener by his name; but it struck me she said it in a lowered voice as if there was something peculiar about it or she didn't like to come right out with it, so to speak. Our daughters must have been listening a little, too, because they referred to this critically at lunch, which was rather an open-air meal, as you might say, on account of the carpenters having torn off the bay-window of the dining-room, that morning, to get its architecture more harmonious with the extension of the living-room. Mrs. Massey didn't mind that; she was flushed and warm with her gardening in the sunshine, and appeared to be pleased with the way things were going, though the girls' criticism embarrassed her slightly.

"What on earth were you calling that man, Mother?" Clarissa asked her. "It sounded too silly!"

"Why, no," Mrs. Massey said. "It was just his name. It's an odd name, just as many of the names about here are, especially in the country-side, away from the village. He comes from a little settlement two or three miles from Mary's Neck and he seems a very good man indeed, though he hasn't had much experience with flowers, I'm afraid. Zebias says that he's the best to be had and that he's entirely reliable and honest, and I get that impression myself; besides, it's rather pleasant to find one of 'em who's talkative and affable."

"Altogether perfectly equipped as a gardener!" Enid remarked, with a touch of sarcasm, you might infer. "We were speaking of his name and we'd better learn what it is since we may have occasion to use it ourselves some time. Just what was it you were calling him, Mother?"

"Prinsh," Mrs. Massey told her, and looked a little disturbed. "When he told me his full name I thought that was the best thing to call him. It's his middle name."

"It sounded perfectly horrible!" Clarissa said, and she took a severe tone with her mother. "I heard you calling him that, and I couldn't believe my ears. I heard you saying, 'Where's the rake, Prinsh?' and calling 'Oh, Prinsh!' when he was in the tool-house, and 'Prinsh' this and 'Prinsh' that, and I did hope the carpenters weren't listening because it sounded as though his name were 'Prince' and you were tight and couldn't speak distinctly.

Just imagine *their* hearing you calling him that when *they* come! It won't do, Mother."

"Well, it's better than anything else," Mrs. Massey said, getting redder, and naturally both girls demanded to know what she meant by that. "I mean better than his other names," she explained. "When he came this morning the first thing he said was that he was the man Zebias Flick had hired for the summer to do gardening here, and then he said, 'I'm Mr. Sweetmus.'"

"What!" both the girls exclaimed together.

"Mr. Sweetmus," their mother told them. "I didn't think of it right away; but the first time I called him that without the 'Mister'———"

"I heard you!" Clarissa interrupted. "I'd have thought you were looking for one of us, or even for Father, except it was so unlike your ordinary vocabulary. How often did you call this man 'Sweetmus' and who heard you?"

"Never mind," Mrs. Massey told her. "I saw at once it wouldn't do because it's so difficult to distinguish between the sounds of 'M' and 'N' at a little distance. So I asked him what the rest of his name was, and he said he didn't like to be called by his first name, though it was a Bible name. There are two Ananiases in the Bible and when his family named him they meant the other one; but strangers never understood that, and it had been a burden to him at times. I thought he was right, too; it would be unjust to call him by a name he objected to, and then he told me that his middle name was Prinsh, which was his mother's family name. So I thought the simplest thing to do was to call him that, though after I'd done so a few times I—ah———"

"Rather!" Clarissa said. "There's only one thing to do and that's to go back to the way he introduced himself, which is certainly what he wanted. Joanna Gillwife says the most tactful summer people and those the inhabitants like the best use the word 'Mister' pretty frequently in addressing the original Mary's Neckers in their employ. He called himself 'Mr. Sweetmus'; as you say, you can't possibly call him 'Ananias', and unless you want people to think you've been drinking you can't go all over the place shouting, 'Oh, Prinsh!' any more. If we put in the 'Mister', there isn't much danger of people's thinking we've gone crazy enough to call a person who looks like your new gardener 'sweetness'! I do wish, though, that one or two of Father's old friends in Logansville could have heard him calling him that, just once!"

"Never mind," I told her. "We'll call him 'Mr. Sweetmus', of course; it's settled."

"I hope so," Enid said, getting up. "He's certainly a sight!"

This word of description interested me, for I hadn't been able to get a clear view of Mr. Sweetmus from my window; so, after lunch, I went out to look him over. He was a fat middle-aged man—pretty bald, because you could see a half-moon between his hair and his old straw hat—and the upper rim of his greenish old trousers didn't look as if it was going to stay much longer on the lower slopes of his gingham shirt that was bulging out above it. He had a shiny brown face, puffed cheeks, and eyebrows that looked like the leavings of a pair of caterpillars that had died half-way up his forehead. He appeared right glad to see me.

"Guess you must be Mr. Massish," he said, stopping work and holding out his hand. "Pleased to make your 'quaintance." I shook hands with him and told him that my name was Massey; but information on this point had no weight with him, then or at any other time. "Nice

place you got here, Mr. Massish," he went on. "Mrs.
Massish, she seems a nice lady, too, I expect, once I git
used to her, maybe. Well, breeze sou'west but looks like
holdin' fair. Too early to say so now, bein' it's only May,
but looks like, come September, we might git a good,
nice Indian Fall. What I mean by that, it's the season
after summer. Guess you might 'a' heard the spression
used somewuz, maybe?"

"You mean Indian Summer?" I asked him.

"Yes—and no," he answered. "By that I mean if you
ast me I'd haf to answer, 'Yes and no.' Seems like I'd
heard the spression used somewuz one way and somewuz
else another way. That's the way things are, Mr. Massish; you go one place and they'll tell you one thing, then
you take and go another place and they'll tell you different. Another thing I was thinkin' 'bout 'fore you come
out hee-uh, it was them mosquitoes. They ain't come yet
and when they do fust come they ain't got the gimp they
git later on. Early in June some years I've had 'em to
kind o' settle on me nigh all over wherever I was kind of
exposed; but they wouldn't take a-holt like what they do
when they git gimped up more. When they're young, like
that, they bite but they dun't eat. Mrs. Massish tells me
she paid high fer this fertilizer; but it looks kind o' dried
out to me, like most o' the goodness was gone out of it.
Once the goodness gits gone out o' fertilizer, why, the
best you can say fer it is it ain't hardly got no goodness
left in it. Course that's only the way it looks to me; I
dun't say it mightn't look different to somebody else. All
a man can do is jest spress his own 'pinion, and then you
go and take and ast somebody else and they'll spress
another—it may be the same or it may be different. You
can't tell till you take and find out. How do you feel
'bout that, Mr. Massish, yourself? You 'gree with me?"

By this time he'd got me a little confused; I wasn't just sure what he meant. "Well——" I said; but he didn't seem to hear me and began talking again before I could go on.

"It's a good deal like you say," he said. "Some people look at a matter the right way and they take and spress their 'pinions same as I would, myself, or maybe the way you would, yourself, Mr. Massish, if you was a mind to —or take Mrs. Massish herself and you might say the same thing 'plied to her or to your two daughters. Zebias Flick told me you had two, and the woman in the kitchen, I ast her and she says they was two, so I guess Zebias must 'a' had the rights o' the matter." Mr. Sweetmus had been leaning upon the handle of a hoe as he talked; but now he appeared to get reflective and rubbed the rounded end of the hoe-handle up and down against his nose as if to polish both. "Well, it's funny," he went on. "It's funny but childern always kind o' take to me. Animals and childern and women. Take to me soon as ever they lay eyes on me, and always did. Must be somethin' 'bout me they like. Funny, but that's the way it always is. B'en that way long as I can 'member; even when I b'en among strangers they'll leave other people and come around me—animals and childern and women. Funny, but that's the way it's always b'en." He scratched his head, leaned again on the handle of the hoe and went back to a previous topic. "Yessuh, breeze sou'west but good, nice weather and it may be too early to say so but looks like four five months from now we might git a nice, good Indian Fall, though's I says, some might p'fer to use some other spression in speakin' o' that time o' the year. It's like you said, Mr. Massish; you go one place and people'll spress one 'pinion and then you take and go some other place and they'll tell you different. Yet on the other hand you can take and look at it this way: if you stayed in the same place all the time it might be jest the same way, some spressin' one 'pinion and some tellin' you different; and yet how could you tell unless you set about to find out? You 'gree with me, Mr. Massish?"

This time I said "Yes" quickly, and added right away that I had an appointment and would have to be moving on. He seemed to regret the breaking off of the conversation; in fact he prolonged his own part in it—raising his voice to reassure me that the breeze was sou'west but that we had good, nice weather and might expect a good, nice Indian Fall—until I had passed around the corner of the house, out of his sight and hearing. Well, of course I could see that at last I'd found somebody I could talk to, or anyhow listen to, whenever I cared for the pleasure; but my conversation with Mr. Sweetmus didn't lighten my pressure at all. That's the way it is pretty often when we get hold of something we've been looking forward to a good while; it seems to fill the bill pretty seldom. Mr. Sweetmus's thoughts struck me as going around in a circle; they confused me and I found myself unable to be clear as to their drift.

I had the same experience with him the next morning when I happened to be in his part of the yard again. He stopped work and began to talk before I was within fifty feet of him, and didn't quit until I went into the house. Listening to him gave me a peculiar sensation; he seemed to mean something by what he said; but most of the time I couldn't tell what it was, and it gave me a feeling like listening to a foreigner speaking half in English and half in his own language. Mrs. Massey said his conversation made much the same impression on her. Unless she kept him pretty busy, she said, he'd talk continuously and in

a way that made her a little dizzy—partly on account
of his peculiar voice—and when she was working in the
garden she'd found that the best way to handle him was
to pretend she didn't hear him except when he asked
questions about the work. Even that didn't always stop
him, she said; he'd call out something about the weather
from one end of the garden to the other, and if a cat
crossed the yard, or they'd hear a rooster crowing somewhere, he'd be reminded of how animals and children and
women always took to him and tell her about it. One
morning while I was shaving I heard Zebias Flick talking
with him, down in the yard below.

"Guess you've often took note of it, yourself, Zebias,"
Mr. Sweetmus was saying. "I mean how animals and
childern and women always like to make over me. Take
these two daughters o' Mrs. Massish and Mr. Massish,
too. You see them two talkin' to me yestiddy aftanoon?
Guess you did. Know what they was sayin' to me? Well,
I'll tell you: said right out they'd b'en thinkin' 'bout my
'pearance. I told 'em that jest seein' me in my gaddnin
clo'es, they couldn't tell; but some Sunday I'd walk up
this way in the golf suit Mr. Carmichael's wife didn't
like him in last year so she gave it to me, and they could
jedge for theirselves. So they says no they liked to look
out o' the window sometimes, and sometimes when they
was out on the premises they liked to look down towards
the gaddin, maybe, and they'd 'joy theirselves better if I
was fixed up all the time. Says they'd like to see me in
good, nice overalls, the kind that fasten up over the
shoulders. Come right out with it and said they thought
I'd look nice in long, blue overalls. See? Funny, but that's
the way it's always b'en."

"They ain't the only ones," I heard Zebias Flick telling him. "Yestiddy I see three four fine handsome

women-folks—automobile tourists they was, top-notch high-heelers—and they was lookin' over the hedge at you while you was at work; but you never took note of 'em. Ast me who in the world you was, and I told 'em. 'My!' they says. Heard 'em say it two three times. 'My!' they kep' sayin'. 'My!' "

"Did they so? Well, it's funny," Mr. Sweetmus told him.

"That wun't all," Zebias went on. "Heard 'em sayin' they wondered where you c'd a-come from. Heard 'em say it right out. Same as sayin' they'd liked to know where you lived, so they c'd make your 'quaintance. I never told 'em though; thought I'd said enough."

"Well, they wouldn't 'a' b'en no harm in your tellin' 'em," I heard Mr. Sweetmus say. "Guess they'll be by again, though, likely. Funny how it keeps on always the same way. Why do you think it is, Zebias?"

"Must be somethin' 'bout you," Zebias told him. "Somethin' that 'tracts 'em."

"Must be," Mr. Sweetmus agreed, and there was a short silence as if he were doing some hard thinking. "One reason that might help to 'count fer it," he said, after that, "why, it's likely because I never put on no airs with 'em. Always easy and natural-like. They might be other reasons; but that's one of 'em anyways. Natural-ness always come natural to me, as you might want to put it. In other words, I'm always jest myself with 'em, same as I am with you or with somebody's dog or if I was anywuz else. You take note o' me, Zebias, when I'm with animals or childern or women, and you'll see. I'm behavin' jest as natural's if I was speakin' man to man. Yessuh, that's part o' the reason they make over me the way they do. 'Counts fer part of it anyways."

CHAPTER VI

M<small>R.</small> S<small>WEETMUS</small> was certainly right about his being natural with animals at any rate, as we discovered an evening or two later. We were just finishing dinner, and for a time I thought a skunk must have got right into the very room with us, though the carpenters had put in a temporary partition. I never before had such a powerful experience with that odor, and it drove us out of the room in a hurry; but conditions weren't better in any other part of the house, upstairs or down. Everybody had to get outdoors and stay there for quite a while, and it was difficult inside the house even after bedtime; I never did know a smell to be so thoroughly distributed throughout a building. Well, the next morning I went out to see how the garden was getting on, and of course Mr. Sweetmus stopped work as soon as he saw me and began to walk toward me, talking about which direction the breeze was coming from, and so on; but as he got nearer I began taking steps backward, so he stopped.

"Guess I still smell of it. Some people dun't stummick it so well," he said, and smiled kind of superiorly. "Take me, fer instance, and I ain't never b'en troubled by it because I've got kind of a natural way with me, and

what's natural with animals and childern and women
dun't never trouble me none, and you take that little
animal and nothin' ain't more natural than fer it to
make anythin' that distu'bs it p'take of its smell. Course
I know, though, that summer families in p'tic'lar dun't
stummick it easy, and that's what I was thinkin' 'bout
last night when I see one a-settin' here in your ya'd. I
says to myself, 'Mrs. Massish and Mr. Massish, too, and
their two daughters, besides,' I says to myself, 'they
wouldn't like this,' I says to——"

I interrupted him. "You did? It was you——"

"Jest like I'm tellin' you, Mr. Massish. Zebias laid
off yestiddy aftanoon and Mrs. Massish showed me a
cellar window that she says was the new fresh air intake
the carpenters had finished to carry nice, good outside
air all through the house. Told me to close that window
jest before I went home, because it looked like the
evenin' was goin' to git chilly; but I fergot all 'bout it until
I was home finishin' supper. So I come all the way back
to 'tend to it, and when I got here it was bright nice
moonlight and they was a young skunk a-settin' right
there on the grass not two feet in front o' that fresh air
intake. They're friendly little animals if you're natural
with 'em—I've had one to follow me as much as a
quarter of a mile after dark, walkin' 'longside o' me,
nice and pet-like—and they wun't do nothin' or even
budge if you 'proach 'em right, in a natural kind of a
way. Course I knowed you wouldn't want one pra'tic'ly
in your fresh air intake, so when I come up to him I give
him kind of a kick——"

"You did!" I said. "You did!"

"Sploded right in my face a'most," Mr. Sweetmus informed me. "Never did git it stronger. Awdinarily, 's I
says, I ain't sensitive to it; but kickin' him like I done

it come on me kind o' like a knife in the nostrils—more'n
I'd looked fer, you might say. Disagreeable. By the time
I'd got back home, though, course it wun't anythin' a
man with a good deal o' naturalness would object to.
He went on 'bout his bizness after I give him that kick;
didn't hurt him none. Course I shet that window 'cause
she'd told me to; but if it had b'en mine I wouldn't 'a'
done it, 'cause after what'd happened 'twould 'a' b'en
better to let the house air out some. Bein's it was her
window and not mine, and she knowed what she wanted,
I didn't see no choice but to take and shet it. Looks to
me jest the same way as 'tis 'bout that gaddin. I got a
love o' flowers jest the same 's I got a love o' animals
and childern and women; but the way I like flowers is to
see 'em growin' natural-like—wild flowers you hear some
people callin' 'em. You've heard that spression used,
yourself, Mr. Massish, I guess; but my own 'pinion is that
it ain't no matter whether you call 'em wild flowers or
jest natural flowers or whatever you might take a mind
to say 'bout 'em, the point is they're handsome to look
at and no trouble to anybody. What I mean by that,
they ain't no trouble if you let 'em alone and dun't take
no trouble 'bout 'em. Course it's *her* gaddin, though, and
she's 'sposed to know what she wants; but if 'twas
mine——"

I excused myself here and got away, though of course
he kept on talking as long as I was in sight; Mrs.
Massey's method didn't work so far as I was concerned,
and my only way of stopping him was to get where he
couldn't see me—I had to keep out of the yard entirely
during Mr. Sweetmus's working hours or there wouldn't
be any garden.

Inside the house there was such a hammering and
sawing and ripping and tearing going on that you couldn't

read, much less think; I don't care to spend my whole time motoring and I expect I've made it clear enough that I didn't have anybody outside the family to talk to —at least not with any great pleasure to myself. Well, you see, I had to do something with my time and that's how it happened that I bought the motor-boat. One summer when we were up on Lake Michigan I'd been out in hired motor-boats enough to understand that I don't get seasick in a boat so long as it keeps going ahead; qualms begin to come over me only when it stops and goes to flopping about in one location, and when that can be avoided I enjoy motor-boating first rate. So one day when the carpenters were pretty noisy at our new cottage I was down on a wharf at the harborside and saw a fine-looking boat, all nicely painted and varnished, with the brass work polished, and about thirty-eight feet long, I judged. It had a nice mahogany cabin forward, a small bridge-deck with comfortable seats for the operator and one other person; there was an ample cockpit with four or five wicker chairs in it, and there was a little rowboat or dinghy swung up on davits—altogether a pretty good appearing sort of a motor-boat. So I asked a man that was standing there whose boat it was.

He was a quiet, likeable-looking man, middle-aged, in a blue suit and a blue yachting-cap, and I was surprised when he answered, "It might as well be yours, Mr. Massey, because it's for sale at a bargain and a good boat, too."

Then I remembered having seen him before and that his name was Captain Turner. He seemed to be another man that was willing to speak freely, but more to the point, you might say, than Mr. Sweetmus did. So we had a conversation and he told me the boat belonged to a summer family he'd run it for the year before; but they'd

gone to Europe and left him the job of selling it and getting himself the position of captain on it again, if he
could. Well, the long and short of it is, I bought that boat
the next day, with Captain Turner to run it for me, and
of course Mrs. Massey and Enid and Clarissa got right
excited. The way they talked about it and the plans they
made, you wouldn't have thought I was going to have
much to do with the Wanda—that was the boat's name
—she was just going to be used for them to give parties
on when "they" got here. Mrs. Massey's enthusiasm was
the quickest to drop; she isn't a good sailor, and her
first excursion on the Wanda was a poor experience for
her. The girls' excitement tapered off pretty quickly, too,
especially as the Wanda only made about fifteen miles an
hour, and within a week if I asked them to go out with
me they usually looked absent-minded and began to make
excuses.

Of course I enjoyed having them along with me; but
I got to liking the Wanda just as well when they weren't.
She had a good engine in her that Captain Turner kept in
fine condition, so my stomach didn't become unsettled by
our having to stop for repairs, and I learned how to
manage the wheel and the controls, myself. I got a good
deal of pleasure out of running the boat, and some out
of talking to Captain Turner, though his mind was
strictly limited to marine interests and I never did get
much response out of him to what you might call Logansville topics. We'd usually go out to sea pretty soon after
lunch and not come back into the harbor until along about
five o'clock, and one afternoon we got back a little later
than usual and were just tying up when I noticed Mr.
Sweetmus standing on the wharf that we used, looking
down at us with his customarily affable expression. "See
you b'en moty-boatin', Mr. Massish," he said. "Jest on

my way home and thought I might 's well stop to find out
how you 'joy yourself. Ain't never b'en on the ocean myself nor into it, neither. B'en to the bathin'-beach, though,
couple times when I was younger to look at other people
goin' into it. Overdo it, they do—leastways that's my
'pinion. Gittin' the whole human body into water, it
ain't natural 'cept fer them fishes. Disagreeable."

"You don't mean to say you can't swim?" I asked him.

"Me?" He looked surprised. "Never see no use of it.
Ain't never b'en in a boat, neither, 'cept two three times
in my life. Nice-lookin' chairs you got there, though.
Wouldn't mind settin' in one myself some Sunday aftanoon when you're goin' out, if so be you'd be willin' I
sh'd 'company you. Ain't got nothin' p'tic'lar to do next
Sunday aftanoon, if so be you'd be pleased to have me."

Of course there wasn't anything to do but to tell him
he could come, though I certainly didn't enjoy the pros-
pect, because I knew he'd talk the whole time, and the
more I listened to him the more confusing I found him.
I mean to say that his whole character perplexed me; he
was the only man I ever saw who would walk up to a
skunk and kick it, and the fact that he would kick one
right in front of a person's fresh air intake and then
casually tell the person about it, without the slightest
appearance of realizing he'd done that person a wrong
or of what the person would be thinking of him—well,
I'm not much of a psychologist, I suppose, and Ananias
Prinsh Sweetmus was a little too much for me.

When I got home, that afternoon, after telling him
he could go out on the Wanda with me the next Sunday, I found one of my family had other boating plans
for the same date, and I thought it better not to mention
my engagement with Mr. Sweetmus. It was Clarissa who
had the plans, and her mother and sister were almost as

excited as she was, because after all these weeks from the middle of April well into May of being 'way up here, left alone among and by the original inhabitants, we were going to have a visitor from the outside world. Clarissa's a nice, bright, sensible girl, always with plenty of boys seeming interested in her, and now and then she appears to get a little excited about one or another of them. This time it was a boy named Paul Bicksit whom the rest of the family hadn't ever seen; but she'd met him at a college dance somewhere in our part of the country and had talked quite a little about him in a conscious kind of a way, so I judged she was rather more upset over him than she usually got. This young Bicksit was in the Harvard Law School down at Cambridge, Mass., by now, and he'd called her on long distance, I gathered, and was going to spend Sunday with us at Mary's Neck, so she'd decided she wanted the Wanda for the afternoon.

"Why, certainly," I told her. "Bring him along."

"Oh," she said, and looked serious. "I only thought that probably you'd be having something else to do that afternoon and wouldn't want the boat——"

"What else to do?" I asked her. "Suggest something."

"Well——" she said. "Something or other."

I didn't take the hint. It had already occurred to me that I wouldn't mind having Mr. Sweetmus along so much if Clarissa and her young friend were there for him to converse with. Probably it was a little inconsiderate of me—maybe you might call it selfish—but anyhow I just said that I'd be on the bridge with Captain Turner, running the boat, and there was plenty of room in the cockpit, so she let it go at that. You could see it wasn't exactly what she wanted; but she decided to make it do.

Young Bicksit turned up in a dusty little automobile Sunday morning right after breakfast, having started, he said, looking at Clarissa, a long, long time before sunrise. He was a tall, nice-looking boy not different from others so far as I could see, though Clarissa was all tensed up with self-consciousness and acting as if the rest of us didn't belong to her. The two of them had the whole morning together, driving in his little car, so by the time they got back for lunch I couldn't see how they'd have anything left to say to each other particularly and I didn't feel selfish any more about their having a companion for the afternoon's excursion on the Wanda.

When we got down to the wharf Mr. Sweetmus was there waiting for us, and Clarissa gave a start at the sight of him. "What on earth's *he* doing here?" she whispered to me. "For heaven's sake, don't say anything that would give Paul the idea he's our gardener!"

She was nervous; but I could see, in a way, why she didn't want the young man to think Mr. Sweetmus was connected with us in any capacity. He was dressed in the clothes he'd mentioned a Mrs. Carmichael's having given him because she didn't like her husband in them, and I haven't often seen anything more inappropriate-looking than Mr. Sweetmus with them on. You could see why Mrs. Carmichael hadn't wanted her husband even to play golf in 'em, on account of their loudness, and Mr. Sweetmus hadn't helped them any by wearing a little stiff summer-before-last's straw hat that somebody must have given him, gladly. Clarissa tried to get us off in the boat without appearing to notice him, though of course he'd already begun to talk and she couldn't have had much genuine hope that young Mr. Bicksit wouldn't find out at least that Mr. Sweetmus knew us. "Hurry! Hurry! Hurry!" she kept saying, pretending to laugh. "I'm simply mad to be out on the sea! Hurry! Hurry! Hurry! I'm simply mad for a breath of salt air!" She kept right on talking as loudly as she could, trying to drown out what Mr. Sweetmus was saying.

The three of us were in the boat by this time and Captain Turner, anxious to please Clarissa, was casting off the lines that held us to the wharf. "Hurry! Hurry! Hurry!" Clarissa said. "I'm simply——" But Mr. Sweetmus, talking all the time, himself, had already come down the steps from the wharf and landed himself with us in the cockpit.

"Nice good pleasant weather," he said. "Nice good day fer a sail, though course that's only my 'pinion. Some people might say it was a nice good aftanoon to take a walk in, maybe, 'count o' their not havin' the stummick they might be called on fer if they went sailin'. They might have their 'pinions jest the same as I and you and the rest of us got ours."

Clarissa looked sort of horrified. "Get him off the boat!" she whispered to me. "Do something!"

I thought it better just to make a gesture that showed her I couldn't do anything, because we were already passing out of the harbor and getting into the ocean chop by then. It seemed to me just as well that she should surmise Mr. Sweetmus had invited himself along, which of course was really the case, so I made the gesture I speak of, and, as Clarissa looked as if she were going to faint, I just hurriedly introduced Mr. Sweetmus to Mr. Bicksit and went up on the bridge and took the wheel from Captain Turner, sitting with my back to the cockpit. I didn't look round for quite a while; but I could hear Mr. Sweetmus talking—I think I've mentioned what kind of a voice he had—and I wondered whether or not Mr. Bicksit was taking him for a friend of the family, gardening not having been referred to.

"Always take to me, Mr. Biscuit," I heard him saying.

"Animals and childern and women. Funny, too; but some think it's 'count o' naturalness. Seems to be part of it, anyways. You take hens, fer instance; it's awful seldom you'll see anybody that's got a pet hen, fer the simple reason why, it ain't natural fer a hen to take to nobody. But *I* had a nice little hen once, and me and her——"

Clarissa had come up on the bridge and bent over me. "Get him out of the cockpit!" she said in a whisper. "Get him out!"

"Me?" I asked her. "I'm running the boat, Clarissa."

"Get him out!" she said. "Can't you hear him calling Paul 'Biscuit'? Get him out!"

"But I——"

"Make him come up here with you!" she said kind of fiercely. "Make him——"

"I can't. There's only room for Captain Turner and me up here, and I want the Captain to stay; I might need him."

Clarissa shocked me. She isn't often sacrilegious; but she said something that maybe could be excused on account of the state she was in. Then she went back to the cockpit and began to try to out-talk Mr. Sweetmus, her voice sounding pretty artificial as she made efforts to choose subjects he wouldn't be able to join in on. Afterwhile I ventured to take a glance back over my shoulder, as if in a casual manner, and I saw that she was looking pretty red. Just as I happened to look, she and young Mr. Bicksit were placing their chairs so that their backs would be toward Mr. Sweetmus; but he was moving his own to be right alongside of them.

"Better position fer the view, as you might call it," I heard him saying. "Kind o' fixes us better towards the breeze, too, as you says, Mr. Briskit. Way I look at the matter, or, in other words, what you might call my 'pinion, as you might want to put it, Mr. Biscuit——"

He went on and I noticed he'd worked round to calling Clarissa's friend "Briskit" and "Biscuit" interchangeably, by this time, which I supposed wasn't pleasing either of the young people very much, but, after that, I couldn't hear their voices at all, so it looked as if they'd given up. I heard Mr. Sweetmus talking extensively about seasickness and his opinion of it, and probably his two listeners hoped he'd be attacked; but he wasn't. It was too nice a day for that, with only a light chop on the surface of the ocean, and I found myself enjoying the run much as usual —selfishly, I suppose, because of course I couldn't get entirely away from a slight consciousness of an emotional disturbance going on behind me inside of two youthful temperaments, especially Clarissa's.

This part of the coast runs east and west, roughly speaking, with rocks and reefs and shoals scattered around mighty liberally; but I'd already learned where most of them are, the day was bright and I had Captain Turner close by in case I needed advice—on the whole I was feeling pretty chipper. I ran to westward, keeping a mile or so out, for about an hour, I judged; then I noticed Captain Turner was looking over his shoulder pretty often and I thought he must have got interested in Mr. Sweetmus's conversation.

"Quite a talker, isn't he?" I said.

" 'Nias Sweetmus, you mean?" Captain Turner asked me. "I wasn't looking at him, Mr. Massey. There's a fog-bank off to the eastud. She'll likely hold off unless there's a change of wind; but I was thinking maybe we'd better get the compass out so's to get our bearings before we're closed in, in case the breeze shifts."

Well, I didn't want to get caught out in any fog, so I swung the boat around right then and there and headed for home, though that bank looked a long way off to the east and there didn't seem to be much danger of its coming down on us. Captain Turner kept looking at it kind of thoughtfully, though, and afterwhile he said, "I believe maybe I better bring that compass up, just to be on the safe side."

It was usually kept in a locker down in the cabin and he went to get it; but he couldn't find it right away because I'd moved it, myself, a few days before, to make room for some bottles of mineral water, and forgotten about it. It didn't seem to me he was down there more than three or four minutes, and nobody could have believed a fog-bank capable of behaving the way this one did in that short a time. When Captain Turner left the bridge I'd have sworn that bank was miles to the east, and then, all at once—and without my being able to see that it was moving—it didn't look much farther off than what in a city would be just a few blocks. Sections of it, like drifts of smoke, began to go by us, and, by the time I remembered where I'd put the compass and told Captain Turner and he came up with it, the solid part of that fog was all over us and you couldn't see a hundred feet in any direction.

Captain Turner coughed a few times; then he asked me, "We didn't pass that spindle while I was down in the cabin, did we?"

"Spindle?" I said. "You mean one of those black poles sticking out of the water? Kind of a buoy, you mean?"

"Well, this was a red one," he told me, coughing some more. "We ought to've gone outside of it, keeping it to port."

"To port?" I asked him. "Port. That would be——"

"It would be to your left," he said. "You didn't notice——"

"No, I was looking at the fog. If you think there's
any risk of our running into that spindle, Captain, perhaps we ought to try to put on a little more speed so as to
get away from it."

"Well, no," he told me. "I was thinking maybe we'd
better slack her up a mite till we can get a better idea
of about where we are. You see——"

That's all the further he got with what he was saying,
because the underneath part of that boat hit something
awful hard just then; the bow dropped down; there
was a most terrible banging and scraping and crashing
and tearing and bumping, and the wheel quit offering any
resistance at all, so I knew that the steering-gear was
among the various things that were getting themselves
broken. I felt flustered because the noise underneath was
kind of dumbfounding, and a voice behind me began yelling and protesting.

"Hee-uh!" it kept on shouting. "Mr. Massish, what
you doin'? _Hee_-uh!"

CHAPTER VII

THE crashing and scraping and breaking didn't last long; then the engine stopped and we seemed to be flopping around in deep enough water, not bumping any more; but Captain Turner looked a good deal disturbed.

"Might 'a' been better for us if we'd hung up on that bunch o' rock," he said. "But now she's banged and scraped all the way over it, and Lord knows what's happened to her under water!"

"You mean there might be a bad leak?" I asked him.

"There certainly might!" he said. "We'd better get that dinghy into the water, the first thing we do, in case——"

I saw what he meant and it made me pretty uncomfortable, because there were five of us on the Wanda; that dinghy was only a little, flat-bottomed rowboat nine feet long and couldn't possibly carry more than three people. If the Wanda had been damaged enough to make her sink, it looked like hard times ahead for somebody.

Back in the cockpit Clarissa was calling to know what had happened and what we were going to do. Mr. Bicksit wasn't saying anything and Mr. Sweetmus was stating that in his opinion we'd hit something which in his opinion was a rock, though others were entitled to their own opinions upon the matter. Captain Turner and I hurried back to the davits, which were at one side of the cockpit, and got the dinghy lowered into the water; then Turner hustled forward again and disappeared down the little stairway that led into the cabin and to the engine compartment under the bridge. Right that same instant, Mr. Sweetmus, not saying anything, rolled himself over the side of the Wanda and plumped down into the stern seat—the best one—in the dinghy.

"What on earth are you doing?" I asked him pretty severely, though the truth is I wanted to do exactly the same thing that he'd done and only controlled the impulse by an effort. "What do you mean? Get back in this boat at once!"

"Why, no, Mr. Massish," he said in a mild voice, and he looked up at me as though he felt surprised and maybe a little hurt by the severe tone I'd used to him. "Why, no. Course it's only my own 'pinion, Mr. Massish; but, the way I look at it, that there vessell you're in got an awful dreadful bump back yonder. Sounded to me like she got all creation busted out of her, and, the way I look at it, the water must be fairly a-pourin' into her on her under side somewuz. Course that's only my own 'pinion and you——"

"Get back into this boat!" I told him. "That dinghy'll only carry three people; there are five of us and we haven't decided which three——"

"I couldn't hardly do it, Mr. Massish," he said argumentatively. "Way I look at it, that vessell you're in is li'ble to take and go right straight to the bottom of the ocean almost any minute. Way I look at it, I'd be awful li'ble to git drowned in that there vessell. I wouldn't be on her right now fer a million dolluhs, Mr. Massish. Way I look at it——"

He went on talking; but I turned to Clarissa, who was pretty white and trying not to tremble. "Get into the dinghy," I told her. "Get in there quick!"

"No," she said, and her voice wasn't steady. "I won't unless Paul——"

But young Mr. Bicksit interrupted her, and I certainly admired him for what he said and the way he behaved. "Don't be absurd," he told her. "Do what your father says and get into the dinghy immediately—you and your father both. Make her get in, Mr. Massey, and go with her, yourself. It's the only thing to do."

That young man looked pretty heroic to me, as he said this, and handsome, too. It seemed to me I'd never seen a better-looking young man—or one with better ideas, either. Of course when he spoke of me I said, "No, no," in a protesting manner, though I didn't want to sound too firm and kind of hoped that this fine young man would go ahead and argue me into doing what he said; but Clarissa was agitated and didn't seem to get his point clearly. It made me nervous, too, the way Captain Turner and I didn't seem to have much place in her consciousness just then.

She stamped her foot. "I won't move one step!" she said, addressing Mr. Bicksit exclusively. "Never! Not unless you come with me! I refuse unless you——"

"Never!" he said, speaking the word even louder than she did; and he took off his coat, showing that he meant to put up a man's struggle before he went down. "You and your father get into that boat and don't talk any more about it!"

Clarissa began to cry. "This is a nice way to treat me!" she sobbed. "Do you think I could ever believe half what you told me this morning if you're going to act like this?" It was curious, but her voice sounded really angry with him, and it seemed to me she was crying more because she was furious over the way he was behaving than because of anything else. "You told me I was the greatest influence in your life," she went on. "Do you think this is any way to prove it? Do you dream you could swim to shore? It's at least more than a mile! In this fog how would you even know what direction to swim in? If you don't get into that boat this second I'll never——"

Young Bicksit stepped toward her as if he meant to pick her up and put her into the dinghy. "You do as I say!" he told her. "Get into that boat!"

"I won't! Never! Never! Never!"

"You will——"

"Never——"

"Hee-uh!" Mr. Sweetmus said, speaking up earnestly and interrupting. "Listen hee-uh!" He was holding to the side of the Wanda with one hand and looked uncomfortable because of the way his weight in the stern made the bow of the dinghy stick up out of the water. "I dun't know nothin' 'bout rowin' and the way I look at it, whoever gits in hee-uh with me ought to be able to row this little boat. Course it's only my own 'pinion, but the way that vessell you're in 'pears to be saggin' down to one side, looks like you better git the matter settled 'mong yourselves one way or 'nother 'fore very long. Better git it settled; better git it settled."

Well, there's no denying that what he said and the way he said it made me irritated with him. I was beginning to be a little seasick, too, on account of the boat's having a soggy sort of roll after she stopped, and I knew I'd be more so if I didn't get drowned pretty soon. Clarissa and her friend didn't pay any attention to Mr. Sweetmus—they were in a state about saving each other and going on with their argument loudly—but I spoke to him with a good deal of indignation. Matters didn't look right to me; he was a bachelor, and both Captain Turner and I had families to support—or at least, in my own case, investments had to be looked after and protected —and Mrs. Massey's garden wasn't so terribly important. She could get along without it if she had to, it seemed to me. "Get out," I said to Mr. Sweetmus. "You get out o' that boat! You climb back here and wait till we decide which three of the five of us———"

"Why, no, Mr. Massish," he told me again, and looked at me reproachfully. "Way I look at it, I wouldn't care to take the risk. That there vessell you're in———"

But just then there was a startling, strange loud sound from inside the boat, as if it was giving a terrible sort of scream. I jumped, Clarissa shrieked, Mr. Bicksit got paler than he had been and Mr. Sweetmus gave kind of a flop in the dinghy and put his other hand on his stomach. But the noise was only Captain Turner coming up the little stairway and blowing a tin foghorn he'd got out of a locker; it certainly gave all of us a turn.

"My Orry!" Mr. Sweetmus called complainingly to Captain Turner. "Dun't you know no better'n to make a noise like that without givin' a man no warnin'?"

Captain Turner had brought a brass bell with him, as well as the horn, and now he began to ring it while he was blowing the horn. "What chance have we got?" I asked him, going up to him and shouting. "How long do you think there's any hope this boat will———"

"Looks fairly bad," he said, letting up on the horn. "Strut's gone, keel's splintered, I think, shaft's busted and she's taking in a good deal of water. If somebody doesn't come along pretty soon and give us a tow, I guess we'll have to get out the rubber boat for you and me. I didn't want to do it because it's quite a job to inflate her with the pump we got; but——"

"What rubber boat?" I asked him. "You mean to say we've got another boat on board?"

"Yes. It came with the Wanda; it's under that after hatch. If we had to, you and I could use it and let the others take the dinghy; but——" He broke off, stopped ringing the bell and peered through the fog. "Guess we won't have to, because we're going to get a tow." I couldn't see anything anywhere; but he put his hands around his mouth and yelled: "That you, Ben?"

Then there was a hoarse voice out somewhere to the right of us. "Lookin' fer a tow, George?"

"Guess you better!" Captain Turner shouted, and a lumbering, grey old fishing-boat with a two-cylinder motor chugging away in it and three men in oilskins, looking uninterested, came out of that thick smokiness and began to manoeuver alongside. Captain Turner passed them a towline; they went ahead, and, when the line tightened, the Wanda gave a stubborn kind of lurch and began to follow, upon which there was a loud complaint from behind, alongside the cockpit.

"Hee-uh!" Mr. Sweetmus called. "Ain't you got no sense? Git me out o' this little boat! Expeck me to drag my arm out of its slockit, holdin' on all the way home!"

For my part I didn't care much what happened to him, because it seemed to me that if I'd ever seen any human being make an exhibition of himself, he'd been the one. He didn't know we had a rubber boat on board any more than I did, myself, which was a fact that made his disgrace apparent to everybody; but you never saw a more complacent expression than his after young Bicksit and Captain Turner hauled him aboard and he settled himself down in one of the comfortable chairs. "Nicer place to set on than that there hard board in the rowboat," he said. "Long as they ain't no more danger, why, the cushion in this chair is pleasanter to set on, though course that's only my own 'pinion."

We hoisted the dinghy back upon its davits; Captain Turner went below to see what he could do about the leak and a temporary repair of the steering-gear so as to help with the towing, and we began to get ourselves kind of settled down again and less emotional. As a matter of fact, though, this remark of mine about getting less emotional mightn't properly apply to Clarissa; she seemed to want it known that she was indignant and had got her feelings hurt. Her face wore that expression; tears kept coming to her eyes, and she wouldn't speak to that fine young Bicksit at all. If he came to her end of the cockpit she'd go to the other, and if he came there she'd go up on the bridge and turn her back to him. Mr. Sweetmus kept talking to both of them, and sometimes she'd answer him right politely to make it more pointed that she wasn't speaking to her young friend. Mr. Sweetmus put his own interpretation upon this conduct of hers and I heard him explaining it to Mr. Bicksit, though the young man didn't seem to take much interest, and very likely agreed mentally with me that Mr. Sweetmus's tone was just about insufferable.

"Animals and childern and women," he said. "Funny, but that's always b'en the way; they'll leave other people anywuz I go and come around me."

He was still talking about this when we got back on shore, and I heard him saying more about it the next morning; but by that time the family'd got excited over something important, and Mrs. Massey wouldn't even come and listen to what I wanted her to.

CHAPTER VIII

Clarissa'd made it up with that splendid young man to some extent, in the evening—he'd started on his trip back to Cambridge by moonlight pretty late anyhow—and in the morning I was shaving by my bathroom window when I heard Mr. Sweetmus, just below, telling Zebias Flick all about our accident. I went to the door and called Mrs. Massey. "Come and listen to this!" I told her. "If you want to hear——"

"No, no," she said in an impatient way. She was in a wrapper, talking busily to Clarissa and Enid who were dressed and had been outdoors. "So they've begun to come!" she said to them, making a gesture for me not to interrupt. "Did you see what they looked like?"

"Only the butler," Clarissa told her. "We were sure he was the butler and he looked English. He was overseeing having a truckload of trunks carried in, and there's absolutely no doubt of that cottage's being opened. It's that long grey shingle one, the fourth from here to the west, and Joanna says their name's Blodgett."

"It's true, Mother," Enid said, and she looked solemn. "They're beginning to come!"

I was more interested in what Mr. Sweetmus was telling Zebias, so I went back to my bathroom window to finish shaving and listen; but by this time Mr. Sweetmus had finished giving an account of what had happened to the boat and himself, and appeared to be summing up, making deductions.

"As you says," he was telling Zebias, "they must be somethin' 'bout me that 'tracts 'em. Always jest myself with 'em. When that accident come about, I was jest myself, same's I always be. All the way back to the habbuh you could see how it 'tracted her. Thought more o' me'n she did him, 'count of it. Naturalness, that's part o' the reason fer it—anyways that's a part of it, Zebias."

"Not the best part, though," Zebias told him, from which I was able to conclude that Zebias Flick was capable of sometimes having a little enjoyment inside of himself. "Not the best part, 'Nias."

"Well, yes and no," Mr. Sweetmus told him. "On some 'counts you might say 'yes', and then on others you might say 'no'. It's all a question of give and take in sech a mattuh. You've heard that spression used, hain't you, Zebias? I mean 'bout 'give and take'? You go one place and you might hear that spression used and you take and go another and you mightn't. Anyway that's my 'pinion. You might have another——"

Well, this was so familiar to me that I stopped listening, finished up my shaving and went downstairs to breakfast, where the family were already eating and talking right excitedly about that grey shingle cottage's being open and a summer family named Blodgett in it. Zebias knew who they were and he'd told Joanna Gillwife and Joanna'd told the girls. These Blodgetts were a man and his wife and two or three young children, it seems, from Little Falls, Mass., and he'd never done any work but just lived on his money, and they'd been at Mary's Neck a good many summers, which, according to Joanna, would be considered an important fact sociably. I got the impression that these Blodgetts estimated themselves to be fairly highty-tighty, and when I saw them driving by, one afternoon, I observed they looked that way—you can nearly always tell. After they'd been in their cottage a couple of weeks or so, Mrs. Massey said kind of worriedly she supposed Mrs. Blodgett would call soon now; but I wasn't surprised when Clarissa shook her head and told her probably not so soon. By this time there were people in maybe eight or ten of the cottages; the weather was warming up and the place began to look inhabited. Then a family named Weeder moved into the cottage next door to our left, and a queer-looking old man and a middle-aged couple were occupying the one next door to our right—though the girls said these last didn't count, being a new family at Mary's Neck the same as we were, and besides, this old man and the middle-aged couple had only rented that cottage for a month and were peculiar anyway.

There wasn't anybody across the road from us, of course, because that's where the Atlantic ocean is, down below the rocks, at least, and most of the cottages front on it in a long, zig-zag line; but our privacy, so to speak, wasn't intruded on any more from the sides than it was from in front. The sociable rush the family had expected to begin when "they" came seemed to be holding off. Well, it kept on holding off. By the middle of June I judged the majority of the cottages were occupied; the hotels were open and a good deal seemed to be going on—except among the Masseys. Every afternoon about four o'clock we'd drive over to the beach and Mrs. Massey and I would sit on the sand and watch the girls bathing; but neither there nor anywhere else did anybody seem to be aware of there being such a thing in the world as a Massey.

Of course it's naturally the fact that both Mrs. Massey and the girls are considerably more up-to-date, fashionably speaking, than I am; but it took them some time to realize that on the sociable plane, as it were, there might have been some mistake involved in a new family's sailing right in and buying a cottage at Mary's Neck, especially a family from the Middle West. Being from a city like Logansville, where we're mighty anxious to increase the population and appreciative and cordial with strangers that come in and help us do it, and where we're glad to get acquainted with 'em and help 'em get settled down among us—especially if they seem to look respectable and don't start in by borrowing anything—why, I used to have the innocent idea that people were pretty generally like that all over the country. So it certainly did surprise me the way the cottagers at Mary's Neck seemed to feel toward us—or not to feel toward us, I might say, because it appeared to be a vacuum.

Of course I understood a good many of them had been coming here for their summers as a regular habit and I could see right away that they might be right likeable but were pretty much a kid-glove-gold-headed-cane-looking sort of people, so to speak, and would have that coldish fashionable manner with strangers you've got to expect at first from citizens of Massachusetts and Philadelphia and Brooklyn and our other points East—I didn't look for them to come pushing right in to see if we didn't want to borrow their lawnmower or an electric iron or something. Naturally, I know how it is with newcomers anywhere; even where people are pretty cordial those that have been longer in a place can't help feeling some supe-

rior to the ones that have just got there. I expect it's
more or less a universal feeling—or maybe you might call
it failing—we've all got it to some extent, and you can see
it in the expression of any country lounger sitting on a
packing-box on the platform of the dinkiest little crossroads railroad station in the world. When the train stops
there, all he's got for the passengers looking out of the
windows is a kind of pity because they know so little about
his crossroads village that he feels they haven't hardly
got a right even to look at it. He's got a kind of instinct
that makes him think they're nothing but a lot of igno-
ramuses. Of course, though, out in our part of the country, if they got off the train and wanted to stay in that
crossroads village, he'd take an interest in 'em right away,
and his interest might still be a little superior but it'd be
enthusiastic.

That wasn't the sort of interest we found anybody taking in us at Mary's Neck, and the fact is, what happened
to us gave me a peculiar sensation. It was a funny thing,
and after a little it began to more or less give me the
creeps to be around in a place full of people, with
neighbors and everything, that didn't know I was there.
It was just exactly as if I'd been made into an invisible
man and had my family made invisible with me. Mrs.
Massey and Enid and Clarissa and I knew we could see
one another and talk to one another and touch one another; we knew we were human and solid and alive so
long as we kept together; but when we got separated we
seemed to have turned into air.

Well, I'm a more or less cordial sort of a man, you
might say, and like to talk to people and act a little as if
they and I had something of the same kind of insides, so
to speak; but of course, being invisible got to be a good
deal harder on Mrs. Massey and the girls than it did

on me. I didn't have anything to do, except to attend to
my business correspondence, since the Wanda's repairs
seemed more like rebuilding and were going to take a
good part of the summer; but the family were worse off
than I was because they were used to being in a popular
rush when they were among people, and invisibility was
quite a shock to them. Clarissa and Enid had always been
pretty much the centre of all the young people's gayeties
at Logansville, and I expect I might say they were used
to being considerably sought after and made much of. I
may be their father; but anyhow I think I'm entitled to
say they're pretty nice-looking girls, lively and friendly
and as well-dressed as anybody of their age you're likely
to see. Mrs. Massey didn't need to tell me that they
were getting to feel more astonished and set-back than
they'd ever been in their lives, because before long Mary's
Neck filled up with quite a sizable crowd of young people
—boys and girls shouting and laughing together on the
piazzas of the cottages and going to dances in the evenings together and tearing about in automobiles and
motor-boats—but not one of 'em showed the slightest
sign of knowing that Enid and Clarissa were alive. They
began to look so disappointed and kind of lifeless that
it worried me. I suppose you might say I showed a weakness, especially after the heavy expense I'd been put to
for the cottage; but one day I called up an automobile
dealer in Boston by long distance and bought a runabout
for each of them. Mrs. Massey said she thought that
would help, and it did seem to—but only for about a
week. Then they got that surprised, hurt sort of expression again.

But one morning at breakfast, along toward the end
of June, Enid said she'd found out that we'd been making
a great mistake. "Nobody except maids and nurses and

children and chauffeurs go to the beach in the afternoon the way we do," she said. "I thought they were a pretty queer-looking crowd there, even in their bathing-suits. Everybody in Mary's Neck goes to the beach about eleven and stays until lunch time; that's when they all meet and have a good time together, and if you don't go then and do go at any other hour it simply shows you don't know —you're all wrong. That's been our worst mistake. People could be here forever and never meet a soul if they didn't know enough to go to the beach at the right time. Joanna Gillwife says she knew it but hadn't noticed we were going in the afternoon. You see what idiots we've been!"

So that morning we drove to the beach at eleven o'clock, all together in the family car and pretty excited. When we got there it looked as if Joanna Gillwife was right again, and I don't know that I've ever seen a prettier sight or one pleasanter to look at than that long strip of sand with all those big, bright-colored umbrellas and the dozens of groups of people in their gay summer clothes and gayer bathing-suits, with the green ocean booming and foaming and the sun so bright and sparkling over everything. We Masseys began to feel cheerfuller right away and when the girls had got into their bathing-suits and we'd stretched ourselves out on the sand we felt better still. Everybody seemed jolly; there was a nice-sounding confusion of voices in the air, with a great deal of laughing going on all the time. Mostly, the younger people and children were running and dancing all over the place, diving in under the surf or prancing up and down the beach, throwing big medicine-balls and lawn-tennis balls to each other, and boys chasing girls and girls chasing boys—it all looked mighty pretty.

I noticed the way the groups of people were sitting

together, though, and when they went down to the water
how they did it more or less in separate clumps that
didn't seem to have much to say to other clumps that
were doing the same thing, and I wondered if maybe the
summer colony at Mary's Neck wasn't kind of clicky or
something. Most of 'em seemed to know one another all
right enough to say howdy and pass the time of day a
little; but it was noticeable that the different groups and
clumps seemed to hang together for the main part of
their sociabilities. Certainly the clump of Masseys did
that and it wasn't long till we realized we were just as
invisible at the bathing-beach at noon as we were anywhere else. Enid and Clarissa got up and took their
plunge together and splashed around a while; then they
came out and played around near the edge of the water.

They chased each other up and down the beach and
threw a little rubber ball to each other and laughed and
shouted and seemed to be having as good a time as anybody; but Mrs. Massey said they weren't, and I declare
it did seem a pity, because even if I am their father they
were the best-looking girls on that whole beach, and I'd
certainly have thought that some nice-looking, elderly
woman would come up to them and maybe say something
like, "I see you young ladies are strangers here and I
would like to have my daughters and sons meet you." But
of course nobody was liable to do anything like that—
not at Mary's Neck!

People were talking near us, and now and then—because it was the first of the season, I expect—we'd hear
somebody asking who somebody else was. They'd ask
this question in a way I never did hear used in Logansville and for a time I couldn't make sense out of it. "Who
are the Thompsons?" I'd hear them say, and then I'd
hear the answer, something like this: "Such nice people!

They're connected with the Thompsons of Dodfield." Or maybe the answer would be: "Terrible! Willy Smith lives within a block of them at home and says he never even heard of them!" I couldn't see at all what the questions meant or how the answers shed any light, and then I heard someone asking who a family named Kirke were. "Kirke?" the other person said, as if wondering why anyone would mention such a family as these Kirkes. "Oh, you mean those Western people!" The word "Western" was spoken in a way that seemed to be enough to say about the Kirkes; and, as Mrs. Massey had told me that Joanna Gillwife had told her there was a cottage of Kirkes from Altoona, Pennsylvania, of course I perceived that coming from Illinois we must be a lot worse Western than they were. It kind of frightened me to imagine what would be said if anybody ever happened to ask who the Masseys *were;* but nobody did. We were too invisible. We stayed that way at the beach (and of course everywhere else) day after day.

Then one morning when Mrs. Massey and I were sitting on the sand and watching Clarissa and Enid playing ball in their bathing-suits, we saw a girl about Enid's age turn away from some boys she was with and go up to Enid and shake her hand. They talked a little while; then Clarissa and Enid brought this girl over to Mrs. Massey and me and introduced her to us. She seemed to be a right nice young thing and she'd been at Enid's school, the year before. Of course she turned right away from Mrs. Massey and me, the way young people do, and began to talk to Enid again.

"Only to think of running into you here of all people!" she said. "And if we hadn't both happened to come to the beach this morning I'd never have seen you at all!

You see, I'm just stopping over one day with the Bull-finches. Of course you know the Bullfinches."

"Bullfinches?" Enid asked her. "Wait a minute. Bull-finches. No—no, I don't *think* I've met any Bullfinches."

"What!" the girl said, and she made kind of a squeal-ing sound. "Why, good gracious me! the Bullfinches practic'ly run everything in Mary's Neck! Mr. and Mrs. Bullfinch began coming here when there were just cow-lots where all of the cottages are now. The whole place just centres on the Bullfinches, and you *haf* to know them. Whatever goes on goes on at the Bullfinch cottage; Janey Bullfinch is absolutely my most intimate friend and George Bullfinch has the only forty-foot motor-boat here and Eddie Bullfinch owns a Dorio-Grecco racing car; they're by far the most important people at Mary's Neck —they and their own particular friends—really they're the only people here. Who *do* you know here?"

"Me?" Enid asked her. "Not any family in particular. You see, this is practic'ly our first summer here and——"

"Listen!" the girl broke in. "If this is your first summer it's no wonder you don't know the Bullfinches because of course——" She interrupted herself there; but it was easy to see she meant that people could come to Mary's Neck for years and years without getting to know the Bullfinches. "Listen!" she went on, "I'm going to take you and your sister over to where they're sitting—they always sit 'way off at the other end of the beach. This isn't the right end, you know. I'm going to take you to meet them right now."

She said this in a manner that made it clear what a privilege she was conferring and how much she was going to do for the girls; and it seemed to me they looked a little scared, which of course was natural enough. After their invisibility, to be marched right up to the Royal

Family of Mary's Neck was almost too much for them; but they trotted along with this helpful young thing and went so far up toward the other end of the beach that Mrs. Massey and I lost sight of them behind the crowd and the gay umbrellas. We didn't see them again for quite a while after that; then Mrs. Massey laughed and sighed with relief at the same time.

"They're started at last," she said, and she pointed down the beach to where a game with a tennis ball seemed to be going on between six or seven boys and girls. Clarissa and Enid were two of them, and everything looked all right. "All I was afraid of," Mrs. Massey said, "was that they'd never get started."

They did seem to be started, too, because they didn't come back to us at all and only stopped for a minute on their way to the bath-houses to dress, and asked if they could go to the Bullfinches' to lunch. Janey Bullfinch had invited them, they said, and Eddie Bullfinch was going to drive them there in his racing car. We said yes, and were glad to see them looking happy and excited, though, after they'd gone, we ourselves felt a little more lonely and invisible maybe than we had been before. That was all right with us, of course, because the parents of fine-looking girls are pretty generally expected to be that way, and we knew we'd better get used to being abandoned as soon as we could. The girls certainly abandoned us that day, and they must have been making a terrible hit with these grandee Bullfinches because they were away all afternoon and telephoned about half past six to say they were going to stay at the Bullfinch cottage for dinner; then about eight o'clock in the evening I was sitting out on the piazza alone when a most disgusting uproar broke out on the ocean road that runs in front of the house, and the Dorio-Grecco racing car that Enid's school friend had talked about came whang-banging up our driveway and stopped near the piazza.

It was a terrible-looking thing with hardly any paint except where the racing number 26 was left on it, and that had been re-painted so as to be more conspicuous. I didn't like the appearance of that machine at all; its open plumbing was sticking out in the air, and altogether it was one of those cars with the look of having been in a good many accidents and going to be in more. Enid got out of it and so did a long, gangling boy who looked just the person to have that sort of a car. He must have been six feet high; but I judged him to be younger than Enid, maybe going on eighteen, and he had grown so fast and was so narrow all the way up that he didn't seem to have had time to get put together the right way—not as yet— or to know how to handle all his parts in conjunction, so to speak. He had a pinkish face with a childish nose in the middle of it that seemed to have been left over from his younger years; his light-colored hair had been soaped back but part of it on top was sprung out of place. He didn't wear any hat and his white flannel pantaloons were not much for shape and had automobile grease on them —all in all, he was the overgrown kind of boy you'd have expected to be as shy as he was gawky. But he wasn't shy; you could tell that right away by his expression: he was the kind of boy that tells a hotel waiter to rack along and make it snappy.

He stumbled a couple of times as he followed Enid up the piazza steps, because he caught the loose sole of one of his spotted white shoes in cracks, and he walked partly into the side of my chair when Enid introduced him.

"Meetcha," he told me.

"This is Eddie Bullfinch," she said. "Clarissa and Janey and George have started to Blue Harbor for a dance, and Eddie and I are going to join them after a while. Is mother upstairs?"

I said yes, and she took this Eddie into the living-room and left him there while she went up to see her mother. Eddie must have been looking things over pretty thoroughly because I heard him bumping around in different parts of the room. It was finished by now and big enough for anybody to walk around in quite a while without re-crossing his own trail; but pretty soon this Eddie Bullfinch knocked a standing-lamp over. "Oh, slush!" I heard him say; and then he seemed to be rubbing himself instead of picking up the lamp.

Enid came trotting downstairs, at that. "Did you hurt yourself, Eddie?" I heard her say.

"Me?" he asked her. "It takes a good deal more than a lamp to do me any harm. That's a bum lamp, anyhow; you needn't fool with it because it's too twisted to be much good any more and there's plenty light in here without it. Listen! How do you like driving round in a Dorio-Grecco? Pretty warm little car, what?"

"It's lovely," Enid told him. "Perfectly wonderful!"

"Look!" he said. "Don't tell anybody, but that car's had three racing drivers put out o' business in it and look it's been right through the front wall of a brick house. That's the kind of a car I like to own," he went on, and he let out a pretty loud, reckless-sounding laugh. "I had to pay fifty dollars down to get it and look I owe two hundred and forty dollars on it yet for the repairs. Don't say anything about that."

"I won't," Enid said, and I could tell by her voice she was impressed. "I won't say anything to anybody about it."

"Don't tell this, either," Eddie said. "Don't tell it and don't let anybody know I told you: I owe over eighty dollars at the hardware store in the village for things I've got to put on the car. Don't tell anybody about that and look don't tell this, either: I run bills pretty nearly everywhere. Don't let anybody know I told you about that, though. Do you know what I tell 'em when they ask me for the money? I say, 'I may pay you next month or I may pay you next year; that's my business. Talk to me too much about it and you'll never get it!' " With that, he gave another kind of reckless laugh, and I judged he must have gone over to the mantelpiece and leaned back against it, or rested his arm on it or something, because there was quite a crash and the tinkling of glass or china getting broken on the brick hearth. "Oh, slush!" he said again.

"It's nothing," I heard Enid telling him. "It's only a lustre vase mother got at an antique store."

"I see," Eddie said. "My mother used to collect those things, too; but she quit. Listen. If you're going to try and pick up all those pieces we won't get to Blue Harbor till after the rest of 'em are there, and I bet George three used golf balls against his striped socks that we'd be there first. Let's go!"

So they came out of the house with Eddie caroming off the side of the front door and the loose sole of his shoe flopping as they went down the steps—I wondered how he was going to dance in it but I don't suppose he let anything like that bother him—and they got in the car and drove away, making about the same noise that a battle would.

Well, I wasn't overly impressed with Eddie Bullfinch, myself, and somehow he gave me kind of a poor idea of his parents, too—which of course isn't fair but on the other hand it's pretty natural—so that I didn't quite share the excitement of the rest of my family over the Bullfinch grandeeship. But the next day nothing else was talked of at our table except what wonderful people the Bull-finches were and what wonderful things they owned and how wonderful it was for a new family like ours to have got to know them so soon. In fact, it seemed that if we didn't make any mistakes—that is, if Mrs. Massey and I didn't—the Bullfinches were preparing to recognize us as a family, so to speak, and even invite us to dinner. That's what happened, too, before the end of that week. We went there to dinner but I didn't enjoy myself particularly because, in the first place, they had steamed clams in seaweed and I'd never eaten any before in my whole life and, living in Logansville, hadn't expected ever to be called on to eat any, and hadn't learned how. In the second place, doing my best to seem appreciative, I ate the wrong part of quite a number of these clams before I noticed how much I was mortifying Enid and Clarissa by doing it, and, in the third place, the clams didn't agree with me at all.

Right away I began to be sick enough to wonder how long I was going to be able to stay at the table; but I wouldn't have enjoyed the conversation much anyhow. Mr. Bullfinch is a tall, thin, scarce-haired man and of course he's right nice and likeable, though, being Eastern, he's kind of coolish at first. Right afterwards, though, as soon as he felt better acquainted, he turned out to be pretty nearly as long-winded as Mr. Sweetmus and of course, after being invisible, I'd have been mighty glad to talk to any man about anything; but Mr. Bullfinch is one of those people who have the habit of working any subject around to themselves. "Good weather this year?" he'd say. "That reminds me: one of my friends asked me the other day, 'Mr. Bullfinch,' he said. 'Mr. Bullfinch, you're the Chairman of the Westfield Industrial and

Agrarian Statistics Committee, aren't you?' 'Yes,' I said,
'I am.' 'Well, Mr. Bullfinch,' he asked me, 'if it's not an
intrusion, would you mind giving me your opinion as to
the effect of last winter's bad weather in the South upon
industrial conditions? You ought to know more about
that situation probably than any other man in the United
States and, if it's not an intrusion, I should like to ask
you if you'd mind stating your opinion upon that subject?' 'Not at all', I told him. 'My position enables me
to be posted upon the subject.' The fact is, Mr. Massey,
it was only at the last meeting of our Committee that
one of the members asked me the same question. He
stood up at the meeting and addressed me, 'Mr. Chairman,' he said, 'may I have the floor for a moment?'
'Certainly,' I said. 'Well, Mr. Chairman,' he spoke up,
'I would like to ask if you feel like confiding to the Committee your opinion upon the effect of the weather in the
South upon the present situation?' I told him I would be
very glad to do so."

He went on like that fairly forever, it seemed to me,
as I sat there wondering just how far those clams were
going with me; and sometimes I could hear Mrs. Bullfinch talking to Mrs. Massey and telling her about the
cottagers, how few really attractive people there were
among them and how there were only two other families,
the Blodgetts and Carmichaels, that she herself looked
upon as really intimate friends. We must meet the Blodgetts and Carmichaels, she said. The Blodgetts had
peculiarities, of course, she went on laughingly, after
talking a long time about how lovely these two families
were, and Mrs. Carmichael was leading a martyr's life
because of Mr. Carmichael's having a little weakness
for the bottle; and besides, people did have to make
allowances for the Blodgett children's being a little

rampageous at times. Anyhow, she was sure we'd find the Blodgetts and Carmichaels really delightful. One trouble with Mary's Neck, she told Mrs. Massey, was that there weren't as many really desirable people here as a person would think at first glance. Mrs. Massey kept nodding her head and exclaiming, with the deferential kind of eagerness a new person in a place always has when the settled potentates become confidential; and Mr. Bullfinch went on with his stories about people asking him his opinion; and at the other end of the table the youngsters made a power of noise, and my clams threatened me so that I wondered if I wasn't going to be a case for a surgeon. But finally we got out of there without anything serious having happened.

CHAPTER IX

W ELL, the next morning at breakfast there was more talk than ever at our home table about how wonderful the Bullfinches were, and Mrs. Massey claimed that before long now we'd be entitled to invite them to dinner at our cottage. I said (to myself) I could probably live through it without complaining too much, if we didn't have clams, though I confess that already Eddie Bullfinch was giving me complicated feelings. He seemed to be spending about two-thirds of his time at our house and for the past week I hadn't often wanted to sit down in some comfortable chair without finding him already in it. Besides, he'd proved dangerous to a good deal of the furniture and bric-à-brac that was at all fragile; he'd put his foot through a French window, and one of the things he'd broken would have been almost impossible for anybody else—it's a thing I hesitate to mention for fear of being thought an exaggerator, because it was a chandelier. It was a glass one, in the dining-room, and when I asked what on earth had happened to it, Clarissa said casually, "Oh, Eddie broke it."

"Why, he couldn't," I told her. "A person can't just bump into a chandelier, especially when it's hanging up over a dining-room table!"

But she explained that he'd been showing a golf stroke with the poker, and I saw that I needn't have been surprised; even a chandelier wasn't too much for Eddie Bullfinch. When Enid was out with him in the Dorio-Grecco we usually had at least the comfort of knowing where she was until the car got some miles away, because we could hear it, and it was never any use trying to take an afternoon nap when the Dorio-Grecco was in that township.

Well, the morning after the Bullfinches' dinner, when we went to the beach, Mrs. Bullfinch introduced Mrs. Massey and me to their friends, the Blodgetts and Carmichaels, and we sat with them and everything seemed fairly agreeable. The girls were bathing and capering with the Bullfinch boys and Janey and a number of others; it was pleasant to watch them, and the Blodgetts and Carmichaels seemed pretty nice likeable people. They were right amiable to Mrs. Massey and me.

"Why, of course!" Mrs. Massey told me, when I mentioned this after we got home. She had a kind of excited, triumphant manner and seemed to be pleased about everything. "Naturally they would be—since we were introduced by the Bullfinches. Don't you see? Why, Mary's Neck's just ours!"

Of course I was delighted to see how much pleasure she and the girls got out of the feeling that after our period of being vacuums we'd all at once jumped into Mary's Neck right at the top. It was a relief to quit being invisible—a relief I felt, myself—and, looking back on it, our invisibility hadn't lasted very long, though it seemed long while we had it. My suspicion was that it might have gone on indefinitely if it hadn't been for everybody's seeing how attractive our girls were, and of course Enid's school-friend's turning up made a power of differ-

ence. Yes, even before the Bullfinches' dinner we'd begun
to feel like flesh-and-blood human beings again; but it
did strike me that even this soon Eddie Bullfinch was
beginning to pall on Enid.

I think maybe she wished he'd dress with more care
and less fashionableness;—by that I mean his white
pantaloons and formerly white shoes practically always
showed contact with the Dorio-Grecco's lubrication system, and I never did see anything just like the knee-
breeches he wore right often. I asked Enid if they were
called ankle-breeches and she said no, they were knicka-
bockers invented on account of the Prince of Wales but
Eddie couldn't do anything except by extremes and she
did think his mother'd be mortified the way his usually
got to looking. Besides this, I think Enid wished he'd now
and then arrange so that his soaped-back sandy hair
wouldn't get rucked up on the top section the way it did,
and maybe she got irritated by his being pretty argu-
mentative and also by his never seeming to move in
unison, so to speak—I don't know, but sometimes I felt
that way myself about him, and she was with him a good
deal more than I was.

She's a couple of years younger than Clarissa, but
light-haired and more severe. She's every bit as good-
looking as Clarissa but less given to susceptibility and
being frivolous with a crowd; she's always been the intellectual one, and, before she was even sixteen, she read
more than most of us do about serious matters such as
biology and people like the Emperor Marcus Aurelius.
Then, for the next two years, before we came to Mary's
Neck, she'd begun to be artistic—not that she dressed
that way, I mean; but she read books that even Clarissa
said were queer and too deep for herself. Besides that,
Enid got puzzling-looking magazines and argued a good

deal about literature and music and the fine arts and
biology and calling a spade a spade, and usually she became a little snappish if we didn't agree with her; but
how can you agree with a person when you don't know
what she's talking about? Mrs. Massey and Clarissa com-
prehended oftener than I did, of course, on account of
these subjects being more natural to women, and for my
part there were occasions when I couldn't tell whether
Enid meant to be sarcastic with me or not. For instance,
she had to call me a Kiwanis three times before I gathered
she didn't mean it for a compliment.

That wasn't what she called Eddie Bullfinch. She must
have made some effort, pretty soon after the start, to
elevate his mind to her level, because I heard them arguing around the corner of the piazza, and she called him
a mere barbarous mechanism and he took it pretty hard.
I think it was right then that I began to get a leaning
toward him, due to sympathy maybe. Besides, you can't
deny there's a kind of fascination in watching one of
these boys that have grown too fast and can't manage
their members. He was expensive around the house, but
interesting, especially in the way he behaved when Enid
walked on him. Part of the time she'd be just a natural,
light-hearted, unsusceptible young girl ready for outdoor
life and gayety; then all of a sudden, when he couldn't
have been looking for it, her intellectualness would break
out and give him a trying time. These uncertainties were
all the painfuller for him, I expect, because he's a little
bit younger than she is and it was pretty plain he'd got
the kind of feeling about her that a boy younger does
get when he feels like that.

These young people in their late 'teens get familiar
with each other with a quickness that stops an older person's breath. I don't believe it was more than ten days

after the Massey family stopped being invisible when Enid said, at breakfast, that the boys and girls at the beach bored her, especially Eddie Bullfinch. She said she didn't want him around any more at all, because of his mind; and about two hours later I was sitting on the piazza and heard her parting with him permanently in the living-room. "I never want to see you again," she told him, "so go on home and don't come back. Any person without intelligence enough to understand 'Biljor', or who would talk about things of beauty the way you do, gives me a pain! I never want to see you again!"

"Listen!" I heard Eddie saying. "I may be a dumbell but if I've got to read any more things like 'Biljor' or else quit going around with you, I'm not goin' to read 'em! Why can't you act like you look?"

"Go home!" she told him. "Go straight home!"

He did it; he flopped out of the house, saying, "Biljor!" over and over to himself, and, although he came back about an hour later, it was easy to see they were on unpleasant terms and that something called "Biljor" was a good deal the cause of it. So I asked her what this "Biljor" was, and she told me it was a "great Work", and it turned out to be a book containing a play, and I read it and was surprised to find that it had cost her three dollars and a half. It was peculiar summer reading; but I managed to get clear through it that night, because I wanted to see what she thought was great and because the plot of it was pretty surprising.

Biljor was the hero of it, or anyhow the one that talked the most; his business was raising hogs out in the country somewhere, and he had a daughter named Tilg and a son-in-law married to Tilg, named Crogg, and there was another woman on the farm, named Lide, who was Crogg's mother, and at first they all talked a great deal about how much they worked around the hogs, and nothing of interest seemed about to happen. But afterwhile it seemed Biljor was in love with Lide, and so was Crogg, which mystified me because this Lide was Crogg's mother. Biljor and Crogg had a terrible fight over her, and Biljor's daughter got jealous and Crogg came in and told how she'd pushed Lide into a vat of boiling lard. It didn't kill her; but she suffered a good deal and seemed to like to talk about it and dwell on how disfigured she was, so Biljor and Crogg put Tilg in the vat and kept her down in it with pitchforks until there wasn't anything left. Then they had another fight over Lide, and Biljor killed Crogg with the meat-chopper, and Lide told Biljor she and his daughter, Tilg, had both always been in love with him. But now that she was a good deal disfigured, Biljor couldn't seem to like her any more, so he put her in the vat and disposed of her the way he and Crogg had disposed of Tilg; and he put Crogg in there, too. Then some neighbors came and he sold them the vat and went on raising pork the same as before. Probably the author couldn't see his way to fix up a happy ending, so he had Biljor break his leg and fall inside the pen so that he couldn't feed the hogs any more, and, as he was too sick to crawl out, they ate him, which was told to the audience by a neighbor.

Some of the language was unusual. For instance, Biljor told Lide, before she had her misfortune, that his heart was flesh stretched over the stars, and she beat upon it, so he said, like a bone pounding the taut cat-skins stretched upon a tom-tom. And she told him something equally peculiar. "i am starvation" she said, using a small letter for the pronoun; I couldn't see why, myself. "i am pangs and slavering and my slavering is like the hot yellow slime on the cobblestones of a chinese slum."

Well, of course I knew Enid was advanced in her ideas on art and literature and I was afraid she'd get nervous with me if I asked her why she'd paid three dollars and a half for "Biljor", especially as the author'd been too economical with capital letters and punctuation, I thought, to warrant any such outlay. So I tried to be tactful and just told her I seemed to be as ordinary-minded about it as Eddie Bullfinch had been. "Another thing that bothers me," I went on, "I don't seem to get the plot quite straight. For instance, Crogg appears to state that he's in love with this Lide; but there are other statements to the effect that Lide is his mother, so I don't——"

Enid interrupted me, looking impatient. "Certainly!" she told me. "He has a mother fixation."

"Oh," I said, and, although I'd never heard the expression before, the idea it seemed to convey struck me as morbid; but I wanted to go on being tactful so I just asked her in a friendly way what pleasure or improvement she'd got out of "Biljor".

"Pleasure?" she said. "One doesn't read great dramatic poetry for mere pleasure."

This surprised me, mainly because I hadn't caught any idea of its being poetry at all, and I told her I hadn't.

"Certainly, it's poetry," she said. "You don't think mere cheap jingle and rhyme and capital letters make a thing poetry, do you? That's as absurd as thinking one reads for the sake of pleasure. 'Biljor' is brutal beauty. It's a welling of damnation and the forbidden out of the soil. It's abysmal reality. It's an engulfment of the human in the psychical demonism of the soil, expressed in masculine verse." Enid talks this way when she gets roused on literature or art, and I think I'm quoting her pretty correctly—because there was something a good deal like what she said on the back paper cover of the book, and I read it over several times, trying to get it. "It's stark elemental actualism," she said.

"I don't understand you exactly," I told her. "If I get you anywhere at all near right, you mean that there are real people outside of asylums quite a lot like these people in 'Biljor', and such things happen as are supposed to happen in this book?"

"Certainly," she said. " 'Biljor' is the drama of the souls of people in close contact with the soil—of primitive, elemental people who sweat and labor close to the soil."

"My goodness!" I said, "I've known a good many farm-hands and suchlike; I never dreamed they were like that. For instance," I went on, "look yonder." We were sitting on the piazza, and Zebias Flick was grubbing around over the lawn on his hands and knees; he had an old case-knife, and he was rooting up weeds and dandelions out of the grass. Zebias usually seems to have been in fairly close contact with the soil, if you judge by looking at him. He certainly was in close contact with it when I pointed him out to Enid and he filled her other conditions, too, because he was laboring some and perspiring quite a little. "Do you suppose," I asked Enid, "do you suppose Zebias Flick ever told anybody that his heart was flesh stretched over the stars like taut cat-skins over a tom-tom?"

She began to look sensitive. "He might have," she told me. "You don't pretend to know what he might say if he were alone with a woman he had a passion for, do you?"

"Well, let's ask him," I said. "Unless maybe you'd prefer me to inquire of Mr. Sweetmus instead?"

Right there she asked *me* a question—a terribly disrespectful one; but I expect everybody understands about the young people being different nowadays. "Are you trying to play the Tomfool?"

"I see your point," I told her. "You mean it would occupy too much of our day if we asked him. We'll stick to Zebias."

So I called him. He heard me of course; but at first the only sign he gave was to stop working and look at the ground for a while. Then he hunted around, still on his hands and knees, till he found a blade of grass that was longer than the one he already had in his mouth. He introduced the longer one and took the shorter one out, got up pretty slowly, scratched his head and the back of his overalls; then he walked over toward us, stopped about ten feet away from the piazza and chewed his piece of grass a while.

"Breeze droppin'," he said. "She's shiftin' to sou'west."

"Zebias," I asked him, "did you ever tell any woman you had a passion for that your heart was flesh stretched across the stars like the taut cat-skins of a tom-tom, and that she was beating on it like a bone?"

He wasn't looking at us; he was staring out at the Atlantic ocean; but the grass he was chewing stopped wagging out through his scattered mustache for a minute. Then it began to move again. "Mebbe she's shifted a mite west o' sou'west," he said.

Enid got up, and it wasn't hard to see she was pretty cross with me; she gave me one of those looks I've mentioned as painful for a parent to endure when being put in his place on such subjects as art or antiques or biology. "I wonder how long," she said over her shoulder as she went into the house, "I wonder how long I've got to live among sparkless literal-minded people?"

CHAPTER X

OF COURSE Enid feels a good deal of intellectual loneliness sometimes; anyhow she tells her mother she does, and her mother tells me. Well, she'd already heard there was an Art Colony—that's the way it was spoken of—over at Mount Jasper, which is a little settlement about fifteen miles back in the country, and, when she came out of the house again, after the discussion between us I've just mentioned, she got her runabout and drove over there. The Jasperites must have cheered her right up because she didn't get back to Mary's Neck until after dark and was all enlivened and enthusiastic. The "Jasper movement", she told us, was the most advanced outpost of the best in literature, art and music. "Modernistic" was her word for the Jasperites; she'd had a glorious afternoon with them and one of them was coming over to dinner with us the next night because she'd invited him.

He turned up early and Enid was pleased, though we could see she was worried about the impression we'd make on him and bothered by Eddie Bullfinch's being at the cottage and keeping on staying—I suppose it was a little unfortunate that Eddie hung around so long he had to be asked in to the table, too. The young man from the Jasper Art Colony was named Carlos Prang; but he wasn't a foreigner. He was from Springfield, Ohio, I found by asking, though he'd lived for the last two or three years in New York. He wasn't homely and he wasn't eccentric-looking, either, and he was dressed like anybody else; he didn't even wear those big spectacles, and the only thing noticeable about him—except that he was pretty sallow and had what you might call burning eyes—was that he began smoking cigarettes with his soup. Of course to me his conversation seemed peculiar; but it wasn't any more so than Enid's, and, after all, I don't know that the word "peculiar" is exactly the best way to express it.

I think I've mentioned in connection with antiques and the fine arts that Enid had a way sometimes of looking as though she knew secrets most other people could never hope to learn, and that in a lesser degree her mother and Clarissa now and then put on a little of this look, too. There seems to be something in all these artistic matters that isn't intended for us men—I mean us customary American business men—and when we try to share in such subjects with our wives and daughters they appear kind of mysterious to us and they're apt to look on us as pretty much dummies. Probably they're right and the way we're constituted doesn't permit us to enter into their feelings in the manner some kinds of foreigners, for instance, can.

Take music: it'll make a man's own wife a perfect stranger to him sometimes. Women are liable to behave as though one of these Frenchmen or Spaniards or Yiddish could do something for them more important than any American husband could ever hope to accomplish. Why, when this Esjago, or what-you-call-him, played at Mozart Hall in Logansville, Mrs. Massey hung around there with about forty or fifty other of the nicest

married women in our city to watch him come out—and
I wish you'd seen what they were looking for! I did,
because I happened to be in the hotel lobby that afternoon when he came in, and my, my! She just couldn't
talk to me when I got home; she always says music takes
it out of her. She was sort of queer, and if this Esjago
had come up to her right after he was playing and told
her he had a longing to settle down somewhere and just
play to her always, I don't know, I don't know! What
I'm getting around to, in saying that young Mr. Carlos
Prang's conversation wasn't exactly peculiar, it's that he
seemed more or less like that class of foreigners I'm
speaking of who appear to have a private understanding
with women on their artistic sides, you might say.

Not that either Mrs. Massey or Clarissa understood
what Enid and young Mr. Prang were talking about much
better than Eddie Bullfinch or I did, and when any of us
tried to put in with some remark or even a simple question we got what you might call a polite sitting-on. Enid
and Mr. Prang didn't insult us exactly; they'd just look
reticent and answer in a hurried, troubled manner pretty
briefly, then go on talking to each other. What they said
was mainly about people with names I'd never heard,
and I couldn't make out very well what the two of 'em
were really telling each other about these people.

For instance, they began speaking of somebody who
seemed to be named Raffeeny, and the way they spoke
of him kind of scared the rest of us and made us feel
uneducated—except Eddie Bullfinch of course. "Do you
feel with Raffeeny?" Enid asked this young Carlos Prang.

"Beyond anything," he told her. "Raffeeny is inevitable.
You feel inevitableness with him. It's elemental inevitableness."

"Yes," Enid agreed, "it's stark. And don't you feel groping, too, with Raffeeny?"

"Immensely," Mr. Prang said. "I put that into my own composition in three dimensions—the one I showed you at the studio, called 'Subsoil'. Didn't you feel it expressed something of that?"

"Immensely," she told him. "I think there's more of that in it than in anything else you've done. It has more that of Raffeeny than Raffeeny himself."

Mrs. Massey was anxious to be polite to Enid's new friend. "Are you a painter, Mr. Prang?" she asked him.

"Well," he said, "I feel for things in color sometimes. At least I feel for them."

I was going to ask honestly and inoffensively what he felt for them; but Enid was probably afraid I'd say something out of the way because she spoke up quickly and didn't give me a chance. "He's not only a painter," she explained to us, "he's one of the very most important modernistic sculptors. He composes music and writes the most searching things in a new type of prose that he's invented, himself. Everybody in the colony is tremendously proud of Mr. Prang."

It was then that Eddie Bullfinch began to make things uncomfortable. "Well, isn't that nice!" he said. "My goodness! Isn't that nice!"

He didn't say it in a way that would let anybody come right out and accuse him of intending to be disagreeable, and yet we all knew perfectly well that he had some such intention, and Mrs. Massey tried to keep him from being too jarring. "Indeed it's wonderful!" she said. "I think it's perfectly wonderful that anyone of Mr. Prang's age could be a painter and musician and sculptor and poet all at the same time."

"Wonderful!" Eddie said. "I should say it is wonderful! If he paints pictures and carves sculptuary and writes poetry and plays the piano all at the same time, he must be a centipede or something!" And he broke into a loud, boorish laugh in order to applaud himself properly.

Enid got red and gave him a pretty fierce look; but young Mr. Prang didn't seem to notice anything, and we got up from the table just then and went into the living-room, so Eddie's rudeness appeared to be passed over and covered up. He was wearing the bitterest kind of expression on his face, and it was pretty incongruous, because Eddie's complexion is a fresh pink and, as I've said, his nose hasn't grown up and settled down yet but has the look of being left over from when he was about ten years old. His eyebrows are so light, too, that they aren't very distinct; and when he frowned in this bitter manner with them I had to look away from him, myself, because I was afraid I'd laugh and hurt his feelings more.

He went over to a chair pretty nearly halfway across the room from the rest of us and slumped himself down there, alone, making some clucking noises in his throat, while Mrs. Massey and the girls grouped themselves around young Mr. Prang and made a polite little fuss over him and asked him if he wouldn't play something for us. He was modest about it and said he hardly felt up to it; but, when Enid asked him if he wouldn't play one of his own compositions, he made up his mind rather suddenly that he would.

"I'll play a thing I call 'Remnants' for you," he told her. "I felt it out yesterday after our talk in the studio."

Then he sat down at the piano and lifted his hands above the keys; but waited until we'd seated ourselves so there would be complete silence. He was just going to begin when Eddie made some more clucking noises in his throat and kept on until Enid stopped him by looking at him in a way that would have hushed anybody. Then all at once young Mr. Prang hit the lower part of the keyboard with a crash almost startling enough to bounce me out of my seat. For about two minutes, he banged the bass notes, with his foot on the loud pedal; you never heard such a noise in a private house, and just when I thought my ears couldn't stand any more of it he quit as suddenly as he'd begun and commenced to tweedle two of the highest treble keys. He went on tinkling those two keys, without touching any of the others, for about as long as he'd banged the bass; then he swept the whole keyboard up and down a few times with both hands. After that, his arms dropped down to his sides, he leaned back, and I could see that Mrs. Massey, though she's mighty susceptible to music ordinarily, didn't get what he'd been doing at all; but she wanted to be polite, so she said, "Perfectly wond——" But this was a mistake, because he wasn't through.

He rubbed both hands over his head, mussing his hair up considerably, shook himself all over as if he'd just been in the water, then lifted his hands pretty high and brought them down again with another crash; then he put them up again and crashed again and kept on crashing for a while; then he tweedled the high keys some more till a person could hardly make out to bear it, and, after that, he more or less settled down to calisthenics with all parts of the keyboard. It went on for seven or eight minutes, I should say, and I couldn't make head or tail of it, myself, try as I would to understand what he was up to.

There wasn't any doubt that he meant something and that what he was doing had significance for him and for Enid, too. Her face wore what you might call a rapt expression, though she couldn't have been hearing anything that I'd been brought up to regard as music. Of course I knew the world wasn't standing still, and that just as only a few people can understand the Einstein theory, so there might be art that ordinary people like myself would probably be ignorant about because it had gone so far beyond the standards of my youth that it couldn't be understood by the multitude, so to speak. Certainly it isn't modest, and usually it isn't wise, either, for a person to set himself up as a judge of what he doesn't understand, and when we try to sweep away everything we don't understand by just booing at it and calling it nonsense we're liable to show our own ignorance and get into as much trouble as Eddie Bullfinch did that night.

So, when young Mr. Carlos Prang stopped playing and sat a minute or two with his towsled head bent forward over the keyboard, showing he was almost exhausted, as was certainly natural after all he'd been doing, I didn't say anything and neither did Mrs. Massey or Clarissa. We thought best to leave comments to Enid, who'd be equal to the occasion.

She gave a great sigh. "It's enormous!" she said. "I like it better than anything you played for me yesterday. 'Remnants' is the perfect title for it. One feels precisely that mood in nature absolutely expressed in your music —the reverberations of that thunder-shower yesterday among the hills of Jasper and the little frightened twitterings of the birds scarcely daring to think that it is over—thunder and crashing winds, and then the little cheepings in the underbrush———"

She was going on; but he swung around on the piano-bench, and his face began to look a little red. "Well, yes, possibly", he said. "But what I meant was more my own mood after you'd gone—strong mental and emotional reactions in me—then little thoughts———"

"Yes, of course," Enid said hurriedly, and she turned a little red, herself. "I meant that. More like the reverberations of an emotional strain—the stronger feelings, and then the little wandering imaginings, like birds' cheepings——"

"Well, no," he said, and he was getting redder, "not exactly like birds' cheepings——"

"No, not like that," she put in. "By birds' cheepings, I meant just the emotions that have that detached feeling about them. Of course it's all mental——"

"Exactly," he said, and he nodded, seeming pleased to find her in agreement. "Yes, you get precisely what I meant."

"Yes," she told him, "I get it because your playing expressed precisely that very thing."

She nodded back to him, and he nodded to her again, and they both looked satisfied and pleased—especially pleased with each other, which didn't please Eddie Bullfinch, as he proceeded to make everybody aware. He spoke up in a voice he seemed to be afraid someone would think wasn't sneering enough. "Ain't it gur-rand!" he said. "It's all about thunder and torrable crashing winds in the mountings—only it ain't! Oh, listen to the little birds cheeping in the underbrush—only they don't!" He turned to me. "I hope that piano's insured because its works are certainly out of business now. My gosh!"

Enid jumped up, and her eyes were flashing; she was pretty mad. "Eddie Bullfinch!" she said.

He got up, too. "Wasn't it wonderful how you knew precisely what Mr. Carlo Sprang was playing!" he said in a coarse voice. "Carlo says he played about going into fits or spasms or something right after he had a talk with you yesterday afternoon, and you say, 'Oh, sweetie pie! what lovely thunder!' My gosh! Which is it,

Carlo having convulsions, the way he would after you'd talked to him, or is it cheepings or something? My gosh!"

Well, Enid was pretty upset with him. "You march out of here!" she said. "Go straight home! Try and get out of the house once without breaking anything!"

Eddie drew himself up, looking as severe as could be managed with a face like his. "I bid you good-evening, Mr. and Mrs. Massey," he said. "I bid you good-evening, Clarissa." Then he stalked out, and would have accomplished this with considerable dignity if his foot hadn't slipped on a rug; but he caught himself before he got clear down and went the rest of the way to the door without further accident. When he was on the piazza, he shouted back, "Oh, what pretty cheepings the birds do make! Cheep! Cheep! Cheep! My gosh!" And after that, we could hear him whistling sarcastically as he went down the road.

Altogether, his outbreak left things pretty embarrassing in the living-room, so Mrs. Massey and I went out on the piazza. George Bullfinch came for Clarissa pretty soon; and then Carlos played some more for Enid, alone, and they seemed to have recovered themselves and to be getting along together first rate.

Enid talked pretty crossly about Eddie Bullfinch, the next day at lunch; but she was unusually polite to me, and once she came around to my chair and put her cheek against mine and talked a little baby-talk to me, so I was fairly sure she wanted something, and she usually gets it when she sets about it that way. I asked her what she was up to, and she invited me to drive over to Mount Jasper with her.

"I want you to see the wonderful things they make there," she said. "They have a communal studio where they all exhibit—a place that's just overflowing with the most fascinating works of art. You will come with me, won't you?"

Well, I wasn't sure I wanted to go; but on the other hand I did kind of want to. That is to say, I was uneasy about it but curious to see the wonderful things; so I told her I would.

CHAPTER XI

JASPER was a right pretty place in a grove of pine trees on a hillside, with some one-story cottages scattered around a larger building that was the studio where the artists exhibited their works and had their concerts and theatricals, Enid told me. We got out and went in there, and it was a big room with a skylight, and the walls were pretty well covered with pictures of all sizes. Besides that, there were some long, wooden tables, and the tables had things on them made of plaster-of-Paris and terracotta and carved wood, which Enid told me were the statuary. Also, there were some people in the room that she said were artists; they were standing around, looking at the works of art they'd made. Two or three of them were right good-looking girls; there were a couple of young men wearing overalls; and there was an old man in black velvet pantaloons, a white sweater and high, black boots. He had white whiskers and pretty long hair and seemed to be a great talker, though he stayed at the other end of the room and I couldn't hear what he said. I didn't try to hear him, for that matter, because I was too much surprised by the works of art to do anything except use my eyes and go staring around.

The first thing I felt about the pictures was that there

was more bright fresh paint on them than I'd ever seen on pictures before, and this gave the whole place a pretty gay and lively effect; but it dazed me a little, too, as if I'd got into a paint factory that had been blown up by an explosion that left the walls standing. But when I looked at the pictures separately, the liveliness I'd felt at first glance wore off pretty fast. Right in the middle of one wall of this art gallery, there was a big painting that made me nervous as soon as I looked at it. It was of a man with no clothes on and a broken neck; anyhow he had his head lying down on his left shoulder in a way he couldn't have accomplished if his neck hadn't been broken; but his expression didn't seem to indicate that he noticed anything much the matter with him. He was bright orange with lavender eyes and blue hair; his legs were not the same length; neither were his arms, and he was standing among some green derricks and other machinery.

Well, I didn't want to talk like Eddie Bullfinch; but when I looked at this orange man with the broken neck and other accessories I couldn't help giving a little jump, as it were, and saying, "Oh, murder!" and I was sorry because I saw that my behavior was mortifying to Enid. Her expression showed that, and she asked me to please contain myself because this picture was one of the finest in the exhibit and had been painted by Abner Lorry himself, who was the talkative old man in the whiskers and velvet pantaloons.

I had a feeling that I'd better go outdoors and stay there and give up trying to gain any education in what Enid felt was art. But even if I'd been alone I don't believe I could have done it, because once a person gets into an exhibition like this he's nearly compelled to see it through. Something holds him and fascinates him. After he's seen one blue-haired, lavender-eyed, orange-colored man, without any clothes but with a broken neck, drooping among green derricks, bright pink cogwheels and violet pistons, he's got to see more; he can't stop there.

The picture next to the broken-necked man wasn't so large but didn't seem to me any more natural; I couldn't make out the subject exactly, although Enid told me the title was "Morning". It appeared to me that something disturbing had happened to a woman. There was a big, two-inch plank—at least it looked like a two-inch plank to me—painted from one corner of this picture catty-cornered down to another corner, and a good many parts of a light-green woman were on both sides of the plank but not connected with the other parts of her. Half of her face, with one eye looking out at you, was on one side of the plank, and, about a foot lower down, the other half of her face was on the other side of the plank, and her arms and legs were scattered similarly up and down the plank on each side of it, but without much corre-spondence. What was pretty bothering, the half of her face on the right side of the plank had an eye in it, and the other half on the left side of the plank had two eyes in it. I had to ask Enid to help me out.

"Would she originally have had three eyes?" I asked her.

She only looked distressed. "Oh, dear!" she said. "Oh, dear!"

"Well, she seems to have been split up by that plank and——"

"It isn't a plank," she whispered crossly. "It's a shaft of morning light. When a shaft of light crosses your vision of anything, you don't see the thing itself. The thing is scattered and you only perceive its meaning."

I tried to take this in, and I went over it in my mind,

looking at the floor so as to be able to concentrate on what she'd said. It was elusive, you might say; one minute it would appear to have some sense in it and the next minute it wouldn't—it was like something slippery that you think you've got grasped in your hand until you look up and see it flipping its tail at you around a stump and disappearing into the underbrush. So I thought it might be helpful maybe to look at the other pictures; but they didn't do me much good. Some of them were of trees that didn't look like trees—that is, you could tell they were meant for trees, or dead weeds likely, or something —and some were of houses that were falling down and had wiggling doors and windows; and quite a number struck me as pretty entirely wild.

Afterwhile I saw I wasn't going to be helped by the paintings to digest Enid's explanation, so I turned to the statuary, and got more confused than ever. There was one something-or-other carved out of wood; it was shaped like a slim banana two feet high, with a copper wire sticking out of the top of it and then running through the middle of about a dozen glass disks, like buttons, and the title of it was "Flight". There were some plaster-of-Paris things, each one with the title "Portrait", that looked something like human heads partly worked on by head-hunters and given up; and there was a terracotta group that upset me almost as much as the orange-colored man had. It seemed to represent a woman maybe and a man maybe—you couldn't tell; neither of them had arms, and the lower part of them was made of square blocks. Their heads were shaped like cylinders, and they didn't have any features; but there was a title at the base of the group: "Card-Players".

This absolutely stuck me. I was timid of asking Enid about it; but I felt as if I'd have to. "If I get what you were telling me," I said, "all these pictures and statuary aren't pictures and statues of things as they are, but represent their meanings. Is that right?"

"It's a groping," she said. "It's a groping."

"But a while ago you told me——"

"I know," she explained. "But it's a groping, too."

"I don't exactly get you, Enid," I told her. "Do you mean that the spectators have got to grope for——"

"Oh, dear me!" she said. "No true artist of this modern day is content with the old worn-out forms of expression. The kind of things you like represent the merely photographic. Mere photography isn't art. The modern in art is the expression of meanings and is also a reaction of the nervous system to objects."

"Whose nervous system?" I asked her, because I was trying to follow her as closely as I could.

"The artist's," she said. "The artist's and the spectator's, too."

"Then if I understand you," I told her, "my nervous system's included, because I'm one of the spectators." I pointed to what seemed to be the picture of a pretty unpleasant chair with the perspective reversed. "For instance, that chair over there—if that's what it is—represents not a chair but the reaction of my nervous system to a chair? Is that it?"

She looked annoyed. "In a way, yes."

"Well, in what way?" I asked her. "Because I don't feel like that about a chair, at all. I haven't got any such nervous reaction to one, and if the person who painted it feels that way about chairs I don't feel as if I'd have any congeniality with him. I wouldn't even like him."

"What's the matter with you?" Enid asked me, and she frowned, staring at me. "You aren't talking connectedly and I don't understand what you mean."

"I was just expressing what I thought was the reaction of my nervous system to one of these works of art," I said. "I was trying to express just what it is, and if you understand them I think you ought to be able to understand me."

"Oh, dear!" she said. "Oh, dear!"

"In other words," I went on, "I'm a spectator, and you said the reaction of a spectator's nervous system is what's expressed in these works of art, and also that the picture of a chair yonder isn't the picture of a chair but is the picture of the meaning of a chair, and besides that, it's a groping. Am I right so far?"

"Oh, dear!" she said, and she looked pretty impatient with me. "That picture is the self-expression of the artist who painted it."

"Is it?" I asked her; but for a minute I seemed to be getting a light on the subject. "I think I begin to see, Enid. The artist just expresses himself the best he can, because himself's what interests *him*. Why, yes, that begins to clear it up; but the trouble is that himself mightn't be as interesting to other people as it is to him. It reminds me of old Macroyd Johnson and your mother's step-cousin, Will, over at Terre Haute. Macroyd used to listen to the poetry Will wrote, because then Will'd have to listen to the poetry Macroyd wrote, and I guess we all feel about the same way concerning each other's self-expressions. But anyhow I'm glad I'm getting the hang of this business, because at first I thought I'd never be able to understand it at all. Yes, sir, when you explain that this artist is expressing himself and not the chair——"

"If you're going to talk that way," she said, "I haven't anything more to say to you!"

"Well, but look here," I told her, "that isn't fair. I

thought I was beginning to find out something you seem to know, and now you're disgusted with me and if you aren't careful you'll get me more confused than I was. Why can't you reason with me a little?"

"Because works of art aren't made to be reasoned about," she said crossly. "You're not supposed to reason about them; you're supposed to feel them."

"So that's it, then," I said. "You aren't meant to think about them; you mustn't let your mind get to working about them at all. I think I begin to understand again, Enid. When you come in here you're supposed to check your brains outside and slide in with only your feelings operating. In that case, ought I to look at one of the works and get to feeling like crying, maybe, or laughing or something?"

She'd have been madder with me, probably, if she hadn't seen that I was speaking in good faith; but, even as it was, she didn't like it. "You certainly are dumb!" she told me. "These pictures and sculptures represent a return to the elemental and the primitive—the absolutely simplest, natural way of looking at things."

"You mean when a child or maybe an Indian looks at a chair, that's the way it appears to him?"

"Certainly. That's the way he'd express it in paint."

"Well," I said, "it's a good deal the way I would, myself, if I tried; but that'd be not because the chair looks that way to me but because I wouldn't know how to paint it any better than a child or an Indian would, and I suspect it'd really look to them about the way it does to me. I guess this thought doesn't appeal to you, though, Enid."

"It doesn't," she told me. "That painting gives forth its elements in the simple, primitive way. In other words, the work is purely subjective, though I don't suppose you

have the faintest idea what I mean. The picture represents abstractions of thought—purely abstract thought
and conception."

"I'm gone again!" I told her. "I thought I was beginning to get hold of it; but I've slipped. If it's abstract
thought, then you don't check your brains outside; it's
your emotions you leave out there. A spectator has to
look at these card-players, for instance, and use his thinking apparatus solely; he mustn't let his emotions get
worked up over the fact that this supposed lady and gentleman aren't playing cards and haven't got any table to
play on, or cards to play with, or faces to use in conceal-
ing what kind of cards they aren't holding, or even arms
and hands to deal with if they did have cards. The spectator is expected to see an abstract conception of what
card-players are really like. Well, I seem to be getting
hold of it again; the thing that bothers me worst now is
that it seems the title is the most important thing about
this work of art, because no spectator on earth would
believe that the group had anything to do with card-
playing except for the title. That bothers me considerably. It seems too much like a little insignificant man that
nobody pays any attention to until he gets people into the
habit of calling him 'Doc' or 'Colonel', and I've always
had an impression that a work of art would mean something or anyway look like something, whether you knew
its title or not. Somehow it doesn't seem just right to me
that the important thing about such a work should be the
title; that appears to me to throw things all out of balance. You see, the trouble is, Enid, if you bought one of
these works of art, for instance, and lost the title and
couldn't remember it, say, then you wouldn't own a work
of art at all; you'd only have a chunk of terra-cotta or
plaster-of-Paris or wood and glass or maybe some lively

paint on canvas. Am I right or am I getting confused once
more?"

I was afraid this would make her mad again; but it
didn't seem to. She took hold of my arm and began to
stroke my sleeve affectionately—a way she has that always pleases me and makes me feel pretty indulgent
toward her. "You're a dear cute old Pops," she said. "I
knew that was what you were going to work around to!"

"What was what I was going to work around to?
That if you bought one of these things you'd have to
keep hold of the title or else————"

"No," she said, and went on, speaking quickly, "I knew
you intended to buy something, and I think it's perfectly
lovely of you, because of course there aren't many people
up to appreciating such things, and the artists have all
made tremendous sacrifices to keep the colony going."
And then before I could get my breath she called to the
old man in the white whiskers and velvet pantaloons,
"Oh, Mr. Lorry, I want you to meet my father. He
hopes to have the honor and pleasure of owning————"

"Murder!" I said, and I began to be scared. "See here,
Enid————"

But by this time Mr. Lorry was shaking hands with
me, and young Carlos Prang had come in from outside
and joined us, and Enid was talking to both of 'em about
which work of art I ought to select. I was most of all
afraid she'd want me to buy the orange-colored man with
the lavender eyes and blue hair among the derricks and
things; but I found I needn't have worried about that
because Mr. Lorry explained that it was a loan exhibit
—merely an example of his earlier manner, he said. It
was owned by a museum somewhere that had bought it
just after it was awarded the Coptus medal, whatever
that was.

"I think I know what would please you best," he said. "I imagine you might perhaps care for one of the more obvious things. My own suggestion would be 'Morning'."

That was the three-eyed lady scattered along the plank or shaft of morning light, and I simply couldn't bear the idea. "It might be—it might be too expensive," I told him, because I couldn't think of anything else to say, right quick. "I don't believe——"

"Oh, no," he said, "it's extremely moderate—only three hundred dollars; but perhaps one of the sculptures——"

"I think he'd like both," Enid put in, and she kept stroking my coatsleeve, and used her prettiest voice. "What we really want are some things of Mr. Prang's —at least to begin with."

Mr. Lorry nodded and looked benevolent. "Mr. Prang is the painter of 'Morning'," he said. "That was one reason I suggested it, knowing your interest in his work."

"Yes," Enid said, "we're going to take that, of course, and I'm simply crazy about his 'Card-Players'. That's the first thing father suggested our buying."

"Well," I said, "I didn't exactly——" I was pretty thoroughly embarrassed, and with my free hand I got out a handkerchief and mopped my forehead. Old Mr. Lorry and young Mr. Carlos Prang seemed to be right nice likeable men, and, though I couldn't comprehend their works, I felt they'd gone to a great deal of pains to fix them up the way they wanted them and were honest in their art beliefs and would naturally be mighty sensitive. I coughed a while, trying to think what to do, then decided my best procedure would be to temporize in some manner until I could get out of there and talk to Enid alone; so after coughing some more I said, "Of course with so many interesting things to choose from it's very difficult to make up one's mind. Perhaps if we'd go home now and come back some other day——"

Enid cut me off; she reached up, patted my cheek and laughed delightedly. "That's just the thing!" she said. "We can pick out a number of things that we'd like to choose from and take them back to Mary's Neck with us in the car, and then some day, as Father says, Mr. Lorry, we could bring back the ones we don't select. That's just splendid! And in the meanwhile we'll have the inspiration of living with wonderful things!" She picked up the terra-cotta "Card-Players" and two plaster-of-Paris "Portraits" and handed them to young Mr. Prang. "Put those in the car, Carlos," she told him, "and we'll take 'Flight' with us. Father will carry that." This was the wooden banana with the glass buttons on top, and she pushed it into my arms while she went on talking. "I'll bring 'Morning' myself, and this wonderful terra-cotta that Carlos did, the one called 'Subsoil'. There! Let's get out to the car with our treasure!"

She pushed me ahead of her, and went on prattling and chattering, and before I knew it—I was so dazed and upset—she had all those terrible things in the rumble of the runabout, with a rug under them to keep them from being damaged by jolting, and we were on the way back to Mary's Neck.

"You cute old Pops!" she said to me. "I knew it was in you! You really have a feeling for art, after all, and you've begun your education. You'll be a collector before you know it, dear old Pops!"

Well, inside, I was pretty cross with her; but she was so gay and happy, feeling that she'd done something for the colony, in general, and this ambitious young Carlos Prang, in particular, I suppose, that I didn't have the heart to cast a wet-blanket over her proceedings, at least not just then. So I only grunted in as objecting a way as I could and decided I'd get Mrs. Massey to do a good deal of sitting on her after we'd got home. When we reached the cottage, though, I helped her and Zebias Flick carry the works in, and we put them down under one of the living-room windows, with "Morning" leaning back against the sill and the sculptures in a row in front of it.

Zebias showed considerable curiosity; he looked at the exhibit quite a while, with his lower jaw moving; then he said, "Them objects ain't antiques. Ef you paid antique prices fer 'em, somebody's made a dolluh!"

I was just going to tell him that nobody'd made a dollar yet with these objects, when Clarissa came in and said Eddie Bullfinch had been waiting around all afternoon to see Enid; and she hadn't any more than told us this when Eddie was heard outside, calling Enid's name.

Enid turned to Clarissa. "My heavens! Lock the front door! I don't want that moron around here!"

Clarissa was willing; she locked the door just as Eddie bumped up against it, and then he rang the bell a while and whistled, but pretty soon seemed to give up, because we heard him tramping down the piazza steps.

"Thank heaven, he's gone!" Enid said. "Clarissa, will you look at these wonderful things Pops is going to give me as the beginning of my modernist collection? Did you ever know anything so glorious?"

Clarissa didn't seem excited at all; but she put her arm around Enid's waist and tried to be sympathetic. "I suppose they're beyond me," she said. "But probably I'm too literal-minded, as you tell me, dear. Anyhow I'm glad you enjoy them, and I think Pops is fine to be so generous with you. Probably you'll want to keep them in your own room——"

She didn't get any further, because something happened just then. The two girls had turned away from the exhibit, and I was starting to go outdoors with Zebias Flick to tell him about some work I wanted done. All our backs were toward the window, which was open, and Eddie Bullfinch had decided to come in that way.

"Somebody must 'a' locked the front door by mistake," I heard him say, as he pushed up the fly-screen; and, seeming to be in a hurry, he tried to vault from outside into the room, and partly succeeded.

Anyhow he landed pretty scramblingly among the exhibit, and, before he got through, the plaster-of-Paris groups were wrecked, the slim banana part of "Flight" was broken in two, with the glass buttons in bad condition, and he had one foot through "Morning". Enid screamed and made a dash for him, and, not understanding her meaning, he squirmed his foot out of "Morning" and did damage to the terra-cotta "Card-Players" and "Subsoil".

"What are you making the fuss about?" he asked Enid. "What *is* all this worthless junk, anyhow?" She told him what it was, in a pretty screeching voice, and added to that a good deal about what she thought he was. He looked right hurt and sat down on the floor and began to examine the pieces and try to fit them together. "Works of art?" he said. "Were they? Well, prob'ly a little glue'll fix 'em." He pulled together the torn edges of the hole he'd made in "Morning" and examined the picture. "My heavens!" he said. "What was all this, anyhow? Was it meant to play a game like parcheesi on or something?"

"Parcheesi!" she told him, shouting. "It was Carlos Prang's masterpiece, and all you've cost my father by stepping into it is three hundred dollars! That's just one item!"

Eddie began to laugh in his coarse, silly way. "Be serious!" he said, and looked up at me. "Mr. Massey, in justice to yourself you oughtn't to let her go around telling people you'd spend three hundred dollars for something like this. You wouldn't, would you?"

"I had hoped I wouldn't," I told him. "Up to the time you called on us this afternoon I still hoped that."

This seemed to startle him. "Why, for Pete's sake!" he said. "Listen! These things look just as well the way they are as they would if you stuck 'em together again; but if somebody's got the nerve to charge you anything for 'em, actual money, why, I expect I'd better get busy. Zebias's prob'ly got plenty of glue out in his workshop in the garage, and he and I'll just pile all this truck in a basket and take it out there and fix it up."

He'd begun to pick up the pieces; but Enid sprang at him, took him by the collar and dragged him away in his seated position. "You let them alone!" she shouted. "Don't you dare! You're nothing in the world but a frightful little vandal, and I never want to see your face again as long as I live! You march straight out of here and go home!"

Eddie got up, looking hurt. "Did you say this was some more of Carlo's doings, like the cheeping birds, f'r instance? Is this the way he puts in his time over at Jasper Mountain, loading up things like this on your father, so that he has to pay actual money for 'em if some accident happens or something?"

"If you say another word," Enid told him, "I'll have Zebias Flick put you out of here!"

"I don't have to be put out by any Zebias Flick," Eddie said, "because in the first place Zebias wouldn't do it unless you paid him a lot extra for it, and he wouldn't do it anyway, and in the second place I'm going myself, thank you! I don't usually hang around any place where some of the family don't care for my society. I bid you good-afternoon, Mr. Massey. Clarissa, I bid you good-afternoon."

So he went out, and Enid, who kept on being in quite a state of mind, began to pick up the pieces of statuary and try to see where they belonged. But after I'd watched her a while I saw that it was a pretty hopeless idea, especially with the sculpture. If you had a regular kind of statue, so to speak, that was broken, you'd know that the legs and arms ought to go onto the body of it, for instance; but with this art you couldn't figure out where any of it belonged, and so afterwhile she had to give up, and I tried to console her a little.

"There's nothing to do," I told her, "except for me to figure out the total and send a cheque over to Mount Jasper, and that ought to satisfy you, Enid, because you'll have the pleasure of knowing you've helped the colony that much anyhow. And though of course it's more expense than I'd expected to be put to, I don't want you to worry about it."

She was wet around the eyes and kind of sniffing over the ruins; but at this, she looked up, surprised. "Oh, yes," she said, "that part of it's all right." And then she kind of choked. "I'll never get over it; such a beautiful little modernist collection absolutely ruined in ten seconds! I'll never, never get over it!"

CHAPTER XII

Bᴜᴛ she did. At least she did temporarily—and only two afternoons later. Mrs. Massey and I had persuaded the girls to take a family drive with us, and we got back home about five o'clock and walked into the living-room to find a surprise waiting for us. Enid gave a loud cry and ran toward the window that had been the scene of the accident created by Eddie Bullfinch, and she dropped on her knees before it. There was another little collection of works of art standing where the first one had been when Eddie landed on it, and I could only surmise that Mr. Carlos Prang had heard of what had happened and decided to make it up to Enid by bringing over some more works of art from Mount Jasper and leaving them for her. It seemed pretty nice of him.

There was a picture quite a lot like "Morning"; it had a man or woman or something on both sides of a shaft of light or plank; but one part of this person's face had two eyes and the other three, all pretty blurry. There wasn't any terra-cotta sculpture in the outfit; but there were five clumps of plaster-of-Paris, and there was a wooden statue that looked a good deal as if a heavy curtain-rod might be the principal element of it. There was a brass strip set neatly down the whole length of one side of it; the base was set into a block of lead, and on top there was fastened what looked to me as if it had once been a glass doorknob, and just below that, a pair of metal wings stuck out of the rod. Two of the clumps of plaster-of-Paris were something like human faces, though not much; the others seemed more like models of a few child's blocks scattered around and molded into plaster-of-Paris; but naturally a title was furnished for each of these works of art, because of course otherwise the spectator would have been in trouble. A card was stuck in one corner of the painting, and it had "Evening" printed on it; there was another card leaning against the base of the curtain-rod thing, and it said "Soaring". Each of the face-like messes of plaster-of-Paris was labelled "Portrait"; one of the others had a card bearing the word "Daffadils"; another was called "Football-Players" and the fifth one, "Womanhood".

Well, nobody could have been more pleasurably excited than Enid was, and of course her mother and sister and I were glad for her, though it couldn't be said that either Mrs. Massey or Clarissa showed much enlightenment about the collection itself, and Mrs. Massey admitted that if the titles got mixed up she wouldn't be able to put them back in the right places. "I think I could get 'Soaring' put back right," she said, "on account of those wings, because they're really splendid; but frankly, I'd be stumped to know which was the 'Football-Players' and which was 'Womanhood'."

"How about 'Daffadils'?" I asked her, and it seemed to me curious that this word wasn't spelled correctly, because I thought both Mr. Abner Lorry and Carlos Prang would have known how to spell it. In fact, there were three things about the collection that made me suspicious of it; one was this wrong spelling; another was the messiness in the way the paint looked to have been put on the canvas in "Evening", because with all the queerness of the pictures over at Jasper I'd noticed that anyhow they had a workmanlike appearance, as if the people that made them knew how to handle their materials; and the third thing that set me to thinking was the fact that the wings on "Soaring" were so much like real wings. Indeed, those wings seemed to have the very photographic quality that Enid had told me wasn't art, and besides this, they had a familiar look to me, so much so that I tried to think where I'd seen them before. Then all at once, I remembered and knew where they came from, which was from the cap of the radiator on somebody's automobile, and it struck me that they were a testimonial to a genuine emotion of self-sacrifice if they happened to have been removed from a Dorio-Grecco. I didn't say anything about this, though.

Mrs. Massey went on in a kind of dreamy way, and said, "It does seem, Enid, that a person ought to be able to tell daffodils from football players."

Enid jumped up. "That's the same silly old criticism," she told her mother indignantly, "the same old worn-out platitude of literal-minded people everywhere that never can reach any higher than the cheap photographic plane! If you can't appreciate true works of art like these, at least I think you could learn not to say anything about them! They're wonderful! They're——"

But here she was interrupted because Eddie Bullfinch crawled out from behind a sofa where he'd been lying, and he looked happy and pretty well pleased with himself. "I certainly feel relieved to hear you say so, Enid," he told her, "because Zebias Flick and I——"

That was as far as he got; she began to scream right away. "Go out of here! Don't let him come near them!

Don't let him get in this part of the room! Take him outdoors! Don't let him———"

Eddie shouted louder than she did. "Listen! Haven't you got sense enough to listen? I'm not coming anywhere near 'em. If I did, I wouldn't be very apt to break 'em, would I, after taking all the trouble to make 'em for you, myself?"

"What!" Enid shouted. "What did you say?"

"Of course I did," he told her, and you could see he hadn't been trying to be funny about the works of art but was in simple, honest earnest. "I didn't want Mr. Massey to stand all that loss just for nothing. I think maybe they're kind of punk, myself; but you've just said these are anyhow as wonderful as the others. They certainly ought to be, because I got Zebias Flick to help me in his workshop because he's supposed to be hired to be working for your father anyway, and we certainly put in many's the long hour on 'em! I don't believe there's two other men anywhere could have made these things any better, in the same time, and, since you like 'em, I'm going to make a lot more for you. It's kind of interesting work, and I and Zebias———"

But by this time she was screaming louder, so he couldn't make himself heard any more, and pretty soon he saw he'd better go; he was only upsetting her worse and worse. "Well, doggone!" he said, kind of desperately. But she was calling on Zebias to come and carry the collection out to the ash-can and didn't pay any more attention to Eddie.

"Mr. and Mrs. Massey, I bid you good-afternoon!" he said, shouting to make himself heard. "Clarissa, I bid you good-afternoon!"

So he went out again, and the truth is I felt more sympathy with him than I'd have dared mention to Enid.

His taking those wings off of the radiator-cap of his Dorio-Grecco for Enid's sake seemed to me to show a depth of feeling that was kind of touching, considering how little good it did him. He must have broken the cap when he took the wings off, too, because next day at the beach I saw and heard him drive up with the radiator steaming in a dangerous way from the vacant hole on top of it. As it happened, this was the occasion when he was criticized to me by somebody besides Enid; in fact, it was the day that the Massey family heard of quite a mistake they seemed to be making not unconnected with Eddie.

"Oh, that's nothing," he told me, alluding to the vacancy on his radiator. "I'm going to make one myself this afternoon. I got sort of a gift for making things." He showed me what he meant for a bitter smile, and added, "When they're not expected to be art, I s'pose."

I gave him a wink, hoping to cheer him up some; but he didn't respond, and Mrs. Massey and I walked on to join Mr. and Mrs. Bullfinch and their special friends on the sand, as we were getting in the habit of doing. Mrs. Massey sat down with them; but Mr. Blodgett took me by the arm and drew me a little aside. "I don't want to alarm you," he told me, "and I'd be obliged if you wouldn't repeat what I'm going to say. Many people at Mary's Neck are very sensitive, because, you see, they come from different places, and when they get here everybody may not know who they *are* at home. Of course Mrs. Blodgett and I are very good friends of the Bullfinches, for instance. They're leading people here and naturally we see a great deal of them; but the fact remains that they are extremely sensitive—especially about their children. I'm not sure that I ought to continue."

I told him to go on, he could trust me, and I was anxious to hear what he had to say. "It's just this," he said. "My own three little daughters are too young to be mentioned in this connection, thank heaven! but if they were old enough I should certainly never let one of them step into that horrible car of Eddie Bullfinch's."

"Well, thank you for the advice," I said; "but I don't think my daughter Enid's been stepping into his car much lately."

"But she does sometimes," Mr. Blodgett insisted. "In the first place Eddie doesn't know how to drive, and in the second that car is dangerous. Just for one thing, it's been on fire three times to my knowledge. I don't know whether or not I ought to be telling you this."

Well, what he said shook me up quite a little. Of course I hadn't thought that Eddie's car was the safest plaything in the world; but on the other hand, not wishing to interfere with my daughter's pleasure, I'd kept my worryings restricted to myself and tried not to be too imaginative. After the conversation with Mr. Blodgett, however, I naturally felt there'd have to be a change and I spent the afternoon trying to work out a way to put the matter before Mrs. Massey as tactfully as possible and get her to tell Enid she'd have to stick to her own car when she got reconciled to Eddie again; but, as things happened, Mrs. Massey was able to help me out in the matter without my doing much.

Mrs. Carmichael had taken quite a fancy to her, it seemed, and called for her that afternoon and carried her off to a big Tea at the cottage of a family named Allstover who lived a little distance back in the country. The Tea lasted a long while and Mrs. Massey must have been having a pretty interesting time at it, I judged, because the girls and I sat down to dinner before she got back; and when she came to the table her face was all flushed, and it seemed to me she was trembling. This was peculiar because customarily when she gets home from an afternoon ladies' party she only has the left-over of a tense excited look and shouts everything she says for half an hour or so and is more or less hoarse.

"Well!" she said, and looked up out of the tops of her eyes and down again and fixed her face the way a woman does when she's heard something pretty paralyzing and is going to let it out after she's led up to it. Then she began to tell us all about it.

At the Tea she'd been introduced to a lady named Parkinson, and it turned out that this Mrs. Parkinson's husband's cousin was the Parkinson that married Mrs. Massey's cousin Georgianna that lived in Elmira, New York State, and so the two felt well acquainted right away and got pretty confidential.

"She asked me who'd brought me to the Allstovers' Tea," Mrs. Massey told us. "And when I said it was Mrs. Carmichael she began to look a little prim, and I asked her if Mrs. Carmichael wasn't as nice as she seemed to be. 'Oh, of course she's very nice,' she said; but she wasn't enthusiastic, and I told her we were newcomers and didn't want to make any mistakes, and she said that she certainly hoped we wouldn't and that she felt perhaps it would be a good thing, since in a way we were distant family connections, if she told me a little about how things *were* at Mary's Neck. So we moved out to a sun-porch together where there wasn't anybody else; and she certainly told me enough! The first thing she said was that the Carmichaels were very nice people in their *way,* though of course Mr. Carmichael did cut up too much sometimes at parties. Then she looked a little funny and said, 'But you see, they belong to the Bullfinch set, I'm afraid'."

"What!" both girls squealed together, and they quit eating dinner right there.

"Those were exactly Mrs. Parkinson's words," their mother told them. "When I showed how surprised I was and told her that we'd understood the Bullfinches practically ran everything at Mary's Neck and were really the great people here, she laughed out loud and wanted to know where in the world we'd ever heard such nonsense. The Allstovers are the real people here, she said. The Bullfinches are all right in their own way and among their own set, probably; but so far as the *real* Mary's Neck is concerned they're just nobody!"

Well, after both girls had squealed again, there was a whole lot of exclaiming and of course they and their mother went on making a to-do in the way women always seem to have to under such circumstances. Clarissa said she'd thought several times the Bullfinches mightn't be exactly "right", maybe, and she told about things that had made her feel that way, and Enid did the same thing, and so did Mrs. Massey, while I had to wait, the way a man always does, for them to pass through this phase. Then, when I finally got a chance, I mentioned that the outcast Bullfinch family had been polite to us; perhaps Mr. Bullfinch didn't have the most interesting conversation in the world and Eddie had certainly broken quite a little furniture and other articles that I'd had to pay for —but nevertheless it didn't seem to me entirely respectable to cut off communication. They were all three indignant with me at once; they weren't snobs, they informed me, and didn't intend dropping the Bullfinches or doing anything radical at all.

"We aren't 'climbers', either," Mrs. Massey went on to explain; and of course she was right about this and entirely sincere. "We aren't considering who are the most important people in Mary's Neck. We don't care anything about that; but for my part I certainly do wish to know who are the nicest people here and who would be the best and most congenial associates for my daughters. If we do come in contact with such people, wouldn't you agree that it would be wise to include them in our circle instead of remaining exclusively intimate with the Bullfinches and Carmichaels and Blodgetts?"

Naturally I said yes to that; and then she went on to tell us that she'd been perfectly charmed with Mrs. Allstover and also with Mrs. Allstover's son, Eugene, who had been present at the Tea. Mrs. Allstover told her that Eugene had spent most of his time at the beach lately watching Enid and Clarissa and trying to invent means to meet them. Eugene felt sorry to see them monopolized by the Bullfinch boys and their set, Mrs. Allstover said, especially as they happened to be the kind of young men whom he couldn't possibly ask to present him to the girls; and then she and Mrs. Massey got so cordial together that they arranged for Eugene to present himself; he was going to call on us after dinner, in fact, and I could see that Mrs. Massey thought this was something of a triumph.

Eddie and George Bullfinch came in before the two girls had begun to quit talking about this last item of their mother's news—both the Bullfinch boys had the habit of just pushing open the front door and shouting to make it known where they were, and if we were at the table they'd come right in and begin to talk, or, if they saw anything that appetized them, they'd eat a little, too; and that's what they did to-night. I was glad to see that Clarissa was just as cordial to them as she'd ever been, though I thought that when George reminded her of a movie engagement they had she looked a little disappointed; but she went with him like a good girl, and Enid seemed to be treating Eddie in about the usual manner.

Then afterwhile, as I was sitting on the piazza in the twilight, I had the privilege of seeing what Clarissa'd missed by going to the movie.

SEVENTEEN

CHAPTER XIII

A LIMOUSINE drove up; the chauffeur opened the door, and a short, thin, sallow-looking young fellow about nineteen got out. He was wearing evening clothes and smoking a cigarette in a long holder, and his expression seemed to me to indicate that he believed himself to be about the right article—as he naturally would, since he was a principal representative of the great Allstover family. He came up the steps and looked over to where I was sitting but seemed to decide that no conversation with me was necessary to his happiness, though he kept on looking at me casually even after he'd rung the bell. Someone let him in, and pretty soon I heard him and Enid and Eddie Bullfinch talking in the living-room. They didn't seem to be getting on very well.

"Listen, Boob!" I heard Eddie saying. "Listen! Enid, did you know his regular nickname is Boob? You won't wonder why long. Look, Boob! When are your puppa and mumma going to let you take lessons how to drive a car?"

"Be a little careful, young Bullfinch," the Allstover boy said in response. "If you talk too much while your voice is changing some of your saw-dust'll spill out through the crack and everybody'll know you're stuffed."

This seemed to stop Eddie for the time being, and Enid evidently tried to fill a pause that was embarrassing; she asked young Allstover if he would rather stay in the living-room or go out and sit on the piazza.

"It'd be all right in here," he told her, "except for the smell of fish."

"Fish?" she said. "Why, we haven't had any fish cooked to-day."

"No, I didn't mean that," he said. "There was a school of minnows along the coast this morning, and I see one of them's flopped up the rocks and got in here."

Eddie seemed to take this rather hard. "Is that so?" he said. "You better look out, Boob, because look, minnows eat mosquitoes. How'd you get in here anyway? Listen, Enid, some o' your family must 'a' left the screen-door open!" He laughed uproariously, and went on, "After you've spent a few more summers here you'll do like the rest of the girls at Mary's Neck do when Boob Allstover is anywheres around. They keep the screen-doors nailed shut all the time! Listen, Boob, weren't your puppa and mumma afraid to let you come out in the night air?"

"Yes, they were," the Allstover boy came back. "They were afraid maybe our car'd get a puncture running over that sardine can you been driving around here this summer. And by the way, young Bullfinch, I told one of our gardeners to let you come in our place the next time you're up that way; he's got a goat that's fond of old tin and he's trying to fatten it."

Eddie didn't seem to like this at all, and he stood up, as I knew because I heard a chair fall over. "Listen, Enid," he said, "let's don't sit around here any longer. Let's drive on up and find George and Clarissa at the movies."

I could tell that Enid was embarrassed and trying to keep up better manners with Eddie on account of the important stranger being present. "Why—why," she said. "If Mr. Allstover would like to——"

"No," young Allstover told her. "I'd rather stay here. It's a pleasant room for two people to sit in."

I imagine that Eddie gave him a pretty hard look, at this, because nothing was said for a few moments; then Eddie spoke up loudly. "Listen, Enid! We don't want to sit around here all evening just because you feel you got to be polite to Boob Allstover on account of not knowing him well enough to tell him where he gets off!"

"Why, Eddie!" she said. "Eddie! You mustn't——"

"Listen!" Eddie said. "I stood Carlo Sprang, and right now it seems to me Carlo Sprang's a bird with something to him. I stood all you said about that, and this morning you said you accepted my apology about the art collection. I been through a good deal on your account, and I've told you more things about myself than I ever told any girl, and if you're going to pass me over for a——"

"Eddie!" she said. "You mustn't talk that way. You mustn't make Mr. Allstover think——"

"Listen!" Eddie told her, and his voice sounded almost as if he was thinking of crying. "After all this and all that and all the times I've taken you out in the Dorio-Grecco and everything, I just want to know once and for all abs'lutely whether we're going to go on up to the movies or stay and sit here? Because look I got to know once and for all whether you wouldn't rather go out in the Dorio-Grecco than sit around here with this Boob All——"

But here young Allstover interrupted. "Untangle yourself," he said. "You've got one foot caught in the arm of that chair you knocked over and in a minute when you start to go home, crying, you're going to break a leg. Untangle yourself."

Eddie didn't pay any attention to him. "Listen, Enid!" he said. "Once and for all abs'lutely are you going to sit here or are you going with me?"

"Kindly don't be so silly!" she said, and her voice showed considerable temper. "I couldn't possibly be so rude to Mr. Allstover as to——"

"That'll be enough!" I heard Eddie say, kind of hoarsely. "I stood Carlos but I won't stand this!" Then there was a crash and a heavy thump on the floor; but he didn't break his leg, and after a minute he came out, limping, and said, "I bid you goodbye, Mr. Massey", then went down the steps and drove away.

This time he didn't come back, either; and the next day young Allstover turned up in the morning with a chauffeur and an open car and drove both the girls to the beach, where I saw him introducing them to some young people they hadn't met before. Mrs. Massey and I met some new people, too; Mrs. Parkinson came over to where we were sitting with the Bullfinches and the Blodgetts and Carmichaels and a Mrs. Dalrymple whose cottage was only two doors from ours, and, after saying howdy to them in a smiling sort of way that seemed to pain her, this Mrs. Parkinson got us to go to another part of the beach and be introduced to Mr. and Mrs. Allstover and sit with them and some friends of theirs. They weren't a very lively set of people and didn't have much to say; they were kind of stiff, I thought, and though they were cordial to us you could see it cost them quite a good deal of effort, like a man with the rheumatism feeling that he's got to make a bow to somebody.

But I could see Mrs. Massey was pleased, and afterwards she told me the Allstovers would probably be calling and asking us to dinner pretty soon, and then we could have them. It was wonderful for us to know just the really right people at Mary's Neck before the height of the season came on she said;—if it hadn't been for Mrs. Parkinson we might have made quite a mistake in our intimacies. The Allstovers were the most charming people she'd ever met, she said, and Enid and Clarissa chimed in with her. They already had a whole new set of engagements with Eugene Allstover and his young friends, so I decided there wasn't any need for me to put my foot down about the Dorio-Grecco. Enid said she'd never go out in that old rattletrap again even if Eddie did come back and ask her.

She spoke so decidedly that I felt kind of peculiar thoughts rising in me about Eddie Bullfinch. It wasn't that I expected to miss him exactly or be homesick for him, as you might say; but still a person can't break all that furniture and bric-à-brac for you to pay for and then just disappear out of your life without leaving kind of a queer emptiness somewhere behind him. It wasn't exactly an emptiness, though, because right then, even while Enid was speaking, we could hear the Dorio-Grecco sounding like quarry-blasting in the distance, and that night about one o'clock it woke me up with its plumbing shooting off right under my window. Eddie let it go on for a while just to make sure Enid was awake, I suppose; then he shut it off so that everybody could hear him singing. He didn't know the song very well; but he certainly made it loud enough.

> "*When you were sweet*
> *When you were sweet sixteen*
> *I loved you as I nev-URR loved before!*"

Then, to show his bitterness, he yelled: *"Nit!* Not in a thousand years!" After that, he uttered a long harsh jibing laugh, turned on his machinery, and drove away.

Well, we were all getting more and more acquainted with everybody, at the beach and elsewhere, and were feeling more and more comfortable, as if we belonged to the place, you might say, and had our human rights to be in it. Now we were getting to know them, the summer residents didn't seem so much like the kid-glove-gold-headed cane brand we'd thought they were, and the better we knew them the more likeable and pleasant we found them. Of course I saw pretty soon that inside themselves they were really just like people anywhere, and the principal things that made them different from the population of Logansville, for instance, were the peculiar conditions of a summer resort of this kind and the fact that the cottagers had mainly been brought up in large Eastern cities.

One thing I didn't get used to right away was their manner of speaking our language. Most of them pronounced their "A's" the way the teachers tried to get us to in our school-days, back in my part of the country, only broader; but I guess the Easterners have the authorities behind them on this question, and the rest of us are wrong. It can't be helped; we'll never be able to pronounce our "A's" that way without trouble. When we hear the seaboard and New England people doing it correctly we feel guilty and a little resentful; but when we try it ourselves, as some of us have been heard to, we miss fire about every third shot and feel foolish. Yet I don't think we're in the wrong about the letter "R".

I thought at first that most of the cottagers were imitating the English or Southerners; but I saw before long that squelching their "R's" was natural to them and not an affectation, and I also gathered that our general American way of pronouncing "R" like "R" and not "ah" is troublesome to their ears. They oughtn't to feel that way, because it's only common sense that every letter of the alphabet has a right to its own sound and needs it. And my goodness! when it comes to playing Crazy Jane with the alphabet some of our seaboard localities win the high prize. Mr. and Mrs. Bullfinch pronounce the word "sore" exactly like the word "saw"—they'd tell you somebody had a saw finger because he'd cut it on a saw— but when they want to tell you they saw something they say they sor it. Mr. Allstover, being from the city of Philadelphia, is different and takes a kind of pride, I understand, in what he does to the letter "H". I heard him, myself, asking his son about their chauffeur: "Ware was he going, witch way did he go and wen did he leave?" As for Mr. and Mrs. Weeder, our next-door neighbors, they're from somewhere just outside of New York and I don't believe the greatest elocutionist in the world could pronounce the word "girl" the way they do unless it was natural to him.

However that may be, Mrs. Massey was going to Teas, bridge parties and luncheons pretty regularly almost every afternoon, by now, and it wasn't long after Eddie's serenade when she came home from one of 'em with a funny look she has that always means she's holding something back until she gets good and ready to tell it. The girls were going to the Allstovers' to dinner but she had a confab with them before they went, and I heard Clarissa shouting, "For heaven's *sake!*" pretty often in her room where the conference went on, and Enid came downstairs squealing back at her mother, "How many more times are we expected to go through this? I'm getting tired of it!" But Mrs. Massey wouldn't

tell me anything until about ten o'clock when I was reading something interesting by a lamp in the living-room
and wanted to go on and had gotten over any desire to
talk at all. The gist of what she had to say was that
she'd found out we might be making a little mistake
about the Allstovers. At these women's parties she'd
been going to she'd been getting a great deal more light
on family standing at Mary's Neck lately, and one of
the ladies she'd been getting confidential with had en-
lightened her upon the real facts of the case.

"The way it began," Mrs. Massey told me, "she said
that though she'd known me such a short time she felt
she just must speak out, because she took such an interest
in my daughters' looks, and she didn't like to see such
sweet young girls beginning to be noticed going about
everywhere with that little Eugene Allstover and his set.
Those boys might be all right in their way, she said, but
the *real* Mary's Neck didn't approve of them at all. She
said she knew how easy it would be for a new family to
get confused about who constituted the real Mary's Neck,
and the Allstover family certainly didn't belong to it.
'Oh, never!' she said, 'Never in the world! Please don't
make *that* mistake, Mrs. Massey!' The people we really
ought to know, she said, were the Ruckleboys."

"Who?" I asked Mrs. Massey. "What sort of boys
did your lady-friend say——"

"Not boys," Mrs. Massey told me. "It's a name,
Ruckleboy. She said the Ruckleboys were the most desirable people along all this section of coast. They're
a historical family, too, because Mr. Ruckleboy had an
ancestor on the mother's side that made a famous speech
in Congress during the War of Eighteen-twelve, denouncing England. She says the Ruckleboys are terribly
exclusive; they don't even go to the beach. They don't

accept any invitations; they practically don't go anywhere or meet anybody, and very few people ever have
the opportunity of even seeing them."

"How do they get their sustenance?" I asked Mrs.
Massey. "Do you suppose if we sneaked up their way
after dark we could get the chance to catch one of these
Ruckleboys creeping out to feed on night herbs, maybe?"

This didn't bother Mrs. Massey; she just looked
dreamy, and went on about what her lady-friend had told
her. "She says the Ruckleboys are Bostonians. There are
other families from Boston here, she says; but the
Ruckleboys are the only Bostonians. They have a
daughter, and two adopted nephews are spending the
summer with them. She says she'd never seen more charming, well-brought-up girls than Enid and Clarissa, and
she was sure they'd be more congenial with the Ruckleboy young people than anyone else here. The only difficulty was that the Ruckleboys kept to themselves so
exclusively it might be almost impossible to arrange;
but she did hope somehow to bring it about."

Well, either Mrs. Massey's lady-friend was pretty
energetic or else the Ruckleboys were in a yielding mood
just then, because it was only about two days after that
when Mrs. Ruckleboy and her daughter called on Mrs.
Massey and Enid and Clarissa and left Mr. Ruckleboy's
card for me, and that evening the two adopted Ruckleboy
nephews drove up in a car that didn't have much on the
Dorio-Grecco for looks, and the only reason it didn't
make more noise was that nothing could. Young Allstover
and two of his friends were there, and so was George
Bullfinch; and, from what I could make out, the party
of young gentlemen had much the same kind of a time
among themselves that Eugene and Eddie had on the
evening of Eddie's latest final departure.

Mrs. Massey stayed in the living-room part of the time; and afterwards, she and Enid and Clarissa were enthusiastic about what superior young men the two Ruckleboys were, and Clarissa and Enid were excited about going on a sailing-party with them the next afternoon. Well, here came in a coincidence I'd hardly believe if someone else told me it had happened to himself, and maybe it couldn't happen anywhere except at Mary's Neck or another summer place of that nature. Anyhow I'll just go ahead and state the facts. The girls were out on the Ruckleboys' sailing-party, and Mrs. Massey and I were sitting on the piazza watching the Atlantic ocean, when a fashionable-looking old gentleman with white hair and a buttonhole bouquet drove up in a closed car and got out and came in and introduced himself as Mr. William Jaffray. I knew that the Logansville Light and Power Company, of which I may have mentioned I'm president, had a few Eastern stockholders, and I recognized the name as belonging to the largest of them. He was a friendly-spoken old fellow, right likeable, and said he'd happened to hear the president of the company had taken a cottage at Mary's Neck and so he'd driven over from Pigeon Cove, ten miles away where he lived, to pay his respects and ask if he could do anything for our pleasure or comfort. Mrs. Massey and I thanked him, and we chatted a while; then he asked us how in the world we'd ever happened to decide on spending the summer at Mary's Neck.

"Of course the place itself is pretty enough," he said, "and so's the view, and your cottage is about the best here. What I mean is the people. I used to come here, myself; but after about five years I couldn't stand it—I couldn't get along with 'em at all. I moved over to Pigeon Cove, though of course in the way of summer residents,

Pigeon Cove is pretty bad and I haven't found it much of an improvement."

Mrs. Massey gave a laugh, for manners, and said we'd found most of the people at Mary's Neck quite delightful.

"What!" he said, and he got red, all at once wearing a right quarrelsome-tempered kind of expression. "Then you certainly haven't learned to know 'em yet! In the first place, there are whole families here that never have a decent word to say for almost anybody, and, for my part, I think that's the only thing they're right about. A summer resort is the worst place on earth for people to get along together, and I'm an amiable man; but I certainly couldn't get along with anyone at Mary's Neck—or Pigeon Cove, either, for that matter, for there are no end of inconsiderate people over there, too, always getting up a feud about something, usually the behavior of somebody's children. But, as I say, Mary's Neck is worse. Except yourselves, there are very few here that aren't virtually just trash."

This upset Mrs. Massey quite a little. "Why, Mr. Jaffray!" she said. "You can't mean that. You couldn't mean to include the whole of Mary's Neck in such a sweeping condemnation. For instance, there's one family we've met lately, the most perfectly delightful people——"

"They must be new here, then," he told her. "You must be speaking of a family that's come here since *my* time! Seriously, Mrs. Massey, if I were you, I'd be careful about having much to do with anybody in the place, especially as I understand you have two daughters to look out for. The only way to enjoy a place like this is to have nothing to do with anybody. For instance, there's a family here named Ruckleboy; they were my next door neighbors and I know 'em like a book! So does everybody else, you'll find, if you make inquiries! They're the pariahs of Mary's Neck——"

"The pariahs?" Mrs. Massey asked him. "The pariahs?"

"Whatever you do," he told her, "for heaven's sake, don't let anybody introduce the Ruckleboys to you! Keep clear of them and, for that matter, of all the people here you can. There's only one family here that really have any standing at all and that you might like to know and could have a little respectable intercourse with; that's the Bullfinches. The Bullfinches are really pretty fairly nice people; but they're the only ones here that are."

CHAPTER XIV

Of course what this spiky old gentleman made us mainly think was that he'd be pretty hard to get along with, himself, after you knew him better; but when he'd gone, I told Mrs. Massey we seemed to have been around the circle and to be back with the Bullfinches again. She didn't say anything and I could see she was disturbed in her mind, and there can't be any doubt she was finding Mary's Neck considerably upsetting sociably, as I suppose most summer places likely are for a new family. But the Neck hadn't finished its confusingness for us—not by any means—and the coincidence I spoke of wasn't over. A day or so after old Mr. Jaffray had made his peculiar remarks, Mrs. Massey and I were sitting on the beach by ourselves;—that is, there wasn't anybody we knew right near us. But a few feet behind us there were two or three ladies sitting and looking on, and we made out from their conversation that they were staying at one of the hotels on their first visit to Mary's Neck. Of course they didn't know who we were, and it happened they began to talk about Enid and Clarissa, who were playing ball in their bathing-suits with pretty nearly all of the boys and young men on the beach.

The Ruckleboy nephews were in the game and so were

Eugene Allstover and his friends, and even Eddie Bull-finch. I noticed that Enid was making up with Eddie again. She put some sand down his back, and he tried to slap her for it and fell down, and I was glad to see this, because I understood it meant I'd have some more break-age to pay for pretty soon, which would be really a small price for the pleasure of hearing Eddie talk sometimes. I didn't have to worry about the Dorio-Grecco, either, be-cause, not hearing it anywhere for over twenty-four hours, I'd asked Zebias if he knew what the quiet was due to, and he came right out with a direct answer. The Dorio-Grecco had gone over a small cliff with Eddie in it, he said, and Eddie had got out of the ocean but the Dorio-Grecco never would, which Zebias considered as valuable an accident as could have happened to the community, and so did I. Our agreement in this and other matters seemed to cement a friendship that was growing up be-tween Zebias and me; he was what I've heard called an acquired taste—you had to know him—yet I found I was getting kind of a fondness for him.

But as I was saying, the hotel ladies behind Mrs. Massey and me at the beach were talking about our girls, not knowing they belonged to us. "Do you see that slim flowerlike young thing?" one of these ladies said. "She's the sister of that lovely dark-haired girl just throwing the ball. They certainly seem to be the belles of the place. They belong to a family that lives in that big cottage the driver pointed out to us yesterday, and of course would never deign to notice us mere hotel people—high-and-mighty cottagers! Their name's Massey and they're just about the leading family here. The waitress at my table told me so this morning."

Well, I looked at Mrs. Massey, and I could see that she was as pleased as pie. What's more, I can't deny I felt that way myself. Of course I knew that the information this lady had about us came from only a humble girl working in a hotel and I also realized from recent experience that there was much difference of opinion about which were the leading families at the Neck; still, if even a waitress had that conception of the Masseys, it seemed to me that the idea might be getting general, as it were.

Naturally, I knew it was soon for us to become a leading family; but anybody could see (as the lady said) that Clarissa and Enid were certainly the leading girls, and, after all, I am president of the Logansville Light and Power Company and concerned with other enterprises in a way that I thought might have become known even as far away from home as Mary's Neck;—for instance, Mr. Jaffray might have let it out to somebody, I thought likely. No; I can't deny that I kind of glossed over all we'd been hearing about other leading families, and, what's worse to contemplate in my own character, I can't help admitting that right there and then I got the beginning of a development inside of me that led pretty promptly to results I'd rather have had otherwise. There must be a sort of vanity-spot somewhere inside most of us. If it's reached just right, the most sensible character seems to go wrong without any loss of time. I'm afraid what that strange lady said on the beach about the leading Massey family reached mine just right.

It broke out on me even quicker than you'd expect. We'd just sat down to lunch, and Clarissa began to say something about how modest the two Ruckleboy nephews were. Some girl had told her. "You'd never in the world hear it from them," Clarissa said, "but during the War of Eighteen-twelve an ancestor of theirs——"

I interrupted her. Of course I laughed; but there'd

been quite a little of this kind of talk in the family and I began to be bothered by it. "Look here!" I said. "You seem to forget that the Masseys were among the first settlers in our part of Illinois, and that Packsburg in our county is named after George H. Pack, my own mother's uncle."

All three of them stared at me and then burst out laughing, and I wasn't very well pleased. In fact, I was a little huffed and didn't go on talking; but after lunch an incident occurred that made me feel better and as if I'd regained the right-of-way over 'em. Mr. Allstover called and asked to see me alone, so I took him round the corner of the piazza and we sat down. He looked affable but serious.

"I was glad to learn," he said, "that you and your family were elected to membership in the Rocky Meadow, Mary's Neck's family club. I'm sure you'll enjoy it."

"Yes," I told him. "I got a notice a couple of weeks ago, I think, and sent in the payments. I've been in there once or twice and everything seems pretty handsome and comfortable. Mrs. Massey and my daughters have been there several times and say they're going to enjoy it a great deal. We were very much pleased to become members."

"Not at all, not at all!" he said. "The board was more than delighted. You may have observed on the notification card that I'm the club's secretary. There was a meeting of the Executive Committee last evening and I should tell you that I am now speaking for that committee. Mr. Massey, you are new to Mary's Neck this season; but it is the club's policy to bring new members—desirable ones —into the active life of the club. We want you there, Mr. Massey. Probably you've not noticed it; but we've been observing you and we want you with us."

Well, I was embarrassed; but it seemed to me he was a right likeable man. I laughed and coughed a little, to be cordial, and told him I appreciated what he said very much.

"Not at all," he told me. "I've come really to bring the news of an honor we wish to pay you. At the meeting last evening we elected you Chairman of the House Committee."

"Why, my goodness!" I said. "I'm afraid I haven't had much experience in the work, Mr. Allstover. I certainly do appre——"

"Not at all, not at all!" he told me. "We want you with us, Mr. Massey; we want you. You're exactly the man we've been looking for—exactly. You see, Mr. Dalrymple resigned the office last week, because—I believe it was because he felt he couldn't be here this summer, except week-ends. Mr. Massey, I'd like to notify the president of the club and Mr. Bullfinch, the treasurer, that you accept."

"I hardly know what to say," I told him, though there's no denying I was pretty gratified and already planning the careless sort of manner I'd use in telling the family about it. "Mr. Allstover, I hardly know what I ought to——"

He got up and leaned over and shook hands with me right then. "Mr. Massey, it's going to be a relief—a relief and a great pleasure to me personally to make the announcement that you accept. You'll certainly allow me to make it, Mr. Massey?"

"Well——" I told him. "I suppose I——"

"Good!" he said. "Good! Do you think you could conveniently assume the active duties of the chairmanship by to-morrow morning?"

"I suppose I might," I told him. "I take it you mean

I'd better call a meeting of this House Committee and preside over it?"

He looked kind of surprised. "Oh, no," he said. "Our House Committee never have any meetings; you'll never be bothered with the other members of the committee. As a matter of fact, I don't remember who they are; they just give the use of their names, you see, and nobody ever pays any attention except to the chairman. You'll be the whole thing of course, Mr. Massey."

Well, I couldn't help feeling that this was more and more gratifying. "You mean I don't have to even consult the other members of the committee?" I asked him.

"Goodness, no!" he said. "You don't have to consult anybody. You just take complete charge of the clubhouse, Mr. Massey. The Chairman of the House Committee has absolute control of the whole place: servants, house-rules, conduct of members—everything. All you have to do is to go over to the club and run it practically as if it were your own property. I suppose there isn't a more autocratic position anywhere, and it's going to be the greatest pleasure in the world that you're to fill it for us, Mr. Massey."

Well, there's no denying I felt some pride in being selected to occupy the chief sociable position, so to speak, in the whole of Mary's Neck. Coming right on top of what the hotel lady at the beach said her waitress had told her, it seemed to me fairly significant, and I guess there's no denying I took it that way. Now, of course we have a golf club, back in Logansville, the same as most of our smaller cities nowadays; the clubhouse isn't much to speak of—mainly locker-room and shower-bath and some bottles of ginger ale in a refrigerator—and I'd have thought it a good deal of a chore if I'd been elected to office there, especially as I don't play the game myself.

No, I can't claim to have ever been much of a clubman; but this Rocky Meadow Club is a different sort of matter, imposing appearing on the outside and calculated to make a stranger feel timid, as if he committed trespass in just looking at it. Well, to be put practically at the head of an institution like that, particularly when such an honor was the last thing I could have been looking for—— No, I've got to admit that right then and there it seemed to me I ought to begin looking at myself in a new light, as it were, and that maybe there were things about me to appreciate I'd theretofore been too simple to suspect.

But after Mr. Allstover left, when I gave myself the pleasure of telling the family about what had happened, I must say they didn't make it exactly a pleasure. All three of them sat staring at me when I'd finished telling them, in the easy, casual way I adopted; then Clarissa broke out, still looking at me.

"Why, I just can't believe it!"

"Why, I should say not!" Enid said, and Mrs. Massey began to appear troubled.

"Are you *sure* that's what he said?" she asked me. "Don't you think you misunderstood him probably?"

They made me a little cross. "I'm not an idiot!" I told them; but they didn't seem convinced, and Clarissa asked Enid a question I thought better to pretend not to hear as I went out of the room.

"What do you suppose is the meaning of it?" she asked her. "Have you heard anything about Mr. Allstover's being a practical joker?"

"Well, that's just the way of things," I thought to myself. "It's always a man's own family!"

But when I went to the clubhouse, the next morning, to take up my new responsibilities, everything got gratifying again. The steward, a man that had made me kind of nervous the few times I'd been in the club, came hurrying forward to meet me and expressed himself in a humble sort of way that was right pleasing to me. "Were there any orders you'd care to give, sir?" he asked me. "All the employees are very anxious to please you, sir, and we hope you'll make your wishes known as to any manner in which it may strike you the service could be improved, sir."

There was only one club member present in the house, everybody being at the beach; but this member was a very nice lady, a widow named Mrs. Hapburn, right good-looking for her age. She came up to me afterwhile and congratulated me on the chairmanship, which you could see she thought was something pretty large. "I know in your position you can't grant any special favors, Mr. Massey," she told me, "But if you *would* let me make just the timidest little suggestion, I think it would be a great deal more convenient if the newspapers could be kept on the table in the reading-room where the magazines are, instead of in a corner over in that lonesome billiard-room where no one ever goes."

I thought she was a pretty nice little woman, and, when I told the steward to do as she suggested, he said, "Instantly, sir!" and did it. Then he came back and asked me if I'd mind looking at the billiard-table. "It's a pity no one ever uses it," he told me. "But you see, the children got it into such a terrible condition last year that nobody would scarcely be able to play on it, and a good many of the members have been complaining about it."

So I went to look at it with him, and the table struck me as being pretty far gone. I said the children should never have been allowed to get it in that condition, especially as I'd been looking over the house-rules of the club, since last night, and knew there was one to the effect that children were not allowed even to enter the billiard-room. "That rule should have been enforced," I told him.

He agreed with me heartily. "It certainly should!" he said. "But if you'll allow me to suggest it, sir, this table was getting rather old anyhow, and if you'd feel like authorizing me to order a new one——"

"Me?" I said.

"Why, certainly, sir," he told me. "It would all rest with you, sir. The club needs it badly, sir, and if you'd say the word I could order a new one by long distance telephone to-day, sir. I think it would be a great thing for club spirit, sir, if the membership could see that now the place is going to be kept up as it ought to be, sir."

Well, I told him to order the billiard-table, because I was certainly going to keep the place up. He said, "Instantly, sir!" again, going right to obey the order; and then Mrs. Hapburn came to thank me in a very sweet, nice way for the great change I'd made about the newspapers.

"Already this whole place seems to have a new air," she told me. "I'm sure the entire membership will feel that at last the club's got a splendid House Committee Chairman!"

No, it can't be denied that incidents like this were kind of gratifying to me, or that it did begin right then to seem to me more or less the way Mr. Allstover had said, and that the Rocky Meadow clubhouse ought to be treated as if it were practically my own property. Indeed, the fact is that before the first two days of my chairmanship were over I was regarding things pretty much in that light. In fact it was only on the fourth day of my chairmanship that I had most of the furniture moved around in a way that suited me better, and it was quite a pleasure to me to see how the steward had my orders obeyed the minute I delivered them. I guess there isn't much doubt it's true that a sense of power in these sociable matters does go to a person's head quite a good deal.

I hadn't noticed any change in myself, of course, and there's no getting away from the fact that I got pretty indignant when Mrs. Massey began trying to point it out. I'd thought all along the furniture in our cottage could be changed around in a way that would be more comfortable; so when I got home after altering the position of the sofas and tables and chairs at the club, I had Zebias and Mr. Sweetmus come in and did the same in our living-room. She was out at the time; but the minute she got back she said, "What on earth!" and began to shove things around, herself, to where they had been. We had quite an argument over it, and she ended by saying she wished we'd never come to Mary's Neck at all. She went so far as to tell me that I was acting like a spoiled child and backed it up by saying that Clarissa and Enid thought so, too.

"Why, you're like a different man!" she told me. "You've got so you just want to run everything, and you're making your children unhappy by interfering in their affairs."

"How?" I asked her. "How am I interfering in their affairs?"

"Why, every way," she said. "You've taken on a dictatorial tone with them you never used before, and you attempt to order them around in a voice you wouldn't dream of using to people working for the Logansville Light and Power Company. Look what you did yesterday to poor Clarissa!"

"What'd she tell you?" I asked, pretty angry. "What'd she tell you I did?"

"You mortified her at the club so awfully that she came home and almost had a fit!"

"What!" I said. "Why, she and two of these boys that tag after her, that Bush Thring and George Bullfinch, they'd been swimming in the pool, then came screeching into the clubhouse, ran all over the place, and then flopped themselves right down in their wet bathing-suits in three of the best chairs I've got there! They ruined the cushions so completely I had to order new ones. I certainly made it clear that I wasn't going to allow such occurrences to be repeated. I reproved her and her friends——"

"Yes, I guess you did!" Mrs. Massey said, cutting me off pretty crisply. "My goodness! I never saw a man get so pompous in so short a time in my life! It wasn't so much over what you said to her that Clarissa had a fit when she got home. What upset her was having her father make such an exhibition of himself before her friends."

"Exhibition?" I said. "Do you mean to say she applied that term to——"

"Oh, please do go on out of here!" Mrs. Massey told me. "I want to get this furniture to rights again, and you're in my way. Go and take a walk with your old chairmanship!"

CHAPTER XV

I THOUGHT it best not to say anything more but just to give her a severe look and go out. It seemed to me that a kind of bothersome change was coming over her, and that she wasn't herself. Up till right lately a man could hardly have asked for an amiabler wife than she had most always tried to be, and so, to have her attack me out of a clear sky, as you might say, made me all the more indignant. If she'd left out one word particularly that she'd thought fit to use, I could have pardoned her more easily; but "pompous" was a term I couldn't help resenting pretty warmly. Just because a man of mature age sees proper to behave with considerable dignity didn't strike me as any justification for his wife's using a term like that.

Well, I walked back over to the club, and I hadn't any more than got inside the door before I saw that some meddler had been interfering with my arrangements there, too, because all the club furniture had been put back the way it was before I'd had it changed around. I sent for the steward; he explained that a number of the lady-members had come in and seen fit to do this interfering, and he hadn't liked to object for fear of giving offense. I was pretty sharp with him and asked him why he hadn't told those ladies who it was that had ordered the arrangement of the furniture.

"I did, sir," he told me. "Would you like it put back the way you had it?"

"Instantly!" I told him. "Instantly!" And he said, "Yes, sir. Instantly!" and while he was attending to it and I was overseeing the job, feeling pretty put-out, that Mrs. Hapburn came up to me again, looking right peevish.

"I don't wish to be critical," she said, meaning she did. "But it does seem to me that when you give an order, Mr. Massey, you ought to see that it's enforced. The newspapers were all carried back to the billiard-room the day after you had them moved, and they've been there ever since."

I called the steward over to where we were standing and asked him why he'd done such a thing. "I didn't," he said. "It's old Mr. Francis. He was quite upset about them being moved, because he says it's quieter in the billiard-room than it is in the reading-room. He carried them back, himself, and said if they weren't left there he'd resign from the club."

"Then let him do it!" I said. "Let him resign!"

But the steward looked worried. "I'm afraid it wouldn't do, sir," he told me. "You see, Mr. Francis is one of the Founders of the club. It would hardly do. Of course though, if you give me orders to move them back to the reading-room——"

"Instantly!" I said. "Take them back there instantly!"

So he did it, and the next morning old Mr. Francis moved them back to the billiard-room and sent me word by the steward that if they were moved again he'd resign. The ladies came in that afternoon, too, and moved the furniture back to where they wanted it, and I had it changed again and the newspapers carried back to the reading-room. Then, that evening, old Mr. Francis carried his darned old papers back to the billiard-room and said more about resigning, and the ladies interfered with the furniture some more, so I began to be pretty hot upon these questions and determined to show who was who in that club, no matter how worn out it got the steward and the other employees.

Of course, though, not being met by the right feeling in my own home, I couldn't talk freely of my troubles there or look for the sympathy a man ought to have first of all from the women of his household when he's engaged in conflict. As a matter of fact, my home-crowd's sympathies appeared to be going to the wrong parties, and Clarissa actually took pains to drag this old Mr. Francis into our domestic table conversation, and all three of them spoke of him admiringly. She said he was a wonderful old gentleman, and so did her mother and Enid.

It made something seem to kind of burn in my stomach; but I just smiled as if I pitied them for not knowing more about what made old gentlemen wonderful. "Who?" I asked them. "You mean the one that scuffs around in rubber overshoes in dry weather and always has cigar ashes on his necktie?"

They didn't pay any attention. "He's descended from a Colonial Governor or somebody," Clarissa told her mother and Enid, in an important, low voice. "He's the only summer person who's ever met the Trumbles."

"Trumbles?" I said. "Who the dickens are the Trumbles?" You see how catching such things can be. Here was I, myself, beginning to ask who people are.

"They live in the big white house with the cupola in the village," Clarissa told me, looking at me kind of absent-mindedly. "They're natives and have never spoken to any summer people, and of course they consider Mr. Francis a mere mushroom but they've let him in their house once or twice for tea. He's the only one."

Then all three of them looked at me in that same absent-minded way as if I wasn't really there. For no reason I felt sort of kerflumixed; all I could think of to say was, "Well, live and let live", which didn't seem to mean anything much nor to help get my family behind me, backing me up in my struggle, where they ought to have been.

Well, I didn't know it but there was worse in store for me than this old Mr. Francis and the furniture-moving ladies. It was getting toward the middle of July and right up to then we'd mostly been having bright, fair weather at Mary's Neck, day after day of it with hardly more than two or three short little showers that didn't keep anybody indoors to speak of. Then one morning—it was the sixth day of my chairmanship—a Northeaster set in, terrible weather with wind howling and rain pouring as if it never intended to let up again at all. Inside that clubhouse you couldn't hear yourself think. Not because of the elements. My goodness, no! The tempest was noisy enough; but what went on indoors outdid it ten times over.

You see, the Rocky Meadow Club is a family club; but in bright weather, when everybody's out in the open air all day, you'd hardly notice it. The minute the rain began to come down, though, it looked to me as if the children of practically every family at Mary's Neck got bored at home and came rampaging into the club to express their animal spirits away from their parents.

I was reading in our living-room, not thinking I'd go out, when the steward telephoned in a kind of quavering voice, asking me if I wouldn't please come right over there; and I hadn't got inside the door before I could hear pandemonium going on. Any time you noticed him right closely, you could see that the steward was a sort of haggard-looking man underneath his outward expression, as you might call it; but now he was showing his worriedness right out in the open.

"I thought it might be better if you were here, sir," he told me. "You see, sir, every one of the children has the feeling that his own special father and mother are pretty much the owners of the club, and yet, as the club is property really belonging to everybody, sir, all the children have the impression that they can do things here that they'd never in the world be allowed to do at home."

"What have they been up to?" I asked him. "I mean besides making all this noise." We were standing in a little hallway, with the door closed that led into the big lounge-room of the club, and a good deal seemed to be happening on the other side of the door. There were two pianos in that room and each of them was having duets played on it with elbows, it struck me; an awful squealing kind of singing was going on, too, and a trompling like a couple of herds of ponies chasing each other.

The steward gave me a ghost-like kind of smile. "There won't be any trouble about where Mr. Francis reads his newspapers if he comes in to-day, sir. Little Paulie Timberlake and Brockie Griggs and some more have got the papers all torn up and the pieces rolled into balls, sir. All the little boys and girls take these balls and stuff them into the paper drinking-cups at the water-cooler, soak them with icewater, then fold the wet cups down around them and throw them at one another, sir. They've had several quite battles, sir, and the Colonial glass lamp, presented to the centre-table by Mrs. Weeder, is gone, sir. It was in the line of fire, and Paulie Timberlake got it after only a few shots, sir."

"Have the lamp replaced immediately," I told him. "Tell the club treasurer to send the bill to Mr. Timberlake."

"I'm afraid Mr. Bullfinch could hardly do that, sir. The Timberlake family is very influential, and we've found by experience that families become very offended when bills like that are sent to them. We've found it makes factions in the club, sir, with members not speaking to each other, and was one of the principal reasons why the last treasurer before Mr. Bullfinch was compelled to resign. I'll have the lamp replaced, sir, since you say so——"

But just then, the noise beyond the door got even louder; there was a crash that sounded like an article of furniture completely giving way and a burst of very loud yelling. "Look here!" I said. "You know the house-rules of this club. Why haven't you enforced them?"

He gave me another ghost-like smile. "I'm afraid it would take considerable muscle, sir," he said. "But if any of us employees intruded in that way the parents would very likely threaten to resign from the club unless we were vacated from our positions, sir. You see, Mary's Neck consists entirely of such influential families——"

"It can't," I told him. "A community can't consist entirely of influential citizens. It's got to have a lower populace for the influential citizens to influence or else they wouldn't be influential."

"They are here, sir," he said. "They're all influential. I'm afraid you'll find it so, Mr. Massey."

Well, I didn't wait for any more talk with him; I opened the door, and, the very instant I did so, a paper cup packed with ice-water soaked newspaper, and feeling like a soggy snowball, landed on the side of my neck. "It was meant for me, sir," the steward told me. "They were expecting me back, sir."

I didn't care who it was meant for; I was pretty hot. I strode out into the middle of that room and clapped my hands together. "Silence!" I said. "Silence in this room!"

The noise stopped and the children all stood still right where they were, kind of solemn and not looking at anything, the way they do when they think maybe they're going to be in trouble about something. "You listen to me!" I said, speaking loudly and sternly. "You all know who I am. I'm the Chairman of the House Committee of this club, and I'm going to enforce order and respectable behavior here. If any of you wish to look at the magazines or books in the reading-room, you may do so; and the rest of you will have to sit down and talk quietly together or be silent. We'll have no more of this uproar do you hear me?"

One little boy standing in front of me, with his hands behind his back, said "Yes, sir" in a respectful tone that I didn't altogether enjoy.

I knew him; it was little Paulie Timberlake, only nine years old. I'd often seen him at the beach but never liked his eye, because whenever he happened to look at me he seemed to be saying quietly to himself, "Now what could I do to this old slob that would entertain me?"

He had that expression pretty strong on him when he said "Yes, sir"; but he didn't say anything more just then, and none of the others said anything. Some of them walked quietly over toward the reading-room, and the rest began to troop out to different parts of the building. There was one cluster of boys near the door that opened into a little hall leading to the billiard-room, and I was just going to tell them that they must keep away from that room and the new billiard-table, when an ice-water soaked ball of newspaper, coming from that direction, flattened itself upon the steward's forehead just behind me.

The room was empty of children before he had time to wipe his face; then he smiled in that wan sort of way he had, and said, "It was Master Paulie again, I believe, sir. He seems to be quite a sure shot."

Then he began to clean the place up. There were dozens of stuffed paper cups all over everywhere; a spindle-legged sofa was broken; one of the pianos appeared to have a good deal of ice-water in it, and altogether the rioting seemed to have been severe. As for me, being Chairman of the House Committee, and having acquired the sense of proprietorship that I've spoken of, I couldn't help feeling personally outraged, especially by Paulie Timberlake. I knew he'd been the ringleader and I had a pretty indignant suspicion that he had a reason for holding his hands behind him when he said "Yes, sir" to me, and also that the last ball of soaked newspaper had not been intended for the steward.

"I shall ask the club secretary to send a notice to Mr. and Mrs. Timberlake," I said. "I'll instruct him to inform them that if they can't regulate the conduct of their child he will be suspended from the club upon the slightest repetition of this offense."

But the steward shook his head. "I'm afraid not, sir; Mr. Allstover wouldn't send it. You see, sir, the club used to try but found it couldn't single out any child in that manner because it merely infuriated the child's parents, and, when it sent notices to all the parents, it roused just that much more feeling against us, sir."

I was beginning to tell him that I didn't care how influential the Timberlakes were, I'd insist on that note being sent, when a sound like thunder broke out in the direction of the billiard-room; and a young man in the club uniform came in, looking kind of resigned. He was supposed to have charge of the billiard-room but didn't seem to be enjoying his position.

"I knew it wouldn't be any use to try and keep 'em out of there," he told the steward and me. "Not after the new billiard-table got here. Now they've got me locked out o' there—told me somebody had lost a dollar on the floor of the hall—so when I came back, they had both doors bolted on the inside. They're using the butts of the cues to see who can knock the balls hardest and make them bounce over the cushions onto the floor. It was the little Timberlake boy that thought it up."

I took those two men with me, went to the door of the billiard-room and demanded that it be opened instantly. The noise going on inside was something that can't be expressed; but I made those boys understand that it was the Chairman of the House Committee who wanted in. I knew they understood because, over everything else, there was a squealing voice anybody could recognize as Paulie Timberlake's. "Chapmin o' the House Committer! Chapmin o' the House Committer!" he kept squealing over and over; but that's all the attention any of 'em paid to me, and we had to go round outside and jimmy one of the windows open with an ice-pick before we could get into that room. The boys scurried out, of course, as we climbed in, and by that time another riot was occurring in the reading-room.

I don't need to go into more details; anybody knows what a whole passel of children will do once they get into that mood and loose in a big place like the Rocky

Meadow Club. The employees were pretty nearly distracted, and, as for me, I began to feel that life wouldn't be the same again until I could actually get my hands on Paulie Timberlake. Of course I knew it wouldn't do to have the kind of interview with him I yearned for, and that made the yearning worse. I tried to call his father on the telephone; but he wasn't home, and I had to talk to Mrs. Timberlake instead. Of course she said she was sorry Paulie was cutting-up a little with the other boys; but you could see what she really felt was irritation with myself. She wanted to know if I'd called up the other children's mothers, and, when I said I hadn't, told me pretty tartly she thought I'd better have spoken to them first as most of the other boys and girls were older, while her Paulie was only nine.

"It seems rather peculiar to single out as small a child as that to get so excited about!" she said. So all the satisfaction I got was making myself madder.

The turmoil went on the whole day all over the clubhouse wherever I didn't happen to be at the moment. Old Mr. Francis and Mrs. Hapburn were the grown-up people who spent most of their time at the club and they were the only adult members who came in. Mr. Francis told the steward that if I didn't resign he would, and Mrs. Hapburn hardly let me alone a minute, she lodged so many complaints. Once when she was talking to me in a pretty cross voice, and I was answering her in the same sort of way, only more so, we started to sit down together on a sofa in the reading-room; but didn't, because somebody hiding behind the sofa reached around and put a sheet of fly-paper there for us to sit on. He scurried out in such a jiffy that we couldn't have sworn who it was; but I knew.

It was a two days' Northeaster inside and outside the

clubhouse, and the children enjoyed themselves maybe more than at any other time since Christmas. Paulie and his friends were perfectly respectful in manner whenever I overtook them and got them face to face with me, and if I asked little Paulie, for instance, "Did you do this?" or, "Did you do that?" he'd look kind of grieved, and answer, "Why, Mr. Massey!" as if all upset to see me so misled.

Then a few minutes later, if I happened to be passing near one of the stairways, or standing out on the terrace under a window, there'd be an explosion behind me, maybe, where four or five electric-light bulbs would be dropped together from upstairs, and I'd jump about three feet and hear a tinny voice squealing, "Chapmin o' the House Committer! Chapmin o' the House Committer!"

By the end of that storm I was thinking almost exclusively of little Paulie Timberlake, and he must have had me in his thoughts a good deal, too, even after the weather cleared, because I heard something that made me judge so at our own dinner-table. It began with my family's dragging old Mr. Francis into the conversation again, but got around to Paulie pretty soon. It was like this: Clarissa said everybody was talking about what a wonderful old gentleman that old nuisance of a Mr. Francis was, and she'd heard him say the most amusing thing she'd ever heard in her life, that very afternoon. So of course her mother asked her what it was.

"Why it was about Father," Clarissa told her in a whispering voice, as though pretending to keep me from hearing. "That dear old Mr. Francis was so cute; he was perfectly furious. 'Massey?' I heard him saying to the steward. 'Massey! Massey! Who on earth's Massey? I've been coming here sixty-one years and never heard of any Massey!' Then I heard the steward mumbling something, and Mr. Francis broke out again: 'What! New this year?' Then I heard him say, almost yelling: 'What! Illinois? Good God!'"

"See here!" I said, and I felt so indignant I brought my closed hand down pretty hard on the table. "We'll have no such language in this house, if you please! If that's what you're learning by coming East, we'll think twice before leaving home another year!"

My remarks didn't seem to take at all. Clarissa and Enid just began to whisper together and laugh kind of surreptitiously in a way that I felt was almost open rebellion, because what amused them went on seeming to be something about myself. I told them that they spent too much time giggling generally. "It's a habit I don't like to see," I said. "It's time you began to display a little more dignity!"

"You mean like you, Father?" Enid asked me; and then both of the girls and their mother burst out laughing. I considered this pretty offensive and I told them so.

"But you couldn't blame us, Father," Enid went on to say;—"not if you'd been there to-day and had seen what Clarissa and I saw."

"Been where?" I asked her. "Been where?"

"Behind the dressing-rooms at the club pool," she told me. "Clarissa and some of the boys and I heard a funny kind of screeching around there and went to see what it was. That clever little Paulie Timberlake was strutting up and down before a lot of the other children, clapping his hands together and with his stomach 'way out in front of him. 'Chapmin o' the House Committer! Chapmin o' the House Committer!' he kept squealing, and the other children were all just howling. To tell the truth, we did, too; we nearly died! He certainly is a bright little child!"

"He is, is he?" I said; and I guess I must have been pretty red, because I could feel my collar nearly burning me. "Why didn't you come into the clubhouse and report it to me? I was there, and you knew I was! I'm Chairman of the House Committee of that club, and it's my business to support the authority of——"

I didn't get any further because Mrs. Massey and the girls began laughing so loudly I could hardly hope to drown them out. I waited till they had quieted down; then I told Enid what I thought of her lack of respect. I was annoyed and I went on talking, getting more and more severe, until Mrs. Massey looked serious and said she thought I'd gone about far enough. "I haven't said half of what I'm going to," I told her pretty sharply. "Girls of this generation don't show any respect for anything; but I don't intend to let my daughters be brought-up in that way. I'll teach them to show some respect, or else they'll look elsewhere for their monthly allowances!"

I suppose it was unfortunate that I said this in such a tone of voice, because Enid took advantage of it. She deliberately burst out crying as if her heart would break and got up and left the room. What made it worse, Mrs. Massey put her fork down on her plate, looked at me, then got up and followed Enid; but made a remark on her way out, seeing fit to add another unpleasant expression to one she had used before. "You've got so pompous and irritable lately I don't wonder the poor girls feel they can barely manage to live with you!"

So Clarissa and I were left to finish that meal alone. I went on eating kind of doggedly, though I knew I was in too wrathy a condition for good digestion, and, just before Clarissa got up, she didn't make me any calmer. She gave a kind of gurgle, the way people do when they remember something funny. "Everybody says Paulie Timberlake is just a natural born little leader," she told me. "He certainly has the most phenomenal powers of mimicry I ever saw in a child."

This last she added when she was already in the next room, and, as she went on out of hearing right away, I was thrown back on brooding upon what I would have liked to do to little Paulie. Even in my own home, which had always, or pretty usually, at least, been a happy and loving one, that child, it seemed, could produce discord. Well, sir, it could hardly be believed that a man of mature age could concentrate as hard as I did on the troubles a nine-year-old boy was making for him. It's actually a fact that when I was trying to fall asleep that night I kept having pictures in my mind, half dreamy-like, of myself getting little Paulie to eat big sour pickles and a box of soft sweet chocolate together, and I saw myself watching what happened after that with a kind of relieved pleasant feeling in my chest. No, sir, if I hadn't gone through it myself, I couldn't have believed it possible that a business man in middle life could get worked up to feeling that way about a bright-eyed little boy nine years old.

When I woke up, I found I had an idea that struck me as such a splendid and satisfying solution I wondered I hadn't thought of it before. I'd make a rule and post it up in the clubhouse absolutely forbidding the use of the club to all minors under the age of fourteen. "That'll fix little Paulie, I guess!" I thought. So, when I went over to the clubhouse I told the steward about it and instructed him to have the new rule printed in large letters and posted up on the bulletin-board in the hallway. He only got that pathetic smile of his on his face.

"What's the matter with it?" I asked him. "Don't you know it's the very thing most of the members would be delighted with?"

"Those that have children over fourteen would, sir," he told me. "Mr. Dalrymple tried exactly the same thing when he was Chairman; but about an hour after he had the rule posted he came to me, kind of pale, and instructed me to cross out 'Fourteen' and write 'Eleven' up, instead. The next day, after a good many people had been talking to him at the beach, it seems, he came in and told me to write 'Four unless accompanied by a nurse' instead of 'Eleven'. It's been attempted, sir, you see, and it doesn't do at all."

So there I was, down again; but determined to fight that thing out to the end. It was the ninth day of my chairmanship—I was Chairman of the House Committee of the Rocky Meadow Club just nine days—and I was still in a grim mood, mind you, when I got back to our cottage after that interview with the steward. In fact I was frowning and had my fighting face on me when I sat down at my desk to look over my mail.

The very first envelope I opened had a note in it from Mr. Bullfinch on Rocky Meadow Club stationery. It said he had to be ready in advance with a sufficient bank balance to pay the club's monthly bills and he'd like a cheque from me as soon as convenient to cover the billiard-table and other articles I had ordered installed. He itemized them, also stating the total amount they came to, and when I looked at it, I thought it must be a horrible kind of joke on his part. Then I read his note twice again and took up the telephone and called him.

"Look here!" I said. "I've received your note but it seems to me all mixed up about club matters. It looks as if you thought I ought to pay for the new billiard-table myself, and also for an expensive new antique glass lamp and repairing a piano and reupholstering——"

"Yes, yes," he said. "What's the matter?"

"Matter! Why, those things were all ordered for the *club!*"

"Well, you ordered 'em, didn't you?"

"Yes; but not for my own——"

"You ordered 'em," he said again, interrupting me kind of testily. "Of course they can't be charged to the club, you understand, because the club hasn't got any funds to meet such expenses. There's a large faction determined to reduce the dues at the next annual meeting and very indignant because the place isn't run more economically than it is. As a matter of fact, that club's insolvent right now."

"Look here!" I said. "Do you mean to say I've actually got to send you my own personal cheque for——"

"You certainly have," he told me. "You ordered 'em of your own free will. The club depends quite a little on gifts like these from members and hasn't any budget to meet——"

"Look here!" I said, interrupting in a tone I expect probably sounded kind of hostile. "Listen! If I've got to pay this bill, I'll do it; but I've been having altogether too much trouble over there making my authority as Chairman respected; and what with one thing and another I tell you frankly if things don't go better pretty soon I'll resign!"

"Oh, for goodness' sake, don't do that!" he said, and his manner changed completely. He'd been speaking with some sharpness but now he sounded kind of frightened. "For heaven's sake, don't talk about resigning!" he went on. "Please dismiss that idea from your mind, Mr. Massey, I beg you, please!"

"I won't dismiss it," I told him. "If things don't go better I'll do it!"

It was just then, as I was hanging up the telephone, that Mrs. Massey came in from outdoors, looking cheerful in a superior kind of way that she does sometimes. "Your right ear certainly ought to be burning," she said. "I've just been hearing such splendid compliments for you from Mrs. Abercrombie, that nice old lady in the green cottage who claims she was the first summer resident at the Neck. You'll be delighted to hear what lovely things she was saying about your chairmanship."

"Never mind!" I told her. "I don't care to hear any."

Mrs. Massey didn't pay any attention; but went right on. "Mrs. Abercrombie says she thinks it was perfectly lovely of you to accept the chairmanship. They'd asked pretty nearly everybody in the place before they got poor Mr. Dalrymple to take it, and when Mr. Dalrymple only kept it three weeks and resigned they were almost distracted, old Mrs. Abercrombie says. They saw that absolutely their only chance to get anybody would be to find someone entirely new at Mary's Neck, who didn't know. She says they'd practically given up when luckily somebody happened to think of you. She says it's the most splendid thing that you were willing to serve, and she hopes you won't be discouraged by all the complaints that are going around, because she thinks you're going to do just wonders in the way of keeping the place up."

"Never mind!" I said. "I don't care to hear any more."

"No?" Mrs. Massey asked me; then she gave a musing kind of laugh and pinched up her mouth in a way she has. "I thought maybe it might help you to get your face back to normal instead of trying to keep it looking like Mr. Mussolini's all the time."

With that, she laughed again and went on upstairs. I

didn't have a thing to say;—of a sudden it had kind of
come over me what my associates in the Logansville
Chamber of Commerce would think if they knew I had
let myself be soft-soaped into a chairmanship nobody
else would take and that had got me trying to order
everybody around, including my own family, and pretty
principally involved me in fighting with a little nine-year-
old boy. It isn't too much to say that after Mrs. Massey
went out what she left behind her, sitting in the chair
by that desk, was mainly a state of collapse. My condition
was a good deal like that of a person coming out of a
coma, or maybe just realizing that he'd been sick for
some days but might get well.

I tried to figure out what it was that had happened to
me, and why it had done so; and about the first conclusion I came to was that communism isn't practical—
at least not for prosperous people in a condition of summer unoccupiedness. I don't know about very poor and
busy people; they might do better at it, maybe. But when
a rich summer community has property in common, its
members, and their offspring, have got the sense of individual ownership too much developed.

In considerable pain I perceived that I had been making a really remarkable mistake about little Paulie Timberlake. For that child had come to be such a disturber
of my state of mind as Chairman of the Rocky Meadow
House Committee, and occupier of the main sociable position at Mary's Neck, I'd begun to feel that if I could just
once and for all put him in his place and excommunicate
him or something I'd be a happy man again. But now I
saw it wasn't so; it wasn't little Paulie I'd have to eradi-
cate in order to be happy; it was something else—something little Paulie had instinctively been having fun with.

Right there, I saw that Paulie wouldn't have had any

effect on me at all if I hadn't somehow let my importance get so distended that it projected from inside of me clear out to where even a nine-year-old child could get at it. How in the world had such a disastrous expansion ever happened to me? Since I hadn't ever been a victim to it before I came to Mary's Neck, the swelling must have had some connection with the place. I could trace the beginnings of it to what the hotel lady said the waitress said; but that didn't wholly account for it. In fact, I wondered if I hadn't got it because maybe it was contagious. I couldn't tell.

CHAPTER XVI

Anyhow, without leaving my desk, I sent a cheque to Mr. Bullfinch and wrote to Mr. Allstover in short, decisive terms, resigning. I didn't do it because of having to pay for the billiard-table and repairs that I'd ordered; I did it to convince myself I was over what had been the matter with me, and I told Mrs. Massey about it right away because I felt I owed her the chance to be superior and forgiving. She was kind and laughed instead, and she said old Mrs. Abercrombie had told her there'd been difficulties about that chairmanship for as much as twenty-five years, always the same kind, and so I mustn't feel too upset. I'm glad to say I was able to laugh with her, and I laughed again on the same subject, though all to myself, some time later, when I saw the new Chairman of the House Committee of the Rocky Meadow Club going by on the board side-walk. He wasn't a cottager; he was staying at one of the hotels for his first season at the Neck—but I noticed he was wearing an expression that made him look a little like Mr. Mussolini, maybe. "Oh, misery me!" I said, just whispering from the hammock, and of course he couldn't hear me. "Little Paulie Timberlake must be having the time of his life again!"

But here, I'm getting ahead, chronologically speaking,

because the day I saw that new Chairman looking expanded was 'way on toward the end of July, and before then quite a little had happened that seems to me worth considering.

The girls reinstated me, you might call it. They teased me a little—just enough to show they took the whole thing as a joke—and then they petted me all up and laughed and were affectionate and did and said a lot of little things to please me. That's the way the family are, and maybe it's the way women are—when you fall down after being disagreeable and give them their chance to walk on you, and you expect now they will, they most likely just turn round and treat you pretty angelically because you're down. My observation is that our opposite sex are indulgent with us men, like that, because they really don't want us to be as perfect as we pretend to be with them, and like us better, and feel they can show they do, when something compels us to admit we're not. When they see we're mortified over something we've done, they're as sweet to us and as anxious to make us all right again as they are when we're sick, and everybody knows trained nursing is naturally a woman's profession. Anyhow, Mrs. Massey and the girls treated my fall from the chairmanship in a big-hearted way that was touching, you might say, and I hope I'll never forget to appreciate it.

But as it happened, being more a father and less a chairman again, I got to worrying a little about my daughters, partly on account of their popularity, with a special reason added. To explain this I'll have to state that even though they're my own children they'd certainly become the most conspicuous centre of the youthful life at Mary's Neck. Pretty nearly every time Mrs. Massey came in from anywhere she'd get red in a pleased way and tell me how somebody'd congratulated her again on being the mother of the belles of the season, and our piazza was usually covered with boys and girls, including Eddie.

Well, the popularity of daughters is a strange thing, I suppose, for a parent to be worrying over (except for his own privacy and comfort) but worrying was what I began to be doing. In Logansville it never would have occurred to me to bother about such a thing. The difference was that I've always known all the young people in Logansville and understand just about what they're like; but these young people here in Mary's Neck were new to me. They're from different parts of the country. I hadn't seen them growing up from childhood the way I'd seen Clarissa's and Enid's friends in Logansville grow up, and so I didn't feel I knew much about the private life, so to speak, of these Mary's Neck youngsters, except by reputation.

What I mean by their reputation is what I was hearing about them from the older people, and never in my life did I hear so much about "wild young people" as I did after we began getting acquainted at Mary's Neck. Of course in Logansville I'd run across something in a newspaper or a magazine sometimes about this wild new generation; but we didn't seem to have any conspicuous examples of that sort in Logansville, so I supposed they must live some other place, and, judging from what I heard the older people saying since we came here, it began to seem to me I'd have to conclude that Mary's Neck was the place.

What puzzled me, I didn't see any of the wildness, myself, and when I asked my daughters about it they just laughed; I didn't get any satisfaction out of them, and, when I tried to, they made me feel foolish. Then for a while I wouldn't worry; but pretty soon I'd hear the older people talking again and I'd begin fretting some more, and it's funny what kind of things will upset a parent and get him to working himself all up over his children. For instance, a talk I had one morning at the beach with Mr. Carmichael did that to me; and Mr. Carmichael's the last person on earth you'd think could upset anybody. He's a fat, bald, harmless man, and his conversation is seldom important.

He was sitting in his loud striped bathing-suit on the sand down where it's wet, letting the foamy water come up over his legs sometimes when a heavier wave rolled in with the tide; and his fat little five-year-old daughter, Helen, was splashing around near him. But when he saw me walking along the beach, he called to me and moved back where it was dry and asked me to sit down for a talk. I did it, and noticed that the air near his head had kind of a tang like alcohol; but he didn't have much hair to put tonic on, so I judged it wasn't from that. He called his little girl over to us and made her sit down in his lap for a minute; but she didn't like it and squirmed away, so he let her go.

"I love that child," he told me, as she held up a dead crab for a minute and then threw it at him from a little distance away. "I love her. It's a comfort to me to realize that she's only five years old. But next year she won't be five any longer; she'll be six, and the year after that she'll be seven, and the year after that she'll be—well, let that go; but last year she was only four. No, she won't be five very long, if you understand what I mean. What I mean, she's happy now and healthy; but when she grows up and comes out her poor mother and I can't expect her to stay that way. Even before she comes out, she could lose her health in a minute, any day, the way things are now. You understand me."

"Why, no," I said. "I don't see——"

"Prohibition," he said. "Unless that amendment is repealed before she grows up nobody can tell what's liable to happen to her and all these other innocent little children playing here, happy and healthy in the sunshine to-day. If Prohibition lasts until they grow up there isn't a single one of 'em that'll be safe. Everybody knows it, and yet everybody just stands around and doesn't do anything about it. Nobody lifts a finger."

I didn't see at all what he was driving at, and I told him I didn't, so he put his wet, left hand on my shoulder and waved the right one in a gesture toward the little children playing at the water's edge up and down the beach. "You see all those children, don't you?" he asked me. "Well, some of 'em are only three years old, some of 'em are four and some of 'em are five, like Helen, and some of 'em are six; and a year from now every one of 'em'll be a year older, just like my little Helen. You get that, don't you?"

I told him yes, I followed him so far.

"Well, you see the danger, don't you?" he asked me. "Every year they'll be just that much older, and if Prohibition lasts till they grow up, what's the exact proportion of 'em'll die from poisoned liquor? And of those that don't die, what's the exact proportion'll have their health shattered? How many of 'em'll have their eyes ruined by wood-alcohol? Do you know the figures? No; you don't, because few people do. But you see the uncertainty, don't you? You see why I hate to have my little Helen get to be even six years old; she'll be just one year nearer the brink!"

He was more than serious; he was solemn about it, and I could see he was really troubled. But I was too astonished to sympathize with him much. "If Prohibition lasts," I said, "and it certainly looks as if it's going to——"

"Yes," he told me. "And every child in the United States is just that much worse off with every birthday it has. Look at my innocent happy healthy little Helen!" He pointed to her, and his voice had a kind of choke in it as he went on, "I'm her father and she's my child. A father doesn't like to think of his child's getting poisoned, does he? But I've got to face it. I've got to let her take her chance, don't I? I've got to watch her walking right straight into it, don't I?"

"Why, no," I said. "I don't see why so. It seems to me that it'd be fairly simple to avoid it."

"What?" he asked me. "How?"

"Why," I said, "if she didn't drink——"

"What! You don't mean——"

"I don't see any certainty of it," I told him.

He stared at me. "Why, my soul, man! Just look at these young people of sixteen and upwards all around us. You know what Prohibition has done to them, don't you? You don't suppose they know how to get good liquor, do you? You know that Youth is the reckless age, don't you? You don't s'pose they bother about getting good reliable bootleggers or having stuff analysed? For that matter, how many of 'em could afford it? Most of these parents here don't give their children allowances that permit it, so how is a boy or girl of sixteen or seventeen or eighteen going to be able to show the right caution, even if they stopped to think about it? I know what I'm talking about. Sixteen to twenty-four is the danger age. After that, they have more money and they're naturally more cautious. Poor little Helen, if I can get her through that age I'll begin to feel that all my trouble in bringing her up has maybe been worth while! But it's a terrible thing to look forward to. It's bad enough to think of any child growing up to behave the way these young people at Mary's Neck do, without having to face the danger of her being exposed to poison."

"But see here," I told him, "you don't think these young people between those ages you mentioned——"

"They're terrible," he said; and he frowned, looking pretty severe. "These young people of to-day are the wildest the world's ever seen. What's worse, they're fresh; they don't respect anybody; they don't show any respect for anything. The way I was brought up, I showed some respect for older people and for older people's opinions and moral judgments. Do these young people do that? Not much! They don't care what we think or what we say to 'em. They absolutely like to shock us, and the more I see of 'em the worse I'm disgusted!"

Then he called little Helen to him again and seemed to want to pet her and feel pathetic over her; but she was more interested in the dead crab and cried when he tried to get it away from her, and he got cross with her about it and spanked her, so I came away.

But, in spite of the fact that what he said didn't seem very logical to me, it did disquiet me quite a little—so much so, indeed, that if I hadn't been too embarrassed I might have spoken to Clarissa and Enid, and asked them if they knew how much wildness was going on in their circle. I did talk to Mrs. Massey about it that evening and got her disturbed over it, too; but she said she didn't feel like speaking to the girls any more than I did.

Well, it's curious how separated even the most sympathetic parents are from their children, on some points, at just the period, usually, when the children need the best advice. But advice is what they can't stand, because that's the very period when they're most afraid of some inter-ference's hampering their independence, and so they commonly get pretty reticent with their parents, because they know that encouraging intimacy is a good deal the same thing as encouraging advice. The generations set themselves apart that way; young people usually have to get to be middle-aged before they can be just man-to-man with their parents, and sometimes it seems as if consider-able changes have been going on before such a point is reached.

Myself, like most of the people of my age, I hadn't been brought up nearly so strictly as my parents had. *Their* parents, who were children of the pioneers and early-settlers, were rigid in matters concerned with church-going and child discipline; those were the days when card-playing, dancing and the theatre were the works of the Devil, and if you didn't believe in hell-fire you were sure to crinkle up in it eventually. The next generation was severe but less so. My grandparents thought it was all right to go to the circus and they played euchre sometimes, and my own parents were re-ligious but a lot livelier and more liberal-minded. Danced when they were young, enjoyed the theatre and weren't hard on me when they found out I'd sneaked off and gone swimming once on a Sunday afternoon—just sighed and said they hoped Aunt Pansy wouldn't hear of it. Mrs. Massey and I had brought our two girls up as well as we could, and of course they'd had the customary church and Sunday-school experiences; but ever since pioneer and early-settler times there's no denying that the gen-erations had been getting more and more liberal-minded

and less and less governed by regular set rules of conduct. According to the old ideas, at least, they were getting less and less religious, you might say, and nobody
could tell just how far the change would go or where it
was going to stop. What Mrs. Massey and I worried
about was whether it had already gone too far or not,
and what was the point at which such a change *would* be
too far, if it had.

But we didn't seem to have any way to find out, so we
just worried along and wondered and let it ride for a
while.

Then all of a sudden a kind of scandal broke out at
Mary's Neck and upset us and all the other parents worse
than any of us had been before. Every Saturday night
pretty much the whole of the place turns out for the dance
at the Rocky Meadow Club, including many of the older
people as well as all of the young ones; it was one of these
hops that was the scene of the trouble, and I was certainly glad that it happened on the Saturday night *after*
I resigned the chairmanship. Mrs. Massey and I weren't
there but it didn't take us long to hear about it, because
the beach was fairly exploding with it the next morning at
the bathing hour.

A boy only a little over twenty years old—his name
was Bush Thring, and he'd often been at our cottage—
got tangled with his partner's feet at the dance so that
he fell down, sitting, and everybody heard something
breaking. He seemed to be in difficulties about getting up
again and when some of the boys had helped him and he
moved away from there he left quite a large pool, easily
recognizable as gin, on the floor, so everybody knew he
must have been carrying a pretty good-sized bottle, and
got it broken. Besides that, he had to be taken up to the
village drug store and have bits of glass picked out of

him and some stitches taken; and the worst of it was that this young Bush Thring was well-liked and formerly had a good reputation, especially among the girls' mothers.

If an accident showed up Bush Thring like this, everybody said, what wouldn't have been discovered about the other boys if the same thing had happened to them! Also, everybody said it proved what terrible conditions prevailed among the young people, and there was a great deal of general indignation expressed.

I asked my daughters if this young Bush Thring had been tight; but they declared he wasn't, and they said they didn't understand why the older people were making such a hullabaloo over it, because Bush Thring was "all right", and the only reason he happened to have that bottle on his person was because if he left it in his car he was afraid it would be stolen. They admitted that his anxiety in this respect had been a mistake; but they insisted that he had as much right to own liquor as anybody else, and it bothered me quite a little that they should stubbornly maintain this point of view, at their age, though I was sure that they themselves would never join Bush Thring, or any other boy, in disposing of such a bottle—at least I hoped they wouldn't.

It surprised me a little at the beach to find that Mr. Carmichael was almost the severest critic of Bush Thring. "That boy ought to be dealt with," he told me and his friend Mr. Blodgett. "The young people can say all they want to about his not being tight. People don't fall down and have to get stitches taken in 'em except in that condition. What I hate is to see a young man of that age not being able to drink like a gentleman. If he can't do that, he ought to stay out of decent society."

"I agree absolutely," Mr. Blodgett said. "But what alarms me is all these young people pouring it down the way this thing shows they do. The idea of boys and girls in the eighteens and twenties getting tight is pretty painful to me, and it's even disgusting. They have no business to drink at all. When they're older and at an age when there's a natural need of stimulants, why, that's entirely different."

"I should say it is," Mr. Carmichael put in. "But what else can you expect under Prohibition?"

"Not a thing!" Mr. Blodgett told him, with strong emphasis. "I don't want the saloon back, myself; but while that law is on the statute books society has got to expect just such disgraceful episodes as this Bush Thring affair continually."

Pretty much the same thing was being said in almost every middle-aged group up and down the beach; all the older people were denouncing Bush Thring and the youngsters and Prohibition, and wondering what the world was coming to. Myself, I got sort of a conscious, guilty feeling over being the parent of two young daughters who seemed to be a conspicuous part of the outfit condemned, especially because I could see that the parents who were going for the "wild young people" didn't mean their own children but the children of the rest of us, which included mine. Some things I heard made me pretty nervous. I went up to where Mrs. Massey and a number of ladies were sitting, and I saw that Mrs. Massey looked flushed; I understood why, too, when I heard what Mrs. Bullfinch, who was sitting next to her, was saying.

"What I want to know," Mrs. Bullfinch said, "is just how far all this has gone? Now we know that all these wild stories about their drinking are true, how much of the other things we hear is true, too? That's what I'd like to know!"

"But surely," Mrs. Massey told her, "we don't know that they *all* drink."

Mrs. Timberlake was severe with her. "I don't see how anybody can defend them," she said. "Not after this terrible thing that's happened. The worst of it was the example it set the younger young people, because there were any number of mere children at that dance. Think of their seeing such things!"

CHAPTER XVII

WELL, there wasn't anything else talked about that morning, and the next night Mrs. Massey and I went to a big dinner-party of about forty middle-aged people at Mr. and Mrs. Weeder's, with whom we'd become right cordial by this time, because they're a mighty nice likeable couple when you get to know them. We found the subject hadn't been exhausted—not by any means. But that party began rather unfortunately for me, or perhaps it'd be more accurate to say I was in plenty of trouble beforehand, because Mrs. Massey and I were an hour late getting there, and she felt that this was my fault and I couldn't argue this impression out of her. The Wanda was in commission again and Captain Turner and I took her up the coast so far in the afternoon that we got back a lot later than I expected, and, as I had to dress after I finally did get home, Mrs. Massey certainly gave me fits.

But the dinner-party had just sat down at seven or eight small tables when we arrived, and Mrs. Weeder made us feel as comfortable as she could and said they hadn't waited at all on our account, so Mrs. Massey began to feel better, especially as everybody seemed very bright and gay and friendly. In fact, the whole party were talking all at once and making a great deal of noise, and seemed to be in the highest spirits, even though most of them, so far as I could gather, were still discussing Bush Thring and the doings of the young people. The lady next to me, Mrs. Dalrymple, a right nice likeable woman, began to talk to me on this subject as soon as I sat down.

"Don't you think it's the most shocking thing you ever heard, Mr. Massey?" she asked me, though she kept smiling all the time. "I don't suppose we can expect anything better, though, until we can get a President who'll be willing to repeal the Prohibition Act or something. What I feel so terribly, myself, is the increase in crime, because I have two little sons of my own. The older one is named for his grandfather, General Francis Dalrymple, and the younger one, Henry, is only eight years old. Do you understand what a mother must feel, Mr. Massey, who has two little sons of that age? When you think of all the hi-jacking and racketeering that goes on, and the terrible things you read in the paper every day about murders and gangsters and all this frightful political corruption, don't you think we're living in a dreadful epoch, and don't you see how a mother feels, Mr. Massey? You're a man, I know, and of course you look at things in a different light; but surely, after such a thing has happened at the Saturday night dance at the Rocky Meadow Club, you can appreciate how a mother would feel about Francis and Henry. I wish you knew my two dear little boys, Mr. Massey, because I think if you did, you'd understand what I mean better."

"I've seen them at the beach—and elsewhere——" I told her, and I was able to restrain any bitterness I might once have felt about their being friends of Paulie Timberlake. "They're nice, good-looking boys; but I don't exactly get your point. I don't see why they'd give you any worries about professional hi-jacking and racketeering, for instance."

"I didn't mean hi-jacking, alone," she said. "I meant the whole crime wave. What a mother has to face is the thought of her innocent, helpless children growing up into a world of law-breaking and law-breakers, under such conditions as have never been known before. And you can't keep these conditions from the children, Mr. Massey. You can't veil their young eyes; you can hardly believe how much they know already about what's going on. Last week, one afternoon, they came back from the movies, and Francis said he hadn't enjoyed it because it was the same old triangle, and he was tired of sex shows; and then only yesterday morning my two little boys were playing outside the window where I was writing a letter, and I heard little Francis shouting, 'Bang, bang, bang, you're dead!' at his brother, and little Henry shouted, 'Bang, bang, bang!' back at Francis, and said, 'I'm not dead, you're dead, yourself!' And then they got cross and called each other little names and had a little fight, so that I had to go out and stop them. Henry had a toy automobile full of empty bottles he'd brought up from the cellar, and it opened my eyes, Mr. Massey, and shocked me very painfully to find what they were playing. Little Henry said he was George Gregg, his papa's bootlegger, and Francis was playing a hi-jacker. Now, I ask you!" She broke out in a fond whooping kind of laugh. "Wasn't it simply too intriguing?" she said. "Don't you love it!" Then she got serious again. "On the other hand, when our own little children are playing games like that, and young people a little older are behaving the way they did Saturday night at the Rocky Meadow Club, isn't anything going to be done about it?"

Mr. Carmichael was at that same table. "If you want to know what I think about it," he said, "it's simply this: there ought to be a Round Robin to the officers of the Rocky Meadow to discharge the steward and get a new chairman of the House Committee. If the club had been run right that thing would never have happened!"

Well, they all agreed to that, and so did the people at the next table; they joined in with our conversation and said Mary's Neck wasn't safe until a steward and a chairman could be found who would prevent any boy from bringing concealed liquor into the club or having liquor in a car outside, for that matter. "The whole Neck is down on the Rocky Meadow Club and Bush Thring," one of them said; and Mr. Carmichael warmed up and said he was going before the club officers and get the steward fired.

"I'm going to tell 'em the Neck won't stand for that fellow any longer, and I won't stand for him any longer, myself; he's got to go. I'm going to do that much," he told us, "because I'm getting pretty tired of everybody talking so much about this Prohibition evil and never doing anything. That's the whole trouble: people don't do anything. We all know these conditions exist, and yet we sit and fold our hands. My daughter, Helen, is only five years old; and I'm her father but I wouldn't let her go out driving in an automobile with any of these young people here for anything on earth. Because I love that child; I love her. And even if I didn't want her to get killed I wouldn't let her get the name of being around in such company. I wouldn't let anyone drive her in an automobile except me, and I've already made that a rule she's got to live by when she gets old enough. She can't go out with any boy in a car, because you can't be sure what a boy's been drinking unless he falls down and breaks it. If my daughter ever steps into an automobile, it's going to be one I'm driving myself!"

He was very stern as he said this; but, right afterwards, he looked mollified and smiled, because the people over at a table in the corner began to sing, just then. This was a table where the host, Mr. Weeder, sat, and the people he had with him there were laughing and kind of cutting-up and having a pretty jolly time. I was a little surprised when they began to sing as loudly as they did, sort of putting their heads together to try and make chords, because nobody'd had anything to drink that I'd seen; and this is what they were singing:

> *"We are pals, happy pals,*
> *We are all just boys and gals!*
> *Whoop 'er up for a merry time togethah!*
> *For we're all just boys and gals*
> *And we love our dear old pals*
> *In every kind of weathah!"*

Mr. Carmichael couldn't look stern and sing a song like that at the same time, which was the reason he had to modify the severity of expression he'd worn when he was talking about not allowing Helen to go out with boys in any car he wasn't driving himself. He sang louder than anybody else.

Mrs. Dalrymple didn't seem to approve and began whispering to me about him: "I feel so sorry for Mrs. Carmichael; he always makes such an exhibition of himself."

But it didn't seem to me that he was making an exhibition of himself particularly; he was just singing like the people at that other table, and keeping time on the edge of his plate with his knife and fork, the way they were, and to me it seemed a pretty innocent kind of jollity. The only thing that surprised me about it was that anybody who appeared to feel so badly and spoke with so much severity about the episode at the Rocky Meadow Club and the dangers of life for young children, could brighten up so suddenly. I was a little depressed, myself, thinking of Clarissa and Enid and the general condemnation applied to everybody of their age; but I tried to look gay and keep myself perked up into the spirit of the occasion. Evidently, this was being a mighty successful party, and, when we left the table and went out to the other rooms and the piazza, most of these middle-aged people began to frolic almost as if they were children again.

Mrs. Massey and I had been to quite a number of small dinners at Mary's Neck; but this was the first big party we'd joined up with, and it was pleasant and surprising to see how jolly and unconscious and informal these people were when they got together in this way. Mr. Weeder and two other gentlemen and three of the ladies went parading up and down the long living-room with their arms about one another's shoulders, and singing:

> *"We are pals, happy pals,*
> *We are all just boys and gals!*
> *Whoop 'er up for a merry time togethah!*
> *For we're all just boys and gals*
> *And we love our dear old pals*
> *In every kind of weathah!"*

Every now and then, they paraded into Mr. Weeder's study, stayed in there a while and came out again, singing louder. There was another group of seven or eight doing almost the same thing; they went into Mr. Weeder's study, too. Then they'd come out and tramp up and down the piazza in the moonlight, singing something about "Drink, Puppy Drink," and one of the ladies pretended to be a jockey riding the piazza railing for a horse, shouting, "Gone-away! Gone-away!" and whipping with the poker, while the rest played they were dogs barking at her. This seemed pretty light-hearted for people mostly around forty or over to be doing, and I noticed that some of the younger members of the Weeder family, a couple of girls and a boy between twelve and fifteen years old, were looking on from out in the yard with some playmates of theirs and seemed to be enjoying it, too. When I went in again, a man was passing around a tray of pretty sizable highballs, and I said to Mr. Blodgett, who was helping himself to one, that it didn't appear to me any artificial stimulus was needed for people already enjoying themselves so thoroughly in their natural high spirits.

"Yes," he said, "it's a lovely evening; but you missed the foundation."

"What was that?" I asked him.

"A solid hour," he told me. "One solid hour of cocktailing before dinner. Divine!"

I didn't take a highball, myself, because I don't like them, and just then Mrs. Dalrymple called to me to come and sit with her and some other ladies; and so I went to join them. They were talking pretty loudly; but they had to, because Mr. Weeder and his group of paraders had begun to play a game they called "Red Dog" at a table right near and were making a terrible noise.

"We're back on the same subject, Mr. Massey," Mrs. Dalrymple said to me. "We were discussing what ought to be done about that boy, Bush Thring, and we want to get your reaction."

Mrs. Allstover was one of this group and she took up what Mrs. Dalrymple was saying. "It's the whole question of the young people, not just this one instance of wildness," she said, and she took some ice out of her glass and put it in an ash tray. "What ought to concern us parents is their general behavior, not merely this Bush Shring sing—I mean this Bush Thring thing. What I mean, being the mother of a son just grown to manhood, myself, the way the girls of this generation try to attract the boys alarms me as much as anything. I simply can't get over the way they dress; and nobody can tell me that the few clothes they wear don't have a most deleterious effect. Why, if I'd done that when I was eighteen or nineteen I think my father would have whipped me!"

"So would mine!" Mrs. Timberlake chimed in. "I often wake up at night thinking of the danger my own son is going to be exposed to from these modern girls. For instance, look at the way they smoke! When a young man and a girl get to smoking together——"

Mrs. Dalrymple interrupted; she was smoking a cigarette herself in a long amber holder, and she laughed. "No, I think we ought to be a little broad-minded about that. I've always believed that a girl has just as much right to smoke as a boy has. It's the way their clothes expose them that I object to, because of their deleterious effect. They can't help but have that kind of effect, because, what I say is, human nature is human nature every time. Don't you think so, Mrs. Bullfinch?"

"Yes," Mrs. Bullfinch answered, "I do. I believe you're right."

"Certainly, you are," Mrs. Allstover put in, and she appealed to me. "Don't you think so, Mr. Massey?

Don't you agree that human nature is human nature every time?"

"Well—I don't know," I said, because I was a little embarrassed by the question. The clothes these ladies were wearing didn't seem to be very different from what they were criticizing, and the way they were sitting around in them made me feel kind of conscious while we were on that subject, and I was afraid they might have the idea I was affected by human nature, myself, which wasn't the case; and I didn't like to commit myself in any way that would make it appear it was. "What I mean," I went on, getting red, "I mean we're all pretty much used to 'em by this time, so we hardly notice any more, and I doubt if the boys think anything about it. My own two daughters——"

But of course all the ladies broke out at me there and said they'd never dreamed of thinking anything about human nature as connected with my girls; they all agreed that Enid and Clarissa were perfect, and they'd never dreamed of criticizing them. They were talking about the other girls entirely.

"It's the whole subject of the younger generation," Mrs. Dalrymple said, "and what sort of men and women they're going to grow up to be—that's the problem we parents have to face." She paused for a moment, because the man with the tray was going around again and stopped beside her. She declined any more, but finished the glass she already had and put it on his tray. Then she went on, "What's brought the question to a head is this Push Shring thing." She coughed, and corrected herself, speaking slowly. "This Bush Thing—this Bush Thring thing. I mean there's one terrible phase that is the worst of the whole situation and it's what we parents ought to regard most seriously of all, because we ought to regard it that way if we have any regard not only for our own children but regard for the future of our country. Don't you all think so?"

She spoke with a great deal of earnestness and pretty impressively, and, though I couldn't quite make out her meaning, the other ladies all looked serious and seemed to agree with her. "Every single word you say is true," Mrs. Bullfinch said; and the others nodded and said indeed it was.

Mrs. Dalrymple looked a little cross. "Wait till I come to the point," she told them. "What I mean is, the most terrible evil of all the evils of Prohibition is the effect on our children and our young people in teaching them disrespect for law. Isn't that what they're learning all over the United States? Aren't all the little children in the land growing up to hold the very Constitution of our country in disrespect and contempt? Isn't that the worst of the evil?"

At that, the whole group broke out with exclamations showing how enthusiastically they agreed with her. "It's just what my husband and I have told each other a thousand times," one of them said. "What sort of citizens is this disrespect for law going to make of our children?"

"It's exactly what Mr. Bullfinch says to me practically every day," Mrs. Bullfinch put in. " 'What right have a few spigots—bigots—' he keeps asking me, 'what right have a few bigots to bring on this crime wave?' Mr. Bullfinch says these bigots——"

She went on; but nobody could hear her, because all the ladies began to talk at once, telling how their husbands said the same thing and how strongly they agreed with them, and besides, Mr. Carmichael came up to the group just then and joined in. He didn't sit down with us; he just kind of leaned on Mrs. Bullfinch, holding his glass over her as he talked, so that she got nervous and changed her seat. But he just leaned against the side of the chair and didn't seem to notice.

"You're absolutely right, Mrs. Bullfinch," he said, and he was frowning severely. "That's what my little Helen's got to face—an utter disrespect for the laws of her country. I love that child. I tell you I love her; and so does my wife love her. Mrs. Carmichael loves her, too. I love her and she loves her and we both love her, and we're her own father and mother. I don't mean the rest of you don't love your own children, because there wouldn't be any reason for you not to, and so you probably do, because they're all in the same boat and have got to grow up with this disrespect for law hanging over 'em; and until that amendment is repealed we can't do anything to abate it—not a thing! We're helpless to help little helpless children. We're helpless to help little helpless children, and they can't help themselves, and we can't help ourselves, so we're sepless."

He went on talking about helplessness that way; but it was hard to hear him because there was so much noise, and Mrs. Dalrymple told me not to pay any attention to him, anyhow. "Everybody has the greatest sympathy for his wife," she told me. "Mrs. Carmichael is a perfect martyr to him, because she can hold so much more than he can without showing it. It spoils all her pleasure in going out."

But Mr. Carmichael was determined to make himself heard. "Can't you ladies listen to anything important for one *minute?*" he shouted at them. "I've got something important to say about this affair of Push—Puss—I mean that boy. Are we going to fold our hands as if we were absolutely helpless?" He seemed to get angry, and he shook his fist at Mrs. Allstover, for emphasis. "You may be helpless, Mrs. Bullfinch," he said. "But I'm not. I'm not a helpsessless man! I'm going to have that steward fired by nine o'clock to-morrow morning, and I'm going to have Puss—or whoever he is—sent away from here on a long, long sailing voyage. Am I right or am I wrong?"

Nobody answered him, maybe because just then a phonograph broke out with the loudest kind of jazz, in the next room, and the racing people came in from the piazza pretty noisily. They were trotting in single file, stooped over, and shouting, *"Hoo! Hoo! Hoo!"* pretending they were Indians. Then some more people came out of Mr. Weeder's study, where they'd been all the time; they were singing about how they were dear old pals and just boys and gals, and they joined the Indians, and all of them went into the room where the music was. And Mr. Carmichael went with them, and he and Mr. Blodgett waltzed together until they bumped into the man with the tray, and all three of them fell down.

Then, just as this happened, a most awful squealing broke out, and at first I thought it was Mr. Carmichael, and that he must be hurt; but he didn't have such a treble voice as this squealing was in, so I saw it was something else. It came from outside a window that opened on the piazza, and pretty soon I understood what it was, because a nursemaid looked in at the window and called to Mrs. Weeder, who was at the card-table with her husband's party. "It's Master Charlie," the nursemaid told her. "I can't get him to go to bed, and he kicks and fights me something dreadful because he says he wants to keep on watching the party through the window."

CHAPTER XVIII

M R. WEEDER pushed over a pile of chips to one of the ladies, and told the nursemaid to bring Charlie to him. So she came round in the door, leading the little boy by the hand, and Mr. Weeder patted him on the head. "Kiss Da-da good-night," he said, and little Charlie did it, and kissed his mother, and then marched off with the nurse like a little man.

Everybody said what a sweet, obedient child he was; then the ladies where I was sitting got back again to the subject we'd been talking about before, and somebody shut the doors into the room where the phonograph and dancing were going on, so we could hear ourselves. "Besides this disrespect for law that they're learning," Mrs. Timberlake said, "there's another angle to it that I see. What I mean by another angle is simply another view of the same proposition. If children aren't brought up to respect the law, they simply haven't any respect for it, and that's the angle I was speaking of as one view you could take of it, if you were looking at it from all the different angles. For instance, if you do look at it from this angle I'm speaking of, what other conclusion can you come to? Mr. Massey, you're naturally a man, and so of course, being a man, you'd probably put it on a man's angle, yourself; but I wish you'd explain all these different angles to us and give us your reaction, unless I'm mistaken. Besides being a man with that angle, you're a father, too, and that would help to explain. Would you tell us, simply and plainly, what angle you react to the most?"

What she said confused me considerably, and I told her I was afraid I didn't understand her question, so Mrs. Dalrymple said she'd make it clearer. "It's like this," she said. "What troubles us is the fudility of it all——I mean the futility of it all; and we want to know how you react to these angles. Mr. Carmichael doesn't often speak very wisely; but there is something in what he said: Are we as helpless as he believes? Are we simply to sit with folded hands and see our children growing up to learn this disregard for our institutions and distress us the way they're going to?"

"Let me understand you a little better," I said. "I'm still mixed up about your question. If I get it anywhere near right, you're asking me whether or not I can imagine anything you could do that would help to keep your children from growing up with a disrespect for the law and the Constitution. Is that correct?"

"Yes," she told me, and clapped her hands and nodded and smiled. "You've hit it, Mr. Massey! Exactly! That's what we want to know."

Well, I didn't want to be a wet-blanket; but since she put it that way, and all these ladies leaned forward as if they thought I might be going to say something important, it seemed to me that I really ought to tell them. I was going to do it, too; but just then the man with the tray came around again; and this time there was a big bowl of bubbling punch, with ice and fruit in it, and Mrs. Timberlake gave a little cry of delight. "Wait, Mr. Massey," she told me. "This is a champagne punch, and

no one in the world knows how to make it like Mrs.
Weeder. Wait till we all get our glasses filled and then
tell us what you were going to say and we'll enjoy your
remarks infinitively more and everything'll be simply delicious! Wait just a minute, Mr. Massey."

I waited, of course; but just when they had all fixed
themselves with supplies, and said they were ready for
me to speak up, somebody opened the doors into the room
where the dancing was going on, and Mr. Blodgett and
Mr. Carmichael came out, dancing together and yet you
might say not together, too, because they were holding
on to each other but dancing different dances; and Mrs.
Carmichael was trying to separate them and make her
husband listen to what she was saying about hiring a
car to go home instead of letting him drive, which she
wasn't going to do because she had some regard for her
life, she told him. Then all the other dancers came out,
with their arms around one another, and singing:

> *"We are pals, happy pals,*
> *We are all just boys and gals!"*

At that, the ladies who'd been sitting with me joined in
the song, waving their glasses, and most of 'em stood up
to kind of swing with the singing and make it louder, the
way people do when they get in the spirit of a thing like
that; so I knew they hadn't expected me to say anything
very useful in response to their question, after all. And
Mrs. Massey came to me just then and said for heaven's
sake let's go home because the noise was going to give
her a headache. So we told Mr. and Mrs. Weeder good-
night, and got away.

Walking across from the Weeders' lawn to ours, I told

Mrs. Massey about the question the ladies had asked me, and she said she was glad I'd had sense enough not to answer it, because naturally they'd have felt that I was some sort of a narrow-minded fanatic or something that wanted to spoil everything, and it would have made me thoroughly unpopular and not have done one bit of good to anybody. I said I guessed she was right, and of course she was; they'd only have thought I was some kind of spigot or something. Then we walked up our own piazza steps, and there in a wicker chair, talking to Clarissa, sat nobody on earth but Mr. Bush Thring. He jumped up right away and said he'd been waiting to see me, which surprised me pretty uncomfortably; but I took him into the living-room and asked him what I could do for him.

Of course I couldn't help feeling a little prejudiced against him, the way anybody naturally does when a whole community goes around saying how terrible somebody is, and besides, when you hear anybody's name as much mispronounced as I'd heard his, that evening, it sort of sets you against him a little bit, even though that doesn't seem right and just. Yet I couldn't help noticing that he was a manly-looking boy, and had a good eye; he was serious and kind of quiet and modest.

"Sir," he said, "I thought I ought to speak with you about continuing to come to your cottage, because I don't want to be here if you don't want me here, and if you don't I'd rather have you tell me yourself than put Clarissa to the embarrassment of having to tell me for you."

"Well, that's fair," I said. "Go on."

He did. "I know that since last Saturday night I've been talked about pretty severely; but it seems to me I might be able to say a word for myself to people whose houses I like to go to, and let them judge for themselves.

I hadn't had a single drink out of that bottle I broke, Mr. Massey, as it happened; but I don't say I didn't mean to use some of it later, because I did. Four or five of the other boys and I were going to have a little party among ourselves down on the beach with cold lobster and something to drink. That's all there was to it, except for the accident of my falling down. I'm twenty-two myself and the other boys who planned the lobster feast are about my age, and what we all are sorry for is that there were a number of youngsters at the dance, and of course it isn't good for them to think that we older fellows are running rather wild."

"So that worries you?" I asked him. "What about the people older than you? Do you think such a thing might have a bad effect on middle-aged people, too?"

He looked troubled. "I hope not," he told me. "I don't think there's much harm, sir, at my age, if we have a little party now and then if we don't carry it *too* far and just have a good time among ourselves. But I do hate to see older people overdoing it."

"Well, then," I said, "so you think the only right age for it——" But we had to stop talking for a minute, because the noise at the next cottage got so loud just then. Besides the singing and music and dancing that was going on, there was a big thumping and bumping and some more louder singing than ever, and then the racket of an automobile engine in the driveway, being raced, and I heard Mrs. Carmichael shouting, "Help me get him out of the car, Mr. Blodgett! Don't let him throw the clutch in!" And Mr. Carmichael was singing some more about how they were all just boys and gals, and seeming to have quite a little fight at the same time with Mrs. Carmichael and Mr. Blodgett, who were using a good deal of language.

"Yes, sir?" Bush Thring said, when there was a chance for us to hear each other again. "You were asking me?"

"Ever since I came here," I told him, "I've been hearing more and more about how wild all you young people are; but I haven't been able to find out exactly how wild you really are. What do you think about it yourself?"

He laughed. "Why, we aren't wild at all," he said. "Of course some of these younger boys haven't got sense enough yet to——"

I stopped him. "It's all right," I told him. "You've stirred things up enough at Mary's Neck without starting any arguments of the kind I see you're thinking of. I admit that somebody else is always the wrong age. Go back to the piazza and talk to Clarissa about it, if you want to."

He said "Thank you, sir" with his expression all cleared up, and went, and I sat down to smoke a goodnight cigar, wondering if I'd done right. Mrs. Massey'd stayed on the piazza while I was talking to him; but she came in and took a chair near me, and Enid, who'd been out somewhere with Eddie Bullfinch, brought him in, too, and began playing backgammon with him. Mrs. Massey whispered to me and asked, "What did you say to him?"

I told her and she nodded, showing she approved; but I said, "I'm not so sure it was the best thing. I don't mean I think there's anything wrong with that young man; but I don't know about one of our girls being around with a young man that's got himself so talked about and——"

"Why, that's all right, sir," Eddie Bullfinch said, and I almost jumped because I'd spoken in a low tone and he was something like forty feet away at the other end of the room, and he and Enid were both making a noise over their backgammon. "I think you did just right about

Bush Thring," Eddie went on, as if now I didn't need to worry any more. "It's only the older people made a fuss about him, anyhow. For that matter, why, if you were going to stop your daughters from associations with everybody that gets talked about, why, where would they be? Take me. Look how I get talked about. By the family and everybody else. Take f'rinstance the way I'm being talked about right now. Why, look it's twice as much as all this and that about Bush Thring."

"It is not!" Enid told him. "Nobody's talking about you at all."

He seemed hurt and cross right away. "They are, too! I can't do a thing without everybody in the place startin' up a clackin'. Why, there was ten times as much talk about the Dorio-Grecco's slipping off the rocks as there is about Bush Thring."

"There wasn't either," she said.

"There was, too!" he told her. "You'd 'a' thought it happened in public, and every old lady at the Neck that can't drive a car themselves any more than they could climb a telegraph pole undertook to criticize me to my mother. There was, too! Why, they'll talk about anything here! You ought to know that, Enid, yourself, on account of the way they criticized your own father when he was Chairman." He looked over at me again. "I guess *you* know it, Mr. Massey. You know that even as conservative a man as you are can get talked about at the Neck, don't you?"

It didn't strike me he was tactful, though I made allowances for his age and open disposition, and managed to laugh. "Well, that's over, Eddie," I said. "I don't believe I'll get talked about any more."

"Don't you think it!" he told me, and I might mention right now that Eddie Bullfinch wasn't far wrong that time! "Look what happened to that poor old man that was here a while the first of this season right next door to you. *He* got it, I guess!"

Well, Enid stopped his remarks at this point, telling him he'd either have to play the game or go home, and he devoted himself to backgammon for a little while until they had an argument over it and he took her at her word and did go home. By that time I was ready for bed, but sat up a while with another good-night cigar, thinking over the evening we'd had and trying to figure out matters that puzzled me.

Not being much of a traveller, as I say, I'd taken it for granted that pretty much anywhere in the world you'd go you'd find people generally a good deal alike and of a fairly close resemblance to those in your own home town. In the fundamentals I still think that's so and that all of us human kind operate about the same; but Mary's Neck was beginning to show me that different places and conditions have an important effect on the operating. Myself, to my shame, I hadn't operated at the Neck altogether the way I did in Logansville, and I judged this might be true of other people.

For instance, it began to seem to me that a summer resort of cottagers is like a village, only peculiarly more so, because you'd have to imagine a village where in the first place nobody's doing any business or going downtown to the store or the works, or ever leaving the womenfolks to themselves practically. Just that alone would make a mighty uncertain village, you see; but you also have to allow for the fact that three-fourths of the time all the villagers are scattered and leading lives unknown to their fellow-villagers. What's more, they don't all come back; but entirely new, mysterious families are found living in some of the houses. You can see right away how natural it is for everybody to be kind of looking everybody else over, which is a thing that pretty often leads to a good deal.

Some of the time it's a little like the way Mrs. Massey is when she and I are on a train. Every now and then, after I've been to the smoker, she'll say to me something of this kind, likely: "She's his wife not his granddaughter. He was an old bachelor from Fall River, Massachusetts, and the reason we thought he was acting so oddly is that they've just got married." Or else maybe she'll say, "It *is* her own hair", or else maybe, "The fat man's had too much to drink again."

Another thing: Logansville is a place where the inhabitants pretty much all feel the best good will in the world towards one another, and where they all work together for the good of the community as much as you could expect; but my soul! just suppose that the whole population of Logansville went down to the Courthouse Square and sat on the grass there in little groups and clicks, looking sideways a good deal and buzz-buzzing considerably about each other for two hours every single day for most of the summer, how long do you think there'd be any Logansville at all? Yet that's what we do at the Neck, only it's the beach where we sit and buzz-buzz instead of the Courthouse Square. It's a wonder the place hasn't blown up long ago.

Well, if I make myself clear, you can understand something of what would happen at the Neck before a new family'd have its status really settled—if it ever did. Take the old man Eddie Bullfinch was mentioning that rented the cottage next door to us for the first month of the season—it's called the Ballinger cottage on account of the owner's name being Ballinger. There was a youngish middle-aged couple, and a funny-looking pale old man, terribly thin, who spent his whole time picking worms and bugs off of the trees and bushes and out of the grass. Mrs. Dalrymple, who lives next door beyond, said she watched him out of her window until two o'clock one night and saw him making snatching motions among the shrubberies. "Ha! Got you that time, darling!" she heard him say, and she spread it all over Mary's Neck that he was a maniac. Everybody said something ought to be done about it, and Mrs. Dalrymple wanted me to go in and tell the middle-aged couple, his attendants, they had to keep the old man confined to the house, because she was afraid he might take a notion to injure her little Francis and Henry. Somebody went to the trouble of finding out that the old man was Professor Albert Thompson, chief entomological expert of the Carson Institute, and the middle-aged couple were his niece and her husband who kept house for him; but nobody could really make much headway against Mrs. Dalrymple's story because she'd got it too well established; and after the Professor's month in that cottage was up and he'd gone away she still kept on telling people what a terrible time she had while there was a lunatic in the Ballinger cottage next door.

But my soul! when I think of how I sat there kind of peacefully having a revery over these matters, when Eddie Bullfinch and Bush Thring had gone home after we'd come in from the Weeders' party that night, it seems to me I hardly knew anything but the mere rudiments of such questions, and maybe if I'd known right then what was about to happen to that same Ballinger cottage I might have decided that business called me back to Logansville. I sat there peacefully, as I say, because the noise at the Weeders' had all sobered down, the dinner-party was all over and everything was quiet. I

yawned, myself, being too lazy to go to bed and I heard
Enid and Clarissa yawning and mumbling out on the
piazza as if they were sleepy, too, and about to turn in.
Then Mrs. Weeder's voice came from out there, sounding excited and newsy. I gathered she'd run over to tell
the girls something, and I wasn't much interested but got
up and went to hear what she had to say. All three of
them were doing the kind of exclaiming women do over
important sociable happenings.

"I couldn't sleep till I told you!" Mrs. Weeder was
saying to the girls. "I knew what a thrill it would give
you, living absolutely next door to it. Think of my husband's knowing it all evening and I being the last one to
know because he'd told everybody else in confidence during the evening and left me out because he said he
couldn't trust me to keep it to myself! And his excuse to
me is that the agent for the cottage told him about it
this afternoon in the strictest secrecy because *she* insisted
that the agent shouldn't mention it until after she comes!
Of course she knows she'll be recognized as soon as she
gets here. I don't believe my husband would have told
me even now if Mrs. Timberlake hadn't shouted as she
was leaving, 'I hope you'll like your new neighbor!' "
Then Mrs. Weeder noticed me. "Well, Mr. Massey,
what do you think of the news?"

"I haven't heard it," I said.

"My, this is exciting!" she told me. *"Who* do you
think has rented the Ballinger cottage next door to you
for the next month?"

Judging by the way she shouted *"Who"*, I thought
it must be at least the Vice-President of the United
States, and, when I gave up guessing and she said,
"Madam Parka!" like an explosion, I was disappointed.

"Madam Parka?" I said. "It seems to me I've heard

of her somewhere. Isn't she some kind of a clairvoyant?"

But the girls just whooped at me, the way they do when I show more than customary ignorance. They told me, both together, that anybody who read the newspapers was supposed to be aware that Madam Parka was one of the most prominent grand-opera Prima Donnas in the world.

CHAPTER XIX

THEY must have been right about that, because at the beach next day I appeared to be the only person in the whole of Mary's Neck that didn't know more about Madam Parka than an automobile dealer does about the president of the company that makes his cars. Where Mrs. Massey and I were sitting, with Mrs. Weeder and Mrs. Dalrymple and Mr. and Mrs. Bullfinch, there wasn't any other topic at all. "You'd think that if a great foreign Prima Donna like Madam Parka weren't going to spend the summer in her own country, at Deauville or Biarritz, for instance," Mrs. Weeder said, "she'd at least select Newport or Bar Harbor. Really her coming here shows what an important resort Mary's Neck's getting to be."

"Yes," Mrs. Dalrymple agreed. "Madam Parka probably likes to be among people of her own sort. She's a Hungarian Countess by birth and——"

"Not at all," Mrs. Weeder told her. "She began life peddling dried sea-horses in Naples."

But Mr. Bullfinch intervened, feeling that he had the right information. He usually does feel that way, I might say. "I can tell you absolutely all about Madam Parka," he said. "Her stage name—all these headline singers take

Italian names—is Fiametta Parka; but her real name is Fanny Parker and she's from California. I know, because a second cousin of mine was well acquainted with this Fanny Parker out there when she was studying music in Oakland. She left there to go abroad; but he heard her sing in New York about three years ago and recognized her absolutely. She's been married four times; her last husband was a Russian Prince; but she's a widow again, because he jumped off a precipice."

"I don't see how she could be an American," Mrs. Weeder said. "Because the papers were all talking about her learning English only last autumn when she came to sing in America for the first time."

"No; you're mistaken," Mrs. Bullfinch told her, in a prim kind of way she has. "No; I heard Mr. Bullfinch's cousin from California talking about Madam Parka, myself, and he said exactly what Mr. Bullfinch has just told you he did. Very odd, such a woman's taking a cottage among so conservative a summer colony as ours. I doubt if I shall call on her."

"But even if she has a pretty mixed-up past," Mrs. Dalrymple said, "people rather overlook these things in great artists."

But Mrs. Bullfinch gave a coldish sort of cough and shook her head. "Whether I decide to call upon her or not," she said, "will depend entirely upon whether she appears to be a lady or not. After she's been here for some time, if her conduct and manners prove she's a lady——"

"Oh, but we ought to decide beforehand," Mrs. Weeder interrupted. "Is the Neck going to call on Madam Parka or is the Neck not?"

Other groups of ladies up and down the beach were already discussing that question, I found, as I walked around a little, saying howdy-do; but I don't think any of 'em got it settled any more than they did whether Madam Parka was from California or somewhere in Europe, or whether she'd had four husbands or not any. The way it looked to me, all of the questions about her (and there were plenty) didn't do anything but get more and more unsettled. I happened to run into Mr. Jackson that afternoon in the village; he's an agent for some of the cottages and does a summer business at Mary's Neck in real estate and insurance and running a 'bus-line. "Hear you're stirring things up down our way," I told him.

"Yes," he said, looking serious. "I've had a good many instructions by wire. Seems things have to be just thus-and-so for these opera stars; but I was glad to get the Ballinger cottage rented again even on piecemeal time. She'll be in this evening and I expect it'll be a big pleasure to you and your family, because you'll probably get to hear her singing when she practises."

Well, I thought that might be so; but the practising didn't begin that evening, though I listened for it. Madam Parka got to Mary's Neck after dark and during a rain-storm, so everybody missed seeing her come. In the morning it was still raining; but afterwhile Clarissa told me there was a man sitting out on the porch of the Ballinger cottage in an ulster and looking at the rain. She said he had dark curly hair, and she and Mrs. Massey and Enid all thought he was right romantic-appearing; but after I'd had a look at him, myself, from our living-room window I didn't think so; he seemed to me to be just a little, thin, sallow man, not especially noticeable.

Mrs. Dalrymple telephoned over from her cottage, later, that he'd been walking in part of the Ballinger yard near her living-room windows and she'd heard a woman's voice calling to him and saying, "Orlando! Orlando, you wish to die of the wet? Orlando, come in!"

There was considerable telephoning, and Mrs. Massey and Mrs. Dalrymple and Clarissa and Enid got it all fixed up between them that he was an Italian tenor in love with Madam Parka and probably oughtn't to be there, exactly. Mrs. Dalrymple said it would be better not to tell Mrs. Bullfinch, and I guess she didn't—not until after she'd hung up on our number and got connected with the Bullfinches'.

It didn't stop raining until about the middle of the afternoon; then the sun came out bright and warm, and, right after that, sitting in our living-room with the windows open, Mrs. Massey and I heard a piano going next door, something wonderful, and a soprano voice that I thought at first was a flute, only it turned out to be a good deal too powerful for a flute. "Practising," Mrs. Massey told me. "I wonder if I oughtn't to go over there and call when she gets through. It really would be the cordial thing to be a little neighborly, I think. Even if the other women here decide not to know her, I do believe I——"

But right there she stopped, because the piano broke off with a kind of crashing and the voice that was singing did much the same; it began to shout in some foreign language, fairly pouring the words out and almost yelling. "Goodness me!" Mrs. Massey said, and, looking out of the window, we saw the Bullfinches' limousine just driving away from in front of the Ballinger cottage.

"Well, I don't know," Mrs. Massey said, after a minute, looking thoughtful. "Perhaps I'd better put off calling until she's had more time to get settled." So we went for a drive instead, and when we got home again, toward evening, Mrs. Weeder came over from her porch, where she'd been waiting for a chance to talk about what had been happening with somebody that hadn't already heard.

It seemed Mrs. Bullfinch had decided to call upon Madam Parka just about the minute the rain stopped and had been informed that Madam Parka was not at home. "Though, as she told me later over the telephone," Mrs. Weeder went on, "she could hear Madam Parka fairly screeching at the maid all the time she was standing at the door. Well, of course I didn't know anything about how Mrs. Bullfinch had been received until later, and neither did Mrs. Dalrymple. Mrs. Dalrymple and I decided to call together, and a maid came to the door and took our cards but told us in a most insolent way, we both thought, that Madam Parka was not at home. The same thing precisely happened to Mrs. Allstover, Mrs. Ruckleboy, Mrs. Timberlake and Mrs. Carmichael, because Mrs. Dalrymple and I were sitting on her porch and saw them go up to the door and come right away, and we talked to them afterwards."

"Well, that doesn't seem so terrible," Mrs. Massey said, a little surprised probably by the excited tone of voice Mrs. Weeder was using. "It isn't so very unusual for people to——"

"Listen!" Mrs. Weeder said. "A little while after I went home from Mrs. Dalrymple's, I was called to the telephone by Mr. Jackson. He said he had a message for me that he didn't like to deliver but his life wouldn't be worth living unless he did it. He said that about every half hour since Madam Parka's arrival he'd been called up from that cottage on account of the plumbing or the furniture or the mattresses or a door's having a squeak in it or goodness knows what; he'd had to come up there five different times, and the last time was the worst. He apologized and said he supposed the best thing was to lay the case before the ladies who had called upon Madam Parka that afternoon; she'd given him our cards and absolutely insisted that he should inform every one of us that she'd come to Mary's Neck because she'd heard it was an obscure place without any social attractions and where she could find perfect quiet. She wished the ladies who had called to inform all the other ladies in the place that she preferred to make no acquaintances and would not submit to any lionizing whatever and that it had better be understood that she didn't accept dinner invitations and then sing to give pleasure. Mr. Jackson said he was minimizing the expressions she used, at that; but he thought probably it would be better, especially for himself, if word were passed around for no more ladies to call. I told him he needn't worry!"

"I should think not!" Mrs. Massey said, looking a little flushed. "I should think not, indeed!"

"Mrs. Bullfinch is the most upset of all," Mrs. Weeder told us. "She says she never would have dreamed of going, especially with that Italian tenor, Orlando, in the house; but she thought she ought to on account of Mr. Bullfinch's second cousin's having been kind to this Fanny Parker when she was struggling. We all feel that a deliberate insult has been offered to Mary's Neck, and from now on the only thing to do is to simply and absolutely ignore her."

Well, that seemed sensible to me, and I supposed the ladies of Mary's Neck would go ahead and carry out the idea, which shows I didn't understand much about what ladies mean when they speak of ignoring. If ignoring a person is making her pretty nearly your sole topic of conversation, then Mary's Neck ignored Madam Parka; and, when she came to the beach the day after the rain and the rebuffing, the Neck ignored her so hard that it almost choked in a large simultaneous gasp.

She got out of a limousine, already in her bathing-suit, with Orlando and a maid dressed like the ones you see on the stage and six little white fuzzy dogs; and this procession, with the chauffeur coming along to keep the dogs in line, walked down across the beach to the edge of the surf, while Mary's Neck kept on giving the gasp I've just mentioned. One of the little dogs stopped to take quite an interest in a spaniel of Mrs. Weeder's that was sitting by me, and, when I shooed him away, Madam Parka caught him up in her arms and kissed him spang on the mouth, so I got a good look at her.

She was kind of surprising; you might say startling—not a bit like anybody else. She had the brightest big black eyes I ever saw, and the most black hair wound around her head, and she was so handsome it kind of made you nervous; she was pretty tall, with almost too much figure, as you might say, and her complexion seemed to be almost too white—maybe because nearly all of it was on view, which is striking, you might say, in a large person. She was wearing something of a bright green jersey, and, besides that, she had on high-heeled, bright green rubber slippers, and a bright red silk robe was blowing back from her on the wind.

She kissed that little fuzzy dog about four more times right on the mouth; then she ran down to the foamy edge of the water and gave Orlando the dog and her cloak to hold, while the maid fixed a black bathing-cap on her head. She went into the surf about the way other people do, took dives through a couple of waves, came out, the maid rubbed her a while with some big towels, Orlando put her cloak on her shoulders, and the procession trotted up across the beach, got into her limousine and drove away.

Until then, from the time it had arrived, I don't believe anybody on the beach, except the children, had spoken ten words; but the buzzing was something tumultuous, once it did break out. I couldn't see, though, why the ladies—Mrs. Bullfinch especially—seemed to feel that this episode constituted another deliberate affront to Mary's Neck. Madam Parka certainly had a right to go in bathing if she wanted to and she didn't wear any particular amount less costume than nearly all the others. She wasn't fat but there was a great deal of her, so to speak, and I've noticed at the beach that the more there is of a person the less there seems to be of these bathing-suits they wear. I mean to say girls like Clarissa and Enid could play around in the surf and on the sand without anything over their backs or much on anywhere and it just seemed natural and lively; but Madam Parka, undressed the same way, was maybe so statuesque and spectacular it made people feel kind of self-conscious. That wasn't her fault, though; she hadn't done anything out of the way or even taken any notice of anybody, and if these great artists like to kiss pet dogs it's certainly their own business. So I asked Mrs. Bullfinch about it;—she was frowning and breathing hard, with her lips all pinched up.

"Absolutely hardened insolence!" she told me, looking at me as if she thought there was something pretty wrong about me for not knowing. "Exhibiting herself before us in that state, after sending us the outrageous messages she did—yes, and daring to flaunt her disreputable little Italian tenor, Orlando, right in our faces!" Then she went on, getting more severe. "Has Mrs.

Massey heard that you're going around defending this Miss Fanny Parker, Mr. Massey?"

That made me a little huffy and I said I wasn't defending her and wasn't even going around, which of course didn't do me any good especially, with Mrs. Bullfinch. A few minutes later she alluded to me as the "knight-defender and champion" but not with any pleasantness in how she said it; and then she asked me kind of poison-ously, calling across Mrs. Massey to do it, if I didn't wish I could sing tenor in Italian and be named Orlando. Mr. Bullfinch took the same position she did about it; he looked kind of pompous and moral and said he didn't see how anybody could stand up for an American woman like this Fanny Parker when she behaved as she did in the presence of her fellow countrywomen. "For my part," he said, "I don't like it, and, what's more, I resent it on Mrs. Bullfinch's account. When this Fanny Parker ex-hibits her Italian tenor in my wife's presence, I tell you frankly I resent it!"

Everybody seemed to feel he'd made a mighty credit-able statement of the rights of the case and deserved a good deal of praise for it, so he went all around to the different families and groups of people, saying the same thing over and getting himself pretty comfortably puffed up and self-satisfied—a good deal at my expense, I might say, because both Clarissa and Enid heard him doing it at different points on the beach and spoke of it later at lunch. They said he had a kind of preface for his quota-tion of himself. "I told Massey," he'd begin, "I told Massey, as I'd tell anyone else that attempted to excuse her, 'I don't like it on my own account and I resent it on my wife's!' That's what I told Massey."

So you see, right from the start, I was getting to be kind of the goat, you might call it, and Eddie Bullfinch hadn't been mistaken at all. One of the queerest things about it was that this Orlando wasn't an Italian—he wasn't even a tenor. The very evening of that first day Madam Parka came to the beach and Mr. Bullfinch gathered so much credit over what he'd told Massey, I was out looking over Mrs. Massey's garden—Mr. Sweetmus being not there that late, or I wouldn't have been. I noticed Orlando looking over the hedge, so I thought it wouldn't be any harm to nod to him, and, as soon as I did, he surprised me considerably.

"Look here," he said, and his voice certainly wasn't any Italian's. "Aren't you from Logansville, Illinois? Didn't you use to be the president of the Light and Power Company out there about fifteen years ago?"

"My goodness!" I told him. "Yes, I use' to be, and I still am."

"I guess you don't remember me," he said. "I was living in Mattoon, myself; but Sundays I use' to sing baritone in the Second Presbyterian Church choir at Logansville, and I know your face like a book. Your pew was fourth from the altar on the left side of the middle aisle."

"It certainly was," I told him. "Well, I'll be doggoned! How in the world did you ever happen to land here in Mary's Neck like this?"

Well right there he told me all about it. It seems he was local agent in Mattoon, where he grew up, for the American Farm Implements Corporation; then he got to be state agent, and, after that, they sent him to Europe to supervise their agencies over there. As he was sort of a musical person himself he got acquainted with Madam Parka in some place that I can't pronounce where she was singing, not being as prominent then as she got later, and pretty soon they married each other. They'd been married twelve years, he told me, and he'd had to give up his business to look after her interests; but it paid, he told me.

"She's from California, isn't she?" I asked him.

"No," he said. "She's a Croat."

I didn't know what he meant, and I don't yet, except that it couldn't be any kind of a Californian. His name was Orlando, though, which was the one single thing Mary's Neck got right—Orlando M. Wilcox, related to the Wilcox family of Logansville. "I'd always spend the rest of Sunday at their house while I was a member of the Second Presbyterian Church choir," he told me. "Old Uncle George Wilcox and I use' to play checkers straight through the afternoon until time for my train to Mattoon."

"My, my!" I said, and I laughed. "Was George Wilcox your uncle? I declare! Old Dew-Dew Wilcox!"

"'Dew-Dew'?" Orlando asked me. "I heard Uncle George use' to be called that around Logansville; but he never would tell me why."

"No?" I said. "He was a mighty fine likeable man but never did anything much in his life except just play checkers around and had the idea he played a pretty strong game. Somebody asked him about it one day and he said, 'Well, maybe I don't dew so much; but what I dew dew I dew dew well.' Never lived it down, and there use' to be people out home that thought 'Dew-Dew' was really his christened name. Yes, sir; Dew-Dew Wilcox never got over the idea he was pretty strong at the game."

"That's true," Orlando told me. "I remember his telling me once that you were the only checker-player in Logansville he couldn't give the first move to and beat."

Well, at that, I kind of laughed. "I should say he

couldn't!" I said. "Old Dew-Dew Wilcox never was a tournament player."

"Do you play much here?" Orlando asked me.

"Goodness, no! Mary's Neck's nothing but bridge and backgammon, which I don't play; though of course my wife and daughters——"

"I've got a checker-board," he told me; and it struck me right then that he'd been looking at me in a kind of wistful manner all along. "Being associated mainly with musical people," he said, "I don't get many chances to play, either; but I always do carry a board and a box of checker-men with me in case anything might turn up. I suppose you're probably busy this evening, aren't you?"

I told him no, and that settled it; we didn't lose any more time but went into the Ballinger cottage—I didn't see Madam Parka because she was upstairs somewhere— and he got out his board and box of checkers and asked me if I'd mind playing in the kitchen. "She can't stand smoke in any part of the house except the kitchen," he said. "We can smoke all we want to out there and be right cosy."

CHAPTER XX

I COULDN'T have asked for anything better, myself, especially as he turned out to be a genuine checker-player and was seven games ahead when we quit at eleven o'clock because I thought Mrs. Massey might be getting anxious about me. She wasn't, as it turned out; but when I mentioned where I'd been spending the evening she and Clarissa and Enid got pretty nearly beside themselves, they were so excited.

Of course they knew I was telling the truth about Orlando and everything, naturally, and you'd certainly have supposed that anybody on earth would have known the same thing; but next morning when we went to the beach and I told Mrs. Dalrymple, Mr. and Mrs. Weeder and Mr. and Mrs. Bullfinch all about Orlando's being named Wilcox, and Madam Parka's being Mrs. Wilcox and not from California but a Croat or something, and how he used to sing baritone in the Second Presbyterian Church in Logansville and everything, they took it in a mighty peculiar way.

Mrs. Dalrymple and Mrs. Weeder began whispering together, and, as for Mr. and Mrs. Bullfinch, you'd have thought I was pretty nearly saying something offensive.

"Do you mean you're trying to tell us," she asked me in a tone I didn't like at all;—"do you mean you're trying to tell us that they deny she's Fanny Parker from Oakland and he's a low Italian tenor?"

"Why, certainly," I said, showing some irritation, maybe. "I mean I'm not 'trying' to tell you, I am telling you."

"Oh, Mr. Massey!" she came back, and she shook her head at me and gave a teasing laugh, the way my Aunt Pansy used to do that didn't like me much when I was a boy. Ordinarily Mrs. Bullfinch was a right agreeable woman; but she didn't seem to feel so on this subject. "No, I think not," she went on. "It's a little too stiff, Mr. Massey. People aren't named Orlando and Wilcox at the same time—not even in the Middle West. I'm afraid you slipped up there, Mr. Massey."

And Mr. Bullfinch said, "It won't do, Massey; it won't do. You're not as gullible as you'd like us to think!"

Well, I was a good deal put out but tried to show I was good-natured by laughing as if I thought they were joking. I tried to tell them all about it again, the way you do when people don't seem to believe you, and this time Mr. Carmichael came up and listened and shook his head, and said he couldn't help agreeing with Mr. Bullfinch and Mrs. Carmichael that this Fanny Parker and her tenor ought never to have been allowed at Mary's Neck or anywhere near.

"It's the young people I'm thinking of," he said. "I'm a man of the world myself and so is my wife; but we have a daughter. She's my daughter and as her father I don't like that sort of thing in her presence; I don't like it. Even though she's too young to understand it yet, everybody says nowadays that all these impressions come out on children during their adolescence and later life and injure them. No, sir, if these things have to be carried on, they oughtn't to be carried on where our children can see them. When they thrust themselves in our children's faces like this, Massey, I protest."

Then Mrs. Bullfinch shook her head at me again and said, "Not Wilcox, Mr. Massey; not with Orlando. Scarcely!"

That's the way they took it; but if I'd thought the thing over sensibly I needn't have been so surprised. Most of us are able to believe almost anything fantastic about people we aren't really well acquainted with or have only looked at or seen something about in the newspapers. Besides, when the newspapers print something mistaken but interesting about somebody else, we don't care to pay much attention to the victim's contradictions; yet if something like that gets into print about ourselves we're shocked that anybody's so foolish and so unacquainted with our true characters as to credit it. I might add that a summer resort's a great place for believing anything, because, though most of the people get fairly intimate, the intimacy's only for some weeks of each year and naturally has room for a good deal of curiosity in it.

So I couldn't make any headway at all just relating the simple facts about Madam Parka and Orlando, because in the first place the beach had got its own impressions so fixed in its mind that it might as well have had cotton in its ears, and in the second it was so wild over the messages Mr. Jackson had delivered from Madam Parka (which was pretty natural of course) it wouldn't have let George Washington himself talk it out of anything it was bound to think it had on her. The more I kept insisting, the more those people seemed kind of irritatedly skeptical towards myself, and kept whispering together. They were practically unpleasant about it, I thought, and the whole thing got me to feeling so pettish that I was grumpy all day, and in the evening I told Mrs. Massey I believed I'd cut going to the beach for a little while.

"I will, too," she said, because of course she was sympathetic. "I didn't think those people acted very nicely about what you told them, myself, and all this talk about Madam Parka is getting rather tiresome. Are you going to play checkers with Mr. Wilcox again this evening?"

Well, I had thought of it; so pretty soon I went outdoors, and he was standing in front of the Ballinger cottage, kind of waiting around for me. "Kitchen's all ready," he said. "I was thinking maybe we'd play more on an even basis if I allowed you first move every game."

Of course that stung me in a sensitive spot, you might say—as I considered myself fully his equal and maybe superior; but we played four evenings until close to midnight before I could convince him he'd better not give me first move as a regular proceeding, and, as it happened, it wasn't until then that I even caught a glimpse of Mrs. Wilcox. That is to say, I mean Madam Parka of course. All of a sudden there was a yapping of dogs and she came sailing into the kitchen in a red and orange and green and yellow and purple and magenta wrapper, with three dogs in her arms and the rest jumping and barking around her. She was chattering to them in her big voice and kissing them with loud smacks; and anyhow whenever she came into a room it seemed a good deal as if the Fire Department was arriving. Orlando introduced me and she made quite a fuss over me, as I could see she usually did over everything. She certainly hadn't learned to speak our language in California, either.

"You are bootifuls for my Orlando!" she told me, and that was the way she said it. "He goes lonely sometime' and you are bootifuls old friend of him to play him some jaker." That's what she called checkers; "jaker" was as near as she could get.

She put down a couple of the dogs and gave me about a dozen pats on the back, praising me some more about the jaker; and she kissed Orlando five or six times, calling him her sweet rooster and her poor little cockatoo, and said she was going to make us a raggoo or something. She did it, too; she cooked up a dish, mostly onions but with a good deal of pretty much everything else in it, singing and stopping to kiss the dogs and Orlando all the time; then she poured it out in two plates for Orlando and me, gave me some more pats on the back, and said, "You are bootifuls for the jaker, my Massey!" That's what she called me, "my Massey". Then she told us to eat quietly and play all the jaker we wanted to but without noise, because she was going to bed, and sailed out with the dogs.

Orlando was pleased; he laughed and said in a kind of lowered voice, "She likes you; she's taken a fancy to you. I'd never think of eating this raggoo if she hadn't."

"My goodness! Why not?" I asked him.

"Because," he told me, "she might have put something in this raggoo that wouldn't agree with us if she didn't like you. She's a terrible practical joker; but always mighty nice to people she likes."

It didn't take long to see he was right about that; she was foreign and peculiar but mighty nice—a big, warmhearted woman, liable to fly off the handle, maybe, but affectionate and fond of laughing. She made us a raggoo every night after that. Once, when she finished it, she began to sing and dance, and I never did see anything like the way she went spinning around that kitchen until she ended by plopping down on Orlando's lap and pretty well obliterating him. You couldn't see him at all; but could tell he was trying to get out, and she laughed till I thought the neighbors would come in.

"Frolicsome," he told me, after she'd left us. "She's always been a mighty frolicsome woman; but that's got nothing to do with checkers." So we went at it again, and it was so much nip-and-tuck between us we played till pretty nearly two o'clock.

He let me out the kitchen door, warning me to keep on the grass instead of the gravel path that led around the house, so I went tiptoeing out to the front gate, and just before I got there I noticed four people standing on the board side-walk in front of the Dalrymples' gate, talking. It was Mr. and Mrs. Dalrymple and Mr. and Mrs. Weeder who had been to some card-party in the neighborhood probably and had walked home together and were just saying good-night. I was going to speak to them when I thought maybe I'd better not—they didn't seem to have noticed me, because it was pretty dark, and from where they were standing they couldn't have seen any light in the Ballinger cottage, so they might have wondered what I was doing prowling around there at that time of night. On this account I just went across the Ballinger front lawn, pushed through the hedge and let myself into the side door of our cottage with a latch-key.

Mrs. Massey was awake when I got upstairs and pretty cross with me. "I ought to know by this time, though, that it's waste of breath to talk to you," she ended. "You never have had any consideration for your health and getting your natural sleep when you've got one of your checker seizures on you."

Orlando and I'd been playing every evening for ten days or so and he'd gone out several afternoons in the Wanda with me and we were having nice sociable times together; then one evening after the last game, he asked me if I'd mind doing a little favor for him—he had to take the midnight train to New York, he said, and be there all the next day on some operatic business for his wife and he'd be obliged to me if I'd escort her over to the beach, since he couldn't do it himself. "She likes to have somebody with her besides a maid and chauffeur," he told me, "because it helps to keep strangers from coming up and speaking to her, which is always liable to send her into sort of a tantrum. She's taken a big liking to you—she really has—and so I thought if you wouldn't mind——"

"Mind? No!" I told him, because the truth was I felt flattered and pleased with the idea. "I consider it a privilege."

That was the way I thought of it at first; but later when I got home I began to feel maybe I was going to look a little conspicuous at the beach next morning. Mrs. Massey said she thought I probably would, but laughed and told me to be brave. She was sorry she and the girls would have to miss it, she said; but they were going on an all-day sailing-party with Bush Thring and Eddie and Janey and George Bullfinch and some other young people. "Stop fretting," Mrs. Massey told me, after I'd gone on talking to her about it some more. "If you feel conspicuous, don't let anybody see it; just act as if you'd spent half your life escorting great Prima Donnas around Logansville."

It was good advice; but, sitting with Madam Parka and her maid and the dogs in her car, next morning, I began to feel doubtful about being able to act upon it. I'd got pretty well used to Madam Parka by this time; but there was something about her always kind of overpowering, you might say, especially in her bathing-costume, and anyhow every little thing she did seemed to be about five or ten times more vigorous than the same thing done by ordinary people. She thanked me for escorting her, as if I were doing something enormous, and kept calling me "my Massey" and telling me I was a "bootiful mans" to be such a friend to her Orlando. Finally, when we got to the beach, she handed me one of the dogs to carry, having another one, herself; then took my arm and started the procession down to the water.

When I realized how many people were looking at us, I don't suppose there was a more embarrassed man in the United States, and yet, walking down across the beach, leaving everybody staring behind us, wasn't half the trial that the rest of my escorting turned out to be. Mr. and Mrs. Bullfinch and Mr. and Mrs. Weeder and Mrs. Dalrymple and Mrs. Allstover, and four or five other middle-aged people, were sitting together in the group that made me feel the most self-conscious. I pretended not to see them; but when we'd gone by them I could feel their eyes like about a dozen ice-poultices plastered up and down my spine. Then I got into kind of a hot stew all over because it was high tide and Madam Parka stopped and handed me her red silk robe right straight in front of those people and only about forty feet from them. She gave me the dog she was carrying, besides, so I had two, and she told me not to put them down because those two weren't well and mustn't get their feet wet; then she went in the water and left me standing there.

Well, sir, I don't believe I could have turned around to save my life, and, as for that row of people behind me, standing in front of them gave me something like the feeling a paralysed person would have in front of an express train. Of course I knew it was ridiculous of me to be that self-conscious, and yet if I'd realized beforehand how things were going to be, I certainly never would have told Orlando Wilcox I'd do this favor for him.

When Madam Parka came out of the water, you could see she felt just splendid; she was kind of dancing and capering, and, after her maid had rubbed her with the towels, she was even livelier. She had the four little dogs that were on the ground all frisking and barking around her; then she grabbed the two I was carrying, kissed them—spang on their mouths, the way she always did—and said they must kiss me to thank me for holding them. I didn't like the idea and was trying to back away, being kind of scared because I could see she was in such high spirits she was getting frolicsome, as Orlando called it; but I might just as well have tried to back away from an affectionate race-horse that wanted to play with me.

She was holding the two little dogs with her left arm and pulled my head right down on their faces with her other hand. "Kees my Massey!" she said. "Poo-poo and Too-too mus' kees my Massey! Kees! Kees! Kees!"

Then she made me put her silk robe on her, turned me around, tucked my arm under hers in a fond, powerful way and ran me back across the beach for her car. She ran me pretty nearly on top of Mr. and Mrs. Bullfinch and those others, we went so close to them. All of them looked red and sort of intense, it seemed to me, the way people do when they feel they're insulted to their faces, and I couldn't take off my hat because she'd put a dog back on my left arm and was holding my right one so tightly. I gave them kind of a hurried, feeblish smile and nod but didn't look long enough to see if any of them responded. "My Massey, you are bootiful mans!" Madam Parka was shouting. "Bootiful mans, my Massey!" she shouted, and I couldn't much doubt that a good many people heard her calling me that, in spite of the noise the ocean was making, because she naturally has a pretty remarkable voice. I certainly felt relieved when I'd got her back to her cottage and was able to flop down in the hammock on my own front porch.

Well, Orlando's trip to New York didn't do his game any good; he'd found out that he and his wife would have to be leaving Mary's Neck almost right away for some western concert engagements before the opera season, and the thought of departure must have thrown him off his form. I beat him nine games straight, the night after he got back, and in his disgrace he turned out to be pretty unphilosophical, because he followed me out to the front gate explaining how accidental the whole thing had been. Of course I taunted him some, and he shook his fist at me as I went on toward our cottage. "You come over here to-morrow night," he said, keeping his voice down, of course, for fear of waking Madam Parka up. "I'll show you who's the best man!"

It seemed to me a pity that he was going away so soon after I'd made myself his master, and I wasn't the only one in our family to be sorry that the Wilcoxes were leaving. Clarissa, it seems, had developed what Enid called a crush on the great Prima Donna, and, the morning after Orlando's checker disgrace, Clarissa left a big bunch of flowers at the door of the Ballinger cottage, and pretty soon Madam Parka sent a maid over for her to come and be thanked. Clarissa had a grand time because Madam Parka took one of her fancies to her, asked her to come back to lunch, kept her with her all afternoon and sang for her and took her for a drive, and then kept her for dinner, too. So that the way Clarissa told us about it when she came home you'd have thought she was the most intimate friend Madam Parka had in the world.

She was even more so the next day because the same thing happened. Clarissa didn't come home until after dinner, when I was just about to go over and give Orlando another lesson. She told her mother and me Madam Parka asked her to call her Fiametta, which Clarissa certainly did, and, as she talked on, it was all Fiametta this and Fiametta that. "I think Fiametta would rather like Enid, too," Clarissa said. "I don't mean to say that Fiametta would ever feel the same intimacy with her that she does with me, because Enid's too young of course; but she said I could bring Enid over before they go, and I'm sure Fiametta'll be lovely to her."

Enid had been out for dinner, too; but just then she walked in and she heard the last of what Clarissa was saying. "No, thank you," she said. "I guess the Massey family had better be a little careful about getting mixed up any more than they are with Madam Fiametta Parka!"

She said it in a snappy kind of excited way, and her mother and Clarissa both asked her what on earth she meant by such a speech. So she told us; and by the time she got through I wished she hadn't.

CHAPTER XXI

SHE'D been to dinner at the Bullfinches'. Mrs. Dalrymple was there and got so busy talking up at Mrs. Bullfinch's end of the table that for a minute she must have forgotten Enid, because she raised her voice and Enid heard the words, "Mr. Massey's misbehavior."

Mrs. Bullfinch stopped Mrs. Dalrymple there; but after dinner Enid got Eddie alone and asked him if he knew what his mother and Mrs. Dalrymple had been talking about, and he said he did because everybody did but he preferred not to tell, except it was something about Madam Parka and a whole lot of talk about that Italian Orlando's being jealous and going to kill somebody, Eddie didn't wish to say who, except that it was a person that had been going there after dark all the time and was often seen crawling out through the hedge pretty late. Enid asked him why Orlando was going to kill this person, and he told her because Mrs. Dalrymple had been sitting by her window one night lately and heard Orlando telling the person in a hoarse voice that if he came round there any more he'd fix him. Then Enid asked Eddie whose hedge the person was supposed to crawl through, and he got so tangled up with the questions she put to him as fast as she could that he had to tell her the whole thing right out. I was the person Eddie hadn't wished to mention; but the whole of Mary's Neck was just seething about it, he said, and Enid had come straight home to tell us.

You could see Enid was pretty indignant but expected to make a big sensation in the family, and she was fairly successful, except with her mother. Mrs. Massey was a little kind of mad at first, maybe; but more struck with the absurdity of the thing and inclined to take it as a good deal of a joke on me. I couldn't see it in that light, myself; I began to feel pretty upset, and the way both Clarissa and Enid took the story didn't make me any less so. Clarissa was furious; she said it was an insult to Fiametta who if she hadn't been so absolutely devoted to Mr. Wilcox could have practically all the attractive men in the United States trailing after her, and Enid said yes, that was what mortified her so and made her most indignant, having all the older people in Mary's Neck talking about her father's making an exhibition of himself over Madam Parka when anybody under forty would know of course Madam Parka wouldn't look at him, even if she didn't like her husband. "Even Eddie Bullfinch himself didn't believe the part of the story about Orlando's getting jealous," she told us.

Both girls got so excited and talked so loudly that afterwhile their mother shooed them out of there because they weren't doing me any good and she could see that I was getting more and more upset. She was trying to cover up a good deal of amusement inside herself, which didn't soothe me particularly, and pretty soon she asked me if I wasn't going over to play checkers with Orlando; but I couldn't do it. The truth is, I was all stirred up and the more I thought about the talk that was going around the worse I felt. I'd been Chairman of that House Committee and of course I knew there'd been criticism; but I had never experienced any of this Don Lothario kind of talk about myself before in my whole life, and it made me feel as mean as if I'd got caught doing something silly. Of course I knew there wasn't any sense in feeling like that; but reasoning doesn't help a man much in such a situation. It seems to me our feelings most of the time ignore the facts and when they get off the track, as they're as likely to do as not, they just go on behaving of their own free will and neglecting all care of their rightful owners until another set of feelings comes along and bumps 'em aside and takes the right of way over 'em. They don't care a plugged nickel for all the common sense in the world.

My condition was low all night. I didn't sleep a great deal and I kept waking up as if I'd just tried to jump out of the way of wild animals that couldn't keep their minds off of me. Then in the morning I had breakfast alone and didn't feel any better. Mrs. Massey and Enid had started out about daylight to go deep-sea fishing with Eddie Bullfinch and wouldn't be back till lunch-time; Clarissa'd had her breakfast and wasn't in the house; but I was glad not to have to talk to anybody, maybe most of all my own family. Afterwards I tried to read the newspapers in the living-room but did more walking up and down until along toward noon. Then, just as I was thinking what an undesirable coincidence it was that I'd taken Bush Thring's place as an outcast in the community, Clarissa came skipping in, her cheeks flushed up and her eyes bright as brass. She told me I had to go to the beach with her.

"You're crazy," I said. "I couldn't any more go over there and face all those——"

"Yes, you will!" she said. "Fiametta says it's the only thing to do, and you've got to!"

"Fiametta says so?" I asked her, my voice kind of hoarse. "Fiametta!"

"She's grand!" Clarissa told me. "I was afraid she'd be terribly offended—of course she got it all out of me, right the first thing when I went over there this morning."

"What?" I said, because when I heard this I felt as if I'd eaten something alive that had got active inside of me. "Why, my goodness!"

"Oh, she wasn't offended at all!" Clarissa told me. "I thought of course she'd be furious; but she was perfectly marvellous! She wasn't even offended by Mr. Bullfinch's having spread the story around that her real name was Fanny Parker from Oakland, California, or that Mr. Wilcox is some Italian. When I told her all the part about you, Father, and what they are saying, she gave a kind of big scream, so that I was frightened for a minute; but she threw her arms around me and began waltzing with me and singing the Blue Danube. Father, you've never seen anybody so perfectly ecstatic in your life! She made me tell Mr. Wilcox all about it, too; then she kissed him and all the dogs and me about forty times and made me dance with her some more. Then she told me I had to bring you to the beach; she said if I didn't, she'd come over and get you, herself, and take you there."

"I won't do it!" I said, "I couldn't—I can't! I won't do it!"

I argued and protested; but finally I did it. I did it partly because I was afraid to face those people—the way I felt then, they were just about ruining me—but I was afraid to have them think I was afraid or ashamed or something. Mostly though, I went because I didn't put it past Madam Parka to march into our cottage and drag me out to her car and take me over there with her. Her manner of listening to this Don Lothario gossip that involved herself—waltzing and singing and laughing and kissing the dogs and everybody—struck me as mighty astonishing. "How on earth could she take it that way?" I kept asking myself, sitting beside Clarissa in her runabout. How could such a thing not have any effect on Madam Parka except to almost tickle her to death?

It must have been something like telepathy when Clarissa gave me the answer. She was kind of partly giggling to herself all the way; then of a sudden she broke out almost as if I'd spoken my question. "You see, Father," she said, "Fiametta doesn't care any more about what these people say than if they were Fiji Islanders!"

That seemed to be the solution. Madam Parka regarded herself as out of their class entirely, superior to them, so nothing they said could do anything to her except make her laugh, and I was able to see that a person doesn't mind talk if the talkers seem to him about like Fiji Islanders, as Clarissa said. But that wasn't my case—far from it!—and when we got to the beach I was so nervous and timid and overwhelmed, as you might say, by thinking of all the people that would be staring at me and chattering about me, I made Clarissa keep to the rear edge of the sand with me, quite a distance behind the crowd, and walked clear up to the other end of the beach, where we kind of stood around, I feeling miserable and she making a fuss.

"This isn't where Fiametta wants you, Father," she told me. "Fiametta said you had to walk right in front of those people, and you'd better do it before she comes!"

"I can't!" I told her. "Anyhow not right now. Just give me a few minutes to——"

But Clarissa interrupted me. "Look!" she said, pointing. "Fiametta's there now! Mr. Wilcox isn't with her and she's standing there, looking for us. You've got to come or else be left poking around alone, because I'm going!"

She started right off and I felt pretty desperate but didn't see anything to do except trail along with her. Madam Parka was standing at the edge of the water, looking around for us, as Clarissa said, and when she saw us she waved her hand for us to hurry, so we did. When we came up to her, she didn't say a word; she just threw me her red robe, splashed into the surf, frolicking around about a minute, then came out, and, while her maid was rubbing her, asked Clarissa a question that seemed to me a natural one, under the circumstances.

"Weech olt rascal is zat Boolveetch weech sinks I am his Fenny Polliker of Kellyfornie?" she said.

Clarissa looked around to where Mr. and Mrs. Bullfinch, the Weeders, Mrs. Dalrymple, Mrs. Allstover, the Blodgetts and some of the others I was most scared of, were sitting on the sand a little way behind us. "It's that red-faced, cross-looking man at the end on the left."

"We go there," Madam Parka said. "We speak weez olt Boolveetch, my Clarissa Massey."

"Look here!" I said, and was trying to back away; but Madam Parka took me by the arm and marched me straight up to those people. You couldn't do anything when she did that.

Clarissa ran up to Mr. Bullfinch. "Madam Parka wants to speak to you," she said, and he got up, frowning. "Who?" he asked her. "*Who* wants to speak to me?"

But Madam Parka was already right in front of him.

She dropped my arm and grabbed both of his hands, with Mrs. Bullfinch and all the others kind of stirring around on the sand and making sounds with just their breath.

"Boolveetch!" Madam Parka said in her grand, big voice. "Sweet, sweet Boolveetch! Ah-ha, sweet olt rascal Boolveetch, you mus' not let your Meesuz Boolveetch hear how you slip to my house when she is not been looking! No one but me and you s'all know you still loaf your dear Fenny Polliker of Kellyfornie so much! Ah, never forget your Fenny!" Then, before he could move, she seized him round the neck and kissed him with a good deal of noise.

"Sweet Boolveetch!" she said. "Sweet, sweet Boolveetch!" And then, just as a kind of gasping broke out pretty much everywhere, and while I was standing almost as kerflummixed myself as Mr. Bullfinch was, she gave him another pretty loud kiss—it was on the side of his nose—and ran up the beach with her red robe flying behind her and her six little white dogs streaking after her.

CHAPTER XXII

CLARISSA and I didn't stay there, either; we got away in the runabout pretty close after Madam Parka's limousine, and she was looking out of the back window, throwing kisses to us. My condition was too astonished for me to be able to respond much, although I already began to have sensations of relief from my troubles, I couldn't tell just why. "What on earth did she do such a thing as that for?" I said.

Clarissa was laughing almost too much to talk. "She's grand! She certainly stirred up the Fiji Islanders for you, Father!"

"For me?" I asked her.

"Why, yes, do you think anybody'll have the slightest interest in that crazy gossip about you *now?* After what's happened to Mr. Bullfinch!"

She kept on laughing, and I began to see what she meant. In fact, I was feeling almost fairly comfortable again, and I felt even more so when Mrs. Massey and Enid got back from their deep-sea fishing about two o'clock and Clarissa and I told them about it. Mrs. Massey laughed but couldn't take much interest—she was too anxious to get upstairs and lie down some more—but Enid was delighted because now, she said, she had some-

thing to tell Eddie Bullfinch about *his* father. She took a narrow view of the matter, I thought, and when Eddie came along pretty soon, bringing back a lunch-basket that hadn't been well patronized, and three dead codfish with it, he didn't show any intelligence at all. He just absently asked Clarissa what in the world Madam Parka wanted to kiss his father for and said he guessed he'd better hop on home and get cleaned up;—but Mr. Bullfinch himself didn't share his son's indifference.

He came in to see me about an hour after the fishing-party's return, and he looked about ten years older than he had that morning. "Why, this is a terrible thing, Massey," he said, as we sat down. "A terrible thing. I don't know how much part you had in it——"

"Not any, Mr. Bullfinch," I told him. "Not any. I was just a spectator."

"I'm glad to hear it, because if you'd had anything to do with it I intended to demand a written statement exonerating me. I would have telegraphed my lawyer to come here and force a retraction from Madam Parka; but Mrs. Bullfinch said that obviously the woman is crazy and heaven knows what she might allege. It's a most annoying situation, Massey."

"See here," I said, "you don't mean to say anybody's taking the thing seriously, do you? For instance, Mrs. Dalrymple and the Weeders and Allstovers and——"

"Listen!" he said, and he gave a kind of shiver. "You haven't the slightest idea of the credulity of people in this place! Why, the nonsense about me that is already going around——"

"Well, but why should it bother you?" I asked him. "You know it's unwarranted yourself and so do your family, and as for the gossip itself, don't you suppose it kind of helps to pass the summer for the people that

spread it? What's the use getting all worked up about a thing like that?"

"You take it mighty calmly," he said. "Of course you know you've been in it, too, Massey. There's been talk about you in that connection. You may not have heard it but——"

"Oh, yes, here and there," I told him. "I heard something of it—just rumors. But in my case, you see, everybody knew it was idle gossip because of course nothing happened to me, the way it did to you this morning on the beach. They'll forget all about my playing checkers with her husband now because now they've got something to get their teeth in. I don't want to be too officious; but I thought all along it was a mistake for you to bring up the fact that you used to know her as Fanny Parker in your old California days."

"What!" he said pretty fiercely, and he half started up as if he intended to leave the house that instant; but he sank back again with kind of a loudish groan. "Oh, my!" he said. "So that's the way it's going around now! Look here, Massey, I give you my word I've never been in California but once in my life and then Mrs. Bullfinch was with me, and my son, George, was a baby and sick the whole time we were there. I never left his side and Mrs. Bullfinch knows it and can prove it. In the first place I never said I knew this Parker woman; I said it was my *cousin*."

"Did you?" I asked him. "Are you sure you said that, Mr. Bullfinch?"

"Listen!" he said, and he got explosive in his speech. "Why, dammit, Massey, I don't believe her name's any more Fanny Parker than it is Julius Caesar. My cousin didn't know what he was talking about; you said yourself she's a Croat. Anybody can *see* she's some kind of a

foreigner. I never saw her in my life before she came to Mary's Neck and I can prove it! As for her being somebody named Fanny Parker and my 'slipping' into her house, the way she said——"

"Now, now!" I told him. "You mustn't let yourself get excited over nothing, Mr. Bullfinch. People live these things down."

"I haven't *got* anything to live down!" he told me, pretty nearly shouting. "Why, my heavens, Massey, don't you believe me?"

"Well, *I* do," I said, "*I* do, Mr. Bullfinch."

That seemed to make him feel even worse, and I suppose maybe I wasn't just exactly a Christian in my behavior to him, even though my own relief ought to've made me conduct myself more charitably of course. He went out to get Mrs. Bullfinch and make a lot of calls to find out once for all who were their friends and who were not, he said; but I imagine their discoveries may not have been any too accurate in the matter. Quite a number of people will do almost anything rather than give up something sensational to think and talk about, because of course it's any amount more interesting to hear that somebody stole a pig than to hear he didn't.

It's a peculiar thing, though, that a gossiper always seems to be the very person who makes the most fuss over being gossiped about; and, when Clarissa and I came back from seeing Madam Parka and Orlando off on the train, just before dinner-time, the Bullfinches were driving away from Mrs. Dalrymple's gate. I went over to speak to her.

"Poor old things," she said, "they're traipsing all over the place to people's cottages demanding to know who's been saying what and denying everything over and over again and trying to explain. Don't you love it! Of course

I told them nobody believed what Madam Parka said when he and she were kissing each other on the beach and that everybody thought Madam Parka must be simply crazy, and not to worry over what everybody thought just a ridiculous piece of nonsense." She gave a kind of laugh. "I guess perhaps it may be just as well, though, for Mr. Bullfinch that this Orlando man has left the place." Then she looked at me with a hopeful sort of roguishness. "And for you, too, Mr. Massey," she said. "I shouldn't be surprised if you didn't feel a little more comfortable to have Orlando gone, yourself?"

"I certainly do!" I told her. "For days I haven't known when I might find a long Italian dagger buried in my back."

Then she gave me some information. "Not Italian," she said. "The last thing I found out about those people is that he smokes cigarettes that your man, Zebias Flick, told our cook couldn't be bought anywhere outside of Mexico. Orlando isn't an Italian at all, Mr. Massey; he's a Mexican."

By this time I knew too much to try to undeceive her; I just felt pleased with myself that I was getting so educated in the ways of people that I could let a thing like that alone, and I walked on back to the cottage in a right cheerful humor.

In the living-room I found Enid having a fuss over backgammon with Eddie again up at the far end; but all the chairs were pushed back to the wall, and I asked why so. Enid mumbled something I didn't catch and went on telling Eddie he was cheating and didn't know the rules. "I wish you had half the sense you were maybe born with," he told her, and happened to look over at me. Something about me seemed to fix his attention, and he said, "Well, I'm glad to see *some*body with a smiling face to-day, Mr. Massey!"

"Even if it's only me, you mean, Eddie?" I asked him.

"Yes, sir," he told me, being entirely honest. "Over at our cottage nobody can say a word without getting their head bit off. It was terrible over there when I got home this afternoon, and Mrs. Massey told me only a little while ago that if I ever mentioned deep-sea fishing to her any more she was going to quit speaking to me. Then I tried to teach Enid a little something about a game she can't even understand the simplest ruddaments of——"

"Rudiments," Enid told him. "Rudiments! Stop talking baby-talk."

That made him pretty angry. "Listen!" he said. "Mr. Massey, I appeal to you——"

"Don't do it, Eddie," I told him, "I'm afraid I'd have to say I think it's 'rudiments' myself", and he seemed to feel I was a traitor to him in the war of the sexes.

"Well, doggone," he said, and sat back from the table and just stared at the backgammon-board in gloom.

"What's all the furniture against the wall for?" I asked again, seeing they'd given up playing.

"Clarissa," Enid told me. "When she came home from the station she felt so deprived over Fiametta's going away she asked mother and called up the Jefferson Inn and found she could get the orchestra for to-night, so now she's telephoning all around asking everybody. I think it's a terrible waste, myself."

"I should say so!" I said, and thought she was speaking pretty sensibly. "It's not only a waste; but think of the horrible noise it's going to——"

"No," she interrupted me. "I didn't use the word 'waste' in that sense. I mean it's a waste of space. What's the use of having a living-room sixty feet long if you're

only going to devote it to dancing and things of the hour?
I don't mean that I'm not capable of enjoying a dance or
mere pastimes myself; but we've had this living-room
over six weeks now and not once has it been put to a use
of the kind *I* had in mind when we agreed on its
dimensions. What this community needs———"

But Eddie interrupted her; he wasn't in the best of
moods. "Ho-hum!" he said, getting up. "I've heard her
on this subject before, Mr. Massey, and I guess you have,
about as much as anybody could stand anyway. If I've
got to come back here to hop around all night I guess
I'd better be getting home for a little food and rest. If she
has her way about what to do with this living-room I
guess you'll see the day when you'll wish nothing worse'n
dancing happened in it, Mr. Massey."

I was afraid he might be right again and later I had
plenty of time to think about that while I was foolishly
trying to get to sleep with my head on a pillow that was
only about twelve feet above two saxophone players, a
piano player and a drum artist. Of course I thought about
other things also—about how I was going to miss Orlando and the checkers and Madam Parka, too, for that
matter, because she'd certainly proved herself one of the
sterlingest women I'd ever met in my life—but most of
the time I was given up to apprehensions combined with
what you might call bodily miseries. Mrs. Massey and I
had a night that makes me think of hours at the dentist's;
even at the time, though, I had an idea that maybe trying
to sleep over a jazz orchestra mightn't be the worst
thing that could happen to a father, as Eddie'd proph-
esied. What Enid had said about the use she had in mind
for the living-room and why *she'd* wanted it to be sixty
feet long, and what this community needed, had a threat-
ening sound, I thought. She'd talked that way before, as

Eddie said; in fact, she'd talked like that so much I couldn't help fearing she might bring matters to a head before long, because she nearly always does. When she gets an idea she carries it out, or at any rate gives it a good try, and, by the time that orchestra died of over-work and the young people downstairs went off some-where to breakfast, I was really more bothered about what might happen next than I was by what was actually going on right then. That's why I say that night was like the time we spend in a dentist's chair: it's what he's going to do next that hurts the worst.

You see, I'd heard Enid thinking aloud about the living-room while the carpenters were still working on it. "Absolutely perfect for lectures and readings," I heard her say in a musing tone. After that, at meals, she'd often given us her opinion that the cottagers at Mary's Neck let their minds stagnate all summer long, because all anybody offered them was mere entertainment and nothing cultural. Yet there were plenty of people in the place who sought deeper things in life than just golf and bridge and jazz and motor-boating, she told us; and only too often she'd gone on to say that if a living-room like our new one were put to use as a cultural stimulant and centre the idle life of the summer would be greatly en-riched culturally.

As I say, I was uneasy; but here's a curious thing—at lunch, the day after Clarissa's dance, Enid said that a party we were all going to that evening at Mrs. Ruckle-boy's was a gesture in the right direction, and I didn't take warning. The truth is, I hardly noticed what she said and didn't think of it until after I'd got to Mrs. Ruckle-boy's and wasn't in a position to leave. Then it struck me that the party was pretty lengthy for a mere gesture. For a man that hadn't been granted much sleep the night before, the folding-chair I sat on for three hours at Mrs. Ruckleboy's was like a bed of roses with the stems on and kept getting more and more and more so.

Mrs. Ruckleboy had eight trained young girls from Boston to do Folk Dances—mostly Olde Englysshe, according to the program—and from about the middle of the audience in the Ruckleboys' living-room I could see their heads, and sometimes even their shoulders, doing a good deal of bobbing around, ending with a May Pole, the upper part of which was in plain view. There was a violin accompaniment by a lady that had trained these girls and must have studied the instrument some herself once, because when they weren't Folk Dancing she stood up and played Olde Englysshe Aires—not omitting any. After that, for a good while, an intense looking middle-aged lady elocutionist gave Readings From Modern Verse, having written a good deal of it herself, and there were some mistakes about the applause because the audience couldn't tell when she had finished any of her pieces unless she coughed and kind of turned away, and she didn't always do it.

She took an encore, because the audience wanted to show the Ruckleboys they were appreciative and thought it couldn't last much longer anyway; but this was an error on our part that we had to pay for because she brightened up and said she would render some old favorites, in the popular vein. She recited "Genevra", "How We Brought the Good News from Ghent to Aix" and one I used to hear pretty often in my youth about Down on the Rio Grande and Life and Love and Lasker. It woke Mr. Carmichael up (he was sitting on a sofa against the wall) and made him cry; but I had an idea that was because the Rio Grande made him think of his little daughter, Helen.

Enid had a talk with the lady poetess, I noticed later during refreshments, and at breakfast next morning said she'd got some splendid ideas from her about who were the most interesting and economical lecturers and readers in the field. What the lady had told her was going to help her immensely in making a selection. I had a conversation with her mother privately, when we left the table, and she was severe with me, telling me I mustn't make objections. Enid was at an age when serious young people are pretty sensitive about being interfered with, Mrs. Massey said, as if she had to tell me. Young people had as much right to carry out their ideas as I had to carry out my own, she said, and this wasn't my affair at all because Enid took great pride in being economically independent, intending to do the whole thing out of her allowance and not call upon me for anything extra; she'd determined to carry this thing through, feeling it would be for the good of the community, and any remonstrance on my part would be considered merely obstructionist. I'd undergone a whole night over jazz for Clarissa's sake, Mrs. Massey reminded me, so I might at least bear an evening of culture for Enid's, and, as the matter was practically settled anyhow, it would be more graceful on my part to wear a pleasanter expression when Enid talked about it.

"Look here!" I said. "She isn't going to have that white-whiskered old Mr. Abner Lorry from that Jasper art colony give the Neck his views on art or anything, is she? She wouldn't do that, would she?"

"She hasn't even thought of it. That wonderful young man, Mr. Prang, isn't there any more. He went to Paris to study, the week after Eddie's breaking those things from the colony studio was such a tragedy for poor Enid."

"Went to Paris, did he?" I said. "Well, I should think he could."

Mrs. Massey didn't pay any attention. "What Enid wants to do for Mary's Neck is to supply a lecture on a broader subject—one that everybody can understand and be interested in. Don't you think, since the whole thing's decided upon, you might show a little pleasure in it, or at least try to appear to?"

Well, having no option I did try to do it. The mail had already been bringing Enid a good many pamphlets and circulars from lecturers, readers, vocalists, quartettes and other cultural leaders; she talked these over with her mother, and Mrs. Massey told me it was touching to see how determined Enid was to maintain her economic independence and do the whole thing, except the refreshments and invitations, out of her regular allowance. Most of the prices for an evening of music, literature and science were too high for her; but she finally had one circular that both delighted her intellectually and fell within her economic powers. Mrs. Massey told me it was a lecture on the Ceramics, Basketwork and Tribal Life of the Ogilluwayas.

"Who?" I asked her.

"The Ogilluwayas," she told me. "They're perhaps the most interesting of all Indian tribes, Enid says."

"Perhaps?" I asked her. "Perhaps?"

"In that sense it means absolutely," she told me, looking annoyed. "Dr. Gilmerding is the expert on them. He gives an exhibition of their earthenware art and basketwork along with the lecture, and Enid's especially delighted because the whole thing's only seventy-five dollars and expenses."

At first this detail struck me as good news; but after thinking it over for a minute or so I wasn't sure.

CHAPTER XXIII

Hᴇ's a doctor?" I asked Mrs. Massey.

"Not the kind that practise. His name on the circular is A. S. Folstner Gilmerding, with things like A. B. and so forth after it that Enid says means we must call him 'Doctor'. She's settled it that he's to come and asked me to look after getting the invitations engraved and sent out to practically everybody right away. She's having a lot of perfectly healthy excitement out of it, so you mustn't spoil it."

I said I'd try not to, and I certainly did my best. On the afternoon of the day of his arrival, the Mary's Neck village undertaker filled our living-room with rows of the same hard-hearted little chairs Mary's Neck had sat on at Mrs. Ruckleboy's, and along about five Enid drove off in our family car with the chauffeur to meet Dr. A. S. Folstner Gilmerding at the station. Her mother and I were sitting at a window upstairs, about half an hour later, when she got back to the cottage with him. There were a number of bulky looking things in coffee-sacking piled up around the chauffeur in front, and more of them behind, so that Enid and the lecturer seemed to be quite a good deal scrouged for room. "Those are the art exhibition," Mrs. Massey informed me. "It's the ceramics and basketwork. I do hope they get them into the house safely."

Enid got out, looking flushed and keyed up, and then Dr. Gilmerding unwormed himself from among the coffee-sacking and followed her. He was a long, pale, limber-appearing middle-aged man, with a thin mustache, not much chin, nose-glasses and a kind of eager, absent-minded expression, although those terms seem to be contradictory. He had on skimpy-looking clothes which I judged were from three different suits, and the first thing he took out of the car was a smallish valise. "What's he doing with that?" I asked Mrs. Massey. "You gave me your word Enid was going to have him stay at the hotel."

"Oh, yes, certainly," she told me. "It probably has some of the more fragile ceramics in it that he wants to bring in, himself. As soon as they get the rest of the exhibition out of the car and into the house she'll take him on to the hotel, of course. Stop worrying, because it's perfectly all right."

Enid had Zebias Flick and Mr. Sweetmus waiting to help, and they began to carry the coffee-sacks into the cottage; but Enid and Dr. Gilmerding walked up the path and disappeared from our view under the roof of the front porch, and then we heard their voices down in the hall below, Enid's sounding excited and deferential. Pretty soon Clarissa slid into the room where her mother and I were looking out of the window; she'd been hanging over the stairway rail and listening, but had to give that up because Annie, the housemaid, was bringing Dr. Gilmerding upstairs, she said.

"Upstairs?" I asked her. "What do you mean? Enid gave your mother her word she'd arrange for him to stay at the hotel——"

"She did!" Clarissa told us. "She expected him to; but I guess she forgot to mention it in her letters. Anyhow I could tell from her voice that she's so excited she's rattled. As soon as they came in, I heard him tell her he'd like to go to his room, and she just didn't seem to know how to say he wasn't intended to stay here. He said he'd like to have a room where he could get at his ceramics as quickly as possible, in case of fire, because they are priceless, and of course she saw that he had no idea of anything except staying here. So she told Annie to take him up to the Blue Room." Clarissa peeked out of the door. "Anyhow he's there now and I guess Father'll have to stand it."

She gave one of those taunting giggles that daughters do sometimes and I was looking at her for it, when something happened downstairs. We could hear Zebias Flick and Mr. Sweetmus stomping across the floor to put the ceramics and basketworks on a long table Enid had fixed for the exhibition in front of the undertaker's chairs, and, being outdoor men and not accustomed to ceramics, they made a good deal of noise. All of a sudden there was a fatal kind of ceramic crash. Clarissa had the door open now and I heard Enid give a choked outcry and Mr. Sweetmus saying, "Well, I declare! Well, well, well!" kind of meditatively. Dr. Gilmerding didn't appear to have heard anything, his door remaining closed; but I went downstairs and found Enid driving Mr. Sweetmus out of the house and telling him in a hushed fierce voice never to come into it again. Clarissa and her mother had run down ahead of me and were trying to pacify her.

"It's only one of those bum-looking baked clay kind of red kettles with some terrible-looking black zigzags on it," Clarissa told her. "I'll send the car down to the drug store for some of that new patent cement and have it fixed up within half an hour so that Dr. Gilmerding'll never know it, or scarcely know it anyhow. Probably he'll never notice it, so stop your worrying!"

Her mother was telling her much the same thing at the same time in the same urgent kind of whispering, and Enid was taking on about Mr. Sweetmus in the same kind of voice. So I didn't have to speak very loudly in order to make myself heard. "Look here!" I said, pretty sternly. "I've consented to undergo the lecture and the art exhibition and I haven't uttered a word of objection, no matter what I've been feeling; but now, the way you've got it fixed, he's not only going to be here for the lecture but for dinner and expects to stay right here in the house overnight and probably for breakfast, too. I'd like to know what train to-morrow——"

At this, they all three turned on me as if I were some kind of object they couldn't believe existed. "Good heavens!" Enid said, and she stamped her foot. "At a time like this! Haven't I got enough on my hands? Have I got to stop and explain that I expected him to go to the hotel but it's an honor for you to have as distinguished a man as that in your house? Your own gardener has just utterly smashed a ceramic he'd hardly finished telling me was absolutely priceless, and now *you* come to me—*you* who——"

Well, that's all I stayed to hear; when any of my family begin to *you*-who at me, I generally do go. Enid seemed to be agitated, and her mother and sister had a strong appearance of agreeing with her, so I didn't wait for her to follow up the *you*-who with any historical facts. I just quietly strolled upstairs to my own room and smoked until it was time to get into my celebration clothes for the party. I'd got 'em on and started another cigar when Mrs. Massey looked in and asked me how long I was going to keep dinner waiting, because it had to be early.

"See here," I told her. "There's only one thing to do: we've got to ask him what he means by 'priceless'. We're responsible for getting that ceramic broken and we've got to pay for it."

She put on one of her worst expressions right away. "For heaven's sake," she said, "don't distress Enid any more than you already have! With the whole responsibility for the evening's success on her shoulders, how much more do you think the child can stand? She said herself that if you took the accident as a mere question of dollars and cents she'd simply go crazy. What upset her so terribly was the mortification of letting a priceless work of Indian art get broken and thinking what Dr. Gilmerding would feel about her if he knew it. It's all right now if you don't interfere, because when Clarissa was mending it she found it had been broken before, and she's got the new fractures cemented so neatly that you can hardly see where they happened. Please try to spare Enid any more suffering over it and be a little tactful, if you can!"

It's curious but tactfulness is a quality my family always seem to be suspicious of me about, so at the dinner-table I tried to show them some. One of Dr. Gilmerding's shirt-studs had broken away from the buttonhole where it ought to have stayed, which gave a kind of embarrassing interior view of him, you might say, and I thought it ought to be fixed before the lecture; but just to prove my tactfulness I decided not to say anything about it to him. He didn't notice it himself, being occupied, in the eager dreamy kind of way he had, with eating a good deal.

I wanted to be genial and lead the conversation around

to his own topics, so, after Enid had finished telling him about how honored all of Mary's Neck felt over having him in it, I said, "I always thought before that lecturers and ministers and actors and so on didn't like to speak on a full stomach. I notice you don't hold with them, Dr. Gilmerding."

Mrs. Massey put her implements down on her plate, kind of deliberately, and she and both the girls looked at me as if I'd been making one of my mistakes again; but Dr. Gilmerding just went on eating, and answered, during the process, "No, I learned during my life with the Ogilluwayas to eat whenever food was placed before me. I think as well during digestion as at any other time."

"Do you mean, Doctor," Enid asked, kind of timidly and blushing, "that your lecture is more factual than inspirational?"

"Both," he said, and right away Enid said, "How interesting!" and Mrs. Massey said, "Yes, *isn't* that interesting!" and Clarissa said, "Yes, *isn't* it!"

I didn't understand what he meant, myself; but I thought I ought to add something, so I asked him, "Now just who are these Ogilluwayas?" Enid breathed so I could hear her, and I understood I must have gone wrong again, so I went on, maybe a little too hurriedly, to cover it up, "I understand they're Indians; but what I mean: Are they people you've seen something of, yourself, Doctor?"

This time it seemed to be a bad one; after I had been shown how the worst type of outcast gets looked at, Enid gave a repellent laugh and said, "You've never heard that Dr. Gilmerding spent twelve years among the Ogilluwayas?"

I tried to cover it up again. "Why, certainly," I said. "That's why I asked him.'

Dr. Gilmerding wasn't aware that any undercurrents of ruction were going on in the family; you could tell he didn't notice. All at once he began to talk, eating all through what he was saying. "The Ogilluwayas are perhaps the most advanced of all the anthropomorphical clusters that have retained their natal formations and habits. They are indubitably a by-shoot of the pre-Aztec southwestward drift. This was suspected by the earlier anthropologists and established by myself, with the assistance of Dr. Leo Zeigner, in Nineteen-twelve in our Work on broncho cephalic tribal skulls. The cultural inertia of the Ogilluwayas permits an accurate study of their ancient arts and crafts, since these exist with almost precisely the same utilitarian and decorative motives to-day. Their tribal customs superbly mark the transition from the primitive into the neo-primitive, and their religious pageantry, dances and ritual, all founded exclusively upon incantations with dried snakes and the entrails of dogs, are splendidly reproduced with a profoundly interesting and really exquisite symbolism in the decorative designs of their basketwork and earthenware. Nowhere in the whole vast field of ceramics and basketwork is there a profounder ethnological revelation combined with the simplest elementals of perfect neo-zoölithic beauty. The fascination of watching this really neo-primitive people—I insist that they are more actually neo-primitive than primitive—at their basket-weaving or in the construction of exquisite ceramics is ever enthralling, and I shall never forget the excitement of one day discovering that the swastika and asterisk decorative motives were known to them. It is not too much to say that I was trembling with agitation as I bargained with the Ogilluwaya who offered me this remarkable piece. I will show it to you later, and I imagine that the same thrill of excitement will come upon you as you study it, because, as I shall point out, the use of the swastika and asterisk in combination is a distinctly modern impulse unknown to the ancient Ogilluwayas and marking an upward trend out of their neo-primitivism, so that we may now behold this remarkable people actually in an evolutionary process of arts and crafts. Moreover, I shall ask you to study with me one by one the examples of basketwork and ceramics in my collection, and I shall point out to you, as we take up one after the other, the different decorative motives that prevail in the ancient pieces. What I wish to make clear to you is that beautiful and priceless as the earlier pieces are, the swastika and asterisk in combination, or even singly, were absolutely unknown among the Ogilluwayas until the present day. Then we shall turn to the Ogilluwaya basketwork, unsurpassed in ingenious workmanship and choice of color, and I think you will agree with me that it would be a crime if the civilized world should allow so fascinating and advanced a tribal cluster to pass out of existence. However, I shall revert to this later, for first I wish to explain in detail the peculiar Ogilluwaya color processes and methods of kiln operation——"

Well, he went right on talking, eating with an absent-minded rapidity and heartiness all the time. Of course I can't say that I've quoted him with exact precision; but anyhow that's a good deal like what he said, and I'm qualified to repeat it by later experiences. I thought for a minute I was going to get interested and be able to keep my mind on him when he mentioned the dried snakes and dogs' insides; but he never got around to them again. It sort of struck me that he was practising his lecture or maybe just didn't have anything else to say, or that it might have been both. Mrs. Massey kept murmuring things like, *"Isn't* that interesting!" and "Now, *that's* something I never knew before!" and Enid and Clarissa would both say, "Neither did I!" and "Perfectly wonderful!" After the poor beginnings I had made, I thought it better to attend to my own business, and so the dinner passed off without any more unfortunate occurrences, though after we finished coffee Dr. Gilmerding was still talking, and Mrs. Massey finally had to interrupt him and take him out, so the servants could begin to prepare the room for the refreshments after the lecture.

The audience began to arrive pretty soon, and Mrs. Massey made me stand in the living-room doorway with her and Enid and the Professor—I mean Doctor—to receive the guests. Most of them came in right brightly, many of course having had cocktails before their own dinners, and feeling pretty cordial, with rosy faces, laughing a good deal and looking forward to quite an evening, some of them probably not understanding much about what ceramics are.

Mr. Blodgett and Mr. Carmichael, in particular, had been having quite a little dinner, you could see, and had a pretty vague idea of the occasion. "How about those Nautch girls?" Mr. Blodgett whispered to me, and Mr. Carmichael said he wanted a seat right up in front for the Hindu dancing and to see how the Fakir conjuring tricks were done, from which I gathered that their wives must have let them follow their own ideas in order to get them there.

The living-room filled up pretty soon, with everybody chatting and laughing and leaning across each other to call to somebody, because they hadn't been sitting on those chairs long enough to be much disturbed yet. Then, when it seemed that about everybody was there and the room had begun to get kind of hot, Enid walked down the aisle with Dr. Gilmerding and they sat down sort of self-consciously a while in two chairs in front of the long table that supported the art exhibition.

"Now we'll sit down ourselves," Mrs. Massey whispered to me; but just then old Mrs. Abercrombie, being hard of hearing, got up and asked her to have a chair moved down in front for her, and while Mrs. Massey was attending to it I thought I might just as well ease myself out to the front porch. I could hear just as well from there, through the open windows, and smoke, too; so I lit a cigar, and when Mrs. Massey came back to look for me I saw her just glance round once or twice and take the chair old Mrs. Abercrombie had vacated.

Clarissa was out on the piazza, too, with some of her young friends, but up at the other end where they couldn't hear anything, and I had to tell them to be quiet when I saw from the window where I was standing that Enid had got up to begin her introduction of Dr. Gilmerding. She was pale and had a rigid smile, her voice showing considerable stage-fright; but she looked pretty and did right well, I thought. She said that of course Dr. A. S. Folstner Gilmerding didn't need any introduction to this audience, he and his work among the Ogilluwayas being so well known, and therefore she would only speak of the privilege and honor Mary's Neck felt in having him as a guest of honor who brought both the invisible treasures of his mind and the visible ones of his ceramic and basketwork Ogilluwaya art collection to delight and inform us with. Then she sat down, and I felt right proud of her because everybody applauded and she really did look mighty pretty.

Dr. Gilmerding got up, coughing and smiling in a pleased sort of way, and it seemed to me I really ought to have told him about his shirt-stud, after all; but as he didn't know anything about it, himself, and you could see he probably never would, I presume it didn't matter much. He began by saying that Miss Massey's introduction made him feel among friends, and probably among those before him there were numbers already deeply interested in the Ogilluwayas and familiar with Ogilluwaya ceramics and basketwork. He hoped, however, that before the evening was over he'd be able to add something to their knowledge of this profoundly interesting people. "The Ogilluwayas," he went on, "are perhaps the most advanced of all the anthropomorphical clusters that have retained their natal formations and habits. They are indubitably a by-shoot of the pre-Aztec southwestward drift. This was suspected by the earlier anthropologists and established by myself, with the assistance of Dr. Leo Zeigner, in Nineteen-twelve in our Work on broncho cephalic tribal skulls. The cultural inertia of the Ogilluwayas————"

Well, he went right on, saying just what he'd said to the family at dinner, so I saw he must have been rehearsing then, which of course was natural enough. I listened for the part about the dried snakes and dogs' insides to come around again, and it did, but of course was pretty short, and after that I found it bothersome to keep my mind on the subject. It took him about half an hour to get to the point where he quit when Mrs. Massey'd got him out of the dining-room after dinner, and I hoped that from there on the lecture would maybe be more exciting; but it wasn't. The chairs were beginning to get to the audience, too, and a good many didn't seem to have anything else to think about. Looking over the people's heads I could see old Mrs. Abercrombie, down in front, and she seemed to feel she must be missing something that was better than what it sounded like to her; she kept asking her neighbors, "What did he say then?" in whispers so loud I could hear 'em clear back at the window. Mr. Blodgett and Mr. Carmichael must have given up all hope of any Nautch girls by this time; you could tell this by their attitudes, and they were coughing a good deal, kind of pitifully.

CHAPTER XXIV

Cᴌᴀʀɪssᴀ and her young friends had left the porch and skipped out in automobiles, probably to a movie, and I took a stroll around the yard, smoking, and didn't come back to the window for about three-quarters of an hour, thinking that by then Dr. Gilmerding must have about reached his peroration. I seemed to be wrong. "Now before we go into the technical phase of the basket-weaving," he was saying, "I wish briefly to dwell on the extraordinary Ogilluwaya dye processes. But before coming to that, let me say I think you will be as astonished as I was myself when I discovered it to learn the fundamental difference between dyes used for Ogilluwaya basketwork and those employed in their ceramics. Also I must first tell you there is a separate ceremony before the mixing of each separate color. The twelve ceremonies used before the mixing of the ceramic dyes deserve description in detail, for each is profoundly symbolic. I will describe them in order, so that there may be no confusion. The first requires six days and nights. Early on the morning of the first of the six days the tribe gathers———"

Well, I knew I was smoking too much; but I lit another cigar and went out in the yard again. In fact, I smoked two more, and Clarissa and her friends were home from their movies and on the other end of the porch again before I came back to the window. Dr. Gilmerding had finished the dyeing ceremonies all right and was beginning to illustrate the lecture by holding up one object out of the art exhibition after another and pointing out the neo-primitive and anthropomorphic details of decorative motives on each at considerable length. Just inside the window I could hear somebody whispering, "Oh, my goodness! Oh, my goodness! Oh, my goodness!" over and over, and most of the audience seemed to have got clear past squirming on those chairs, which looked to me like a bad sign. Just after I looked in, Dr. Gilmerding picked up a red and black earthenware bowl about twice the size of a bucket and held it up high, leaning forward pretty far.

"This is the exquisite ceremonial cauldron I have mentioned," he said. "I will hold it so that all may see the perfect neo-primitive motives in the decoration. In spite of its massive appearance, as I have told you, it is so delicate that, instead of a fire, ceremonial hot stones or boulders——"

But just there a little accident interrupted him; he was holding the bowl by the rim and the lower half of this ceremonial cauldron dropped off into Mr. Carmichael's lap first and from there to the floor, because Mr. Carmichael didn't show any presence of mind. Enid was pretty red, knowing that Clarissa's cement had failed in this mortifying way, and she began hurriedly picking up the pieces; but Dr. Gilmerding said that this piece had been broken by an expressman in Passaic, New Jersey, last year, and that what had happened was of little consequence as fresh cement would repair the damage. He was right nice and innocent about it and I couldn't help feeling kind of guilty over Mr. Sweetmus's part in the matter.

Well, he put down the broken bowl and said he must now pause to make a plea for subscriptions to a society he and Dr. Leo Zeigner had formed to prevent the extinction of the Ogilluwayas, who are fast dying out, it seems. He said Dr. Leo Zeigner was the treasurer of the society and gave his address, hoping that many of the friends before him who had not heretofore appreciated the importance of preserving the Ogilluwayas would feel it really a privilege to send substantial subscriptions for this cause. He briskened up quite a little on the subject here, and you could see how sincere he was and how kind of childlike and hopeful. But he didn't seem anywhere near the end yet, so I went around in the back yard for quite a while, and this time it was a mistake because when I came back there weren't any automobiles in front of the house; it was all over, the audience had hurried through refreshments and gone home, Dr. Gilmerding was up in his room and nobody was left anywhere except Mrs. Massey and the girls standing in the hall.

Clarissa and her mother were talking to Enid. One of them would say, "Mrs. MacGruber said *she* liked it, Enid", and then the other would chime in, "Yes, Mrs. MacGruber told me so, too, and so did old Mr. Carter, the Ruckleboys' uncle. Mr. Carter said *he* liked it, Enid. He said he thought it was over the heads of most of the audience, and he said he thought it was just the sort of thing that Mary's Neck needed." Then the first one would start over again. "Mrs. MacGruber simply couldn't get over it; she said it was simply perfect and she did wonder how you'd ever learned to stand up before an audience with so much poise at your age, Enid.

Really nobody could have been more enthusiastic than both Mrs. MacGruber and that dear old Mr. Carter. And, oh, yes! Mrs. Carmichael told me that *she* liked it, too. Why, there were just any number——"

They went on, and I stepped into the living-room through the window and closed it behind me and began closing the other windows and putting out the lights as if I'd been around doing my duty all the time, so I got by with it. They didn't pay any attention to me as I passed them on my way through the hall to go up to my room. Enid was flushed and excited, you could see, and her mother and sister were going on remembering other people that'd claimed to have enjoyed themselves and telling her about it, so altogether it seemed to have been a pretty successful party, no matter what.

Next morning at breakfast Dr. Gilmerding was right exhilarated by the lecture's having gone off so well and told us all about the society for preserving the Ogilluwayas. He was sure there would be a gratifying response from last night's audience in the way of subscriptions sent to Dr. Zeigner, he said, because he felt he'd shown how necessary it was to get the work under weigh of preserving such a splendid tribe from extinction. I asked him if he had an idea approximately how many were left or did the census give the figures on the question or anything. He looked kind of surprised and said he personally knew all the Ogilluwayas there are. Three had died since he was out there, and now there were only thirty-four left.

Enid got very enthusiastic over the society's work and said what a splendid cause it was and that a branch of the society ought to be organized at Mary's Neck. They did quite a little talking about it; but somehow it didn't look to me as if it was going to amount to much. Anyhow they got off the subject afterwhile and into Ogilluwaya ceramics generally.

Dr. Gilmerding hadn't said anything about when he wanted the car to take him and the exhibition to the train, and, at eleven o'clock, when Eddie Bullfinch came by to go to the beach with Enid, she and the Doctor were talking about basketwork on the front porch. Eddie looked kind of blank when she and Dr. Gilmerding both got into her runabout with him. The three of 'em came back to lunch about half-past one, and afterwards Enid said sort of nervously perhaps Dr. Gilmerding would care to go for a drive, and he said he would like nothing better, so they went, with Eddie looking pretty perplexed and oppressed but sticking along. I supposed they'd be back in time for Dr. Gilmerding to catch a late afternoon train, and, as a matter of fact, they were; but he didn't say anything about any train—all he said was that he'd better go up and wash his hands before dinner.

At dinner he got back on basketwork some more, but wandered from the subject long enough to say what fine air we had at Mary's Neck and if he'd known how bracing it was he believed he'd have had his wife and children come along with him. He had kind of a dreamy look as if he thought maybe it wouldn't be too late to send for them yet—at least that's how his expression struck me—and after dinner, Enid having taken him with her and Eddie to a moonlight clam-bake, I asked Mrs. Massey what she thought about it. She got right fierce and intense with me before I even finished inquiring how long she thought he was going to stay.

"How do *I* know?" she said, kind of passionately. "Do you suppose I've asked him, especially after our getting his ceremonial cauldron broken for him?"

"No, but Enid———"

"See here!" she said. "Haven't you any idea that this situation's embarrassing enough for Enid without your adding to it? She can't ask as distinguished a man as that how long he expects to stay, can she? Hasn't she assumed the whole burden of entertaining him, herself?"

"Well, no, not at meals, and for my part—well, I admit that anybody can see he's a nice, well-meaning, kind of harmless soul; but as a talker he makes Mr. Sweetmus seem pithy and if I have to hear any more about the Ogilluwayas and ceramics and basketwork I feel that I'm liable to lose my grip on my faculties."

"What about Enid's? She told me he'd talked the whole solid day about Ogilluwayas to her and Eddie Bullfinch. He told her that it was perfectly inspiring to him to be with people who took the same interest in the Ogilluwayas that he did, himself, because there are so few that do, and at home his wife and children hadn't anything like the enthusiasm for ceramics and basketwork that he'd found here in Mary's Neck. If he stays over to-morrow you've simply got to give her a little rest from this responsibility; it won't hurt you to take him out on the Wanda for a few hours in the afternoon."

Well, I did it. After the first few minutes Dr. Gilmerding hardly noticed the ocean; he didn't seem to really know it was there, and we had a complete Ogilluwaya afternoon. When we got back he asked me to go into the living-room with him because the art exhibition was still there on the long table and he wanted to illustrate another point he'd been making to me about the swastika and asterisk decorative motives in combination; and afterwhile, when he stopped for a second or two to cough, I thought I saw a chance to make a point of my own, kind of delicately.

"Oh, by-the-by," I said, as if something had just occurred to me, "these priceless ceramics and basketworks ought to be put back in the coffee-sacking. I'll have it attended to right away, so that they can be shipped to where you're going from here, if you'll give me the address."

He looked kind of surprised. "Well, no," he said, in his dreamy way. "I've left them out here on purpose, for exhibition. You see, some of the friends who were at the lecture may wish to come in and examine them more in detail, from time to time."

All I could say was, pretty feebly, "Oh, I see", because I felt a sort of collapsing in my inwards. Then all at once I got a kind of inspiration that one reason he was staying might be because he hoped I'd do something handsome for the Ogilluwayas; so right there I determined it would be worth the price and sat down and wrote out a pretty sizable cheque for Dr. Leo Zeigner. Dr. Gilmerding looked gratified and thoughtful as I showed it to him and told him it should go in the next mail; but it turned out to be as poor an inspiration as I ever had. He borrowed the telephone book to take up to his room and when he came down to dinner he'd made an alphabetical list of all the summer residents at Mary's Neck and surrounding resorts. He was just beaming and said the results of his lecture were already proving so financially beneficial for the Ogilluwayas that the thing to do was to strike while the iron was hot and organize the branch society Enid had spoken of; the work ought to be done while the interest was at its height. He said he knew young Mr. Bullfinch would be glad to help and go around with Enid and him on their canvass of this alphabetical list; they could begin with the "A's" and "B's" tomorrow —people were always more interested in personal interviews, he said—and they could get the branch society organized and hold some of the earlier meetings right around the art exhibition in the living-room.

Enid swallowed and said it was a perfectly splendid idea. Well, everything was certainly her own fault; but I couldn't help feeling some sympathy for her because her eyes looked sort of glassy. I certainly regretted my inspiration about the cheque, too—not that the cause wasn't really a good one, and you could tell as soon as you looked at him that Dr. Gilmerding was as sincere a man as ever lived, and I was pretty sure that Dr. Leo Zeigner was just as much so. I was sure the Ogilluwayas would benefit by the cheque; but it certainly hadn't accomplished the results I hoped from it.

I won't go into the details of the alphabetical canvass of Mary's Neck made by Enid and Dr. Gilmerding and Eddie Bullfinch. It makes my throat kind of dry, even now, to think of it. By the end of the week they'd only got well into the "E's" and "F's", because if Dr. Gilmerding was one thing he was thorough on all Ogilluwaya matters, and if people were out when the canvassers called—as most of 'em certainly were after word had passed around—he insisted on going back until they gave up and were found in, though there was still a scattering of "D's", "C's", and even a few "A's" and "B's", that hadn't been run down yet. Eddie Bullfinch was beginning to look pretty peevish and Enid's eyes had that glassy appearance all the time, though Clarissa was a good sister and spelled her for two mornings and one afternoon.

At meals Dr. Gilmerding was always excited and optimistic. "I'm pretty sure Mrs. Abercrombie is going to come in," he would say. "I think we'll get both her and Mr. Carmichael, if we show a little persistence. Mrs.

Dalrymple seemed to get the feeling, too, I thought. I'm sure we'll get her before we're through with her, and even that queer old Mr. Francis, too, though of course when he wouldn't let me explain and kept telling us how he hated Indians it seemed discouraging. But that's the very kind of man I like to work on—something to get your teeth into!" Then, after he'd finished going over the whole canvass up to the point they'd reached, Dr. Gilmerding would remember something interesting he thought he'd forgotten to tell us about the Ogilluwayas, and tell it.

They laid off over Sunday—that is, they laid off on the canvass; but the topic of Ogilluwaya ceremonials came up at breakfast and went on except during a nap he took in the afternoon—and Eddie Bullfinch got me out on the porch for a private interview, that evening. He seemed pretty sore.

CHAPTER XXV

"Look there's just one question I want to ask you, Mr. Massey," he said in a severe tone. "I guess I can stand being unpopular in this summer re˙ort and having everybody avoiding me—I'm perfectly willing to be stuck with all these rebuffs, and anybody can see what a nice man Dr. Gilmerding is and probably it would be a good thing if the Ogilluwayas got encouraged to multiply instead of letting themselves die out; but the simple fact is, about all that interests me, outside of Enid and outdoor sports, is mechanics and engineering. It may be a lack in my nature, but since I was about nine years old I haven't taken any interest in Indians at all—absolutely not the slightest. On the other hand, this doesn't mean that I'm criticizing you, Mr. Massey, and Dr. Gilmerding and Enid and maybe that old Mr. Carter, for spending all your time talking about these Ogilluwayas—you may be perfectly right and I may be entirely wrong—but I simply can't get up any interest in 'em to save my life. Listen!" he went on, speaking louder, because by this time I was trying to interrupt him. "Look, Mr. Massey, I simply want to ask you the question: How much longer is this thing going on? You ought to be able to see by this time that we can't finish the canvass this summer and probably couldn't next summer, because by now everybody in Mary's Neck is on the lookout for us. Even Enid herself says the whole canvass mightn't have happened if you hadn't shown all that financial encouragement and stimulation to the Ogilluwaya cause, and I don't like to be the bearer of ill tidings, Mr. Massey, but I think you ought to know that the whole of Mary's Neck thinks you're simply crazy if you still believe you can get the summer population worked up to the pitch that you are. Look the honest truth is I heard a good many of 'em, myself, even right after the lecture, saying they never did take and never could take any interest in these Ogilluwayas or their old ceramics. Now here!—I'm simply asking you to be reasonable, because look after all the work we've done the only members we've got for the society are Enid and Clarissa and Mrs. Massey and me and old Mr. Carter and you, yourself. Mr. Carter's absolutely the only one we've persuaded to come in, outside of our own group. Now how much longer do you expect——"

He was going on; but I stopped him there and I'm afraid I spoke pretty irritably to him. He kept retorting to all my explanations by saying, "Then what in the world did you think you'd gain by making that big subscription to the Ogilluwaya cause?" He kept telling me he couldn't understand my not knowing the effect it would have; I was supposed to be a shrewd business man, he said, and with lots of experience, and he simply could not understand my not having perceived results that any schoolboy and so forth. In fact the only excuse for the way Eddie talked to me was that he was in a pretty worn and nervous state over the canvass. I made allowances for him; but finally preferred to go back into the house. Enid had got up to her room and Mrs. Massey and

Clarissa were spelling her, sitting around the Indian exhibition with Dr. Gilmerding, who had begun to teach
them the Ogilluwaya sign language. They had note-paper
and pencils and he called to me to say he had some for
me, too; but I said I had to go upstairs a minute.

When Mrs. Massey came up, pretty late, I told her
my nerves wouldn't stand any more. I worked hard at my
business through the fall and winter and spring and what
I was entitled to at Mary's Neck was a little rest and
recreation, which I needed and wasn't getting any of, so
if I was going to take care of my family I had to take
care of myself first. I invited her to go on a motor trip
with me, starting the next morning before breakfast.
Well, you could see she was simply crazy to go; but Mrs.
Massey is a mother before all. She just looked at me and
said I ought to know myself that the way Mary's Neck
had talked about Madam Parka and Mr. Bullfinch and
me showed what public opinion of her would be if she
went away with me and left the girls unchaperoned with
Dr. Gilmerding visiting in the house. She couldn't see any
light, she said, because the only thing that would get him
away before completing the canvass would be something
happening to the Ogilluwayas. The most unfortunate
thing, next to my cheque, she said, was the fact that
when Enid first mentioned organizing a branch of the
society she was really sort of enthusiastic and had told
Dr. Gilmerding she didn't have an earthly thing to do the
rest of the summer and would love to devote her time to
it. Except for that, we could have all gone on a motor
trip and just let him take the cottage; but the way things
were, if I had to preserve my health, I'd have to do it
alone.

Of course I felt pretty selfish; but women do bear up
better under certain strains than men are able to. They

can go through things that we can't, and I think the manful thing is just to admit it right out in so many words. I borrowed Clarissa's roadster and the chauffeur, the next morning, and, after a hurried breakfast in the kitchen, started for the White Mountains, feeling a more lightened sensation of freedom in my breast than I had known since before Enid got her first idea of the lecture. Of course I had to keep thoughts of my family out of my mind; I did it by an effort of will power and looking at the scenery. Once when we passed a bronze memorial tablet on a hillside Fred, the chauffeur, said it probably marked the spot where early-settlers had been massacred by Indians; but I told him we must keep our minds on more cheerful topics. We had a fine drive and stopped that night at the Sunrise House on Mount Fitzpatrick, feeling just superb.

After dinner I ran into the W. D. Patterson family from Columbus, Ohio, in the big, comfortable lobby of the hotel and sat down with them. The W. D. Patterson family had relatives in Logansville and often visited there—mighty nice people and I was glad to come across them again. I hadn't much more than joined them, though, when a Mrs. Nettleby, a big, handsome, kind of important woman that had a cottage in the summer colony on Mount Fitzpatrick came in to call on them. I didn't take to her, you might say, because she had the sort of personality on her that is cold to strangers, and, not knowing my status, left me out of the conversation and treated me as an unnecessary accessory to the Pattersons for quite a while. I took a dislike to her, you might say, and felt quite an increase of it when the coincidence occurred of her beginning to talk to the Pattersons about Indians and basketwork.

She said there were some descendants of the aborigines

in the neighborhood, and she did hope the Pattersons would become interested in their birch-bark baskets. She'd been struggling for years, she said, to get the Mount Fitzpatrick summer people interested in the beautiful and simple Indian arts and crafts, and then she drifted off the subject and pretty soon began talking about how too disappointing it was that the Kinvorzorfsky Quartette that she'd engaged to give an evening's entertainment at her cottage next Friday had fallen down and couldn't come, so to-morrow she'd have to begin sending around and withdrawing her invitations.

Well, it was just like a dazzling stroke of lightning in my head; the thing came over me all of a sudden, and this time right from the start I had the feeling of having got a good inspiration that would make up for the other one. "Speaking of basketwork and ceramics," I said, and I was on firm ground here, knowing pretty well what I was talking about. "I am sure, Mrs. Nettleby, that you are probably familiar with the exquisite decorative motives of the Ogilluwayas, because the Ogilluwayas are perhaps the most advanced of all the anthropomorphical clusters that have retained their natal formations and habits. They are indubitably a by-shoot of the pre-Aztec southwestward drift. This was suspected by the earlier anthropologists and established by the most celebrated of them all, Dr. A. S. Folstner Gilmerding in Nineteen-twelve in his Work on broncho cephalic tribal skulls." I didn't go on with it semi-verbatim from there; I thought best just to give her this tid-bit and branch off into something like my own way of talking. "Dr. Gilmerding carries with him for his lectures the most priceless and enthralling collection of Ogilluwaya ceramics and basketworks, ancient and modern, ever seen in the world, and, as for Dr. Gilmerding himself, of course I probably needn't tell *you* anything about *him,* Mrs. Nettleby, with your interest in Indian arts and crafts and all. You've probably heard Dr. Gilmerding any number of times——"

"Why, no," she said, looking at me all at once with a good deal of surprise and any amount more affability. "He hasn't been lecturing in this part of the country lately, has he?"

"Why, yes, certainly," I told her. "He's been resting at Mary's Neck after a——"

"You don't say!" she said, and she already began to look eager. "Do you think he's still at Mary's Neck? I don't suppose it's possible——"

"It was your saying you'd never heard him and your interest in Indian topics that made me think of it," I said. "Yes; he's still at Mary's Neck—at least he was still there when I left and I have his telephone number. I don't know about his engagements for next Friday, if you were thinking of putting him in instead of the Quartette you mentioned; but I do happen to know that he has this Wednesday open. Of course that might be a little trouble for you to substitute instead of your Friday entertainment, the time being so short, but——"

"Why, no," she said, getting eagerer and eagerer. "Do you think we could get in touch with him this evening? I might at least be able to see whether——"

I jumped right up. "I'll get him for you on long distance in five minutes," I told her, and then, kind of flushed with success and feeling I'd like to do poor old Gilmerding a good turn and make up a little for what Mr. Sweetmus had done to the cauldron, I said, "The whole thing, lecture and art exhibition, ceramics, basketworks and all, is only two hundred dollars and expenses." This wasn't reckless at all, though you might think I took a big risk; but I judged by some pearls she was wearing and her bracelets that a seventy-five dollar lecture would have made her suspicious, and I was right. Two hundred was just the figure to suit her both ways.

I got him on long distance for her; but not until I'd had Mrs. Massey first and told her to tell him that his future lecture price had to be two hundred dollars and that this one had to be Wednesday. Well, I never took part in a more successful coop; it was just like clock-work. When Mrs. Nettleby came back from that telephone she was all excited. Dr. Gilmerding was coming with all the art works and baskets and ceramics on Wednesday morning, and she had to rush off right now to get out the cards announcing the change from Friday and the alteration from the Quartette to the Ogilluwayas.

"But first," she said, "Mr. Massey, do tell me just a little more about them. Of course I know in a general way how important the Ogilluwayas are and how remarkable they are with their pottery and basketwork; but even over the telephone it's easy to see what an enthusiast Dr. Gilmerding is, and I thought that as he's to stay at my house and I'd like to draw him out on the subject as much as possible, maybe it would help if I knew a good many details of Ogilluwaya tribal customs and their arts and crafts, beforehand."

"I'd better leave it to him," I told her. "I'd just butcher it." I looked at her, and I hadn't taken any great fancy to her; but just then, knowing I wouldn't ever see her again, which would be better, too, I had at least what you might call kind of a fellow-feeling for her. "He'll tell you, himself, Mrs. Nettleby," I said. "The Ogilluwayas'll come to you all the fresher for your not knowing their details beforehand. You won't have any trouble in drawing out Dr. Gilmerding about them——that won't be any trouble to you at all."

Now here's another thing that just shows how peculiar human nature is: when I got back to the house on Wednesday after he'd gone, I kind of began to sort of miss him. Yes, sir; the living-room looked queer to me without the collection of ceramics and basketworks, and after that, for a while, it seemed queerer still to have whole days pass without hearing anybody even mention the Ogilluwayas. I spoke of this to Enid; but she didn't seem to understand me or even to hear me, because a pretty terrible thing, altogether different, had begun to happen to her just about then. But before getting on that subject I'd better explain the rest about Dr. Gilmerding.

He'd been gone a little over two weeks when we got a perfectly lovely letter from him; it was addressed to Enid but meant for all the family. It was written from Mrs. Nettleby's at Mount Fitzpatrick. He wanted to know how our branch society was getting on and said he and the Nettleby family had been doing splendid work among the friends at Mount Fitzpatrick, organizing another one; but he wasn't going to be able to remain until the organization was completed because Mrs. Nettleby had made a wonderful arrangement for him to deliver the lecture at the house of some delightful relatives of her husband's in Utica, New York, and what seemed really quite like Aladdin's lantern she'd arranged for the price to be three hundred and fifty dollars and expenses. You could see how happy he was over the whole thing, because he added about seven pages more of facts he said he thought 'he'd forgotten to tell us about the Ogilluwayas.

CHAPTER XXVI

I'D BE the last father in the world to dwell critically on
the characters of my daughters. I don't speak of them
with any critical disposition at all—in fact, it's the very
reverse with me; but on the other hand I'd not like to get
going too far in the way of sounding their praises, because that's the very thing that starts a listener's preju-
dice against a parent's children. In saying this, I'm trying
to lead up to what I mentioned as a terrible occurrence
happening to Enid and to explain that in speaking of the
difference between the two sisters I don't mean anything
invidious toward her, or toward Clarissa either; I just
mean they're so different from each other that they're all
the more interesting to me as a father, though I don't
want to get to talking like Mr. Carmichael.

I've already mentioned a number of ways in which the
two are unlike each other; but I suppose the main contrast between them is in their susceptibilities. On that
point Clarissa seems to be either more experienced or
more fortunate in natural bent, it's hard to say which;
but she practises being more a general belle with all of
'em. She seems to know how to keep her affections scattering from one to the other in pretty quick rotation, and,

when she does appear to get centred upon one object for a while, such as that estimable young Bicksit, her mother and I don't become fretful over her, because we've found it doesn't interfere with her eating or anything while it's occurring. Clarissa just goes on having a good time all the time.

But Enid has a more severe nature, as I may have mentioned. She dances every bit as well as Clarissa does, though, and she dresses just as prettily, I think, but appears to be above talking as much about it as Clarissa likes to with her mother. Now, as to her susceptibility, she never seemed to have the faintest glimmer of any— you'd have thought she didn't know what it meant. In Logansville, if the boys showed any signs of susceptibility toward herself she just couldn't stand it. Any of these symptoms on a boy's part appeared to her as samples of mental defectiveness and yet kept her from feeling the tolerance she'd have shown to a patient in such an institution as she said ought to have charge of him; she'd get so angry and so contemptuous that she'd pretty well drive any susceptible boy away, and, if he still hung around, she wouldn't have anything to do with him.

Well, here at Mary's Neck she was just the same; she could have friendships of course on either an outdoor basis or an intellectual footing, such as the interest she'd taken in young Mr. Carlos Prang. Of course her association with Eddie Bullfinch wouldn't come exactly under either of these headings; it seemed to be more just a kind of mutual habit, due to Eddie's always being around. At first, I think, he showed a few signs of sentimentalism but became mainly and mutually peckish with her instead; they got into the habit of quarreling about two-thirds of the time, and this seemed to suit her all right. In fact, they appeared to get along best when they weren't speaking to each other——they'd even go places together when that condition prevailed between them.

Outside of Enid, Eddie's principal interests are in mechanics. The complete drowning of the Dorio-Grecco in forty feet of water was a great loss to him in that line, of course; but he'd rigged up a shop in the Bullfinches' garage and tinkered around in it a good deal——sometimes with Enid assisting him by pointing out defects in his methods, I gathered. After his loss he'd got hold of two junked automobiles somewhere; they were complete wrecks except for the rusted engines, and he put in a good deal of time and hard labor——some of the labor was furnished by his mother's chauffeur——preparing these engines for marine purposes. Then he traded around for an old sail-boat about thirty feet long, and he and the chauffeur had put the engines in it just before Eddie's time began to be occupied exclusively by the canvass on behalf of the Ogilluwayas. When Dr. Gilmerding left, Eddie was free to devote himself again to more congenial pursuits, and so he did.

He said he thought he could get up some real speed with the twin-screw arrangement he and the chauffeur attached to the engines, and Mrs. Massey spent some nervous hours on our front porch with a spy-glass, watching that boat flop around with Enid in it out on the Atlantic ocean. It's a funny thing about young people, how they like to get into patched-up contraptions they've put together themselves, and I suppose we parents ought to be glad that the time hasn't quite come when young boys like Eddie can get hold of the materials to make crazy-quilt airplanes and take our daughters up in them. Enid was entirely indifferent to the Wanda——didn't care to go out in her with me at all——but I suppose she liked the awful noise Eddie's boat made and the excitement of not knowing whether they'd get back or not unless some-body towed 'em in, as I had to several times with the Wanda.

But one afternoon Eddie's boat got to working right well, as Captain Turner and I saw, ourselves, we being out and keeping not far away. It didn't get up any speed particularly; but it did splash along for quite a little while without stopping, and Eddie was able to get it going again every time it broke down, so they actually came back into the harbor under their own power. Eddie seemed to regard this as quite a triumph, and on shore he told me he guessed he'd showed a few people what was what.

"They all said I couldn't do it," he told me on the wharf. Enid had driven home in her runabout to change her dress, which was pretty wet. "A lot o' people around here thought they were going to have a chance to laugh at the Shooting Star but I guess to-day showed 'em!" Eddie said.

" 'Shooting Star'?" I asked him.

"That's the new name of my boat," he said. "Her original name was the Mrs. Calvin M. Flick when I bought her from a fisherman; but it didn't look right on a twin-screw motor-boat. That's why it's painted out; I'll have 'Shooting Star' on her by to-morrow. Some of 'em may think they can laugh at me for naming her that; but look wait till I get those engines tuned up just right!"

"About how much time will it take you to get 'em tuned up the way you want 'em?" I asked him, just not to let the conversation flag, and I was rather surprised when the question seemed to have a depressing effect upon him. He looked gloomy, made sounds in his throat and tried to scratch a place on his back that he couldn't get at.

"Why, doggone it!" he said. "I'd have those little hummers tuned up absolutely within the next four or five days if that wet splash wasn't coming to visit me."

"What's coming to visit you?" I asked him, though he seemed to think I'd comprehend him without his explaining.

"Mush Sloppy Weather," he said. "Old Sloppy Weather Mush Turpie. Sloppiest weather I ever had anything to do with anywhere."

"You mean it's a person, Eddie?"

"Why, yes," he said, looking surprised. "Anyhow, he thinks he is. It's a fellow named Mushmelon Turpie; at least that's the name we had for him at school. What he's got on his calling-cards is 'Mr. Lathrop Mallowfield Turpie'. His mother calls him 'Mallie', and my mother says I've got to begin now and call him that, too, instead of 'Mushmelon', because he always hated being named 'Mushmelon' terribly, his mother wrote to my mother, and it'd be disgraceful to make my own visitor uncomfortable. That's the position my whole family take—that just because he's my age and I went to school with him he's supposed to be coming here to visit *me*—when I wouldn't have asked him myself in a thousand years and would a good deal rather have some animal or something visit me!"

Eddie spoke with such bitterness that I got a little interested. "But if you feel so uncongenially toward this young Mr. Turpie I don't see how it happens he's to be your guest."

"My guest!" Eddie said. "Why, that's just what I've been explaining he isn't! Only he's going to think he is and my family keep insisting and pecking at me and I'll have to drag him around with me and entertain him and everything or his mother's feelings'll be hurt! She's my mother's most intimate old girlhood friend, and she was getting afraid his mother's feelings'd be hurt about our never having invited him here, except once five years ago; so my mother wrote and asked him to visit me without telling me anything about it beforehand or giving me the slightest chance to argue."

"But won't he be interested in helping you tune those engines up?" I inquired. "Can't you take him on as mate, or something, of the Shooting Star?"

"Who? Mushmelon?" Eddie said, staring at me. "Look I wouldn't any more let Mushmelon Turpie touch those little hummers than I would some camel. He can't do anything on earth except smoke somebody else's cigarettes all up and call heads or tails right so that he always gets into movies at other people's expense. Right almost on top of all the toil I had to do for the branch society, this is going to be an absolutely terrible interference with everything, and one of the worst things about it is the way Enid's going to treat him, because he's the girling kind that just make her absolutely sick and she's already told me not to bring him around her at all. Well, if he has to be kept away it means I'll have to stay away with him a good deal, and, besides that, the family'll insist that I've got to bring him anyhow to call, and, if I do, she's going to get disgusted and prob'ly quit speaking to me again."

He was so dejected about that I couldn't help laughing, but tried to cheer him up a little. "Well, if she does, she's pretty sure to begin again sometime," I told him. "I've noticed she usually does, and anyhow your young friend's visit will only be a temporary obstruction."

"Look!" Eddie said. "The last time he visited us he

was only about fourteen years old but he stayed six weeks."

Mrs. Massey came for me in the family car just then and Eddie climbed back in his boat to do some more tinkering. I was a good deal amused over his troubles and also kind of faintly curious to see the cause of them, wondering a little bit what this Mushmelon boy, Mr. Lathrop Mallowfield Turpie, looked like.

It was only a day or two before I found out, though; Mrs. Massey and I were sitting on the piazza in the bright twilight after dinner, Clarissa wasn't home and Enid was inside, reading in the living-room, when Eddie came up the porch steps with another boy and said nervously, "Mr. and Mrs. Massey, this is my friend Mush— I mean Mallowfield—I mean Mallowfield Turpie. Where's Enid?"

It's curious and unreasonable the way we all feel kind of an objection to people, sometimes, at first sight; but those two boys hadn't any more than reached the top of the steps before I was in complete sympathy with Eddie Bullfinch's prejudices in regard to his visitor. That Turpie boy was handsome in a pear-shaped way; I mean his face was fattish at the base, so his head looked smaller, and he had thin, blondish hair that he didn't seem to mind having curl some around his forehead. His complexion was pale and dampish looking; he had a pink mouth that appeared to be too small, I thought, and too curving; and the expression on it was what you might call complacent. That is to say, he struck me as looking like an only child that's never had any trouble believing all its mother has ever said to it about itself. When he saw Mrs. Massey and me sitting on the porch, and while Eddie Bullfinch was introducing him, he put on one of those stony, repellent looks, like an aristocratic beauty suspecting insult, only more so, the way some boys do to show strangers that the slightest intimacy is going to be unattainable.

He didn't say anything; just allowed Mrs. Massey and me to split a slight nod between us, then walked coldly into the house with Eddie. From outside on the porch we couldn't hear much that went on at first in the living-room; they were talking fairly quietly, as sometimes young people do for a little while, except at parties, until they get better acquainted. After that, the Turpie boy seemed to be holding forth at considerable length in a treble voice, and his subject must have been agreeable to him, because finally we heard Eddie break in, pretty nearly shouting, and beginning with loud, scornful laughter.

"What'd I tell you, Enid?" he said. "Didn't I tell you if you ever let him once get talking about himself you couldn't stop him except you'd hit his little old nob of a head with a sledge-hammer? For heaven's sake, Mush, talk about something pleasant!"

Sounds of repartee and altercation followed, and it seemed to me in his irritation Eddie was neglecting his family's instructions upon the proper treatment of a guest; then we heard Enid speaking sharply to him, and, not long after that, the three of them came out and got into Enid's runabout to go somewhere and dance. It was dark by that time; but we could hear Eddie remonstrating down on the driveway where the car was waiting. "My goodness! You aren't going to let old Sloppy Weather sit *there*, are you? Get out o' that, Mush; get back in the rumble where you belong!"

There was a sound of scuffling and Enid spoke angrily. "No! Mr. Turpie is a visitor. Sit in the rumble, yourself!"

"What!" we heard Eddie saying in a plaintive way. "Me? Well, my goodness!" Then they drove off, and I felt pleased with Enid for her good manners and proper instincts.

"It shows she's a kind-hearted girl," I told Mrs. Massey. "It shows she's sorry for a boy as kind of deficient as this one appears to be, and doesn't intend to let Eddie Bullfinch make the poor thing feel too uncomfortable, though I must say, judging from his expression, her efforts in that line might be unnecessary. Still, it's to her credit."

I felt even more this way at lunch the next day when Enid said she thought it might be nice, on account of our knowing the Bullfinch family so well, if her mother would let her give a little dinner or something very soon for young Mr. Turpie. Mrs. Massey said she could, and I told Enid I thought she was showing a benevolent spirit. "I'm glad to see it," I told her. "Especially because it proves you're able to stifle your own prejudices, Enid."

She gave me a surprised, frowning look and asked what I meant; so I explained how Eddie'd told me she'd said he mustn't bring the Turpie boy to call on her or anything, and, at that, she frowned more and spoke with what seemed to be indignation.

"It was before I knew him," she said. "Eddie gave me an absolutely false impression."

I was a little mystified by the decided way she spoke; but I didn't say anything more and didn't think much about the matter because that was the day I had to leave Mary's Neck on a trip out to Illinois to attend a Directors' meeting and look after some other business affairs. Well, sir, the first person I saw when I got home, along in the afternoon about a week later, was this Lathrop Mallowfield Turpie sitting up on the front porch smok-

ing a bent cigarette and evidently waiting for Enid, because she came out in a new dress just as I reached the
top of the steps. It struck me right away she was kind of
peakid-looking and different somehow, I thought first
maybe because of a new way she was wearing her hair;
but, what seemed peculiar and dampening to an affectionate father, she didn't appear to have any realization that
I'd been away at all.

She just said absent-mindedly, "Mother's upstairs if
you're looking for her" and trotted off to her runabout
with this Turpie boy holding to her elbow and me staring after her.

I never knew her to act like that before, because she'd
always made quite a pleasant little fuss over me whenever I got back from a trip anywhere;—the truth is I
was a good deal kerflummixed. She was as changed a
girl as I ever saw and the only thing I could think of,
right then, as a reason for it, was that maybe the strain
of Dr. Gilmerding hadn't worn off but had done something peculiar to her.

CHAPTER XXVII

Is ANYTHING wrong with Enid?" I asked Mrs. Massey, after we'd talked a little while upstairs; and right away she looked up at the ceiling and then down but said she thought Enid's health was all right.

"Is it?" I asked her. "I thought maybe the strain she was under on account of the Ogilluwayas——"

"No," she told me. "This hasn't anything to do with that."

"Then it *has* got to do with something," I said. "What is it?"

"I'd prefer for you to come to your own conclusions," Mrs. Massey told me. "You'll have a good chance at dinner to notice her because she's going to bring him back with her and of course she'll ask him to stay."

Mrs. Massey wouldn't say another thing then, largely because I said her hint was preposterous and just laughed at it. Enid was an intelligent girl, not crazy, I told her; but when dinner-time fulfilled her prediction that the Turpie boy would be there I began to feel a little disturbed. I felt more so, the more I noticed Enid and listened to her; it was plain as could be that she wasn't behaving very naturally.

When we sat down at the table she began talking excitedly about nothing at all and dropping her "R's", something I'd never known her to do before, because she'd always been a girl that fairly abominated any kind of showing-off or pretentiousness. She kept interrupting her own chatter by laughing in an affected way that sounded too musical, as if she'd practised it; and she referred to me several times as "funny little Pops", not meaning little in size, of course, but seeming to imply that consequential people ought to take me more or less as sort of a joke. The consequential people involved appeared to be herself and Mallowfield Turpie, not including her mother or Clarrisa, because pretty soon she went so far as to speak of her mother as "funny little Mums" and of Clarissa as "funny old Clarissa". Then, spang in the middle of something she was saying, she stopped; all her excitement and laughter and talk wilted right down like the water of a garden-hose somebody else turns off unexpectedly at the hydrant. Nobody had said anything; there wasn't any visible cause—she just suddenly quit doing everything except sit and look across the table at that Turpie boy, with her mouth partly open.

She did this all through the meal. She'd chatter and laugh a while, not giving anybody else a chance to say a word; then, right when she seemed most wound up to continue permanently, she'd have another seizure of looking at him, usually with her mouth partly open. He seemed used to it and kept right on eating, though looking back at her approvingly quite a little and getting kind of more dampish on his face, I thought. I didn't make a very good meal of it, myself, on account of getting disturbed enough not to feel so well inside, and Enid's not being herself at all got her mother and Clarissa and me to feeling so constrained that it was quite a relief, at first, when Eddie Bullfinch came stumbling in while we were eating dessert.

He had sort of a hard look on his face and didn't join us at the table but sat down in a chair against the wall. "No, thank you," he said, when Mrs. Massey asked him if he wouldn't have some dessert with us. "I'll wait here; I guess it won't do any harm my just waiting, in spite of the fact that it's customary when any girl invites somebody that's visiting to dinner to also invite whoever they're visiting, instead of sending word that their host can come around after dinner and sit in the rumble to go to the movies with them! Not that it makes any great difference to me, because I'm just as able to take food at home as some place else where I'm practically requested not to!"

Enid looked furious and gave a contemptuous sort of sniff; but Mallowfield Turpie didn't show any symptoms of being interested at all—just went on finishing up his second plate of Floating Island—and the rest of us felt pretty embarrassed. Mrs. Massey murmured something about being sorry Eddie hadn't come to dinner with his guest, to which he responded by saying, "Yes'm; it wasn't *your* manners I was alluding to. Ha-ha!" in such a harsh, cracking voice that I was glad to see Mrs. Massey get up to go into the living-room for coffee. He came in there with us, of course, but sat off in a corner, staring at the ceiling, while Clarissa went to the piano and tried to be tactful by playing something to relieve the constraint.

"That was pretty," he said, when she finished a piece. " 'Tea for Two', wasn't it? Somebody ought to make up some old song about tea for three or movies for three or sundaes and sodas for three, and the same person being allowed to come along in order to have somebody to pay for it. Otherwise there wouldn't be any, prob'ly!"

Then he said, "Ha-ha!" again, not laughing but just saying it harshly, and went on, turning in his chair toward
Mallowfield, "Well, Mush, old Sloppy Weather, if you
wouldn't mind letting me have one of my own cigarettes
I might as well smoke a while until you and the lady
get ready for me to go down to the movies with you and
buy the tickets."

Mallowfield Turpie didn't respond to Eddie's suggestion about the cigarette. "I'm smoking my own, thank
you," he said. "I bought 'em this afternoon, and don't
spring that old stuff again about its being the first time!"
And he added, with a kind of spiteful little laugh in his
treble voice, "Try and think up something brighter, old
gooseberry!"

Eddie looked dangerous over being called a gooseberry—active trouble seemed to be imminent right there
—but Enid jumped up, pretty red, and said it was already
late for the movie they were going to. So they went out,
with that Turpie boy holding to Enid's elbow even before
they got to the door, and she let him. All I could do for
a minute was to sit staring from Mrs. Massey to
Clarissa and back again, while both of them nodded their
heads and then shook them solemnly, as if answering me.
"Why, this is the worst thing I ever heard of in my
life!" I said. "That is, it is if it's what it looks like."

"It's what it looks like," Clarissa told me. "Only it's
worse. Haven't I always said that if Enid ever did get
this way we'd have a perfectly fearful time with her?"

"Why, my goodness!" I said. "It's got to be dealt
with! I can't understand how such a thing was ever per-
mitted to get started!"

Clarissa gave a hoot. "Started! Father, don't you know
yet that when it happens at first sight it's already too late
to do anything about it by the time anybody notices it?

Don't you s'pose Mamma and I have tried everything
we *could?* Don't you s'pose we pointed out his defects
to her? That was easy, because he hasn't got anything
else; but all the effect it had on Enid was to make her
rave at us for letting Eddie Bullfinch poison our minds.
Then we tried making fun of Mushmelon and telling her
what all the other boys say about him; but I had to stop
because it began to make her think I was jealous!"
Clarissa jumped up, there, because an automobile horn
was rasping for her outside, with half a dozen boys and
girls whistling and calling her name. She put her head
back in the door after she'd gone out, though: "You say
it's got to be dealt with, do you, Father? Gracious! I do
hope I get the chance to watch you dealing with it!"

Well, I got up and began to walk the floor. "It's got to
be stopped!" I said. "How much time is Enid in the habit
of putting in with this Turpie?"

"Only her mornings and afternoons and evenings!"

"Why, good heavens!" I said. "What on earth do they
find to talk about?"

"That's a complete mystery," Mrs. Massey told me.
"You can see for yourself he's another of those boys
that never say anything at all when we older people are
around but just look as though we were impediments
that ought to be very temporary. I asked Enid if he ever
said anything worth listening to, and she instantly got so
excited she wanted to know if I could quote anything
George Washington ever said. I told her certainly; that
he said, 'I cannot tell a lie'. She asked me if I thought
that was worth listening to, and told me it wasn't so,
anyhow, because no serious historian believed he ever
said it."

"Good heavens!" I said. "Comparing this Turpie boy
to George Washington! People'll get the idea Enid isn't

in her senses. It's beyond all reason for a girl that's always held as aloof from sentiment and has had as many fairly attractive, normal boys interested in her, without giving one of 'em a glance—Why, for an intellectual, capable, artistic girl like that to pick out the very last one you'd ever think, the dumbest, spongiest lummox that ever——"

Mrs. Massey shook her head, looking pretty despondent. "No, Enid didn't pick him out; you don't understand. It just happened to her. It does, with young people, pretty often—it just happens without anybody on earth's being able to explain it. I've done everything I could; but, as Clarissa said, it only makes Enid furious. For instance, when I mentioned that so far as I could discover he hadn't ever read a single book in his whole life and might be rather dull company for such a reading girl as Enid, she asked me how long it was since I'd seen *you* reading anything except newspapers."

"Why, that's terrible!" I said. "Comparing that lummox even to her own father—and when I was away on a trip, too!"

"Oh, my, yes!" Mrs. Massey told me. "There've been a great many such comparisons, none in your favor. She said that if I thought I had a right to attack him to her, she certainly had a right to attack you to me."

"What!" I said. "What!"

"Oh, my, yes! I thought there was one thing might rouse her pride, and that was about his closeness. His mother gives him a large allowance, it seems; but he never spends a penny of it if he can possibly help it. Enid's always despised the slightest sign of stinginess in anybody; but when I tried to point this out to her she said you had declined to give anything to the Indigent Improvement Fund last year, and, when I told her that was because I knew the Fund was a fraud and I wouldn't let you, and that you were ordinarily much too lavish in your contributions, she said that proved you didn't know how to save in a proper way. She said Mallowfield had the most generous nature she'd ever known. He'd told her, himself, about large expenses he'd been put to by other people; but he certainly didn't intend to be imposed on, especially not by Eddie Bullfinch, particularly when it was Eddie's place as host to be doing the entertaining and not screeching every time it cost him anything. You see, the slightest hint—no matter how gentle and reasonable—that he isn't absolute perfection only makes her surer that he is and sets her wild with everybody else."

"Yes," I said, "if it isn't done properly."

Then, when Mrs. Massey wanted to know what I meant by this, we had a long discussion, and, after I'd pacified her, she contended that Enid was in such a state of mind that nothing at all I could do would have any weight with her. But something had to be done, I said, and done right away; and I declined to believe that my daughter's mental condition was already such that I couldn't rouse her to the perception of what a grisly mistake her untrained sentiments were leading her into. Mrs. Massey said gloomily, all right, I could try if I wanted to; so, being alone with Enid, after lunch the next day, I did.

I began by asking her, cheerfully and casually, what she'd been up to while I was away, and, when she didn't hear me because she was looking out of the window too anxiously, I said I thought she might pay a little attention to me after my absence. I spoke affectionately. "Don't you ever have a thought in your head any more for your poor old man, Enid?" I asked her.

"What?" she said dreamily, not hearing a word; then she jumped and started for the door. "G'bye," she said, and through the window I saw Mushmelon coming along the board side-walk in the distance.

"You wait a minute!" I told her, kind of loudly. "I want a few reasonable words with you, Enid, about that young man. I just want to say——"

"What!" she interrupted, and turned on me like a flash, pale right on the instant and breathing fast. "What!"

"Now don't get excited," I said. "I haven't spoken a word against him and I'm not going to."

"Oh, indeed!" she said. "Oh, aren't you?"

"Certainly not," I told her. "I merely wanted to mention that I couldn't help noticing you look kind of peakid and not your usual self. Now, when that happens to a daughter of mine, I can't help feeling disturbed, especially when I could hardly fail to see the cause of it. All I want to say is that it can't help making me feel a little uneasy, Enid."

"Why?" she asked me. "What makes you uneasy?"

"Why, that young man does," I told her; and I can't deny I got a little confused about what I intended to say, her manner was so intense and sharp. "In the first place," I told her, "I admit I don't know anything about his character except what I've heard, and I haven't seen anything of him much, myself, except at dinner last night when he certainly didn't say anything very noticeable. I was only thinking, Enid, that if you'd take a better look at him, yourself, you'd see he isn't exactly—that is to say, his appearance isn't exactly——"

But she cut me off right there. "So you don't think he's handsome!" she said, getting paler and breathing harder. "That's your charge against him, is it? Even

Mamma and Clarissa haven't dared to say that! You admit you don't know anything whatever about him; but you object to him because in your expert eyes he isn't handsome!"

"Look here!" I said, naturally a little provoked. "I don't care whether he's handsome or not; it's what he looks like that I object to!"

At that, she got even fiercer with me. "I knew you'd join in this persecution!" she told me. "Do!" Then she lifted both her arms up, kind of violently. "Oh!" she said, pretty nearly shouting. "It's unbelievable how small the natures of people can be when they find themselves compared to something beyond them!" Then she said, "Oh!" again, banged the door behind her and ran out to the board-walk.

Well, sir, the way she'd flown off the handle, almost completely taking leave of her proper senses, as you might say, left me in a pretty astonished condition. What's more, practically the same thing happened every time I tried to reason with her upon that subject; I couldn't penetrate to her intelligence at all. I tried logic; I tried pleading; I tried sarcasm; I even tried over-praising him; but after expending all my resources I acknowledged that her mother was right about my not accomplishing anything. Mrs. Massey and Clarissa began to say nothing would do Enid any good except taking her to Europe, where I didn't believe I wanted to go; I thought it would be better if we could get Mushmelon to go to Europe or Mexico or Halifax or somewhere, and one day I asked Eddie Bullfinch, with a good deal of feeling, how long his visitor intended to keep on visiting.

Eddie was wearing that hard look on his face pretty much all the time, and what I said seemed to intensify it. He stared at me as if I'd brought an accusation against him he couldn't bear. "Why, see here!" he said. "Look! I put a dead sculpin in his mattress and he didn't find it for three days. Right along, besides all I've merely said to him about himself, I've done everything to his room and his hair-brushes and tooth-paste and laundry that anybody in the world could possibly be able to think of. There's only one thing left; but he's such nuts on himself it won't worry him any, except right while it's happening—but, well, it might be useful some other way."

"What other way?" I asked Eddie.

"Well, I don't know," he said, looking thoughtful, and I could see he was unwilling to answer directly. "He hasn't been out in the Shooting Star yet because she's been out o' commission on account of engine trouble; but it's all right now, and I'm going to take Enid and Mush quite a long trip in her to-morrow. Mush hasn't ever been in any small boat right out on the ocean, and if to-day's wind keeps up it might get a little rough." Eddie looked at me, then, with a plaintive kind of hopefulness, and as if he thought there might be something of a bond between us created by mutual trouble. "Would you like to go along instead of going out on the Wanda just this once, sir?" he asked me.

Well, I thought I saw a gleam in what seemed to be his idea; so I said I'd go.

CHAPTER XXVIII

THE breeze freshened up overnight, and when the four of us sputtered out of the harbor in the Shooting Star, right after lunch, it was pretty exhilarating for a while; that is, it was until Enid and Mushmelon began singing "Boy of my Dreams, I want You". He had one of those High-school tenors of the sort I'd often heard Enid mimicking and making fun of; but now it just put her in a soft glow, painful to look at. Eddie tried to join in the singing and ruin it, kind of howling; but they didn't appear to know he was there.

We went about four miles, not moving very rapidly—Eddie explained to me that only one of his engines was working—then he steered the Shooting Star into a channel about half a mile wide behind a low, rocky island, where there seemed to be cross-currents and the water was unusually choppy. He said he hoped we wouldn't break down anywhere in there because the island would likely keep other boats from sighting us and coming to tow us;—he was tinkering with his one working engine as he spoke, and right that very minute it made a flopping sound inside, and stopped. Enid and Mushmelon, up in the bow, didn't seem to notice this right away but went on talking, and, with the engine quiet, we could hear what they said.

Mushmelon was speaking. "I like the ocean," he said. "On a railroad train you have to keep on the tracks; but on the ocean you don't."

Well, it's hard to believe; but Enid looked at him as if he'd said something so intelligent it was startling. "That's a wonderful thought!" she said. "I see what you mean—the freedom anything vast and trackless gives you —the freedom to be a gypsy of the sea! Mallowfield, your mind never stops working for one instant, does it?"

He frowned and puckered up his little curvy mouth. "No, I can't say it does," he said. "No, I can't say it does."

"You're wonderful!" she said. "Wonderful!" And she gave him a worshiping look that I wished she hadn't, because it was the sort of look that would tend to sicken any father who saw his daughter doing it. It's a fact that I felt an actual qualm inside of me, one that stayed there. I turned to Eddie Bullfinch.

"Let's get out of here," I said. "Start that engine and let's get back home."

From where he was tinkering with a monkey-wrench, he looked up at me kind of brightly. "Well," he said, "we will as soon as we get going again. The way it seems to me, something appears to be jammed."

"Hurry!" I told him. "Hurry!" I did wish I hadn't listened to Enid and Mushmelon, or seen her give him that look, because I couldn't get it out of my mind, and it seemed to be increasing my qualm. The Shooting Star had begun to roll and pitch uncomfortably, too, as soon as it lost headway, and, as we couldn't feel the breeze any more, the sun felt too hot and the engines had an unpleasant smell. "Hurry!" I told Eddie, though all at once I didn't feel like speaking. "Hurry!"

Something in the way I said it caught Enid's attention and she turned and pointed at me. "Why, look at funny little Pops!" she said; and she broke out laughing as if I'd been the most humorous thing she'd ever seen in her life. "Why, Pops!" she shouted. "Pops, you're going to be seasick!"

"I'm not!" I told her, and I spoke sternly. "I'm not going to be seasick!" I was right, too, and the effort I made to look severe probably did a good deal to make me right: I wasn't going to be sick. I already was. I just said, "Hurry!" again, in a kind of whisper, and the worst began to happen.

After that, I whispered "Hurry!" whenever I could, and every time I said it I could hear Enid break out giggling again.

That is, I heard her for a while; but I got into such a condition that my impressions of external matters were dimmed and facts had difficulty in penetrating to me; then I became vaguely aware that Enid wasn't laughing any more and wasn't sick herself but was in great distress about something. I heard her moaning. "Oh, heavens!" and scolding Eddie Bullfinch for not having any ammonia or other remedies on board, and for not being able to start his engine. I heard her saying, in gentle tones, "Here, let me hold my cool wet handkerchief on your poor forehead. How horrible that you should suffer so!"

From this and other things, I discovered that somebody else was beginning to share my illness. Eddie Bullfinch mistakenly thought I would be interested in hearing about it, for he got up and leaned over me, speaking in a low, tense voice. "It's going to work!" he said. "You

just watch! He's commencing to be something terrible!
If she could ever stand to let him come within a mile of
her after this I'd sell the Shooting Star for forty cents!
You just watch!"

Well, I managed to say, "Watch!" in a voice I barely
hoped might convey a little of my opinion of himself. It
wasn't Mushmelon I was disliking by this time; it was
Eddie Bullfinch. I wouldn't have cared, just then, if
Mushmelon and Enid had got actually married the minute we stepped ashore, just so we stepped ashore, and,
the worst of it was, my whole misery was absolutely use-
less. We rolled and tossed in that channel for more than
two of the worst hours this world's ever seen, and the
longer we stayed the greater was Enid's anguish on
Mushmelon's account and the tenderer her ministering to
him.

Finally I heard Eddie Bullfinch speaking in a desperate
voice. "Well, doggone it!" he said; and the next minute
he had the Shooting Star going again.

As soon as we touched the wharf where Eddie kept his
dam boat I limped right off home to lie down, without
even looking back; but that evening, feeling feeble but
better, I had a talk with Eddie alone on our front porch.
He was in low spirits. "It didn't do any good at all," he
said. "They're absolutely different from men."

"Who do you mean?" I asked him.

"Women," he said. "I never dreamed but that if she
just once saw him going it the way he did—and he certainly did—it would wean her away from him right the
minute she saw him that way, absolutely. It ought to have
done it, too, because you know, yourself, hardly any man
could keep his ideal of some girl if he had to be around
with her under those circumstances for two hours in a
thirty-foot boat. Isn't that right?" I thought it was, be-

cause it seemed to me that if such a thing had happened to even Mrs. Massey during the early stages of our courtship it might have made a critical difference in my emotions. "Yes, sir, it ought to've worked," Eddie went on, getting gloomier. "I'd have kept that boat out there till now if I hadn't seen there wasn't any hope of it. Look I'd have kept that boat out there until even I got sick myself———"

"Don't say that, Eddie," I told him. "I hope you wouldn't have gone to such an extreme."

"I would!" he said. "But the longer we stayed the more she nursed him and the mushier she got over his suffering so until finally it was so absolutely sickening I started up the engine and came back, because I just couldn't stand it. The way it looks to me, when a girl gets that way about a wet splash like old Sloppy Weather Mushmelon, why, the more anybody in the world does to him, and the more awful he is, himself, the more she seems to think of him!" He groaned and scratched his left ankle with the side of his right shoe—it seemed a kind of desperate motion, the way he did it. "Well," he said, "it was the last thing I could possibly think up, and it didn't work. Everybody's tried everything and it only makes her worse. It certainly looks bad!"

I agreed with him, and so did Mrs. Massey and so did Clarissa, when I talked our trouble over, later, with them. Clarissa didn't offer any hope but seemed to feel she understood the case better than her mother and I did. "Didn't I tell you nobody could do anything?" she said. "From the way Enid was always ready to scalp any boy who showed any symptom, I knew all along she was only piling up symptoms in herself that would all break out together some time on the slightest excuse. You couldn't find a slighter excuse than Mushmelon Turpie, of course; but that didn't matter. He just happened to walk in when the breaking-out time in Enid couldn't be postponed any longer. When that time came it didn't make any difference what kind of a boy walked in—just so it was one she wasn't used to—he was certain to be it. Father thought that kind of thing could be 'dealt with'! Well, we've all done every bit of the dealing with it we could, and if you think it's ever going to do any good just go in her room and look at the frame she put on his picture this afternoon! I ask you!"

Enid was out somewhere—with Mushmelon of course —and after a little while Mrs. Massey and I followed Clarissa's suggestion; we went into Enid's room and looked at the frame she'd bought for his photograph. She'd ordered it from a jewelry-house in New York, and I've seldom experienced more despairing sensations than when I saw Mushmelon's kind of softly piggish features ensconced, as you might call it, among those surroundings of ornamental solid silver. Mrs. Massey told me Enid had paid seventy dollars for that frame, buying it out of her allowance in preference to a dress she wanted, and if you could forget what was in it nothing could have been more beautiful.

"I give up absolutely!" I said, when I saw it. "She sees him in a frame like that all the time; that's why she bought it. She couldn't possibly have brought herself to offer that sublime face anything less. It's beyond us; we've been trying to administer remedies in a case where there couldn't be any."

That was my conclusion at the hour of my lowest ebb in regard to Enid's delusion; but by the grace of Divine Providence it's the fact that most of our lowest ebb conclusions aren't conclusive. It was true that we'd certainly provoked the disease to greater extravagance by our

efforts to administer remedies; but that didn't prove that
there wasn't any possible remedy, though it might have
signified to us that we weren't the persons to apply it.

Mushmelon over-ate himself at a clam-bake and re-
mained in bed for several days during which we didn't
experience much relief, because Enid kept the telephone
going most of the time, worrying the Bullfinch family
about his condition, which she attributed to ptomaine
poisoning. Then Eddie came in one noon and brightened
her up by telling her that Mushmelon was so far con-
valescent that he had breakfasted on grape-fruit, cereal,
bacon, eggs, buckwheat cakes and syrup. Eddie stayed to
lunch with us, and his expression and general manner
were pretty bitter. "Mush'll be out to-morrow," he said.
"It's a good thing for my family's grocery bills that he
was sick for a *few* days!" Then he looked at Enid and
asked her, "You been in the Spruce Tree Gift Shop since
Mush took sick?"

"No," she said, looking surprised. "Why?"

"Oh, nothing," he said. "Nothing at all."

"Why?" she asked him again. "What are you struggling to insinuate?"

"Nothing—nothing at all!" he told her. "I don't
s'pose you'd be interested, though a good many of your
girl-friends and some of the boys have been in there and
come out laughing."

Enid frowned at him. "What are you talking about?
What do I care who goes in the Spruce Tree Gift Shop
and comes out laughing? What's the matter with you?"

"Nothing," he said. "Nothing at all. It's only that
they've got the photograph of yourself you gave Mush
down there on the counter. It isn't so much the photograph everybody goes in there to laugh over, though."

"What!" Enid said. "What!"

"Oh, nothing," Eddie went on. "Mush took your photograph down there, and he couldn't make up his mind between a nice white celluloid frame and one made of birch-bark with a picture of an owl stitched onto the top and an Indian in a canoe on the lower part, terribly artistic. This was the one he wanted; but they asked him two dollars and a quarter for it, and the celluloid frame is only a dollar and nineteen cents, though the picture would have to be cut down some to fit it. He offered them a dollar and sixty cents for the birch-bark one, and then went up to one-sixty-five; but they stuck out for the full price, so he said he guessed he'd have to take the celluloid but would think it over and not decide until the next day. But that was the day he stuffed himself too full o' lobsters, clams, sweet-potatoes and corn and everything, so they've been waiting for him to come in ever since, and they've kept the photograph out on the counter in the artistic birch-bark frame, hoping it would attract him so much when he saw it again that he'd make up his mind to come through with the full two and a quarter. Pretty near everybody goes in to see it and ask the Spruce Tree people to tell 'em about it."

Enid just sat staring at Eddie while he was talking, and, when he'd finished, I don't think I ever saw her eyes wider or her face redder; she was breathing fast, too. "You made it up!" she said. "It's every single word a falsehood!"

"No, it isn't," Clarissa told her. "I heard about it this morning at the beach, myself, only I thought it wouldn't do any good to mention it."

"What!" Enid said, and she jumped up from the table. "If you heard it, then it was only because Eddie Bullfinch had been around circulating it. I'll soon show you

what a story-teller he is! It won't take me long to prove
that!"

Then she ran out of the room and out of the house,
and within half a minute her runabout shot past the
dining-room windows and turned toward the village. She
was back before we'd finished the meal; but she didn't
come into the dining-room—she ran up the stairs and
then we heard the door of her own room flung shut. So
pretty soon Mrs. Massey went up there and came back,
looking troubled. She said the door was locked and Enid
had told her nothing was the matter but wasn't coming
down. She kept her door locked all afternoon and didn't
come down to dinner, or during the evening, either.

The next day Mushmelon came around about lunch-
time, looking condescending and anticipatory. I was out
on the porch; but got up and went inside when I saw him
coming, and Mrs. Massey told me later that he seemed
astonished and kind of cross with herself when she had
to tell him that Enid had gone for an all-day excursion to
Lodgeport with Eddie Bullfinch. She also informed me
that Enid's waste-basket had contained, that morning, the
remnants of a birch-bark picture-frame and two photo-
graphs, the pieces being about as small as anybody could
tear them.

"My goodness!" I said, "We were wrong about there
being no remedy, after all. The trouble was, it took
Mushmelon himself to administer it."

"No," she said. "It took Enid. It wasn't Mushmelon
or even his bad taste about the frame—not even his
stinginess. All that wouldn't have changed her if nobody
else had known anything about it. What she couldn't
stand was being made ridiculous."

"What! Why, how could anybody be more ridiculous
than she's been ever since——"

"Oh, yes; she knows that *now*," Mrs. Massey told me. "But of course she never could have known that her being in love with him was ridiculous until she saw that she *looked* ridiculous, herself, because a *picture* of her was being made to look ridiculous. Come and see what she's done with that beautiful silver frame she bought."

So we went into Enid's room, and there on her pretty little desk was that magnificent frame; and when I saw what the dear child had put in it I stood still and swallowed and began to feel ticklish around my eyelids. "Well, I declare!" I said. "I certainly think that's pretty touching!"

Mrs. Massey looked absent-minded. "I was pleased, myself," she told me. "But I'm afraid it was mostly because that President of the Logansville Chamber of Commerce picture of you was the only loose photograph around the house. I suspect it's temporary. Now she's started, there isn't any telling who'll be the next to occupy that frame—maybe even Eddie Bullfinch himself!"

CHAPTER XXIX

Well, sir, I never in the world would have expected to become attached to the Atlantic ocean; but that's exactly what's happened to me. Living the most of my life out in the flat prairie farm-land part of our country, I always felt that no body of water could be pleasanter to look at than Sycamore Creek or Plunket's Run—nice shady streams with old swimmin'-hole turns in them where they curve around sand bars—and I never will get over my attachment to them, either, and the feeling that out there, around Logansville, is where home is. But on the other hand I can't deny there's something about the Atlantic ocean that's got hold of me.

Of course I mean just the edges of it around Mary's Neck—the view of it from our piazza and windows, and going out on it a little way in the Wanda, and the rocks and the surf and easy fishing sometimes where the seaweed lifts up a little on the ocean swell to show you a pink starfish and then drops down over him again. No, sir, there's a kind of fascination about it, and the smell of it that suggests clams and crabs and lobsters groping about underneath is another thing I know I'll miss sometimes when we're back in Logansville for the fall and winter.

I expect there's something else I may be picturing in my

mind then, too, at times. The truth is, I begin to see now that when we first got here, I didn't have my appreciations developed, you might put it. The village at Mary's Neck and these old white houses with green shutters, that Mrs. Massey and the girls were so excited over, all looked too kind of plain and old farmer-like to suit me right away; but gradually they got kind of a hold on me and I can't deny it. There's something about white houses and elm trees, and their both being old, that gets into your system afterwhile and seems to mean to stay there—maybe because they make you remember that your great-grandparents lived in such places and must have had quite a feeling for them before having to ride away to the struggle of opening up the West.

Yes, sir, it's really no wonder people from our part of the country get to thinking about these old houses and even about the kind of furniture that's in them—so much so that if I thought it good policy to be downright honest all the time with my family I'd have to confess that I've been back to those old Cheevers' house two or three times, by myself, and it's the naked truth I'm the owner of the high boy Mrs. Massey and the girls decided was too expensive. It's a matter between the old couple and me, and I think next spring will be about the right time to tell the family and have the high boy moved to the cottage. Of course, though, this is as far as the antiquing fever, as you hear it called, will ever go with me; but it does seem right to mention that I do begin to have some comprehension of it, and that there's something about this old New England village here that reaches the pleasantest part of a person's nature.

Besides this, I presume I've conveyed the idea that I found these Yankee inhabitants right perplexing at first; but the more I've seen of them and managed to get them better accustomed to me, so that they understood I didn't intend any particular sharp practise or overbearing manners with them, why, the more I saw that there was something mighty attractive and likeable about them. They don't start right in with a stranger and take him on his face value, it's true; but I've come to comprehend they have their own reasons for this—they've had experiences that have ground it into them not to be too impulsive with their cordiality, and naturally quite a number of us people from elsewhere that camp on them in summer strike them as more or less queer till they get used to us. No, sir; the original inhabitants of Mary's Neck are as likeable as you'd care to know.

A summer resort has peculiar attributes. Sociably speaking, it presents all the problems you'd find in your own town but with many of them accentuated and new ones added, for reasons I think I've spoken of. That reminds me: it was only last night that the family jumped on me and told me I had the habit of misusing the word "sociably". I was speaking of these very subjects—how I'd come to have a right hearty liking for both the original inhabitants and the summer people, and how, looking back on these months at Mary's Neck, I thought everybody'd got along together even better than might have been expected, considering our all coming from different places and having different bringing-ups and impressions of ourselves. I said I thought Mary's Neck had a fine class of summer people and I liked them all; then I went on to say how I appreciated their friendliness to the Massey family and the kindness they'd really shown to us sociably.

Clarissa broke out and shuddered and said she couldn't stand my misusing that word any longer; she said I meant the word "socially" but for heaven's sake not to use it either, because nothing could be worse taste. So I expect the only way out is for me to avoid any topics that bring up this class of thinking.

Clarissa was more sensitive about me than usual, because young Mr. Bicksit was due to arrive this morning for a short visit at the cottage before he goes back to the law school, which opens pretty soon after Labor Day next week. We're going home ourselves then; but we're coming back to Mary's Neck again next year of course. The family have planned to get back into the cottage almost as early in the spring as we came this year, and the honest truth is I didn't offer any objection—I want to be back that soon, myself. You can't deny it's a place that gets a hold on a person.

I was glad to see Clarissa's visitor when he got here this morning. You understand I'm speaking of that fine manly young Mr. Bicksit—a splendid, intelligent young fellow who knows how to say the right thing at the right time and do the right thing at the right time, as I've seen proved, myself, in a moment of crisis. Of course they're both a little too young for definite arrangements; but I'd be willing to countenance the matter some day if Clarissa decides to concentrate her intentions to that extent. Likely she may; I heard her ask him what seemed to me a fairly leading question under my window just after lunch.

"What I wanted to know," she said, in a voice she doesn't use to the family, "I wondered why you changed about coming here after writing me at first that you thought it was going to be so difficult to talk your father out of making you take that trip with him. You must have made quite a special effort to get here—and I just wondered why."

"It was Mr. Sweetmus," young Bicksit told her. "I couldn't bear the thought of not seeing him again."

Then I heard a slap; but when I saw them later in the afternoon they were sitting on the piazza steps trying not to laugh at Enid and Eddie Bullfinch, who were swinging in the porch-swing together but not speaking because they'd had a quarrel.